House of Skin

Look for these titles by
Jonathan Janz

Now Available:

The Sorrows

House of Skin

Jonathan Janz

SAMHAIN
PUBLISHING

Samhain Publishing, Ltd.
11821 Mason Montgomery Rd., 4B
Cincinnati, OH 45249
www.samhainpublishing.com

House of Skin
Copyright © 2012 by Jonathan Janz
Print ISBN: 978-1-60928-921-8
Digital ISBN: 978-1-60928-913-3

Editing by Don D'Auria
Cover by Angela Waters

First Samhain Publishing, Ltd. electronic publication: June 2012
First Samhain Publishing, Ltd. print publication: October 2012

Dedication

This book is for you, Grandpa. You survived the Great Depression, and you served your country in World War II. But your greatest accomplishment is your unwavering devotion to your family. Thanks for being a grandfather, a father figure, a role model, and a loyal friend to a boy who needed those things in the worst way. I love you dearly.

Acknowledgments

Every horror novel has a lineage. Some of the stories that made this one possible are the following: *Ghost Story* and *Julia*, by Peter Straub; *Earthbound*, by Richard Matheson; *She Wakes*, by Jack Ketchum; *All Heads Turn When the Hunt Goes By*, by John Farris; *She*, by H. Rider Haggard; and "Nona", by Stephen King.

I'd like to thank Don D'Auria for his continued support and guidance. Thanks to Tim, Clay, and Pete for reading this book and helping me improve it. Thanks to my three incredible children for loving me and for being excited about my writing. And thanks most of all to my wife. We met the summer I began writing this novel. You believed in the story then and have never stopped believing. Thank you for that and for everything else. I couldn't have done it without you.

I met a lady in the meads,
Full beautiful—a faery's child,
Her hair was long, her foot was light,
And her eyes were wild.

John Keats, "La Belle Dame sans Merci"

She will find him by starlight, and her passion ends the play.

William Shakespeare, *A Midsummer Night's Dream*

Before

She waited.

Book One

Julia

Chapter One

As he drew closer to her, Brand's grip on the wheel tightened. She wasn't a blonde, but she would definitely do. Girl had the body of a swimsuit model. Tall, curvy, athletic. Maybe he wouldn't need to go to the bars after all.

Rolling down the window he said, "Excuse me, miss. I'm sorry to bother you, but I'm sorta lost." He leaned forward and looked up at her. From where she stood she'd be able to see his sports coat, his starched white shirt open a little at the collar. His Rolex.

She showed no sign of having heard, continued walking. He idled the black Beamer beside her and asked, "Did you know Myles Carver?"

That did it. She stopped and cast a sidelong glance at him.

"That looks like a yes." He smiled what he hoped was a winning smile. Then his expression grew grave. "As you might have heard, Myles passed away last week. His nephew is arriving in town this evening to take possession of the estate."

For the first time, the woman spoke. "Someone's moving in?"

"That's my understanding. My law firm, Walker, White and Brand, handled the Carver will, and since I'm our most junior partner it fell to me to drive down here tonight to drop off the key."

She'd be impressed, he was sure, with his status as a partner at such a young age. They always were. And who could blame them? He'd been made a partner the previous fall and at forty-two, he was one of the youngest in the city.

The woman was watching him. He couldn't read her expression, but even in the wan light of the April dusk he could see she was a stunner. Her long dark hair was parted in the middle and swept over her shoulders. The high cheekbones gave her an exotic look. And even from this distance he could see her green eyes glowing in the sundown light.

"Anyway, I'm a bit lost and I was wondering if you could help me find the house."

In truth, he'd been there twice already. When the old man was still alive he'd insisted on Brand's firm coming to him rather than the old man coming to the city. They would have balked had he not been willing to pay.

Maybe, Brand thought, the girl would want a tour of the place. If she'd never been inside the Carver House it would sure as hell impress her. Maybe he'd try to bag her right there. That would be a hell of a way to celebrate Carver's demise.

She pointed down the road. "You follow this road through the stop sign, go about a mile and when the woods get really thick you'll see an opening to your left. The house is down that lane."

Brand was so focused on her lips that he caught little of what she said. They were full and pink and a little curved at the ends so that he couldn't tell whether she were amused at something or annoyed at him for interrupting her stroll.

"Would you like a ride?" he asked, his right arm cradling the passenger's seat.

"I walk home every day," she said.

"Oh." He laughed. "You look like you're in great shape, so I'm not surprised." He grinned deprecatingly. "I'm just really bad with directions. Since you know where I'm supposed to be going, maybe you could ride with me to the house. Then I could drop you off at your place. They're in the same direction, right?"

She fixed him with an appraising stare. Was she wary of him or was she debating his proposal? Probably both, he guessed.

"I swear I won't hurt you." He raised his hands. "I'm harmless."

The corners of her mouth rose slightly. "I suppose."

He pushed open the passenger's door and waited for her to get in. He extended a hand. "Ted Brand."

"Julia Merrow."

She shook his hand and nodded toward the road.

"My house is a couple of miles from Watermere by road, but only a mile if you go through the woods."

14

Ted did his best not to grimace. Houses with names reminded him of *Gone with the Wind* and his wife's weird attraction to Clark Gable.

"Straight here?" he asked when they came to the stop sign.

Julia nodded. She smelled like some sort of body lotion, but not cloyingly so. Just a hint of citrus that reminded him of a tropical drink on a hot day. He breathed it in, turned to her.

"So where were you walking home from, Julia?"

"The library."

"You go there to read?"

"I work there."

"And how is that?"

She shrugged. "Fine."

She wasn't much of a conversationalist, he decided. It was a good thing she was so good-looking.

Ted chuckled. "Carver's nephew is a strange guy."

"Why do you say that?"

"I don't know," he said. "He couldn't move in any other time but tonight." He checked his Rolex to make sure she'd seen it. "He won't even get there until one or two in the morning."

"What's wrong with that?" she asked.

Talking to this girl was like extracting a splinter.

"Nothing's *wrong* with it, I guess. It's only that it seemed strange to me that he couldn't wait until tomorrow for one of us to meet him there. I mean, the guy calls as we're closing the office and insists we drop off the key tonight because he's got to move in immediately."

"Maybe he's excited."

"Obviously."

"I'd be excited."

He softened his tone. "Yeah, I could see that."

For the first time, she was growing animated. "Watermere is lovely."

"Yeah." He gave her the smile. "It is very nice."

"Nice? It's *sublime*. The ballroom and the marble foyer. And the master suite." Her green eyes blazed.

"I like the library myself," he said, going with it.

"I do too," Julia said, and as she said it she actually touched his arm.

Bullseye, he thought.

"Yeah, the fireplace and the paintings..."

"And the books," she threw in. "Have you ever seen so many wonderful books? They make me feel like Belle in *Beauty and the Beast*."

He grinned. "It *is* like that, isn't it?"

He hated that fucking movie. Ever since Linda bought it for the twins, he swore it was on twice a day. He ever got the makers of it alone, he'd kick their asses.

"It's been so long since I've been to Watermere," she said.

"You're welcome to go in with me."

Her eyes flared brighter, then grew doubtful.

"I thought you were just dropping off the key."

Brand winked. "I've got time."

Paul left Memphis for the last time.

He shifted in his seat, uncomfortable because his cargo shorts kept riding up. He cursed himself for allowing Emily to talk him into the Civic, a car he was sure had been designed by dwarfs. His lower back a tangle of knots, he tried to mold his six-foot-two body to the seat. But no matter where he rested his rear end, his head was still too near the roof and his knees were too close to the steering wheel.

He wiped his brow. Though still only April, the southern air was humid, stifling. He rolled down the window and willed the outside breeze to cool him.

Squirming, he realized he needed to urinate.

Some day he'd conduct a study on the correlation between violent crimes and the amount of urine in the bladders of the perpetrators. There had to be a connection. People could talk all they wanted about childhood traumas and full moons goading men to violence, but his money was on the need to piss. Nine times out of ten, when he got annoyed with anything—a bad driver, an inextricable knot in his tennis shoes, a movie director who joggled the camera so much you couldn't see what the hell was happening—it had something to do with the tingly burning in his abdomen.

It was the reason that despite the cooler temperature the outside air brought on, he still found himself on edge. He needed a bathroom. As if in answer, a green sign proclaimed GAS ONE MILE.

He checked the gauge: three-quarters full. No matter. He'd empty his bladder, load up on caffeine and be on his way.

Not for the first time since he passed the city limit sign, a sense of unreality washed over him. He was leaving the only life he'd ever known, the only people and places familiar to him, driving ten hours north and beginning a new life in a house he'd only seen in pictures. Had anyone, he wondered, ever done this before? Was he, as Emily claimed, insane for going through with it?

Signaling a left turn, he made his way off the interstate and pulled into the gas station.

A longhaired guy working the counter stared at him balefully. Copious tattoos, faded blue by time and God knew what wear and tear, grew like ivy on the man's veiny arms. The pendant on the guy's necklace was a skull with curled horns and long fangs.

Paul realized he'd been staring.

"Help you?" the man asked. His tattooed hands held a *Hustler* magazine. From where Paul was standing, he could see two women in the upside-down picture locked together like a Yin and a Yang. The attendant's eyes followed Paul's gaze to the picture. When he glanced up again, Paul could see the maze of blood vessels webbing the man's eyes and a prurient grin wrinkling his lips.

"No thanks. I just need to use your bathroom and get some coffee."

"Coffee's over there," the man nodded to Paul's left. "Bathroom's outside."

"Do I need a key?"

"Yeah. Might need a gas mask too." The man grinned, revealing a mouth full of coffee grounds. As Paul took the key dangling from a wooden club, he realized the coffee grounds were tobacco.

He went around to the bathroom and was assailed with one of the worst odors he'd ever smelled. It was as if the smell of human shit had been distilled and blended into the dingy white paint. Even the pink urinal cake gave off a fulsome stench. Managing to void his bladder while stealing quick breaths through his mouth, Paul stumbled out of the bathroom and gasped for air. After depositing the club on the counter and receiving a grunt from the attendant, he poured himself a large Styrofoam cup of coffee and grabbed two Mountain Dews. As he checked out, he threw in a bottle of caffeine pills, as well.

"You a trucker?" asked the man.

"No, but I have a long drive ahead of me."

"Where you headin'?" The red-webbed eyes studied him.

"A little Indiana town called Shadeland."

The man shook his head, losing interest. "Never heard of it."

"It's really small."

"Need anything else?" The attendant's fingers drummed on the sixty-nining blondes in the magazine.

"No, I think that's it."

"Need a bag?"

Paul glanced at the items on the counter. "Sure."

The man rolled his eyes, bent down and reached under the counter.

Beside the open *Hustler*, Paul spied a rack of discount CDs. *ROCKIN' SEVENTIES*, one of them read. He pulled it out and skimmed through the names of the bands. Impulsively, he tossed the disc on the counter and asked the guy to add it to his purchase.

"Already run it," the attendant said with a shrug and handed back his credit card.

"Can't you run it separately?"

Sighing, the man rang up the disc and took the credit card. As they waited for the card to go through, the man's grubby fingers tapped on the sex mag. Paul leaned on the counter and stared at the credit card machine. He wished the guy would relax. It wasn't as though the women were going to finish pleasuring each other and put their clothes back on.

The transaction done, they parted wordlessly. Paul guided the Civic back to the highway and sipped the bitter coffee, which was even worse than he'd expected.

His cell phone rang. Paul picked it up, saw who was calling and silenced it. Emily was the last person he needed to talk to right now.

He waited until it stopped ringing and then switched the phone to vibrate. A few days ago he'd worried about his unpaid bill, but now the fact that his cell phone contract was about to end seemed like a blessing. In fact, he didn't plan on getting a landline in his new home either. There was something delicious about being unreachable.

Smiling, Paul accessed his voicemail and before Emily's voice could launch its attack, he deleted her message.

As they drove away, Ted marveled at how easy it had been. From the moment they opened the front door to the moment they climbed back in the Beamer her eyes had glimmered with something approaching ecstasy. For someone who claimed to have only been an occasional visitor to the Carver House, she knew her way around pretty damn well.

In the house he got a chance to see what a stunner she was. Girl looked like a Playboy model done up to look like a professor or a lawyer. Like those hot young Hollywood actresses. You could try to make them look smart and sophisticated, but it never quite took. No matter how hard the wardrobe guys tried, their sexiness rubbed through.

At first she'd been reserved, making sure she didn't let on she might be enjoying herself. Looking back on it, there'd even been moments he suspected the old house might be conjuring bad memories for her. When they passed the basement door, for instance, she'd shivered and gone a sickly olive color.

But her transformation upon entering the ballroom was dramatic. She had danced, literally *danced*, across the ballroom floor, and though he felt like a schmuck, he let her grab his hands and lead him around in a kind of awkward waltz.

Driving away, he felt very good about his chances. Any girl who got carried away that easily was a prime candidate for a one-nighter. He thought of the little girly way she'd acted. She'd laughed and danced with him to the accompaniment of an unseen orchestra, and if that wasn't worth a screw he didn't know what was.

He remembered the way she looked climbing the front porch steps: big tits, tight little ass and a set of legs that went on and on. She had high cheekbones like an Indian or something, and her skin was dark like that too.

The eyes bothered him though he couldn't pinpoint why. They were a nice shade of green, very light, and they were always considering something or measuring you and it made him wonder how long she'd lived alone out here in the boonies without someone to lay the pipe to her now and then.

As they rolled into her drive, she thanked him for the ride and made to get out of the car. Panicking, he stopped her by asking if he could use her bathroom. She said of course, he didn't have to rush off. She had some iced tea, would he like some? Sure, he said, with lots and lots of sugar. She didn't say anything to that, but man, she didn't have to. A girl invited you in for iced tea—*iced tea* of all things!—the work was over. She wanted him and he couldn't wait to get her clothes off, take a look at that killer body.

Inside, he couldn't believe the barrenness of her house. The only furniture in the living room was a rocking chair, a baby grand piano, a DVD player and an old-fashioned console television. The baby grand was adorned with a lamp and a bust of William Shakespeare.

She'd told him where the restroom was and as he stood there taking a leak he heard the piano start to play. He finished and as he checked his hair in the mirror, he twisted on the faucet in case she was listening to see if he washed his hands.

When he came out, the mood in the living room had changed. It might have been the light from the piano lamp shining on Julia's smooth neck; it might have been the song she was playing. But something about the scene before him turned him on in a way he hadn't felt in years. It wasn't just the tingling in his pants, though there was that. This was something greater, something that excited his imagination as well as his dick. Ted glided toward her, the music invigorating his steps. Her long fingers caressed the keys and the song made him put out his hands and slide his fingertips along her bare arms, over her breasts, and then she was standing and hugging herself.

"*What are you doing?*" she shouted.

Shocked at her overreaction, he replied louder than he'd intended, "Why don't you relax?"

"What makes you think you can touch me?"

Her eyes widened with disbelief.

"I thought that's what you wanted."

"What made you think that?"

And now, standing here in front of her accusing stare and open mouth, he couldn't remember why he'd thought it would be a good idea to touch her tits.

"I guess it was the song," was the only thing he could think to say.

"The song?"

"Yeah. The song. I heard it when I was in the bathroom. It was very pretty."

What the hell was he saying?

If he left now he'd still have plenty of time at the bars. Linda didn't expect him home until midnight. He'd told her Carver's nephew would want to talk about the estate, that he'd have to humor the guy and not seem rude. Share a couple beers with the lucky bastard to celebrate his inheritance.

"You thought my playing was pretty?" she asked.

Was she buying it?

"Sure. That's why I touched you."

And miracle of miracles, she was moved by his line of bullshit. She was actually tilting her head and allowing him to move in to give her a conciliatory hug.

"I usually don't play for people," she explained into his shoulder.

"I'm glad you played for me."

"Me too," she said, nodding over at a pewter stein on the bookshelf. "Your tea's over there."

Ted thanked her, but he had no intention of letting go of her, of drinking out of that heavy stein. What the hell was she, a Viking?

Her firm breasts pushed against him. Ted slowly rubbed her back. If he was going to do this, now was the time. He pulled away, leaned in and kissed her. At first she was wooden, unsure of what to do. Soon, though, she was moving her tongue with his and from her trembling he guessed it had been awhile since she'd kissed a man. A shame, he thought. A pretty girl like this, probably in her late twenties. How had she managed to remain single?

Now he was letting his hands roam over her body, under the rim of her shirt where he felt how curvy and muscular her back was. Over her hard round ass. He pushed his crotch into hers and she was just the right height for him, probably about five-ten or eleven. Her hands were probing also. They felt his neck and ran along his jaw and onto his shoulders, which was good because they were broad and women always liked them. Their kissing grew feverish and wet and now her hands were on his sides over his sports coat pockets and he felt her pause, tensing, and he realized his mistake and by the time he moved to push her hand away she'd already broken from him and retreated.

"Julia..."

"What's in your coat pocket?"

"It's just a ring my father gave me."

"Then why is it in your pocket?"

"I don't know." He fought the blush that burned at his throat. He knew it would condemn him, but it was already climbing up his neck. "I get tired of wearing it, I guess."

"Show it to me," she said and held out her hand. There was a sharp edge to her voice he didn't like.

"Why should I produce it like it's a piece of fucking evidence?"

"Why should you worry about showing me the ring if it isn't a wedding band?" Hand out, she took a step toward him.

"Because it's none of your business," he replied. Where did she get off interrogating him?

She closed her eyes. "Goodbye, Ted."

"Huh?"

She turned to the piano. "You heard me."

"Yeah, I heard you," he said, approaching. "Bitch."

"What did you say to me?"

"You heard me," he said, drawing closer. A hateful grin twisted his lips.

Her eyes glittered with latent tears. "What's wrong with you?"

"Not a thing, honey. The problem's on your side." He bit his lower lip, caressed her shoulders with his fingertips. "Built like you are and a fucking prig. Goddamned tragic."

She took a backward step. "I'm a prig because I won't sleep with a man I just met?"

He snickered darkly, enjoying himself now. "No, you're a prig because you invited me here under false pretenses. That makes you a cocktease too."

He saw her eyes filling with tears, her mouth working.

He stepped closer, forcing her back near the bookcase. "Fucking waste of time," he said, driving it in further. "You're a shitty piano player, too, but hey, at least you're hot."

"Get away from me," she said in a low voice.

He clamped her shoulders, drew her roughly toward him, the bitch. Show her who's boss. "C'mon, sweetie, let's be friends."

He didn't see the slap coming. It caught him hard, *fuck*, right on the ear.

He belted her with the back of his hand, sent her staggering into the bookcase. An empty candleholder tipped and plummeted to the floor. Her hands were on a shelf about waist high, and at first he thought she was steadying herself, that he'd dizzied her when he gave her that smack.

Then he saw her reach for the stein of iced tea. She lifted it and for a crazy moment he thought she was going to make a toast, but it continued to rise, a foot above her shoulder now. He noticed there was a face on it, William Shakespeare. *Big surprise*, he thought.

He asked, "What are you doing with that?"

She took a step forward, and he realized she was taller than he'd thought. He was about to comment on this when her hand swept toward him and slammed the bottom of the stein against his face.

Chapter Two

10:06, the dashboard clock read.

Ahead, Paul spotted his exit. He wasn't sure if it was a good idea to take a state road instead of the interstate, but he craved something to break the monotony of the trip. He'd listened to *ROCKIN' SEVENTIES* three times, and by contrast the silence was pleasing. He took the exit ramp and turned onto the state road. The smooth highway appeared deserted, a welcome departure from the constant roar of the interstate. Twisting off the bottle cap, he swigged the rest of the Mountain Dew and tossed it onto the passenger's side floor with the empty coffee cup.

As he picked up speed, he noted the thickness of the foliage around him. It reminded him of the pictures his uncle's executors had sent him of Watermere, his new home.

Paul drew in a deep breath. It was incredible. The things he'd always wanted—becoming a writer, the chance to get some peace and quiet, a place to spread out instead of being cramped inside a shabby apartment—were only hours away.

He yawned and wondered how despite the surfeit of coffee and Mountain Dew rushing through his system, he still found himself growing groggy.

He remembered the caffeine pills. He fished the bottle out of the bag and wrestled with the cap. Managing to stay on the road while he shook out a pair of yellow pills, he popped them into his mouth and waited for them to head off his lethargy.

For a moment Paul had the weird sensation that his leg was falling asleep. He tapped his thigh to rid himself of the uncomfortable needling and realized it was his cell phone, which he'd left on vibrate. With a rueful grin, he leaned back and lifted his hips so he could extract the phone from his pocket, and as he did, one leg bumped the wheel. The Civic veered over the center lane. Dropping the phone with a gasp, he flailed for the wheel and actually pushed the car farther into the other lane before jerking it too hard to the right.

"Shit," he muttered as he fought the fishtailing back end. He turned into the skid, but that meant staying in the middle of the damn road rather than returning to his own lane. There were no headlights racing toward him, but he was approaching a hill, and if a car suddenly appeared from the other side he wouldn't have to worry about moving into his new house, he'd become a roadside cross instead.

The Civic overcorrected again, thrusting him so far into the left lane that his tires swished over the soft grass shoulder.

"Come on," he growled through clenched teeth.

A dim glow spilled over the trees flanking the road. A car was coming.

For one delirious moment the wheels on his side of the Civic descended the grassy shoulder. Then, without allowing himself to think about the vehicle barreling toward the hill, Paul hit the gas and arrowed toward the double-yellow center of the road. The Civic hopped agilely off the shoulder and rocketed toward the yellow lines, while from the impending rise Paul watched the glow increase with exponential rapidity.

The right front bumper of the Civic crossed yellow, the driver's side momentarily fixed in the lights that splashed over the hill and drowned him in a freezing white sea of panic. A horn blasted deafeningly but Paul hadn't the energy to jerk the wheel. His car continued an almost leisurely diagonal into the right lane, and just when he had closed his eyes, certain the other vehicle—a dark-colored SUV, he noted distantly—would smash him broadside, he heard the screech of swinging tires and felt a stunning whoosh of air sweep the Civic as the vehicles passed within inches of a terrible crash. In his own lane now, he risked a glance in the rearview mirror and saw how well the other driver had managed it, the SUV hardly shimmying as it resumed a normal path, its receding horn now hammering out a staccato goodbye.

At least, Paul hoped it was a goodbye. He could only imagine how livid the other driver was, how irate he himself would have been had the situation been reversed, the sort of anger only possible when one has been dealt a mortal scare.

25

The cell phone vibrated on the floorboard between his shoes. He'd apparently dropped the damn thing during his near-death experience.

Paul knew who it would be even before he raised the phone to eye level—no losing sight of the road again, not after what had just happened—and saw the name on the phone's illuminated exterior window.

Emily.

He could ignore it again, but she'd keep calling. Even if he shut the damn thing off she'd find a way to get through. Telepathically, perhaps. With a palsied hand, he opened the cell, put it to his ear. "Hey."

"Took you long enough."

Christ.

"I was trying not to have an accident."

A pause. "You're on the road?"

"Yeah."

"So you're going through with it," she said.

"We're not doing this again."

"It's that easy for you?"

"I never said it was easy. You're just saying that to make me feel guilty."

"You're right, Paul. You're only throwing away three years of time together. Three years of memories and emotional deposits. Why should you feel guilty?"

He knew he shouldn't argue with her, knew it would only rip the fresh scab off their relationship, but he couldn't help himself. "I told you the move isn't about us, it's about me hating my life. Doesn't that matter to you?"

Her voice grew plaintive. "Won't you miss Memphis?"

"I'll miss certain things, sure. I'll miss seeing you, some of the guys. I always loved Barbecue Fest."

"I'd say you loved it a little too much."

Paul restrained an urge to chuck the phone out the window. They'd had half a dozen good experiences at Barbecue Fest, yet all she remembered was the time he'd drunk too much beer and ended up sleeping it off at a friend's while Emily called every official agency in Shelby County convinced Paul had been killed or abducted. He thought she'd let it go after a while, but here they were two years later still talking about it.

"Nothing to say?"

He blew out weary breath. "I'm just ready for a change."

"Running away isn't really a change for you," she said. When he opened his mouth to respond, she added, "So tell me more about Waterworld."

Paul's jaw clenched. "Watermere," he said. "The house's name is Watermere."

"Explain to me why it's called that when it's not on the water."

He opened his mouth to tell her, for the third time, about the creek running through the grounds, that there was indeed water near the house if not exactly beside it, but he decided not to take the bait. She knew the answer, she was just finding another way to mock the place without even seeing it.

"You're awfully quiet," she said.

"That's because there's no point in arguing," he said, glancing in the rearview mirror to make sure the SUV hadn't turned around to exact revenge on him. "We've said all there is to say about my leaving." *Which is why*, he wanted to add, *I haven't returned your calls the last couple days.*

"Everything except the real reason you're running away."

"Please stop saying that."

"Or what?" she said, and for a moment he could almost see her on the other end, hand poised on cocked hip, mouth open in a defiant sneer. God, he was glad to be rid of her.

He heard her sigh tremulously, the fight going out of her. When she spoke again, her voice was almost free of spite and derision. "I don't understand you."

He waited.

"Don't you think what you're doing is a bit weird? Your whole family agrees your uncle was a lunatic."

Keeping his eyes on the road, Paul opened his second bottle of Mountain Dew and took a long swig. Replacing the cap, he asked, "What would you do, refuse the inheritance? Say 'Hell no, I don't want money or a free house'?"

"I didn't say that. Keep the money—of course you should keep the money. But why not sell the house? You said it was falling apart."

"I said it needed work."

"How would you know, Paul? You've never even been there."

"I'll be there in a few hours."

Her voice went small. "Do you enjoy hurting me?"

"Emily," he began, but then fell quiet. What could he say? That any life was better than the life he had? That his relationship with her had become an emotional undertow that only worsened his drinking problem. That the bank—Jesus, how amazing it felt to tell his father he was quitting—was a maelstrom of ringing phones and coughing workers, his apartment building a sarcophagus of noise. That nothing about city life felt good to him. That he wanted to be alone, without another soul in the world, where he could shout at the top of his lungs and not worry about being heard. Where Emily could no longer make him feel like a failure, even if he was.

"Paul?"

"I don't enjoy hurting you," he said, "but I've gotta go now."

Her voice went hard. "You'll regret it."

"Maybe."

"You'll be back by year's end."

Don't count on it.

"We'll see, Emily."

"But I won't be waiting for you."

Paul held his tongue.

She hung up on him.

"That went well," he said and shut off the cell. He glanced at the mirror again and saw the road behind was clear. The SUV hadn't followed him.

With luck, Emily wouldn't either.

Through the heavy stein Julia felt his cheekbone collapse and heard the sound of mashing cartilage. A gout of iced tea splattered over his face, his chest, her shoulder and arm. Even before her hand fell his body crumpled and twisted, his knees buckling. He landed in a sitting position before his head lolled back, his eyes showing white and his tongue resting on his bottom lip like a dog's. His shoulder blades rushed the floor. The back of his skull bounced on the hard wood.

She watched him closely. He didn't move.

A tide of horror washed over her. *My God*, she thought. *I'm going to get the electric chair.*

He moaned, a faint, pleading sound.

It startled her. His brow knitted and his hands circled like he was swimming. Then, he was still.

Julia began to shake in huge, rolling tremors that undulated through her body like waterbed waves, and when she thought she'd lose consciousness, succumb to the nausea and the awful guilt for what she'd just done, she let her knees buckle and plopped down a few feet from where he lay.

She'd only inflicted violence one other time in her life, and then, just as she'd felt a moment ago, it was as though another person had inhabited her body and controlled her limbs. It couldn't have been her arm that brained Ted Brand with a drinking receptacle.

Yet she knew it was. And she knew if she sat here and did nothing, he'd eventually awaken and then she'd be in jail awaiting an attempted murder charge with a team full of city lawyers pushing for the harshest sentence possible.

The thought of a relentless cross-examination got her up, got her body working again.

She had to get him out of the living room.

Julia set the stein on the bookcase, hooked Brand under the armpits and dragged him to the open basement door. She shot a glance at Shakespeare's image on the stein, but looked away when she noticed how accusatory the Bard's stare had become. She nearly slipped on the lake of tea slicking the wood floor. Her feet squelched in it, and the smell of the liquid, normally pleasing to her, now conjured thoughts of some nauseating sugary confection. The feel of Brand's large, limp body appalled her. It was as though she were dragging a cow carcass through a blood-soaked meat locker. She shivered at the thought, and for a moment she forgot what she was doing and covered her face in her trembling hands and his head, unsupported, crashed to the wood floor again, bouncing heavy as a bowling ball.

The panic gripped her. She knew there was no stopping it now. All she could do was get him as far away from her as she could. She hurried around to his feet. Lifting his legs so they were at a right angle to the floor, she reared back and shoved, using her right foot to push his lower back as it came up from the floor. Then she caught herself in the doorway to ensure that she too didn't go toppling end over end down the long stairway the way Ted's boneless body was. His large form somersaulted a third time, a fourth, and then sprawled in a heap at the bottom of the stairs.

She slammed the basement door and began to cry.

She wished she'd never met Ted Brand. Thinking how close she'd come to sleeping with him, to losing her virginity to him, made her feel ill, yet what right did that give her to attack him, to smash his face? What the hell was wrong with her? Yes, it was self-defense, but still...

She hadn't meant to hurt him, not as badly as she had, but that didn't matter now. Intent meant nothing to people like Brand, and now that it was done, she knew her options were few. Let him go, he'd tell on her, lie about what happened. The jury would believe whatever he told them. He was a lawyer, after all.

As terrible as it was, she knew Ted could never leave her basement alive, and it was this thought more than anything that sent her to the kitchen sink to vomit.

Paul's head jerked up, his lungs sucking in frightened breath. He gripped the steering wheel, shook the sleep out of his head. Stifling a yawn, he checked the digital clock.

2:14.

He'd sue the pill makers. Who the hell heard of a guy falling asleep after a handful of caffeine pills?

He thought of checking the map, though he knew he was nowhere near his destination. He'd be lucky to make Shadeland by dawn. What had possessed him to drive at night? In retrospect, didn't it make far more sense to leave early in the morning and arrive in the afternoon?

Too late now. He was already most of the way there and he wasn't about to turn around. It occurred to him to pull over and catch some shut-eye, but that would be conceding defeat. He'd finish what he'd started if that meant driving all night.

He jolted. He'd been dreaming again. Good lord, what was the matter with him? How long had he been out? Ten seconds? Thirty? He imagined himself cruising along at sixty-five miles per hour with his mouth open and his hands dozing on the wheel, a rolling missile careening toward whatever poor son of a bitch happened to be in the other lane.

He had to keep awake. If stimulants couldn't do it, maybe music would. He opened up the storage box under his armrest and plucked out his CD case. Most of what he had was either country or classical, and Paul trusted neither to keep him alert. Finally, he flipped to Metallica's *Ride the Lightning.* If that wouldn't do it, nothing would. He thumbed in the disc and fast-forwarded to "Creeping Death."

Paul's chin bobbed. The situation was growing dire. He checked the clock.

2:26.

He'd never make it there alive. Desperate, he rolled down the window and let the wind blast his greasy hair. It didn't help. The fragrance of the pines bordering the road lulled him deeper into that soft, tranquil place. Paul whipped his head to stay awake. He'd never been this tired before. His fatigue was an undertow sucking him toward the comforting blue depths of sleep. His blood was suffused with caffeine, his ears assaulted by heavy metal, his skin pelted with frigid air; yet the combination of these things only underscored the futility of his resistance. Sleep, an inexorable crawling glacier, plowed through every barrier, freezing his blood and flattening his defenses. The road seemed a million miles wide. For as far as his dimming eyes could see there were no cars, no houses, nothing but a measureless wasteland spreading out in the darkness.

A jarring thud and a high-pitched scream. Shocked into wakefulness, he threw a puzzled glance at the road, then at the clock.

2:31.

Had he been out the entire time? Surely the car couldn't have steered itself for five minutes. For some reason, the sight of the overhead mirror made his stomach feel loose and quivery. He spotted nothing in the road behind him to confirm the sick fear backstroking in his belly, yet he wondered what he'd have seen had he checked the mirror immediately after the thud, the scream.

The bile in his throat demanded he slow the car and turn around. Paul made a U-turn with hands he couldn't feel.

His racing thoughts conjured a hitchhiker's limp body, bloodied and broken, balled into a lump in the middle of the highway. The Civic would arrive there just as another car pulled up and discovered what he'd done. The police report would show that Paul had veered onto the shoulder and clipped the man, sent his shattered body skittering end over end. His dream of beginning a new life as a writer with money in the bank and a large estate would be replaced by a decade in prison for manslaughter.

His headlights splashed over a dark shape in the opposite lane. He glimpsed something large and motionless surrounded by two or three smaller moving shapes.

Then he was closing his eyes and whispering thanks, for the large shape was a mother possum and the moving objects around her were her surviving children. Under normal circumstances he'd have felt terrible for orphaning these baby possums, but the sight of them now made him feel like opening a bottle of champagne.

Delirious with adrenaline and relief, he pushed open the car door and moved toward the carcass. Swollen from her recent pregnancy, the mother's stomach loomed white and large in the headlights' glare. Scattered about her broken body lay four of her dead children. Three looked peaceful and intact, as though they'd lain down in the road for a moonlit nap. The fourth was torn in half, the two sections of its body connected only by a shiny string of intestine. The eye-watering scent of fecal matter enshrouded him. He shielded his nose with the side of his hand.

Three more babies were crawling about in a daze. All three were slathered in a patina of blood, yet Paul couldn't tell whether it belonged to them or their mother. The giant possum lay unmoving inside a spreading pool of blood. Sickened and fascinated by the mother's enormous body, Paul sidled around to get a better look. He felt his gorge leap.

Two little legs, besotted with blood, kicked and strained, flicking little droplets on the highway. A surviving baby possum was digging into its mother's stomach. Transfixed, Paul watched the little blood-covered baby worm its way through cartilage and sinew as it tried to burrow inside the corpse.

At first he didn't want to credit the smacking sounds for what they were, yet the sounds and the frenetic twisting of the baby possum's body could only be the little devil feasting on its dead mother. Buried as it was from the shoulders up, it was inching its way to the heart.

Appalled by the burrowing cannibal and forgetting his revulsion, Paul endeavored to yank the baby out of its mother's corpse. Try as he might to get a finger hold on the kicking feet or the twitching tail, the baby eluded him. He didn't want to get too close, lest its crimson head appear and bite his finger. At this thought, he felt the mother's body shift.

Paul cried out and stumbled away as the mother's face rose and snapped at his arm. He landed on his rump and stared at her in shock. She bared her teeth at him and hissed. Then, instead of batting away her feasting child, she lay back and appeared to rest. Soon, two more surviving babies were swarming over the dying mother and digging out scraps of flesh on which to feed. The smallest possum chewed on one of the mother's teats and drank the blood that sluiced forth instead of milk.

Paul looked down and found that his heels were resting in the pool of blood. He shivered and scrambled away. Then, hearing the sounds of lips smacking and voices chittering, he drew himself to his feet and scuttled back inside his car. As he drove away from the scene of the accident, he found that he was fully awake.

Chapter Three

When Paul came to an opening in the forest, he made out a wooden mailbox whose carved, ornate letters spelled out WATERMERE.

Finally.

He signaled despite being the only living soul for miles. When the Civic left the thick gravel and disappeared into the woods, its wheels aligning with the twin tire paths that doubled for a road, he felt an odd twinge of recognition. The hickories and oaks and maples leaned over the road like knights with swords drawn, admitting their king.

And wasn't that the truth? Unless the pictures the lawyers had sent him had been doctored in some way, Paul was about to take possession of a mansion. He chuckled, giddy with disbelief. He was a modern-day baron, a landed count.

Bushes thwacked the Civic, reeling him back toward reality. He'd need to do something about the flora threatening to overtake the lane. He knew Myles had been an old man, but he still could have employed someone, a local kid maybe, to keep the road from going to seed.

The woods opened up, and all he could do was stop the car and stare.

Watermere was beautiful.

He couldn't believe that this sprawling Victorian home was his.

As Paul pulled forward, he took it all in. Though majestic, the house needed work. He noted the way the porch awning sagged, the cracks in the brick façade, the dead ivy. He doubted the old man had spent much time on upkeep in his twilight years. He studied the detached double garage up ahead and wondered whether either side was occupied.

Paul stopped, threw the car into park. Getting out, he entered the side door of the garage. Flicking the switch, he saw it was empty. The closed air smelled vaguely of kerosene. He scanned the wall for the automatic door opener but couldn't find one. Then, he spotted the rope attached to the garage door lying there on the floor. He crossed to it, bent and lifted.

The garage door roared up on its tracks. It made a frightful racket, but something about the noise appealed to him, as though he were announcing his ownership of the house by startling it awake.

Climbing back into the Civic, he shifted into gear and rolled into the stall. He cut the engine and got out, relishing the simple pleasure of housing his car in a garage. It was the first time, other than parking garages, he'd had the Civic indoors. He patted its roof fondly and went out.

Paul stared up at the house. He'd never imagined he would live in such a place. In fact, he never thought he'd own a house period. His father always told him how silly it was to waste money on rent, but Paul feared ownership, as though purchasing a home in the city would somehow bind him to it for the rest of his life. It was admitting defeat to buy a home near his family, he reasoned, so he kept his crackerbox apartment. Now he understood the pride his father had talked about.

He trotted toward the porch and mounted it in three strides. It winded him. He stood there panting, his belly drooping over his waistband.

He resolved to get into better shape.

Cupping his temples, he pushed his face close to the beveled door window and discerned a foyer made of checkered tile.

A manila envelope lay at his feet. He picked it up and ripped the top open. Bypassing the papers crammed inside, his groping fingers found the key, pulled it out. Taking one more deep breath, he sighed and slid the key into the lock. A dull click sounded. He thumbed the steel button.

Paul went in.

Ted waited, his head pounding like a gong, for her to come down the stairs. He tried to call to her in a reasonable voice.

It was difficult to muster.

First of all, he was in a goddamn basement. He had to bellow just to be heard. Secondly, she'd positioned him on his stomach so every word he spoke seemed to peter out and die on the dirty cement floor. It was getting hard to breathe. His chest flat on the ground, his lungs pressed flat, he felt like a goddamned turtle. He'd waited long enough for her to come down here and loosen his bonds. Now he was through with the nice-guy approach.

"If you don't get your skinny ass down here right now to untie these ropes, I'm going to swear to the police that you tortured me. You'll do a life sentence. *Mark my words.*" He continued that way, hurling every vile insult he could muster.

The clanging in his brain was like black death. He couldn't stand this much longer. He glanced again at his right hand, his left, tugged with both feet, but they wouldn't budge. The ropes around his limbs were firm, unyielding. Their scabrous threads chafed like barbed wire. The iced tea coating his skin wasn't painful but the cloying scent and clammy feel of it were terribly annoying. Like when his kids ate too much cotton candy and their goddamn faces became grime collectors, dirty human Band-Aids that insisted on following him around and soiling the legs of his pants.

Brand's fury grew.

He knew he'd pissed her off but that didn't give her the right to tie him to the floor. What the fuck kind of a freakshow was she?

Light washed through the basement. He blinked to adjust his eyes. As he whipped his head around to take in his bearings he heard her feet padding down the stairs.

She was barefoot. Resting his cheek on the dirty cement, he strained to make out the rest of her. A white sports bra and tiny black shorts. Where were the rest of her clothes? he wondered. Did she think she was going to play some weird S & M game with him? The time for all that was gone. All he wanted now was to get to the nearest police station. Now that the light was on, he could see the blood on his wrists where he'd cut himself pulling on the ropes. The scent of his own blood, like sheet metal slicked with rain, deepened his outrage. His Rolex was gone, he noted without surprise. She hadn't commented on it when he showed it to her in the car, but the bitch had probably been eyeing it all evening.

"Let me go," he said.

She gave no answer but her toes rubbed against one another. He watched them and felt his anger wax.

"Why did you tie me up?"

There was a feral edge to his voice he couldn't disguise. *Just as well*, he thought. *She needs to know how pissed you are. It's fair warning for what's going to happen to her the moment she lets you go.*

Ted grinned and thought how easy it would be to slaughter the bitch down here in the basement. He already had the rope marks on his wrists and ankles to prove she'd confined him. The jury would see he'd acted in self-defense, that the woman was a violent lunatic. In fact, if she stood a little closer to one of his hands he could seize her, put a vise-grip on her ankle that would make her squeal for mercy.

And then?

His grin shrank. If he managed to grab her, just where would that get him? Could he hold her there with one hand and force her to untie his bonds?

He swallowed, unsure of what to do. Had she heard the things he'd screamed at her? He thought she probably had. Why else had her coming down here so closely coincided with the most outrageous of his insults, the accusations about blowjobs and goats?

Whatever the case might be, he had to keep her down here, had to keep this woman from losing her temper again. He remembered her eyes just before she bashed him over the head with that damned stein. The indignity of it infuriated him—knocked unconscious with a beer stein. But he had to keep that rage dormant and work to win back the side of her with whom he'd spent most of the evening, the girl that had danced with him, kissed him.

"Look," he said as kindly as he could, "I'm sorry for the way I acted. I'm a married man and I should have been up front with you about that."

He waited to see if he'd made a dent. She stood silent.

He spoke to her ankles because he couldn't see any higher. "And if I hurt you I apologize. I'm also sorry about the things I've been yelling but you must understand that this is very uncomfortable. I'm in a lot of pain, Julia."

Was she going to let him lie here and talk to himself all night?

"As you can see, my wrists are bleeding and that knock you gave me on the head probably gave me a concussion." He became aware of a throbbing in his hip. "And I dare say you weren't very gentle in bringing me down here. The fact is, I'm in trouble, Julia. I need medical attention."

He felt her kneel beside him and he craned his neck to look up at her. From the way she was crouching, her buttocks resting on her heels, he could see how defined she was. The muscles in her legs were long and slender and hard.

She was holding a hypodermic needle.

"What are you doing with that?" he asked, voice tightening.

"I have to do this," she said. Her voice trembled a little.

He realized it was the first time she'd spoken since entering the basement. He wished she'd stayed quiet. Her fear, he realized, could be good or bad. Good if she could be frightened into letting him go. Bad if it made her irrational.

Judging from the needle, his money was on the latter.

"Julia, just let me up so we can talk about this."

"Please stay calm," she said.

"You're joking, right? You knock me out and drag me down the stairs—hell, maybe even *throw* me down the stairs. You tie me to the *floor*." His brow creased as he followed the ropes to where they connected—the stairway, two water pipes, the workbench fifteen feet away. He saw something gleaming on the edge of the workbench, some sort of large knife, and the fact that he couldn't even hope to reach it made his teeth grind together.

He felt himself tottering precariously on the brink of panic. "Look, Julia. Don't you think this has gone far enough? I know I offended you, but I've apologized for it and I think I've paid for it in spades." He laughed a little hysterically. "Don't you think I've endured enough crazy shit to learn my lesson?"

"Please hold still," she said, and he could tell by the intent sound of her voice that she was concentrating on finding a vein in his arm.

"Can I at least ask what you're putting in me?"

"It's safe."

"I fucking hope so, for chrissakes." He shook his head. "'It's safe.' How about you tell me just how the hell this is supposed to help me."

But the needle was already sinking into his arm, the silver tip piercing his vein as easily as it would a string of warm licorice.

"Almost done," she said and depressed the plunger. "This will give me time to think." The milky fluid flushed into his open vein.

He yanked his arm away and the hypo nodded in his flesh like a road sign swaying in a strong wind. He cursed her for as long as he could but soon the liquid reached his brain and the words lost their momentum, congealed in his mouth, and his head felt heavy even after he let it rest on the grimy cement.

Chapter Four

The night of the first death, Myles Carver was trying to bed his brother's wife. He stared at her through the French doors, the partygoers buzzing around him like gnats, his own date Maria tugging at the lapel of his best black jacket like a goddamned kid.

"Myles," she said. He smelled the sweet tang of wine on her breath, studied the large breasts peeking out of her dress, but those things did nothing for him.

Annabel did.

She was out there on the veranda, leaning forward so her rump stuck out, taunting him, the pale skin of her shoulders luminous in the night air.

He moved away from Maria, thought he'd escaped her when she gripped his arm. Then she was jabbering away at him and he realized she was drunk. Despite the band playing next to them atop the ballroom stage, her shrill, slurry voice bit through the noise and turned heads.

"Why can't you respect your brother? Why can't you leave her alone?"

Jesus. Airing their dirty laundry out here in front of everyone.

"Look at me, Myles." Both hands on his lapels now. "She doesn't want you. If she did she wouldn't have married David." Maria threw a sidelong glance at the men and women gawking at them. "That's right, I said she doesn't want you." Getting into it now that she had an audience. "So why don't you leave like your little brother. Robert knew she'd never have him so he left for Memphis. Why don't you run away too?"

She needed a good smack in the mouth. Painted little whore with a little boy at home watched by his grandma tonight because his mother would rather have a man between her legs than a son on her lap.

He thought of saying all that, thought of saying what everybody already knew about her, but he didn't. Instead, he said, "You've no room to talk," and walked away.

As he shut the French doors behind him he heard her say, "You're a coward." But she said nothing more because she was afraid of Annabel. Little Maria with her big mouth shut up quick whenever Annabel was around. Lovely Annabel.

Myles stood watching her.

He knew if he didn't say something soon he'd lose his nerve, so standing beside her he said, "Smoke?"

Elbows on the cement wall bordering the veranda, she stared quietly at the forest, making no sign she'd heard him or was even aware of his presence.

Playing it cool, Myles tapped one out for himself, lit it. He leaned there beside her showing her he was comfortable with the silence too. He stole glances at her, though, because he couldn't help it. Thin, sculptured nose below large blue eyes with lashes so long she needn't cake them with that black shit Maria smeared on hers. Annabel had her blond hair pulled back tonight. Myles realized his hands were shaking. He had to say something.

"Where's David?" he asked.

"I'm not sure," she said. As it usually was, her delivery was toneless, maddening.

"It'd be nice if he came to his own party." When she said nothing, he added, "And paid some attention to his wife."

Had there been the slightest hint of a smile? Without looking at him she said, "He does."

"I don't mean in the bedroom, I mean when there are fifty people at his house drinking his liquor and having sex in his rooms."

"They're your rooms, too, Myles."

"And I'm here, aren't I."

Annabel turned and moved toward the veranda steps.

"That's it?" he said and despised the plaintive note in his voice.

She descended the steps into the lawn, and for the first time he noticed she was barefoot.

41

He was about to shout at her, tell her that David didn't deserve her, that he was probably off in the woods with another woman, when a cry erupted from within the house.

It wasn't a normal cry, like a man who'd been cuckolded or a woman who'd been groped. It was a cry of anguish, of heartbroken doom, and as he pushed through the crowd gathered near the bandstand he realized it was Maria's wail he was hearing. It rose up to the chandeliers, knifed through his eardrums, and he spotted Maria's mother then, old and haggard and covered with blood. He thought at first she'd been stabbed, but then the crowd opened up and he saw Maria kneeling there in a lake of blood, her little boy clutched to her blood-shiny chest, her dead little boy whose throat was slashed so deeply it hung open like the mouth of some toothless animal.

Myles turned to look for his brother, for David, who would know what to do in a situation like this. But David wasn't around. Everywhere he looked were shocked faces, weeping men and women who were too stunned to move. Myles turned, not wanting to face the grotesque spectacle any longer but unable to block out the sound of Maria's wailing, and as he did he beheld a solitary figure standing in the open French doors, leaning there in a shimmering white dress.

It was Annabel, and she was smiling.

Chapter Five

Sam Barlow was in the middle of a nightmare when the phone rang. He sat up, disoriented. He slapped the snooze button on the alarm clock, dropped onto his side, but the ringing persisted and he realized something was wrong.

He'd run for sheriff expecting to have many dreams interrupted by the ringing of the phone, but the truth was, Patti rarely bothered him at home. Shadeland had its share of domestic disputes and ornery teenagers, but all in all, he knew he had it good.

"Um-hmm?" he asked.

"Patti here."

"Yeah. I figured as much." He couldn't bring himself to be annoyed with his secretary. She bothered him too seldom for that.

"We've got a bit of a situation down here, Sam," she said, sounding flustered. He found himself waking up fast.

"What kind of situation?" he asked.

"A missing person," she said. Then, quieter, "Well, he's not technically missing. He's only been gone for a few hours, but still…"

"Who is it?" Sam scooted up against his headboard, rubbed crust from his eyes.

"A lawyer. His name is Ted Brand."

"Never heard of him."

"He's not local. He came to deliver something to the Carver House."

"The Carver House?" Sam slid forward, his bare feet slapping the cold wooden floor.

"For the new owner."

"I didn't know there was a new owner." Sam reached over and twisted on the lamp. It was black, and there was a hula girl on it. He'd seen it at a garage sale a few years back and liked it. The half-naked girl watched him, frozen in mid shimmy. Had he married, he never would have been allowed to keep it.

It was little consolation.

"...and she really seems distraught, so I figured—"

"I'm sorry, Patti," Sam broke in. "I missed part of that."

"The lawyer's wife is here. She's convinced something bad happened to her husband."

"She giving you a hard time?"

"It's not that," Patti said. "She's very civil." A pause. "Look, it's probably better if you come down here yourself, Sam." Patti's voice went lower. "It's probably a matter of the lawyer stepping out on his wife, but I can't very well tell her that."

Barlow smiled, whatever unease that had been building since the phone rang vanishing under the light of Patti's logic. *She ought to have been a cop,* he thought. *She'd have been better than me.*

"Be right over," he said.

"Thanks, Sam. Sorry."

"Don't worry about it. You'll just owe me one."

"Uh-huh," she answered, and he could see her grin through the telephone.

Being on the wrong side of fifty wasn't much fun, he thought as he plodded through the gloomy bedroom. He splashed cold water on his face, careful not to notice the graying hair at his temples.

He was still active—he ran three times a week—and once he got moving, the years seemed to fall away. But the recovery periods were longer, and the mornings after a long run were an aching hell.

Sam refused to be one of those guys who denied their age, though. He simply wasn't going to let his body fall apart. They could keep their artificial hair dye and their erection pills; he'd manage in those areas just fine. Besides, Patti told him the gray at his temples made him look distinguished, and he figured he might as well believe it. As for his hard-ons, well, they weren't as frequent as they once were, but the old dog still managed to stand up and bark when he needed it to.

Ten more minutes and he was pulling into the station. He could see one of his deputies, Tommy McLaughlin, sitting across from Patti.

On the green vinyl couch next to Patti's desk was a woman who looked a little younger than his secretary. Forty, maybe. Not a knockout, but comely enough. Her curly brown hair looked tousled.

"Hi, Sam," Patti said.

Sam nodded. Tommy McLaughlin got up and gestured for Sam to follow. On the way into his office he could feel the lawyer's wife's eyes studying him, searching for signs that he would be her salvation.

He closed the glass door and nodded at Tommy. The young man's handsome face was careworn, a strained look replacing the cocky good humor Sam had grown accustomed to. Tommy's blond hair was darkened with sweat and matted to his forehead, reminding Sam of a little boy who's just awakened from a nasty nightmare. As often happened when he was with Tommy McLaughlin, Sam felt a moment's regret at never having children, never getting the chance to take a boy fishing or walk a daughter down the aisle.

"I assume Patti's filled you in already," Tommy said.

"Not really," Sam said, his mind clearing. "She just said the lawyer—what's the guy's name?"

"Ted Brand."

"Patti just said that Brand was missing and his wife was worried over it."

Tommy grunted. "Suicidal's more like it."

"How long has Mr. Brand been missing?"

Tommy glanced through the window at Mrs. Brand. "She said her husband left the office at five o'clock yesterday afternoon."

"And he was coming here?" Sam said.

"He was transferring the ownership papers to the new owner of Carver House."

Sam said, "It takes about two hours to get from Indy to here, right?"

"At the most," Tommy answered.

"So even if Brand is alright—which he probably is—we might not have good news for his wife."

Tommy nodded, examined his shoes.

"Why don't you check the hotels. See if Brand checked in somewhere."

Tommy didn't argue, just nodded again and went out. Sam sat down next to the lawyer's wife on the green vinyl couch.

"I'm Sam Barlow," he said, shaking the woman's hand. "Patti and Tommy tell me you're worried about your husband."

"Yes," she said. "This has never happened before."

Careful to keep anything insinuating from his voice, Sam asked, "He ever come home late?"

"He works late sometimes, but that's normal," she said. "Lawyers have to do that."

"What's the latest he's ever been?"

"Eleven," she answered. "Eleven-thirty at the latest."

Sam checked his watch. Seven-thirty.

"Does he know anyone in this part of Indiana?"

She drew back a little. "Why do you want to know that?"

"I'm just wondering if he might have stopped off somewhere."

"Why would he have stopped anywhere?"

It was the first time the woman's control slipped, and experience told him three things: Brand's wife was a nice lady, he treated her like dirt and though she knew deep down that he was cheating on her she'd never heard the possibility verbalized. She was staring at him now above a crumpled Kleenex. Sam felt for her, for the fact that there had to be women like her, as well as men like her husband.

"No one's saying he did stop, Mrs. Brand," he said in a gentler voice. "We're just talking hypotheticals here."

"Hypotheticals."

"That's right." He reached over and grabbed a box of tissues from the end table. Handing it to her, he asked, "Is there someone back at your house who will call if Mr. Brand comes home while you're gone?"

Her eyes held his. "Yes. My mother's there. With our two sons."

"What are your boys' names?"

"Majors and Macky," she answered.

Sam tried not to cringe.

"Those are good names, Mrs. Brand." He leaned forward. "And the best thing for you right now is to be home with them. They'll be worried enough if they wake up without their father home."

"But I don't want to go home," she said without much conviction.

46

"I know that. And I know you're worried about your husband. I appreciate your feelings, Mrs. Brand, but what good will come of you sitting around this office?"

"You think Ted's cheating on me, don't you?"

"No one said that, Mrs. Brand. In fact, I'd guess there's a perfectly reasonable answer to this thing." He forced himself to make eye contact. "How can you be sure he didn't check into a hotel here or somewhere else on the way home? People get tired when they drive at night."

She was shaking her head before he'd even finished. "No, Ted never does that. He can drive all night. On trips or wherever. He never gets tired."

"Isn't it possible?"

"I'm sorry, but no, it's not." She stared up at him, her eyes appealing.

"Okay, Mrs. Brand. Can I call you by your first name?"

"It's Linda."

"Alright, Linda," he said. "Let's talk a little more about your husband."

As Linda Brand began to talk, Sam thought more and more about the lawyer stepping out on her. Granted, it was possible he had crashed his car somewhere or gotten mugged. But Sam's money was on the guy screwing another woman.

"Tell me what Ted looks like."

"He's very handsome. Tall, athletic. He was a pitcher in high school..."

And as Linda Brand went on, Sam began to nod.

Ted's first thought upon waking was that his face itched. He moved his hand to scratch it, but the rope caught and reopened the cut on his wrist.

His head began to pound. What time was it? he wondered. He remembered his days as an undergrad, a psych class he'd taken. They studied a lot of boring shit in that course, but there had been one interesting lesson about prisoners in solitary confinement, how darkness and time deprivation led to panic. Now Ted could see why. Down here in this fucking dungeon it could be noon or midnight. He had no idea how much time had passed, but he was certain by now that Linda would be looking for him.

He tried to remain calm but felt himself slipping. He was trapped, would soon be dead if he didn't escape. But what the hell could he do?

That fucking stupid cunt, she had no right to do this to him, had no right to behave like a Spanish inquisitor, and why did his face itch like it was full of bugs and what was that crap tickling his lips and getting in his mouth? What the hell, had the iced tea transformed into a cadre of flesh-eating bugs bent on driving him insane?

"Let me out of this fucking hole!" he bellowed.

She must have been upstairs, waiting for him to call to her because seconds after he'd screamed, the light flicked on, blinding him. He heard footsteps on the stairs. His eyes adjusted to the light, and he was about to demand she release him when he realized why his face was itching and what it was he'd been spitting out.

Ants.

He was acrawl with them. They teemed over his face and body, and through his writhing and spitting he glimpsed her standing there with huge eyes and knew she was as surprised as he was, and he didn't give a good god damn whether or not she'd meant for this to happen, it had, and the moment she let him out of the ropes he'd make her pay for it.

Then his voice was rising because she was backing away, her hand on her mouth, climbing the steps, saying something about a needle, and his teeth clenched savagely as he blinked away the ants, and the last thing he said to her before she reached the doorway above was that he'd peel her skin off and let the ants eat her raw flesh.

Then she was gone, and Ted was alone with his agony.

The ballroom was grand.

A floor laid with white hexagonal tiles and sprinkled with smaller black ones spread out before him, magnifying the size of the great hall. The curved staircase beside the ballroom led to a long balcony. Beyond the wooden balusters, the rooms that overlooked the dance floor reminded him of an upscale hotel.

He decided to investigate the bar. Pushing a stool out of the way, he hopped onto the dusty wooden surface, swung his legs over the edge and landed on the other side. Squatting, he inspected the cache of liquor.

Paul smiled.

The cherry-wood shelves were fully stocked. There were three kinds of everything. Gin, vodka, scotch, bourbon. Everything. He peered to his left and found two full fifths of Jim Beam, his favorite. The varied bottles of alcohol faced him with bright smiles, eager school children ready to participate in the day's lesson.

It was wonderful. And terrible.

Emerging from behind the bar, he trailed a hand over one of the burgundy crushed velvet couches and moved toward the curved staircase. It was like being on a movie set. Pausing at the top of the stairs, he grasped the wooden banister of the balcony and gazed down, marveling at his good fortune.

It was all his.

He couldn't believe it.

A week ago he'd lived in a tenement. This was a palace.

He opened a door and gazed at the old-fashioned wallpaper, the canopied bed. Moving to the next room, he found the same thing, except the wallpaper was different.

Eight thousand square feet, he remembered as he moved to the third door. What the hell was he going to do with eight thousand square feet? Maybe turn the ballroom into a basketball court, the upstairs into a brothel.

Exploring the rest of the hallway, he discovered a sitting room, two bathrooms, another bedroom. At the end of the hall he mounted the back staircase and felt the temperature warm.

He scanned the third floor corridor. There were fewer doors here, which meant larger rooms.

He opened the first door, flipped on the light. To his right sat a sewing table and an old black Singer that looked like a miniature oil derrick. Paul glanced at a cabinet festooned with enamel animals and other curios and decided he'd not be spending much time here. He moved on.

Behind the next door sat a large mahogany desk and a Tiffany reading lamp. The study. Leaving the door ajar, he moved to the window and raised the blind. The view was majestic. The grassy backyard was the size of a city block.

This, he decided, would be his writing room.

The next door was some distance away, and as his hands found the switch inside the door, a multitude of lamps flared into brilliance.

As impressive as the ballroom had been, the library was the copestone of Watermere. The walls of the rectangular room were a deep crimson, the built-in shelves a pristine white. As copious as the bookcases were, no space on them was left unfilled. Paul had no idea how many books were here, but judged they numbered in the tens of thousands. The books imbued the room with a faintly musty smell that Paul found pleasing. In the center of the library were two segmented islands of furniture, each set containing a pair of chairs and a pair of couches, multiple end tables and reading lamps. Dual chandeliers hung illuminated over the reading islands. Tall floor lamps blended into the walls and spilled light on the ceiling. On and around the three walls of bookcases were paintings and sculptures, most of which were unfamiliar to Paul. One painting he recognized as a Bosch. As he glanced about, he realized that all the artwork depicted demons and gargoyles and other malign creatures. In one painting a woman was being ravished by a grinning, simian-looking demon and a white-eyed horse.

The outer wall faced the expansive back yard. Multiple windows, now shuttered, promised another fabulous view. He was, he judged, in the middle of the house. From here, he would be able to gaze out on the maple trees as their leaves changed to red and yellow and fell to earth. Savoring the feel of the room and the thought that every single volume in this library belonged to him, he imagined how the place would feel in the winter. The fireplace that bisected the outer wall was covered with large stones of many colors. Come December he'd sit before this hearth with a book in hand, his eyes occasionally taking in the snow falling on the treetops fringing the yard.

He frowned. The bare space above the fireplace was strange, incongruous with the rest of the room, which was covered from floor to ceiling with books and art.

He stood before the fireplace. He saw now that there had once been a painting or a mirror hung here. The red paint in the empty rectangle of wall was sharper than the paint around it. It seemed to leer at him, daring him to venture closer. Paul stared back at it, musing.

A knock sounded downstairs. Loud, insistent.

He left the library and wondered what could be this urgent at—he checked his watch—eight-thirty in the morning.

He turned the corner, moving down the stairs, and the pounding accelerated. Whoever was hammering on the door was double-fisting it, as if he were trying to bust out of somewhere rather than get in.

Maybe, he thought as he puffed around another turn, he'd invest in an elevator. How the hell had a man in his eighties gotten around in a place with all these stairs?

Wondering if someone was hurt out on the road, Paul crossed the foyer, opened the door.

A policeman stared back at him.

Though the pale morning light was just beginning to filter over the eastern forest, Paul could see the cop fairly clearly. The man was large, powerfully-built. Though his face was kindly, the cop wore a neutral expression. He took off his hat and said, "I'm Sheriff Barlow. You rather talk inside or out here?"

Paul's throat went dry. "Out here, I guess."

Paul followed the sheriff onto the porch. Staring out at the yard, Barlow said, "Is Ted Brand still here?"

The name rang a bell, but for a moment, it eluded him.

Barlow glanced at him, impatient.

Paul started. "The lawyer, right. I haven't seen him."

"That's not what I asked."

"What I mean is I never saw him. We talked on the phone, and he dropped off the key to the house, but we never actually met."

"Can you explain why his car is on your property?"

Paul glanced down the lane.

"You can't see it from here. It's about halfway to the road."

Paul opened his mouth, closed it.

"You're telling me you didn't see it on the way in?" The set of Barlow's mouth said *You gotta be kidding me*, but his eyes were deadly serious.

"It couldn't have been," Paul said. "I would have seen it."

"That's what I'd have thought."

Paul stared at Barlow. Was the sheriff mocking him?

"Has something happened?" Paul asked.

"I don't know," Barlow answered. "Has it?"

And with that the sheriff turned, went back to his car and drove away.

Julia finished up in the basement, smashed as many of the ants as she could while Ted was still under. It was hell getting the hypo in again, but once she did, he went down fast.

His face had been covered in bites, so much so that she hardly knew where to start when cleaning him up. She'd never noticed the ants before. If she had she certainly never would have put him on the basement floor. There never would have been so many had she not added so much sugar to his drink, which she'd only done because he'd asked her to. My God, she'd been trying to be nice to him.

But he didn't believe that, and if she tried to convince him of it he'd only shout cruel things at her.

She thought of how he'd feel when he awoke, his murderous eyes as he glared through the angry red bites at her. To get her mind off it, she set about getting ready for work.

After she'd driven Ted's car over to Watermere, sleep hadn't come at all. Neither had a solution to her problem. By tying Ted down, she'd bought herself a day or two at most, and that was only if Sheriff Barlow didn't come knocking. If he did she'd just have to tell him the truth, about Brand and the way he'd treated her. She'd go to jail then, she knew, but perhaps the jury or the judge would go easy on her.

No they wouldn't.

They'd bury her in a maximum-security ward, throw away the key. Ted would laugh at her as they took her from the courtroom in handcuffs, her face lowered in shame and the knowledge that she'd wasted her life, thrown away her freedom with one flurry of terrible decisions. There was no avoiding it. As long as Ted Brand was alive.

Julia started at her reflection. Seeing herself in the mirror, she couldn't believe it. It was like another woman had taken her place, another woman thinking like a criminal. She took deep breaths, waited for her fear to bleed away, for rational thought to return.

When she looked at herself again, she was glad to see that nothing had changed. No, she wasn't a psycho. She still had options, ways out of this mess.

Killing him was out of the question. For now.

Unaccountably, she found herself back in Watermere last night, and though Brand had been right beside her at the time, the sound of his voice was now a muffled echo, his figure a faded shadow.

What wasn't vague—what came to her now more clearly than her mirrored face, the sound of the dripping faucet—was the way the floor had creaked under her tennis shoes in Watermere. She remembered the clammy sheen of sweat coating the back of her neck, the exaggerated smells of the old house, moldering drapes and stale air. She reached the basement door before she realized it was the source of her sudden dread, and without thinking she drew closer to Brand, his tall, athletic frame reassuring at the time.

She heard his words through a muffling wad of gauze, the words she somehow knew he'd say, on some level recognizing even then what a vacuous schemer the man was. His arm around her, his face almost kind: "You look like you've seen a ghost."

That's when she'd pushed away from him, her extended hands seeking support on the first thing they touched, the old rose-patterned wallpaper, the steadying wall beneath.

"*Hey,*" he said, going to her. A hand on her shoulder, his voice a distorted baritone. "*Hey, are you okay?*"

She couldn't even pretend, could only wait for equilibrium to scatter the malignant stare of the basement door.

"Julia?" he asked.

"Give me a second," she said, and as she leaned against the wall some of her composure had begun to return.

And then it had happened, the sensation that had to have been spawned by her fear, her irrational terror, a cruel trick of her imagination that got her moving, compelled her into the ballroom where a new set of associations took hold of her.

Beneath her right hand...the wallpaper under the pads of her middle and index fingers...

No, she thought, and stared fiercely into her bathroom mirror. *A thousand times no. You go down that road and you're done for sure. What gossamer-thin strands of sanity you have left after what you've done to Brand will snap like overstretched guitar strings if you let yourself believe that something actually—*

A howl of pain from below made her teeth clench, her hands grasp the sides of the sink.

The anesthetic had worn off.

Paul couldn't return to the house. Not after what the sheriff had said.

He had no idea how far down Brand's car was parked—the house was about a mile from the road—so instead of jogging down the lane, he took the Civic.

He rounded a curve and beheld a black BMW sitting in the tall grass beside the lane. It sat next to the woods on his right, its back end facing him, as if it had tried but couldn't bring itself to leave after its errand was over. Had Brand's car broken down after he delivered the manila envelope? It certainly appeared so, but if it did, why hadn't he gone back to the house to use the phone?

Because there is no phone, his reason answered.

But did Brand know that?

He parked, walked around the side of the car. The forest was unnaturally quiet, the only sound the crunching of his sneakers on gravel. He stopped and looked at the car's bright black exterior, tried to explain its presence here.

Brand broke down, knew there was no phone back at Watermere and didn't feel like waiting for Paul to show up to drive him into town. He probably had a cell phone, but it might not have worked way out here.

So he walked. He left the car here and headed into town. What was so far-fetched about that?

Nothing, other than the fact he'd never made it into town, had disappeared somewhere along the way. Or been picked up. Otherwise, none of this would be happening.

Remembering the stories his parents used to tell him and his brother about people who picked up hitchhikers, he tried the driver's side door. It was locked. What if this time the scary tales were true? What if Brand really had hitched a ride and met some grisly fate?

It was as plausible as anything else he could think of.

He froze.

He'd touched the door handle, left his fingerprints. What was he thinking? He wrapped his hand in his tee shirt and wiped off the handle, sure that at any moment the police would roar down the lane and catch him in the act. That done, he straightened and stared down at the Beamer.

He heard a car approach.

When Paul spied the cruiser coming down the lane, he felt his cheeks flush, as though his presence here in the near-darkness of the forest was reprehensible.

Wait a minute, he thought. Why shouldn't he be looking? The black car was on his property. Didn't he have the right to investigate an abandoned vehicle on his own land?

The cruiser pulled up cattycornered to the BMW and halted. Barlow killed the engine, the sounds of the cruiser door opening and shutting amplified in the stillness of the woods.

Barlow wasn't wearing a hat this time, and Paul was afforded a better look at the sheriff. He had large features, but they were only in proportion with his frame. Standing next to him, Paul could see how big he was. He looked like he was in good shape too. He wore regular cop clothes, though they were wrinkled.

Barlow's expression was hard to read.

"Morning," the big man finally said.

"Morning," Paul answered and stared at the gold badge that said SHERIFF.

Barlow paused beside the black car. Hands on knees, he squinted into the window and asked, "You still don't remember passing this car on the way in?"

"Why do you think I'm out here?"

The sheriff stepped back from the Beamer, examined the ground beside it. Then, his eyes scanned the empty lane.

"You ever kill anyone?" he asked.

Paul's heart thumped. "No. Of course not. "

The cop stared down the lane a moment longer, then walked around to the passenger door and peered in. Paul could only watch him, his heart stampeding.

Stepping to his left, Barlow bent and inspected the back seat. "When's the last time you saw Ted Brand?" he asked.

"I've never seen Ted Brand. Like I said, we only talked over the phone."

Without looking at him the cop answered, "Uh-huh."

"You don't believe me?"

For a moment, the sheriff seemed about to say something. Then, he put a large hand on Paul's shoulder.

"Let's walk."

Through his swollen eyes he could see the basement growing brighter. If Linda hadn't started checking around about him yet, she soon would. That would lead them to Shadeland, to the Carver House.

Whether that would lead them here was another story.

If the police in this godforsaken little burg weren't halfwits—a proposition in which Ted had little confidence —they'd be going door to door before nightfall, which meant he only need stay alive until someone came knocking. Julia had evidently gone to work, which said a lot about her mental state. By leaving him here she was doing all she could to avoid the problem.

To avoid the man tied up in her basement.

Fucking whore.

If she worked normal hours she'd return home at about five o'clock, which was the same time Ted would be declared missing. If she worked late, an officer might come by before she got home.

Ted's breath caught as he remembered her lack of transportation. She worked at the library, he remembered. She had to walk home. Hell, last night she hadn't gotten halfway home before he met her, and that was six-thirty. It was entirely possible that she wouldn't even get back before seven, which gave the cops a full two hours to search for him.

He wondered if his car were still here.

Surely not. Surely she wouldn't have been that stupid.

She was stupid enough to leave you down here in a swarm of ants, wasn't she? Or maybe that had been intentional.

Damn right it had been intentional. Her little act upon finding him had been convincing enough, but hadn't she been acting since the very first? Pretending she had no idea what he wanted from her. Acting like a coy little schoolgirl as they toured the Carver House. Feigning shock when he made his move.

The slut. She knew exactly what she was doing all along. The pick-up, the assault. She lured him here and knocked him out and tethered him and let those bastard ants crawl all over his face.

Ted's fists clenched. If he got his hands on her. If he got a sliver of an opening he'd take it. He'd tie her up. He'd take what she damn well should have given him last night.

Then he'd make her regret ever fucking with him.

Alone in the silent basement, Ted Brand began to laugh.

Chapter Six

As they walked along the lane Sam sized him up. Paul Carver was taller than his Uncle Myles, but softer, less sure of himself. The guy didn't look like a murderer, but not all murderers did.

Too much of this didn't make sense. If Carver had nothing to do with it, how was it he never spotted Brand's car on the way to the house? Grogginess was one thing. Passing by a shiny new BMW, the only car parked beside a narrow forest lane, without noticing it was just too improbable.

But that was how Carver had told it as they moved down the lane, and that was more than Sam thought he'd get out of him. He rarely had a suspect go this long without asking for a lawyer. He had to keep him talking.

"So you left for Shadeland when?"

"Five thirty yesterday afternoon."

"Memphis on the same time as us?"

"Yes."

"Then what?"

Carver sighed. "As I said, I stopped at a gas station—"

"But you don't remember which one?"

"No, I don't."

Sam led them farther down the lane, half a mile now from their vehicles.

"Aren't we going back?" Carver asked.

"Soon. For now I'd like to walk."

Pretty soon, the guy caught up. They walked to County Road 500 and back, Sam's shoes scuffing dust and the occasional stone. He could hear Carver's breathing as they moved around the final turn toward the cars, the guy puffing like a bellows in the cool morning air. Carver had no wind at all. Sam knew it was petty, but he couldn't help taking satisfaction from seeing this guy fifteen years his junior struggling to keep up.

"You a smoker?" Sam asked.

Carver shook his head.

"Oughta get more exercise."

Carver said nothing.

"Course, it's probably too hot down in Memphis to do much of anything."

"That and I'm too lazy to get in shape."

"So you drove straight through from the gas station without stopping again."

"No," Carver said, an edge to his voice. They'd gone over all of it already, and he'd asked Carver everything there was to ask. Now, he was going through it a second time and the guy knew it, knew Sam was probing for inconsistencies.

"Like I said," Carver went on, "I stopped for gas again—the Civic's tank doesn't hold much—but it was a pay-at-the-pump and I didn't get a receipt."

Sam asked, "Why's there blood on your bumper?"

He could tell he'd rattled the kid. Then Carver laughed but not as though he thought anything was funny.

"I hit a possum last night. A family of them actually."

"You saw them before you ran them over?"

"Of course not. I didn't even know what I'd hit until I drove back to make sure it wasn't a hitchhiker."

"Were you drinking?"

Carver watched him, sweat bleeding steadily out of his face. "I didn't drink a drop last night."

Sam stopped and regarded the guy, wondering at his reaction. "Those tiny red blood vessels in your nose." He pointed. "That's rosacea. Often it's from drinking too much."

Carver touched his nose self-consciously.

"I'm guessing you like to toss back a few after work, take the edge off," Sam said.

Carver looked away. "That's none of your business."

"It is if you were drinking last night. Maybe you ran Ted Brand down by accident. Maybe he was walking to his car and you didn't see him. Eyes were too blurry." Sam allowed himself a small grin, needling the kid.

"I think I need to talk to a lawyer."

Damn, Barlow thought.

"Come on," he said in a lighter tone. "It's only the guilty ones need lawyers."

Carver watched him, eyes narrowed. "That's not true and you know it. A person doesn't have to commit a crime to be blamed for it. Just look at me."

"How do you know a crime's been committed, Mr. Carver?"

"Why else would you spend two hours interrogating me? I haven't even had breakfast yet."

They got moving again.

"When's the last time you saw Myles Carver?" Sam asked.

"I never saw him."

"You never met your uncle."

"No."

"Yet he left you his entire fortune."

"I know it's crazy. I can't believe it myself."

"Why you, then? You his only living relative?"

"No, there were others." Carver's breathing grew strained. "Like I said, I never even met him. My grandpa once told me I looked like Myles."

"Do you?"

"I told you I've never seen the man."

"Not even in pictures?"

"No."

The sheriff watched him a moment longer. In front of them the trail opened up and Sam saw the three cars sitting on the lane.

Sam said, "Whatever's going on, it started after Brand did what he came here to do. How is it you didn't see his car on the way in?"

"I don't know," Carver said. "I don't think the car was here when I got in last night."

"You said that awhile ago, and it didn't make any sense then either," Sam said, dismissing it. "Who saw you after you left Memphis."

Carver sighed wearily. "I didn't see anyone." He snapped his fingers, remembering. "There was a man. At a gas station along the way. He was reading a porn mag with two women going at it."

Barlow wrote that down, asking, "You go in for that sort of stuff?"

"Porn mags or two women?"

"Either. What was the name of the gas station and the exit where you stopped?"

Paul shrugged. "I don't remember. It was a place outside Memphis."

"How late?"

"Around six, I think."

"Describe the man and the gas station."

Carver paused. "Do I need a lawyer?"

"I don't know," Sam said. "Do you?"

"I haven't done anything wrong, if that's what you mean."

"You said that earlier. Descriptions?"

"Oh man," Paul said, and gave Barlow the details he could recall.

The sheriff continued asking him questions as they moved toward the lane, Barlow scribbling his answers on a small notepad. Sam said he'd be in touch, climbed into the cruiser. Just as he was about to key the ignition, a thought occurred to him. He got out of the car.

Barlow said, "The reason why you and I will never be best buddies has nothing to do with you and everything to do with things that happened years ago. You say you never met Myles Carver. Fine. You say you were told that you take after him." He moved up close and pinned him with his eyes. The two were the same height, but Sam was much broader. He felt Carver shrink against the car.

Sam said, "If you're like your uncle, things aren't going to be good for you. Not with me, not with anyone else." He tapped Paul on the chest. "You better hope you're nothing like that son of a bitch."

With that, he turned and moved back to his car. After he'd started the engine, he said out the window, "But like I said, none of that's your fault. It's just better that you know where you stand. Some things a

61

person can't forget."

"You seem distracted, Honey."

Julia glanced up from the computer screen. Below her gray hair, Bea's face was a fretful mask. "Did something happen to you last night?" she asked.

Julia thought of the man in her basement. Her mind flailed, grasping for something believable.

"I was going through my old sheet music, and I happened to come across part of Beethoven's Seventh Symphony. He was my mom's favorite."

"Oh, you poor girl." The older woman cupped her chin. Julia could smell the rosewater on the woman's clothes. "I hate that you're all alone."

Looking up at her, it wasn't hard for Julia to despair. She had no idea what to do about Brand.

"Thanks. You're a good friend," Julia said.

"Oh," Bea waved it off. "You don't need a friend. What you need is a husband." The librarian turned and recommenced her labeling of the new magazines.

Julia said, "Can I ask you something?"

"Of course."

"You kid me about turning into an old maid. Do you really mean it?"

"Of course not."

"You sure?"

"I don't know if I feel like talking about something so serious before lunch," Bea said, looking back at her. "Does this somehow relate to your mother?"

"No," Julia said and stared at her feet. "Not directly."

"Because you know she was quite a beauty."

"I know."

"And you're even prettier."

"Come on."

"So the chances of your becoming an old maid are slim. Unless," Bea glanced at her watch, "you spend all your time here with a boring old woman."

Julia looked at the clock. "We don't close for another couple hours."

"No. But you've been acting strange all day. Why don't you take off early?"

"Bea, you really do act like my mom sometimes, you know that?"

"Well, someone has to." The woman grimaced, realizing her gaffe. "Anyway," she hurried on, "you know we're never busy on Tuesdays. And since I know you won't let me drive you home when we get done, you should at least do me the courtesy of taking the rest of the afternoon off."

Julia scratched the back of her neck, debating. She was anxious to get home but mustn't act it. "I don't know."

"I insist. With the weather as clear as it is this afternoon, no one's going to waste their time at the library."

Julia thought about arguing, remembered that the sedative had likely worn off hours ago. Brand could already be finding a way out of the ropes.

"Okay, Bea. You talked me into it."

When Linda Brand left for home to check on her children, Sam breathed a sigh of relief. He didn't like to admit it, but he'd avoided the station for most of the day because of her. Seeing those reddened eyes and that wan face, he felt like he was being accused by a mourner, as though the station were already haunted by the ghost of her husband.

It was this, he knew, that lay at the heart of his unrest.

Something was terribly wrong with Ted Brand.

Sam had no tangible reason to believe that Brand wasn't just playing hooky. Who was to say that a man couldn't lock his keys in his car, walk into town with the intention of finding a locksmith, but instead find some other diversion?

But if Brand had gone for help, he would have used the roads, not the forest paths. Sam had drawn a pretty distinct character sketch of

Ted Brand, and Davy Crockett the man was not. He would have stuck to blacktop and unless he was a complete idiot, he would have made it into town.

Perhaps he'd picked up a local gal at one of the bars. From the pictures Brand's wife had shown him, Sam could see he was a good-looking guy. Maybe, figuring his car was a lost cause for the night, he'd hooked up and had himself a screw.

Yet there were a number of facts that shot that theory to hell. For starters, none of the bartenders he'd talked to had seen a man in his late thirties or early forties last night, at least no one they weren't used to seeing. Secondly, Brand hadn't sought out anyone to get his car unlocked. Wouldn't he, at some point, have called a locksmith, the fire department, someone?

Third, well, third was the sinking feeling Sam had in his gut, and for his money, that was the strongest evidence. When he got these feelings, they usually meant something. The sinking feeling told him that Brand was in deep trouble, if he wasn't already dead. The same feeling rendered it impossible for his eyes to linger on Brand's wife for more than a couple of seconds.

It was the sinking feeling more than anything that prompted him to call the state police and declare Ted Brand missing.

Chapter Seven

Paul sat on the front porch, fingers tapping cement.

He knew the sheriff would be back soon, perhaps even more suspicious than before. Brand was still missing, had to be, and it was this thought that muted his excitement about his new start. The feeling he'd had on the drive up here, the feeling that all of this was too good to be true, was confirmed with each passing moment.

He checked his watch: 6:45 p.m.

If nothing was wrong, why didn't they call him? If Brand had been found, wouldn't they do him the courtesy of letting him know so he could cease brooding out here?

These were his thoughts as the sheriff's cruiser drifted down the lane.

It was almost dark now. As the big man climbed out and approached him, Paul felt his insides turn to jelly.

"Evening," said the sheriff.

"Hello," he returned.

"Any sign of Brand?" Barlow asked.

"No. He hasn't turned up?" Paul asked and regretted his wording.

The sheriff didn't reply. He glanced toward the woods, the skin around his eyes wrinkling.

"So," Paul said, "are you going to take me in or what?"

Eyes still trained on the soundless woods, Barlow replied softly, "Should I?"

"That's up to you."

"You're right," Barlow said.

Paul watched the man watch the woods.

"Let's go for a walk," the sheriff finally said.

"Wonderful," Paul said. "Another walk."

Though the path was wide enough for both of them, Paul kept a little behind the sheriff. Barlow walked with the air of one who has nothing better to do. Moving in this direction, the woods to their left were darker than the woods to their right. Paul longed for the sheriff to veer toward the light, but when the path forked, Barlow went left.

Gloom spread over them. Paul was unnerved by the stillness pervading the woods. May was nearing, which meant the forest should have been teeming with life. Instead, the air here had a funereal quality that reminded him of winter, of dead things.

Moving even with the sheriff, he glanced at Barlow's profile to read what was going on behind the man's knitted brow.

"What did you mean earlier?" Paul asked to break the silence.

Barlow watched his feet stepping over packed dirt, an occasional root. He extended a big hand, his fingers brushing over tree trunks and bushes. Distantly, he heard a harsh flutter of leaves and the death cry of some small animal as a hawk snapped its backbone.

"What did you mean when you talked about the reason for not liking me?" Paul asked.

"I heard you the first time."

"Well?"

"What do you know about your uncle?"

Paul regarded the path. "I know my family hated him. Especially my grandparents. My grandpa left Shadeland when he was still in his twenties."

"Did you ever hear why?"

"No," he said, "not really. Nothing specific, I mean. They just treated the subject like it was taboo. We weren't to mention it, so we didn't."

"Why do you think that is?" Barlow asked, leading him.

Feeling the branches snicking against his flannel shirt, Paul stuffed his hands in his jeans pockets. "I wouldn't know that. That's how my family is. They don't talk about certain things and they don't talk about why they don't talk about them."

"If he were in my family, I wouldn't claim him either."

"Are you going to tell me why, or are we going to talk in code all night?"

The sheriff stopped and turned his back to him. Thinking they were setting off from the path, Paul moved to follow him when he heard the sound of Barlow's zipper. Urine patted the ground, steam rising up from the muddied soil. Paul stood there, hands in pockets, and wished he had to pee as well, share in the moment. Instead, he moved down the path a couple of paces to give the sheriff room to do his thing. He heard Barlow finish, zip up.

The sheriff said, "Your uncle was the most despicable man I've ever met."

Paul laughed, a forced sound in the quiet forest. "Isn't that a bit extreme?"

"If anything, it's an understatement."

"What did he do that was so terrible?"

"You name it."

Paul stopped. "Why didn't you arrest him then?"

"I wasn't sheriff until Myles Carver was in his late sixties. By that time most of what he'd done was in the past."

"You haven't even told me what he did."

Barlow appeared to think. Then, he said, "I'll tell you one story I heard. One of many. Then you can decide for yourself. Some of the things I know are true because I witnessed them. Other things I only heard about, but the people who told them to me, for the most part, are people I trust. Ralph Trask, the old doctor who's down at the nursing home now, he's the one who told me this story. He was a couple of years younger than Myles, so he'd know." He glanced at Paul. "And before you doubt Trask's credibility, write him off as a crazy old coot, keep in mind he was fifteen years younger when he told me this, and he's still perfectly lucid."

It was full night now. The April chill lay hard on the forest.

The sheriff got moving and continued: "This was a long time ago, years and years before I was born. Back then, as you're probably aware, some schools had different grades grouped together, so that the older ones sat in the same room with the younger ones. Your uncle was young, twelve or thirteen. Samantha Hargrove was four or five years his senior, but for some reason, she liked him."

Paul thought he heard bitterness in the sheriff's voice as he went on: "Even in his older years, women thought Myles was a good-looking man. He wasn't the kind of guy other guys liked. I always thought he was too pretty, like a mannequin. But the women around here, they couldn't get enough of him. Samantha Hargrove was only the first in a long line of them."

Paul looked up at Barlow, but the sheriff was gazing down the trail, lost in his thoughts. The bunched shadows that hovered over the trail reminded Paul of a dead man's gaping eye socket, the eye itself having long ago been ravaged by worms and microbes. He shivered, made himself focus on the sheriff's tale.

"It started with her helping Myles with his studies. As smart as he was, he couldn't do bookwork to save his life. Or he feigned ignorance because he was lazy. Either way, he got himself a tutor, and that tutor was Samantha, the preacher's daughter.

"According to Trask, Samantha was a real looker. A raven-haired beauty. Before long she was disappearing from her house for hours at a time. Your uncle was, too, but according to Doc Trask, that was normal. It seems his parents—your great-grandparents—didn't like having Myles in or even near the house most of the time. Trask told me stories about why, but I'll save those for another time.

"Anyway, you can probably guess what's coming. Within a few months of their meeting, Samantha shows up at school in tears. She cries every day but won't say why. Then she starts to get sick, misses school. Even misses church. Finally, her mother gets wise to what's happening and confronts Samantha with it. The two were in the kitchen at the time.

"The next part of this story is third-hand, but I still believe it. Doc Trask was best friends with Samantha Hargrove's little brother Billy, and Billy heard the argument from where he sat on the back porch."

The sheriff halted and reached into his coat pocket. He produced a bag of chewing tobacco, scooped some out and stuffed it in his cheek. In the gloom of the forest, the wad looked to Paul like a leafy turd. Despite its foul appearance, the tobacco scent reminded Paul of harvest apples and hayrides.

Chewing a little, Barlow went on, "According to Trask, Mrs. Hargrove—Samantha and Billy's mother—was a fierce woman. She wore the pants in the family despite her husband's position as the only

Methodist minister in town. She must have suspected it for a while because when she did bring it up, she really let her daughter have it. Samantha was already distraught, and having her mom screaming at her probably didn't do much to calm her down. The more Mrs. Hargrove yelled, the more Samantha cried. Doc Trask said that Billy wanted to help his sister except he was afraid of their mother too.

"Billy Hargrove said he heard the faucet turn on and then he heard Samantha screaming. Afraid his mom was killing his sister, he got up to look through the window.

"She wasn't killing her daughter, but she was dragging her by the hair toward the sink. The water was splashing up out of the basin, and in trying to get her under the pouring water—to cleanse her of sin, I guess—Mrs. Hargrove kept ramming Samantha's head into the steel faucet. Billy could see that his sister was bleeding a little from the cuts she'd gotten from the faucet, but she was otherwise okay. Mrs. Hargrove had at least left the drain open so the water that wasn't splashing out onto the floor was pouring down the drain."

The sheriff regarded him. "She wasn't trying to drown Samantha anyway."

He waited, watching Barlow work the tobacco around his mouth. The sheriff spat, a trifle too close to Paul's sneakers, he thought.

Barlow went on, "Mrs. Hargrove was a big, robust woman, and she finally got Samantha's head under the running water. Her daughter's hair got caught in the drain and clogged it so the water level was rising. Through his sister's screaming, Billy could hear his mother asking Samantha who the father was. At first, the girl could only cry. Then she could only choke and splutter because the cold water was splashing all around her and into her open mouth.

"At this point, Billy walks over and pleads with his mother to stop. Samantha was trying to answer her mom's questions but she couldn't catch her breath long enough to say anything. Mrs. Hargrove pushed her daughter's head under a couple more times, and Billy said these were the worst because each time his mother dunked his sister's head, she'd bear down with all her weight and Samantha's head would thud against the steel basin. Without letting go of her daughter's hair, Mrs. Hargrove pushed the faucet to the side so that instead of pouring down the drain it poured onto the counter and onto the floor.

"Dazed, hurting, Samantha finally came to enough to tell her mom the only lie she could think of. That the baby was Lucas Bramer's, a boy she'd dated earlier that year."

Barlow spat and wiped his lips with his coat sleeve. "Samantha figured this would buy her some time because Lucas Bramer was a few years older than her, which would make her look the victim rather than the seducer of a twelve-year old boy.

"But her mother flew into a rage. Trask knew old lady Hargrove and said that Samantha was doomed whether she said Lucas Bramer, Myles Carver, or Immaculate Conception. No father was good enough for Mrs. Hargrove because it was impossible to her that her only daughter, not even out of school yet, had gotten herself pregnant, had let some boy put his thing in her. Her mother started slapping her and boxing her ears, and that was when Billy intervened. He stepped between them and Samantha saw her chance to escape. She only took a couple of steps before her mother reached out, snagged a handful of her long black hair and yanked back hard."

Barlow fell silent. Paul walked beside him, waiting. He wished he had a flashlight. The woods had grown dark very fast, the sky above the path now an indigo snake winding its way through a tenebrous black sea.

"Samantha fell. Billy said her feet swept out from under her and up in the air like she'd slipped on ice. When the back of her head smacked the floor, he said it sounded like someone had stomped on an egg. Billy stumbled away and leaned on the kitchen table, and as he watched his sister's motionless body lying there, the water pouring off the counter and flooding the floor around her, he felt like he was watching a dead body floating down a river. He and his mom stood and stared as the blood trickled from Samantha's mouth, the back of her head. From between her legs. All of it leaking out and swirling and joining together, and pretty soon the whole floor around her was stained bright red."

"Samantha died?" Paul asked.

The sheriff shook his head. "No. Though that would have been better. She lost the baby, of course. She was only three months from carrying it to term, so Doc Trask's father, the original Doctor Trask, had to deliver it stillborn."

They walked then without speaking, the trail taking them gradually eastward. Paul wondered if they'd end up back at the house.

The sheriff had flicked on a flashlight. That, at least, was something.

Barlow continued, "Samantha spent a good while in the hospital and even more time in bed. Lots of people came to see her. In a few weeks, she began to recover. Billy Hargrove had achieved something like celebrity status because of the scandal, and he loved telling people the gory details. He was a good boy, but according to Trask he couldn't shut up to save his life." Barlow stopped and spat. "Of course, you could say the same thing about Doctor Trask."

He regarded Paul grimly and after a moment, went on. "With Billy talking like that and the town being so small, word was bound to get around to Myles Carver about what had happened.

"Now..." Barlow's voice grew quieter. "This is where the story gets strange. Not to be cold-hearted or anything, but I would think that a boy of twelve would be relieved to have a burden like that lifted from his shoulders. That sounds cynical, I know, but hell, what kid that age wants to be a dad?

"But apparently, Myles did. He was incensed. What little time he'd spent at home before was now spent stealing into the forest. He stopped showing up at school altogether."

"Then, one night Billy saw him standing in the Hargroves' back yard, staring up at the house."

They moved down a hill, and Paul just avoided tripping on a root that grew like a varicose vein across the trail. Though he'd never seen Myles before, he imagined his uncle as a boy, face livid and watchful in the moonlight.

"This frightened Billy, as you can imagine. Carver was rotten to the core, so there was that to worry about. But what scared him even more was that Myles wasn't watching Samantha's window. He was watching his mother's, Mrs. Hargrove's."

He could smell the tobacco on Barlow's breath. It smelled like apple cider. Paul put his hands in his pockets to warm them, listened.

"Reverend Hargrove and his wife were the kind of couple that had different rooms, for who knows what reasons. That was why one night Reverend Hargrove wasn't with his wife when he heard a bloodcurdling scream."

Barlow went on, quicker now. "Billy and his father stumbled out of bed, disoriented, scared, and rushed down the hall to Mrs. Hargrove's room. When they opened the door, the light from within flooded over them, and they discovered Mrs. Hargrove standing there in her nightdress clawing at her throat and shrieking at the top of her lungs. They went to her and fought with her to get her to stop scratching her throat, which was torn to ribbons, but the woman was hysterical. As Reverend Hargrove wrestled with his wife, Billy swiveled his head to see what she was staring at, and he told Trask that he puked before he even realized what it was."

Barlow's voice had softened now to scarcely a whisper. Not for effect, Paul thought, but because the words he was uttering were so terrible.

"The Reverend got a strong enough grip on his wife to turn and look at what it was that had so shaken her. When he saw it his face went ashen. He stood staring, and let go of his wife, who backed out of the room and bumped into Samantha, who had finally made her way down the hall. Her father was blocking the bed, so Billy said his sister had to push by him to see.

"The sight of her dead baby, dug up from the cemetery, bloated and purple and muddy, lying there in the middle of those white sheets, was too much for her.

"Samantha started to laugh, and then she clapped her hands. Then she was moving over and lying on the bed beside the dead baby. She gathered up the corpse, tucked up her knees and laughed.

"Billy said it was awhile before his father told him to go find his mom, who'd disappeared down the hallway. The Reverend, sitting quiet as a ghost beside his laughing daughter on the bed, cursed his son and told him to go and, damn it, tend to his mother right now, which Billy did, or tried to do. The last he'd seen of her she was backing out of the room toward the stairs. He had the terrible feeling that she'd fallen, but when he got to the staircase he could see that the landing below was empty.

"Billy moved down the stairs and through the house trying to find his mother. He even called her by her Christian name—Elizabeth—yet no one answered. She wasn't in the kitchen, so he searched for her in the living room. She wasn't there either.

"Billy could see plainly that unless she'd taken refuge in a linen closet or the pantry, his mother had left the house. He opened the back door and stood on the stoop, listening. What he heard didn't reassure him.

"There came a succession of sounds. There weren't any footsteps or voices, but what he could hear was coming from the direction of the woods. The first thing he recognized were the sounds of a struggle. As he crept toward the trees, he heard the struggling stop, and it was replaced by wet sloshing sounds that made his sour stomach feel even worse.

"He couldn't begin to guess at what it all meant, and the last thing he wanted to do was investigate. But he knew he'd have to. His sister had lost her mind, and she hadn't been in very good condition to begin with. Who knew what the shock had done to her? His dad was too busy keeping things upstairs from getting any worse, so it fell to him to restore order and find his mom.

"When he found Elizabeth Hargrove, she was lying in the grass, clearly limned by the moonglow. Someone had gotten to her."

Paul wished they'd go back to the house, get warm. He had no sense of family, really, but he didn't like thinking about someone he was related to exhuming a dead fetus. He noticed with some unease how the trees bordering the trail leaned over them like ghouls trying to absorb all the story's lurid details.

"Billy was wailing so loud his dad found him and discovered what had become of his wife. The minister fell to his knees and wept.

"Her entrails were spread out around her, her abdomen a bloody mess. Whoever had done it, he'd torn out her uterus."

Paul gaped at the sheriff. "Good Lord," he said. "And you think Myles did that?"

"I know Myles did it."

"How do you know? He was only a boy."

Barlow's voice rose. "Because I *knew* him."

Taken aback at the sheriff's tone, Paul was quiet for a moment before asking, "Did they find the murder weapon?"

Barlow looked at him sourly. "Just another reason why there was no conviction."

"Myles was tried for it?"

"There was no trial," Barlow answered and spat black juice. "Things then weren't like they are now, so there was no way to tell whose baby it was. It wasn't like they could do a blood test on what was left of that fetus. There was no reason to suspect Myles, save for the whisperings of children. No one paid the kids much mind when they insinuated it could have been your uncle because the thought of a girl four years his senior being interested in him was incomprehensible."

"Didn't Billy Hargrove tell the police about seeing Myles in the yard?"

"Uh-uh. He was too scared of what Myles would do to him. Only person he told was Doc Trask, just before Billy and his dad left town for good."

"What about Samantha?"

Barlow said, "I'm getting to that."

They were moving deeper into the woods now, and as the earthen trail grew darker, the odors became more distinct. The earth underfoot smelled of wet leaves and young buds. Lilac tinged the air, a smell he usually found pleasant. But now it seemed cloying, oppressive.

"Standing there by his wife's mutilated body, Reverend Hargrove and his son held each other and wept. The minister didn't know what to do. Cover his wife, carry her back with him, or go get help. He dared not send Billy to do it because whoever butchered his wife might still be in the forest, waiting.

"Though the sight of her was terrible, he couldn't leave her lying there in the woods for the bugs and animals to get at her, so he gathered his dead wife into his arms and made for the house with Billy holding the tail of his night shirt.

"They'd made it to the edge of the yard when they heard a shriek and a crashing sound. Then there was a sickening thump. When Reverend Hargrove saw what his daughter had done, he dropped to his knees and bellowed into his dead wife's chest. Samantha had apparently leapt from the upstairs window and landed face-first on the ground. He didn't have to go to where she lay. The way her neck was twisted, she was dead as winter."

Paul peered up at the moonless sky but found it had darkened to the same inky shade as the oak trees that rose like crooked spires around them. To their left he could see what looked like a break in the forest, though it was much too dark to be certain. He wished Barlow would let him hold the flashlight. He felt like a child whose father didn't trust him with the remote control.

The shrill warble of some unseen bird sent cold fingers down his back. Impatient to have the story ended, Paul said, "So the trauma of it all caused Samantha Hargrove to take her own life."

Barlow shook his head. "I don't think so. The Reverend was bawling over his dead wife and daughter, but Billy was staring up at the window. He told Doc Trask it was the worst part of the night, the worst thing he'd ever seen."

"Let me guess," Paul said. "It was Myles, grinning demonically at him through the jagged edges of the window."

"No. Myles was gone by then. What Billy saw was someone else." Barlow's voice grew thin. "A woman. A blonde woman in a white gown."

Paul imagined it, imagined her in the window. He thought about asking who it was, but before he could the sheriff added:

"But you were right about one thing."

"What's that?"

"The woman was grinning."

They fell silent, the only sounds in the forest their footfalls. Ahead of them, the trail broadened and Paul beheld a white farmhouse in the middle of a large, overgrown yard.

"Who lives here?"

"A girl," Barlow answered.

"Care to be more specific?"

"No."

"Are you going to question her or something?" Paul asked.

Barlow ignored him.

Paul breathed in the honeysuckle reefing the backyard, but he couldn't enjoy it. Finally, he said, "So why are we here?"

Barlow nodded toward the house. "This is where Reverend Hargrove used to live."

Paul peered up at a second story window. "That the window Samantha jumped out of?"

"Was pushed out of, you mean," Barlow said.

Paul waited and the sheriff shrugged. "Could be," he answered.

Paul stared at the dark windows. "And this is where Myles killed Mrs. Hargrove?"

"Over there." Barlow pointed back the way they'd come. "Beside the trail."

But Paul was staring at an upstairs window where a woman was watching him.

"I see her," he said.

The sheriff looked, then stared at him. "There's no one there," Barlow said.

Paul frowned. He could have sworn he saw a face, ghostly pale, watching him.

As they moved away, he asked, "Who was it Billy saw in the window?"

Barlow fell silent. He was silent for so long Paul thought he was going to ignore the question. When they were well away from the farmhouse, he said, "Someone I don't care to discuss."

She watched them from the second floor window, thankful she had waited to go down to the cellar. It wouldn't do for Ted to scream and rouse the sheriff's suspicion.

Their voices receded into the forest.

She went through her checklist again. Everything she needed was packed in two suitcases. It was depressing, actually. She'd been alive for nearly three decades, and all she cared about could be crammed into two suitcases.

Julia waited, counted slowly to fifty, before turning and leaving her bedroom. On the way to the cellar, she grabbed the fresh needle. The way she saw it, she couldn't set him free without sedating him first. She couldn't kill him. He was a lousy human being, but he didn't deserve to die.

The important thing was to give him enough morphine to knock him out for a good long while, but not to give him so much that he'd overdose. If she let him awake too quickly she'd be caught, and with his connections she'd get the maximum sentence, whatever that was. He had her on kidnapping, battery, incarceration against his will and whatever other charges he could think of. Mental anguish, maybe. Cruelty. Assault with a British playwright.

It was decided then. She'd give him a double dose and hope he wouldn't die.

Ted must have heard her open the basement door because he was already yelling about what he would give her if she'd let him go. Cars, jewelry, a new house. He promised it all.

Trembling a little, she flipped on the light.

She could see him blinking, his head turned awkwardly up at her.

"I'll give you anything you want, Julia. Just let me out of these ropes."

She strode down the steps. "Okay, Ted."

It stopped him. "What?"

"I said okay. I'm letting you go."

His voice grew hoarse. "What is that needle for? Christ, I feel like a pincushion already."

"I have to sedate you to make sure you don't kill me when I untie the ropes."

"Kill you? You're my only way out of here." He chuckled. Unconvincingly, she thought. "You die, I die, right?"

"You'll turn me in." She crouched in front of him.

"I won't turn you in. People make mistakes. I just want to get back to my family."

"Just hold still." She looked for a vein.

"Whatever you say, Julia."

She paused, watching him. His tone was different. It worried her.

"Don't move, Ted." She stuck the vein, flushed the morphine inside.

"Sure enough," he said, his voice going sleepy, "whatever you say."

His breathing was slow and deep. She set the needle on the ground.

She waited.

After thirty seconds had passed, she untied first his right hand, then his left. She was moving toward his feet when she felt the needle stab her Achilles tendon.

Julia screamed and reached for the hypo, but Ted was already bear-hugging her legs, dragging her down like some animal in the wild. She saw his eyes then, his bared teeth. His body was twisted, his feet held down by the ropes, but his upper body was free. He should have

77

been under by now, groggy at least, but his arms felt like steel, harder than she would have thought possible. He heaved and she felt herself hip tossed over his shoulder, the concrete knocking out her wind. She kicked at him. He punched her hard in the kidney. She tried to crawl away, get out from under him, but he seized her ankles, began reeling her back. *Please God let the morphine work*, she thought.

He hauled her back under him, grabbed the hypo sticking out of her ankle, and began stabbing her in the calf. She screamed, feeling her pants begin to bunch in his grip, and she didn't care, anything to get away from the stabbing needle. He dropped the needle and got ahold of her with both hands. His weight pressed down on her legs. He pinned her and yanked down her pants. She reached for something, anything to help her fend him off, but nothing was within reach, she'd made sure of that when she tied him up. He was biting her now, his incisors sinking into her thigh. The pain was excruciating.

Julia tried to crawl away, but his teeth held her, tearing, ripping at her leg. His hands fastened onto her sides and pulled her under him, but what she expected didn't happen. He was not reaching between her legs or fumbling with his crotch.

His hands were closing around her neck.

She batted at them, certain he was weakening, all that morphine pulsing through his body, but his grip was unyielding. The basement went gray. His hands were releasing her then, but she could barely feel them, and though she knew her chance to get away from him had come, she knew she was too weak, too faint, to crawl out from under him.

The last thing Julia thought before the gray tide pulled her under was how heavy Ted was, how hard it was to breath with his suffocating weight on top of her.

The grandfather clock in the foyer was chiming for the tenth time when Paul got back to Watermere. He ambled over to the bar, slid a hand over the tired mahogany. He thought of the dirt paths he'd just walked, the vastness of the estate. How odd it seemed that Sheriff Barlow knew the forest so well, as though the place were his.

As Paul stretched, his back popping dully, he thought of the sheriff's broad frame, the man's wise brown eyes.

Barlow seemed convinced of his innocence, but that didn't mean Paul was in the clear. The coldness of the night, the grotesque story, the woman he glimpsed in the window of the old Hargrove house, it was all catching up with him. His nerves were frayed.

A drink would help soothe them.

Sure it would, Emily's voice spoke up. *And it would lead to another, and another, and how many more until you wake up not knowing where you are or how you got there?*

Paul grimaced and dug the heels of his hands into his eyes to grind away the chiding voice. He moved to get a better view of the bar and felt his stomach flutter faintly at the many rows of bottles. Were Emily here now, she'd never let him drink without some form of remonstrance.

But she isn't here, is she?

No, he thought and smiled. *She isn't.*

Bending, he selected the first bottle his fingers touched. He raised it and cocked an eyebrow.

Whiskey.

The glasses were on the shelf above the bottles. He chose one, used the inside of his shirt to wipe out the dust, and placed it on the bar with a pleasing clunk.

Paul unscrewed the cap, poured himself half a glass and sipped. The whiskey carried a smoky aftertaste that compelled him to sip it again.

All things considered, he thought as his insides responded to the heat, maybe allowing himself a minor transgression wouldn't be such a bad thing after all.

Julia opened her eyes. The dank air of the basement filled her nostrils.

She had no idea what time it was. It could have been minutes or hours since she'd lost consciousness. She remembered Ted, their struggle, and felt his leaden body pressing down on her. His body odor rolled over her. It smelled sour and cruel just like his personality.

Summoning what strength she had, she wriggled back and forth until his weight shifted to the side. Straining, she shoved against him and felt his torso slide just enough for her to inch her way out from under him. Disoriented and coughing, she pulled her pants up and thanked her stars he'd not violated her. *He didn't want to violate you,* she reminded herself. *He wanted to kill you.*

Her throat ached. Badly. She needed water.

Julia staggered to the stairs and climbed them as swiftly as she could, hands on the wooden rails to brace her weary body as she made her way up. Her throat felt mangled. It was as though his hands were still there, squeezing, bruising, crushing her windpipe. She got to the kitchen and turned on the tap, but it was more than a minute before she could control her coughing enough to take a drink.

God, she'd been sloppy. She had no idea how long the morphine lasted, nor did she have any idea how potent it still was. After sitting in her mother's nursing cabinet all those years, it might have no more usefulness than a bottle of cough syrup. One thing was certain, though. There was no way Ted Brand would be unconscious long enough to give her safe passage. She'd have to tie him up again, get on a bus, then place an anonymous call once she was safely away. Maybe she'd make the call from Mexico if she could get there soon enough.

Julia got her coughing under control, drank half a glass of water. It still burned going down, her throat a throbbing ache, but it calmed her nerves. She realized she was now doing what she should have done in the first place. Ted would be fine. People lived without food or water for a week before dying, she'd once heard. One more day wasn't going to kill him.

An anonymous call then. Julia descended the stairs.

Flipping on the light at the base of the stairs, she stared down at where Brand's body had been.

Its absence, the blood-soaked but empty concrete inside the quadrangle of ropes, had scarcely registered when she heard a roar behind her. She whirled as Brand came at her from under the stairs, the carving knife raised above his head, his body impossibly large in the yellow glare of the basement light.

She dodged away as he sliced down at her, the knife blade cleaving the air inches from her face. He cried out as his balance betrayed him and toppled him onto his side. She lunged across the basement to the workbench and scrabbled for a weapon. Her hand closed on a screwdriver, and brandishing it, she turned to see him get to his feet, still clutching the knife. He grinned murderously at her, his ruined face crusted with ant bites.

Julia met his stare, tried to remember the things he'd called her. She was furious with herself for being so careless. She clenched the screwdriver handle.

She was about to stick him with it when the knife came whooshing down at her. She hopped away as the blade descended. The knife chunked down on the wooden surface of the workbench, but Brand's hand kept traveling downward, his still-clutching palm slicing itself on the edge of the blade until his hand slammed on wood. Brand screamed, jerked his hand away. Crimson bloomed in a neat line on his palm. As he stared at the welling blood, Julia pumped the screwdriver sideways and buried it to the hilt in his ribs. He uttered a shrill yelp of surprise, pawed at the screwdriver handle, and tried vainly to extract it.

She no longer felt in control of herself, was shocked at her own ferocity. She knew there was no going back now. One of them would die down here. She swiped at him, and when her fingernails caught in his temple and cheek, she raked down with all her might, his skin peeling into pink curls as the nails harrowed his face.

Howling with pain, Brand balled his good hand into a fist and caught her in the cheek with a haymaker. She landed on the floor, her vision graying.

Still holding the screwdriver in his side, he used his free hand to yank the knife from the workbench. She pushed up from the floor and tried to parry the blow. It was too late. He swiped the knife backhand low and hard, the skin above her pubic hair erupting in fiery pain as the blade slashed her. She stumbled backward, felt herself going down again. Her head smacked the floor with a sick thud.

Through her reeling vision she watched him advancing on her, and at once her mind's eye saw him turning the tables, tying her in the ropes, cutting off her clothes, raping her, torturing her over a period of days, weeks. And as he advanced, knife raised, she saw in his eyes the confirmation of her fears. He was a fiend, had always been a fiend, but only now had the chance to let his madness express itself with complete abandon.

He was almost upon her now. She rolled over, her vision clearing, and as she lay on the floor below this monstrous, screaming man, her eyes passed over the implements stored on the shelves under the workbench. The vise clamps. The coffee can full of nails. The broken post-hole diggers.

The tree loppers.

She looked at Brand. He was above her now, feet braced wide, carving knife gripped with both hands above his head, the screwdriver handle still jutting crazily out of his side.

With a roar he brought down the knife, its shiny surface aimed at her throat. She leaned one way and shoved with all her might. Rolling, she watched his body strike the space she'd just vacated and heard the jagged protest of the knife tip snapping on the concrete.

Julia seized the loppers.

From under the workbench she turned and saw him stand. He peered about the basement for another weapon. He paused, his back straightening. He was looking at the wall a few yards in front of him. Julia followed his gaze and discovered the axe hanging there.

Her breath caught.

She had to reach him before he reached the axe. If not, she was done for.

On elbows and knees, she shuffled across the dusty floor, the loppers clutched in her hands. She felt rivulets of blood soaking into her pants above her pubic hair, the fresh wound glacial and pulsing.

He was almost to the axe.

Frantic, she scuttled toward him, the wound in her abdomen protesting. He stopped and reached for the axe. His hands closed on its wooden handle.

She wasn't going to make it.

He turned and spotted her below him, and when he noticed the long wooden handles of the loppers his eyes danced with mirth. He grinned and lifted the axe. She thought of jabbing forward before the axe fell, of lopping off his genitals, but there was no time. The axe was already descending.

She dove forward between his legs as the blade hit the concrete behind her. She rose to her knees and spun. She jabbed the loppers with all her might, felt them sink into the flesh of his back. He bellowed in agony and the axe clattered to the floor. He writhed, unable to free himself of the lopper blades buried in the muscles of his back. With a cry, she brought the handles together and squeezed. Brand's cry rose and broke as the tree loppers crunched through his spine.

Then he was tumbling forward, the loppers going with him.

Lying there on his face, he hardly moved, a low keening gurgle the only sound coming from his mouth.

Julia stood.

She walked around his body, the lopper handles sticking straight up out of his back. She picked up the axe.

"God help me," she said, and brought it down on his head.

Chapter Eight

Paul awoke at a quarter of eight with a sense of anticipation he'd not felt in years.

The time had come.

Pencil in hand, notepad and coffee atop the mahogany desk where he sat with his eyes wide and his every nerve ending alive with possibility, he took a drink of coffee, and though it wasn't very good—he suspected the Folgers can he'd discovered in the pantry was long past its prime—he could still feel it doing its work, surcharging him with energy, readying him for what he was about to do. He breathed deeply of the musty den and the fragrant spring air coming through the window, commingling scents that fused the best of both worlds, the realm of thought and the realm of nature.

He exhaled, scooted under the desk.

He stared at the paper.

And wondered what to write.

Julia walked to work in tears. She thought fleetingly of Watermere, of the new owner. Though both mind and body were numb, she was able to speculate about her new neighbor. She scanned her memory for the few details she could from her conversation with...

(Ted Brand, his name was Ted Brand, the man you killed)

...the lawyer, the fact that Paul Carver was in his thirties, had lived in Memphis until recently, and that he had a girlfriend, but no, they weren't yet engaged. Julia tried to picture him, and in this she was moderately successful, the tears in her eyes that blurred her vision actually making it easier to focus on her inner sight, the man similar in build to Myles Carver, perhaps even possessed of similar features. She thought of Myles Carver's handsome face, his piercing blue eyes. His insatiable libido.

Which brought her back to Ted Brand.

It fell on her like a leaden blanket: dead, the man was *dead*, and *she* was his killer. Julia choked back a sob. God, she hadn't even recognized herself last night after showering off the blood.

Murderer.

The word sounded obscene.

It was the way she felt after the adrenaline of the fight drained out of her and she was left to gawk at Ted Brand's still, silent form on the basement floor. Seeing the ants crawling over him, biting his corpse, made her sick, sick at the sight and sick with herself, her shocking barbarity.

Who was this person, she wondered now, who was capable of murder?

What terrified her was how little she'd thought while doing it. It was another pair of hands lifting the axe. It was another woman, one without a conscience, who ended a man's life.

The sight of his body, the bloody back and shit-caked legs, hand sent her up the stairs to the shower, her whole body trembling wildly as she tried to deny what she'd done, tried to negate the act.

Even after, staring in the mirror, her hands still sticky and her victim still dead, she couldn't believe she'd killed him.

At that point in the morning, and well into the day, she told herself if Sam Barlow paid her a visit, she'd tell him everything.

Paul sat staring at the paper. On it were scrawled the words PIZZA, BEER and POPCORN.

He tore off his grocery list and set it aside for later.

He stared at the blank page, his mind flailing about for literary inspiration. What he needed to do—damn it—was come up with an *idea*. Most of what he'd read was horror, so he might as well start there. Problem was, all the good ideas were taken. That fucking Stephen King had used up half the ideas himself.

Paul liked all kinds of stuff, so maybe it was best to eliminate the plots that had been done to death, the storylines that made him roll his eyes they were so familiar.

Take vampires.

There were some great vampire novels out there, but there were stinkers as well. Many that were supposedly great he just found boring. Anyway, what was the use in covering the same ground?

Werewolves were old hat, too. Same with zombies, cannibals, ghost stories, demons, serial killers and flesh-eating cockroaches.

So what did that leave?

He stared at the blank sheet of paper, willing words to appear. Its bland white face gazed back at him as if he'd already bored the shit out of it. A good first line was all he needed. Come up with that, he'd be home free.

He sniffed, face scrunching.

The den smelled like fungus. That semeny, curdled salt smell he associated with the ravine behind his house growing up. He could open another window, but there was a wind today. It would flutter his papers, tickle his hair, generally distract him. What he needed was a change of scenery.

Collecting his pencil and paper, Paul went down the hall to the library.

At the library Julia pretended to go through the late returns, stared at the circulation desk computer.

Wondered what to do about the dead guy in her basement.

Not having slain a man before, she was unsure whether or not she'd done the right thing by leaving his body in the basement. Remembering her Poe, she considered how to get rid of the corpse. Walling him up was out of the question, as was chopping him into pieces and putting him under the floorboards.

The thought came again, for the hundredth time that day: *What's wrong with you?*

How, she wondered, could she think like this, examine the different methods of discarding a corpse? Her hands were shaking again. She put them under the desk so no one would see.

She sighed, wishing she'd never met Ted Brand. If she suffered through nightmares until she was eighty, so be it, but dammit, she wouldn't give up her freedom or her life because of one mistake.

Barlow was smart. He'd be thorough, she knew. It was only a matter of time before he came to question her. She had to focus.

She could bury Brand's body somewhere, but how to do that and make sure no one would find it? Weren't there dogs trained to do just that? She imagined a German Shepherd sniffing through the forest, moving unerringly to wherever she'd tried to conceal the corpse.

Of course, there was history between her and Sam Barlow, and that could only help her.

Then again, maybe it wouldn't.

The thought was enough to tighten the skin around her eyes, set her imagination racing. What if the things he might or might not know made him more suspicious? What if the past came back to bite her?

She was thinking this when Barlow appeared in front of her.

"Hey, Julia," the sheriff said and leaned over the desk. "How's life?"

Though she could feel her heart racing, his familiar manner lessened her anxiety a notch.

"Not bad, Mr. Barlow. Just going through the stragglers." Good, she thought. Her voice had come out even.

"Am I one of them?" he asked, craning his head to look at her monitor. Though he didn't have a chew in now, she could smell the Red Man on his breath. Like overripe apples. Normally the scent appealed to her, but now it made her feel closed in, like the walls were creeping nearer.

Prison walls.

She cleared her throat. "Well," she said, scrolling through the list of names, "it doesn't look like it. You've got four more days before your books are due back."

Barlow smiled. "Good. I'm only done with half of them."

"Extra busy lately?"

He paused. "Unfortunately, yes." His face sobered.

"Really?" she said, sitting back from the keyboard. "Has something happened?"

The sheriff regarded his hat, which rested on the counter. As he did, Julia noted the gray hairs mixing in with the black, the age showing around Barlow's tired eyes. Seeing these things, it wasn't hard to forget he was in detective mode, was a regular guy and a good man, saddened by what he was doing, questioning her about a missing person.

Keep your guard up, a voice cautioned.

"We don't know what's happened, Julia." He glanced up at her, chin down. "Have you heard of a man named Ted Brand?"

She shook her head, forced her hands not to fidget. "No, that name's not familiar."

He watched her a moment longer. Then, he seemed to dismiss something and stared at his hat again. "You wouldn't have, unless you have a police scanner you listen to."

She waited, her heart sledgehammering in her chest.

He smiled at her. "But you're not really the police scanner type."

She allowed herself a sheepish grin. "I'm a bit out of touch."

"Why is that?"

"I guess I'm just a homebody."

His sigh said it was a shame she never married. She got that sigh a lot, from Bea mostly.

"What I'm wondering about," he said, coming to it, "is whether you walked home from work Thursday night or caught a ride."

"I always walk home from work."

He grinned. "I know you do. I finally stopped offering you rides even though I hate to see you all alone on the shoulder."

She shrugged. "I like walking."

"So the other night, did you see a black BMW pass by, heading south?"

Not wanting to answer too fast, she paused, frowning at the wall beside her. "Not that I remember. It's possible one went by, but if it did I don't remember it."

"Think hard now," Barlow said. "Did a man maybe stop and offer you a ride?"

"No," she said, "I would have remembered that."

Barlow looked disappointed but unsurprised. "If you remember anything, will you call me?" He wrote down his number on a temporary library card.

She took it.

"That's my cell phone," he said. "I hate the damn thing, but everybody's got one now and my secretary says I have to keep up with the times."

"How is Patti?" Julia asked.

"She's fine," Barlow said, straightening. "I better get going."

"I hope everything works out."

The sheriff put his hat on. "Me too."

And with that, he left.

Staring after him she let out a long, fluttery breath. She shut her eyes and pushed herself up in her chair. She'd done well, she knew. Barlow didn't suspect her. She was just another neighbor, a formality to be gotten through. He no more suspected her of Brand's murder than the Kennedy assassination.

All that was left now was the body.

Chapter Nine

July, 1950

After the murder of her child, the only restraint on Maria's wantonness was removed. She bedded a new man each week, often on consecutive days. More than once in the same night.

Myles observed this with detached interest, caring little for his former girlfriend, caring less for the marriages she ruined, the homes she destroyed. Sleeping with men from all stations, politicians and policemen, idlers and drifters, she cut a lecherous swath through the fabric of the town and became anathema to any woman whose man had a wandering eye.

Then, she made her play for David Carver.

Myles knew nothing of the affair, save the lingering stares Maria leveled his brother's way. He could never tell whether or not the interest was mutual, for David was difficult to read. Myles couldn't imagine his brother wanting any woman but Annabel.

One sleepless night Myles arose from bed and went outside.

The night was warm and bright, the gardens redolent with jasmine and sage. Through the dewy lawn and into the hollow Myles went, a slight breeze worrying his thick black hair, caressing his bare chest.

He was upon the lovers before he noticed them.

In a bright patch of moonlit bluegrass, Maria sat astraddle his brother, back arched, hands behind her gripping David's hard calves. Her upturned nipples shone like gems, her entire body rose and fell, a fleshy arch, as David thrust up into her from below.

Unaccountably, Myles felt a pang of jealousy. The satisfied, dreamy smile on her face infuriated him. For as active a lover as she was, she'd never shown much pleasure in having sex with Myles, treating it instead like a pleasant but forgettable diversion.

Maria moaned as his brother drilled up into her splayed legs, his large forearms rippling as he kneaded her hips, her breasts.

Shaking, Myles turned and strode away. All he could think of was Annabel home in bed, her husband in the woods banging the town slut. The thought of Annabel, her icy blue eyes lidded in sleep, the covers pulled down to reveal her pale skin, her sinuous body clad only in a satiny nightgown, lent speed to his steps. He rocketed through the hollow, bare feet padding the smooth earth. Myles hadn't the strength of his brother, but what there was of him was hard and lean, and as the image of Annabel became clearer in his mind, his strides lengthened, his thin body become a white wraith darting around the trail's bends in the moonlight.

When he entered the house he took care to keep the screen door from slamming. If Annabel awoke, he'd have to explain himself, and his opportunity to take her would be lost. When she found out what was happening she'd be eager to confront the pair. Though she feigned unconcern Myles knew deep down that beneath the aloof exterior lurked unfathomable darkness. He'd seen it on the night of the boy's death, again when she heard of the second child slaying in Shadeland, less than a year later.

The sweat dripped from his hair, which hung in lank sheathes over his temples. He twisted the doorknob and let himself in. Though the night was preternaturally brilliant, the thick oak tree outside the bedroom window partially stifled the moonglow, leaving Myles illuminated and Annabel in shadow. The bedclothes were twisted and bunched around her still form.

He crossed the room, the shadows swallowing him. A starling lit on the sill and stared incuriously through the window. Myles reached out, grasped the bedclothes, drew them down and beheld the empty place where her body had been, where he'd watched her from the keyhole many a night, looking past the muscular mound of his brother and gazing upon the one thing life had denied him, the only thing he wanted.

But she was gone. His head swam with longing and rage as he returned to his room. Shutting the door he turned and saw Annabel lying on her side, nude, in his bed. Her back to him, her long blond hair tied up so that her creamy neck glowed, she lay there, waiting, on the white sheet. Myles stepped over the covers, which were pooled at the foot of the bed, and slipped off his boxer shorts. She bent forward, extending *her buttocks, her elbow sliding down the sheet toward her knees. Lying on his side behind her, he slid down low enough to enter her, and as he felt her warmth slide around him, he heard her whisper one word, "Mine," and knew it to be true.*

Chapter Ten

When the phone rang, Sam hoped it would be good news. Then he heard Daryl Applegate say, "Howdy, Sheriff," and his hopes were dashed.

"Yeah?" Sam asked, making no attempt to conceal his irritation. It was six in the morning. He'd planned on sleeping until seven.

"They're searching Brand's car."

Sam switched the phone to his good ear, sat up. "Any prints?"

"We haven't heard anything else, just that they're going through the car," Daryl said.

Sam scraped a hand over his whiskers.

"Hey, Sheriff?"

"Go ahead," Sam said. He stood and walked across the lightless room to his closet. He guessed he'd dress without showering today, though doing so always made him feel dirty.

"What I was wondering," Daryl said as Sam zipped up, buttoned his brown shirt, "is whether or not you wanted me to interview Brand's girlfriends."

Sam pulled on his socks. "Deputy McLaughlin will be in charge of that. Plus we only need to see if one of them heard from Brand around the time he disappeared."

Daryl's voice grew plaintive. "But Tommy gets to do everything. Why do I get stuck being your secretary when Patti's not around?"

"We all have to man the desk sometimes," Sam went on, by rote now. It was the same old crap. Applegate wanted none of the responsibility, all of the glory. Sam didn't have the heart to tell the dumb bastard he wouldn't have a job if it weren't for his father pulling strings. Guy wasn't qualified to scoop shit in a henhouse.

"But Tommy's the youngest. He should have to pay his dues like the rest of us."

Sam felt himself growing agitated, glared at his reflection in the bathroom mirror. Now he was up, he wanted to brush his teeth, get on with his day.

"Age has nothing to do with it," he said. "And Deputy McLaughlin does just as much grunt work as you do." He couldn't stop from adding, "And he doesn't bitch about it either."

"I'm not bitching," Daryl said, but his voice was sullen. "I just want out of the office."

Squeezing paste on his vibrating toothbrush, Sam said, "Patti's coming in at eight, when your shift ends. You can get out of the office then."

By telling Bea she'd gotten a doctor to come to the farmhouse, Julia had bought herself a few days. If Barlow came to the library looking for her, it would look bad, but what else could she do? If he noticed how red her eyes were, how her nerves had degenerated over the past few days, and started asking questions, she might as well kill herself, save the state the trouble.

In the five days since she'd killed Brand and disposed of his body, she'd spent most of her time reading or playing piano. But neither of those things took her mind off of what she'd done, what could happen to her if she were found out. Barlow could roll down the lane at any moment, knock on her door. *Your boss says you've been home sick this week. How come? And what are those blisters there, the ones on your hands? You been digging holes?*

The only thing she found to take her mind off it was to walk in the woods. After she got used to it, the rain didn't bother her. With May right around the corner the air was warmer, the denseness of the forest helping to hold the heat in. Julia watched as a sparrow flitted into view, zigzagged through the boughs of a maple tree, then vanished as abruptly as it had appeared. The bird made her aware of the forest life around her, inchoate now but rapidly gaining fresh vitality. As if to confirm this idea a chipmunk darted out of an uprooted oak trunk and crossed the sodden trail mere inches from where she stood. The smell of the soil, fecund and redolent with budding vegetation, permeated her nostrils.

As she continued on she thought about the Carver House, about Watermere. When she first heard someone was moving in she was disappointed. She'd pictured the place uninhabited, herself the lady of the house by default.

The more she thought about it, though, the more she wondered what kind of man Myles's nephew would be. She was thinking about this man she'd never met as the clearing came up on her left.

She risked a glance that way, at the break in the trees and the large oval space within, and despite the warmth of the woods, what was buried there made her shiver.

He was sitting under a sycamore tree near the edge of the woods, thinking, when he heard a car roll up the lane. It was Barlow, in plain clothes this time, looking like a regular guy. Larger than average maybe, but otherwise normal. His black tee shirt was tight around his thick biceps, his jeans old and faded. As Barlow approached, Paul tried to reconcile this new man with the sheriff he'd walked the forest with last week, the man who was all business.

Paul got up and approached Barlow.

"Howdy," the sheriff said, meeting him at the edge of the lawn.

"Afternoon," Paul said.

"How are you adjusting to your new surroundings?"

"Pretty well, I think." Paul glanced about the yard, wishing he'd done more to it. It was strewn with weeds, and he hadn't mowed yet.

Barlow nodded at the house. "Looks like you've got a shutter missing."

"That one and two on the other side," Paul answered without looking. He'd thought of doing something about the state of disrepair the house was in but had no idea where to begin. The thought of paying someone to fix the place up seemed wasteful, but he couldn't rouse himself to do the work.

"You've got some holes in your screens too."

"Uh-huh."

The sheriff stared at the house. "Lotta work keeping up a place like this."

Paul glanced at him. "I'm getting around to it."

Barlow grunted and knelt on the grass, forearms resting on one knee. "I wanted you to know your story checked out."

Paul spoke to the crown of the sheriff's head. "That's good to hear."

"So unless something new comes up, you're in the clear."

"That's why you came?"

"It's been awhile since I talked to you last," Barlow said. "I just wanted to check in."

"I see."

Barlow remained kneeling. His fingers spread out and caressed the tips of the grass. Paul watched the thick, strong hand whisper gently over the lawn, saw the man's blue eyes follow his hand as it moved.

When the sheriff spoke his voice was softer. "You've heard of women's intuition, I'm sure, but I believe men can have intuition too. Especially cops who've been at it a long time "

Paul watched the hand, waited.

"I don't like it," Barlow went on, "but I believe something bad happened to Ted Brand. What's worse, I believe it's just the start of more badness to come."

Paul watched the sheriff guardedly. "Like what?"

"Who knows? The last murder I had to deal with was a long time ago. Things have been good in Shadeland since then, but things never stay good forever."

Against his better judgment, Paul said what had been on his mind since the first time he'd met Barlow. "My coming here is what started it. That's what you think."

The sheriff's silence was all the confirmation he needed. Barlow rose and strode toward his car.

"I'm not my uncle, you know," Paul said to the man's broad back.

The sheriff turned slowly and regarded him, the deep cobalt eyes penetrating Paul's.

"No, you're not," Barlow replied. "But you do favor him."

The sheriff was right. In the pictures Paul pulled from the office shelves, his uncle appeared to be a better-groomed, healthier version of himself. Of course, if the stories were true, that couldn't be right. Myles Carver had been a debauched ghoul who drank to excess and indulged in every sin imaginable.

So why were the man's features sharper than his?

Looking at his uncle, whose face exuded confidence and virility, was depressing. The man's suave appearance made Paul feel inept. There were pictures of Myles everywhere in the albums, yet none of his wife, whatever her name was.

Paul thought of Barlow, of how he'd omitted all mention of the woman, the same way she'd been omitted from the albums. Flipping back through the browning pictures, Paul was amazed to see many of them had been doctored, cut in half. In one photo, taken at some beach when Myles was in his thirties, the effect of her excision was dramatic. His uncle lay on the sand, propped up on an elbow and mooning for the camera. She'd been lying behind him, pushing herself up so as to be included in the shot, but all around his uncle's shoulder and face, the picture had been trimmed, and the arm she'd let dangle over his stomach was replaced by a white stripe where the pale background of the photo album showed through.

Was the pain of her death so bad as to make the sight of her unbearable? Paul thought of his ex-girlfriend, of the regret he felt when thinking of Emily, and could imagine throwing out her letters, her pictures. But he couldn't envision going so far as to cut around his own image to rid himself of her. It bespoke of narcissism. If not, why not toss out the entire picture? Wasn't the white stripe across his uncle's stomach a reminder of her as surely as her picture had been? Paul couldn't imagine sorrow driving a man to do that. Now hatred...hatred was another matter entirely.

Pushing the albums back inside the roll top desk, Paul strode to the bathroom. The sight of his full jowls made him flip off the light switch. He leaned over the pot, one hand bracing himself on the wall, and voided his bladder. When he finished he found the effort to push away from the wall had worn him out. *Jesus Christ*, he thought. *I get winded taking a leak.*

To cheer himself up he ambled down to the library and cast about for something diverting. The rain pelting the windows soothed his jangled nerves. As he moved through the library and breathed the fragrance of aged paper, he searched for something scary, something as creepy as this house often felt.

Titles like *A History of Hell, The Book of Werewolves, Astral Projection,* and *Secret Voices: A Guide to Automatic Writing* jumped out at him. He shook his head. His uncle had been into some weird stuff.

He came to a novel that looked good—Peter Straub's *Ghost Story*—and began reading.

He'd read a hundred pages before he realized his stomach was rumbling. There was no working clock in the library so he'd no way to tell, but he was sure it was close to noon. Rising, his knees and back popping, Paul carried the book with him down to the kitchen.

He read more as he ate his bologna sandwich.

The horror story, he was finding, was doing something to him, stirring some long-dormant part of him. Reading it reminded him of why he'd wanted to write in the first place. He wanted to do to people what this book was doing to him.

Determined now, he retrieved a paper grocery sack from under the sink and marched grimly into the ballroom. The bottles of whiskey clanking inside the sack, he made his way out to the garage and deposited the sack in a cubbyhole next to the large rubber trash container. That done, he mounted the porch steps, trotted up the stairs, made for the library. On his way by the office he traded the novel in his back pocket for a spiral-bound notebook and a pen. *Holy crap*, he thought, *I'm actually going to do it.*

Thinking this, he sat in the red silk armchair and wrote down the first words that came to him:

He missed her lovely sapphire eyes.

The sound of his own snoring woke him up.

Wiping the drool off his cheek he sat up in the silk armchair and looked at the page. Seeing the one sentence written there was little consolation, like finding one unbroken egg in a new carton.

He felt like shouting, rending the notebook to shreds and stomping on the remains. He had everything he needed—solitude, atmosphere, financial security. The one thing he lacked was talent.

Check that, he thought. He also needed discipline, and that had never been his strong suit either. He'd been in this place for a week now and it looked no better than when he'd first arrived. He'd resolved to quit drinking, had even taken the alcohol out to the garage. *But it isn't gone yet, is it?* a voice asked.

Back off, he thought. Trash collection wasn't until Monday. What was he supposed to do? Smash the bottles to shards just to prove he was serious about beating his drinking habit? That was juvenile. He had more than enough will power to abstain from the sauce for a few more days. He need only channel his thirst into his writing.

He read the line he'd scrawled: "He missed her lovely sapphire eyes."

Now what the hell did that mean? He tore out that page, crumpled it and tossed it aside. He stared at the notebook, waiting for another, better first line to come.

Twenty minutes passed.

The first time he heard the noise, he was staring at the blank sheet of paper. Grateful for the diversion, he forgot for a moment his enormous writer's block and regarded the wall before him.

He heard it again, a flurry of scrapes and taps, faint but very real. For one wild moment, he imagined a woman trapped inside the wall with barely strength to scratch for help.

Shaking off the thought, he sat forward and listened.

It came again, fingernails on tin.

Then the sounds swelled and quickened, expanding throughout the room like spiderwebbing glass. Paul stood, alarmed.

The clatter ceased.

He held his breath and waited.

The tapping sounded once more, accelerating, urgent. He edged toward the wall and tried to account for what he was hearing. Bugs were out because the taps were too thick for creatures so small, and though he shuddered at the idea, the scrapes and slithers he heard as he pressed an ear to the wall could only be made by rats. Large ones.

God help me, he thought as he backed away from the shivery sounds, *I've stepped into a Lovecraft story.*

Half relieved to be shut of the burden of writing for the day, Paul dropped the notebook and put ear to wall again, careful to keep an eye on the fireplace, lest a flood of squirming black rodents come gushing out of the aperture.

On cue, the sounds in the wall increased. He felt his skin crawl as he imagined the size of the things, the finger-thick rubbery tails. Amidst the weird swish and rustle, he thought he could make out the minute clicking of tiny claws. The image of them scurrying around behind the wall bare inches from his face made him jerk away, sucking in air. Not only was the notion of a rat problem revolting, he now needed to hire someone to rid his house of them.

Paul's cell phone contract was done, so he had to use a pay phone in town to call the exterminator. By mid-afternoon, a white van crunched to a stop in the driveway and a fat man with a red beard and a white work suit climbed out.

"Thanks for coming on such short notice," Paul said as he descended the porch steps.

"Not a problem," replied the man. Through his beard he grinned up at the house, removed his plain white ball cap, and ran a sweaty hand through his thick red hair, which was curly and matted by the cap. The guy smelled bad. Awful, in fact. Like a package of bologna left out in the sun for a few days.

Breathing through his mouth, Paul introduced himself.

The exterminator offered a sweaty hand. "Another Carver, huh?"

"Myles was my uncle," Paul said, then added, "though I never knew him."

"And he left you this place."

"That's right."

The exterminator waited a beat, sizing him up, before grunting noncommittally. Turning, the fat man lumbered around to the rear of the van and produced a short, fat silver canister from which sprouted a black hose and nozzle.

Following him, Paul nodded at the canister. "Pretty potent stuff?"

"It'll knock you on your ass."

Setting down the container, the man made for something inside the driver's side door.

"I didn't get your name," Paul said to the man's wide back. He could see dark wet circles spreading from the stained armpits. When there was no answer Paul said, "The ad in the phonebook only said

Triple-A Exterminators."

"Name's Snowburger," came the reply.

"Good to meet you."

Snowburger produced a clipboard, and Paul caught another whiff of rancid bologna.

Paul said, "We didn't talk price over the phone."

Without looking up, Snowburger said, "Shouldn't be much. No more than a thousand."

"A thousand dollars," he said, appalled.

"That's a lot of house," the exterminator said and gestured toward Watermere. "I usually just charge a flat rate of a hundred-fifty an hour, but for a job this big I'll be using extra poison."

"You haven't even been inside yet."

"I got eyes, don't I? There's lots of nooks and crannies in that place. The thing's gotta be over a hundred years old."

"That's not what I meant," Paul said. "What I mean is, how can you be sure rats are even the problem when you haven't been inside?"

"Correct me if I'm wrong, Mr. Carver, but weren't you the one told me you had a infestation?"

Paul laughed. "Yeah, I said I *thought* I had one."

The red eyebrows rose. "I'm only going by you."

"I understand that, but shouldn't you confirm it yourself before you charge me a thousand bucks?"

Snowburger scratched a sweaty temple. "There's others more expensive than me, Mr. Carver. I'm just trying to save you money."

Paul grunted.

"Look," Snowburger said. "You said you heard rats running around in your walls. You said you heard a bunch of 'em when you put your ear against the wall."

"I know what I said, but I'm not a rat expert."

"Don't need to be one to know that. What else could it be, ghosts?"

Angered by the icy tendrils that tickled his spine, Paul glared at the exterminator. "No, I don't think that at all. I simply asked how you could be sure without checking the house yourself."

Snowburger's jowls shook as he giggled. "Mr. Carver. I've been at this gig going on eight years now, and believe me, when a person hears sounds like the ones you described over the phone, it can only be one thing. And it ain't ghosts."

"Wouldn't there be droppings?"

"Probably are. You just haven't seen 'em yet." Snowburger scratched his large belly. "You will though if you don't do somethin' to get rid of the problem right away."

Tired of the conversation, Paul said, "Fine. Do I pay you now or later?"

"Always get paid up front."

"Of course."

Shaking his head, Paul turned toward the house. "I assume a personal check is acceptable."

"Yep. Make it out to Bobby Snowburger for a thousand fifty."

Paul stopped. "You said a thousand."

"That was before taxes."

Paul wrote the check and handed it to the exterminator, who grabbed his gear and trundled up the porch. From where he stood in the driveway. Paul heard the screen door wheeze shut.

Feeling useless, he stepped inside the garage. He wondered what he'd do to kill time. It was an overcast day, hot and muggy, and he was certain rain wasn't far off. Though there seemed little to do in the garage, he was glad he hadn't brought a notebook and pen. This way he could idle away the time without the guilt of avoiding writing. He thought of going into town but remembered he'd left his keys inside the house.

Paul tinkered around with Myles's old tools and wished he had a television out here.

After a time the fat man emerged from the house, white suit drenched gray. As he passed by, Paul caught a whiff of rotten cheese.

"Done?" Paul asked as Snowburger opened the van's rear doors.

"I wish," Snowburger said and unscrewed the canister's lid. Taking a transparent tube from the base of a larger plastic container and feeding it into the mouth of the silver canister, the exterminator turned a handle and both men watched the clear liquid pass through the hose.

"Is that toxic?" Paul asked to fill the silence.

"Toxic as hell," the fat man agreed and hawked a green wad of spit into the gravel.

Staring at the unnaturally green gob, Paul said, "I take it you have a little more to do inside."

"Little more? Hell, I'm just now finishing the first floor."

"You're kidding."

"Hell, no, I'm not kiddin'. I'm not a magician, Mr. Carver, it's only three o'clock."

Paul was crestfallen. He'd been certain it was later than that.

He followed Snowburger back toward the house.

"Where you think you're going?" the exterminator asked.

"I need to get some things from inside."

Snowburger laughed. "You can't go in there, Mr. Carver. It ain't safe."

"But I need some things." He nodded toward the white mask hanging from the fat man's neck. "I could borrow that for a second."

"What's so important you need it right now?"

Paul's right temple began to throb. What gave this guy the right to patronize him?

"Like a goddamn drink of water, for one. I'm parched."

"Use the spigot on the side of the house."

"I'm hungry too. Should I graze on the lawn?"

"There's restaurants in town."

"Yeah, and my keys are in the house."

Rolling his eyes as if Paul were the one being unreasonable, the fat man said, "Alright, since it's so important to you, I'll bring the keys out to you after I finish the second floor."

"Why can't you do it now?"

"Because I'm busy."

"Then I'll go in and get them myself."

"Like hell you will. Can't go in there for twenty-four hours."

"What?"

"Less you wanna die, you can't go in there until tomorrow afternoon."

Paul looked around helplessly. "Then at least bring me my keys so I can drive into town."

"I told you I'll bring them out when I'm done with the second floor."

"Bring them out now," Paul said, climbing the porch steps toward Snowburger.

But the fat man was already inside. "Now don't get your panties in a bunch. I'll be out soon enough."

The slamming of the heavy door punctuated Paul's shock. He was amazed to hear the lock turn and the chain snicker into place.

He'd been locked out of his own house.

Paul paced across the front yard and perspired. His clothes stuck to his skin like cellophane.

He told himself to be patient as the day darkened and the time dragged sluggishly on, but he soon grew tired of cupping his hands under the spigot to satisfy his thirst, of hearing his empty stomach rumble. Setting aside the aged power washer he'd been trying to start up, he stalked around to the back door, hoping he could get in through the kitchen.

The knob wouldn't budge.

Before his hand fell from the door, his whole body began to shake with outrage.

At the kitchen table, the fat man sat eating one of Paul's microwave pizzas. Pepperoni grease slicking his lips, the man gobbled down half a slice in a bite and was about to fill his greasy maw again when he looked up and froze.

Before Paul could think of something to say, Snowburger was up and out of the room.

Paul stood, waiting.

When he reappeared in the kitchen, Snowburger wore the white breathing mask and carried his silver canister. Paul stepped away from the door expecting the exterminator to exit the house, but was stunned to see the black nozzle spitting gouts of poison about the room. Did the thieving bastard think he was still employed?

"*Hey*," Paul cried, arms spread.

The fat man let dangle the nozzle and raised his hands, palms up, to indicate he either couldn't hear or couldn't do anything to help the situation, and as he did so, the nozzle squirted poison all over the kitchen counter. Not stopping, Snowburger drizzled a colorless stream of liquid over a bag of bread, an open box of crackers.

Paul hammered on the door and shouted to be let in. Snowburger gestured vaguely toward his facemask and went on spraying.

Wondering if the exterminator had thought to lock the side door, too, Paul leaped from the porch and chugged around the house. By the time he climbed onto the veranda, a ragged stitch was piercing his ribs. His morbid state of cardiovascular health fed his heightening indignation. To make matters worse, Snowburger had locked the French doors too. Paul's hands clenched into fists, and for a wild moment he debated stoving in one of the windows just to get his hands on the smug prick.

A couple minutes later the exterminator made his way down the front porch steps. Paul pulled up next to him. The facemask hanging loose under the sweaty folds of his neck, Snowburger's round face betrayed no sign of remorse. As he sidestepped Paul en route to the back van doors, it was as though the incident in the kitchen had never occurred.

"How was the food?" Paul asked.

He stepped over to the driver's side door and planted himself there so Snowburger would have to face him before driving away. He heard the exterminator tinkering about in the back of the van, stowing his equipment.

"I asked you a question," Paul said. He'd not be made a fool of. He'd paid this charlatan over a thousand dollars, yet he was by no means certain Snowburger had exterminated anything other than a pepperoni pizza. For all he knew the man had been squirting tap water all over the house.

The clinking sounds ceased, yet Snowburger did not reappear.

Paul said, "I want a refund."

When no response came, he moved around the van. The impotent frustration he felt gave speed to his steps, and he nearly collided with the exterminator as he stepped around the rear van door.

Snowburger held an aluminum baseball bat.

"What—" Paul started to say when he saw the bat rise and whoosh down at him. Paul stumbled, landed on his butt and pushed himself backward through the gravel.

Snowburger's face contorted in a mask of paranoia and loathing. "You stay away from me, you little cocksucker. No one wants you here."

"Just take it easy," Paul said, one palm extended.

"No, *you* take it easy. I help myself to a little food and you act like I stole your credit card."

"You didn't even ask."

"That's right. And I could take anything else I want from this place and no one would believe you. I'm a known man in this town." Snowburger jabbed a finger at him. "You're the one no one wants."

"What the hell's the matter with you?" Paul's head was swimming. The heat, the lack of food, the exterminator's crazy talk. It made him dizzy.

"You don't know that, you're even dumber'n I thought. Related to the rottenest son of a bitch ever set foot in this county—" he jabbed a fat finger into Paul's chest, "—the same son of a bitch that probably had something to do with all those kids gettin' killed—" he raised the bat, "—one of which was my *grandma's little sister*—"

"Jesus," Paul said and stumbled away from the raised bat, the mad hatred in Snowburger's eyes. "I have no idea what—"

The man advanced and for a horrible moment Paul was certain the crazed exterminator would brain him with the Louisville Slugger. Then he stopped, his moon face spreading in a contemptuous smirk. "That's right, asshole, you better walk away." He turned toward the van, said, "And the next time you need help with the goddamn rats, you call somebody else. I wouldn't set foot in that place again for a million bucks."

Snowburger flung the bat into the van and climbed in after it. Gunning the engine, he dropped it into gear and drove in a looping circle, between Paul and the house.

As he passed he shouted, "You try to cancel payment on that check and I'll tell the sheriff you talked about killing that lawyer."

Paul watched the van, open-mouthed, as it rumbled away. Its back wheels pelted him with gravel.

The fat man extended his middle finger by way of farewell and disappeared down the lane.

His bout with Snowburger left him restless, itchy for something to do. Problem was, of his choices—toiling in the yard, going for a jog, organizing the garage—none appealed to him.

He'd not thought to commandeer a pillow or a blanket from the house before Snowburger poisoned its atmosphere, and short of walking, he had no way into town. To complicate matters further, the skies were cloud-filled and gravid with rain. With the weather so warm he'd planned on sleeping out under the stars, but now even that possibility was closed to him.

He scanned the garage bleakly, hoping to find something to cushion the unforgiving concrete floor.

When he spotted what was shoved in the corner of the large, cluttered space, he moaned. The liquor, of course, was right where he'd left it. The brown paper sack of bottles now favored him with its impassive stare, predicting his impending failure.

What was worse, Paul knew it was right.

To hell with it, he thought, and made for the sack.

He was shocked at how quickly the alcohol affected him. He'd never been one to drunken easily, yet here he was only five sips in and already feeling the whiskey's effects.

Outside the open garage door, he heard the trees rustling as little breezes adumbrated the storm. A squirrel bolted across the driveway, paused on its haunches to throw a glassy-eyed glance at Paul, then chattered belligerently and disappeared into the forest. Moments later, the rain drops began to tap the roof with wet, accelerating fingers. Soon the entire estate was awash with the shower.

Paul drank to the storm and wondered how late it was. With the sky so dark and oily, it could be early evening. As often happened, the alcohol seemed to expand time around him. It felt like he'd been drinking for hours, but experience told him he'd been at it for less than thirty minutes.

Grasping the Jim Beam bottle like a pistoleer, he went over and stood under the open garage door.

The large lawn was sodden with rain. The brick house, too, was painted gunmetal gray by the deluge. Inches from his nose fell steaming drips of rainwater that splashed into puddles at his feet and doused his sneakers. The warm metallic scent of the rain made a nice counterpoint to the cool pine fragrance breathing out of the forest.

The mist rising from the ground felt good on his face. Toasting it, he tilted the bottle once more. The brown liquid gurgled. He wiped his mouth, stuck out his hand to wash off the whiskey and was surprised at how warm the runoff from the roof felt on his skin. Inspired, Paul took a step forward and planted himself under the overhang's edge, letting the rain and the runoff sluice over his shut eyes. The giddiness he felt made him toss back another guzzle of whiskey, and while his skin felt cool, the alcohol burned off the chill from the inside out. Metallic rainwater flooded his throat. Coughing and sputtering, he weaved back inside the garage and cast about for something to dry himself with. All he found was a rag soiled with suspicious looking brown streaks. He set aside the bottle and scooped up the rag. Hoping the substance on the faded blue fabric was motor oil and not something worse, he scrubbed the moisture off his face. Feeling clammy and drunk, he peeled his tee shirt off and slapped it onto a paint-spattered sawhorse. The motion disturbed his balance. In trying to right himself, he knocked over an ancient coffee can and sent a rusty assortment of bolts and screws clattering. Just as he was about to topple over into the spray of junk, he caught himself on another sawhorse and waited out the carouseling garage.

He was drunker than he'd thought.

Carefully this time, he stepped out of the mess on the floor, picked up the whiskey bottle and moved to the workbench, his sneakers squishing uncomfortably. Pressing his backside against the coarse surface of the bench, he managed to pull off his sneakers and socks without falling.

Outside, the sky grew darker.

For a time he tried to occupy himself by puttering around with his uncle's tools and lawn equipment. He got some amusement from the old newspapers Myles had put under the sawhorses to catch paint. He drank as he read about Imelda Marcos and Dexy's Midnight Runners.

When Paul finished reading about Reagan's first term it was full dark outside and he'd finished all but a thin line of whiskey. He knocked it back.

The garage canted sideways. He staggered toward the receding wall to his right. He let his momentum take him that way, thinking to flip on the garage light when he got there.

His foot caught on something and before he had a chance to throw out his arms he was diving head first into the wall. The side of his head smashed into a supporting beam, his body crumpling below him in a heap. Before he could raise his hand to touch the golf ball lump forming on his brow, the murky garage pixilated and dimmed. Soon, he was resting facedown in a corner, the rain only a drizzle now in the driveway five feet away.

He awoke to a barbwire drill shredding the base of his skull. He opened his eyes and stared into darkness. *Bad one*, he thought. It was still nighttime and the hangover had already begun. The raw sizzle in his gorge meant he'd soon puke, and though there were few sensations as unpleasant, he knew he'd feel better afterward.

As terrible as the thought of vomiting was, he was more concerned about his churning intestines. He didn't know if he was capable of defecating in the woods, especially in a storm, but he couldn't go inside the house until the fumes settled, and he couldn't void his bowels in the garage. He thought for a moment of propping his ass cheeks on a sawhorse, of aiming for the rusty coffee can, but dismissed the idea as too ambitious.

At least he wasn't disoriented. He remembered clearly the argument with the exterminator, the way he'd guzzled the fifth of Jim Beam. He could not but remember the rain, for it had swum into the garage entrance, surrounding his head in a shallow lake. The water lapping against his shoulders smelled like withered grass and old dirt. Pushing himself up, Paul glanced out the open door and into the rainy night.

He'd no idea what time it was, but he was sure it was late. His eyes were bleary, which had to be the reason he saw a woman standing in his yard.

Blinking, he got to his feet and peered through the gloom into the large back yard. There, just visible around the corner of the house, stood a woman in a white dress, staring up at the third floor.

Alcohol had caused him to imagine things before, but never to this degree. Nevertheless, his soaked body and roiling stomach told him he wasn't dreaming. His pounding head made it tough to see clearly in the stygian darkness, but he knew what he saw: a woman in a short white dress.

When he stepped out of the garage into the driveway, he hardly felt the limestone gravel biting his bare feet. The sight of the woman mesmerized him. He was forty yards away, yet he was already nervous he'd frighten her into flight. *A deer hunter must feel this way before the kill*, he thought.

Lightning flashed and he distinguished her outline more clearly. The garment was a negligee rather than a dress. The drizzle made it cling to her body.

And what a body it was.

He wondered if her face, currently obscured by the distance, would be as striking as her large breasts and slim waist.

He moved closer.

If the lightning flashed again, she'd be sure to see him, near as he now was. Paranoia surged through him. Would she think him a rapist? A rain-drenched sexual predator? He supposed he looked like one, with only a pair of wet cargo shorts on. And, he realized, a raging erection.

For the woman was astonishing. This was surely a fantasy his lonely brain had conjured. There couldn't be a gorgeous girl, long black hair tossed back over her shoulders, breasts large and visible through her white nightie, standing soaked and half-naked in his backyard.

When he got within ten yards of her, lightning flashed again. As it strobed it cast the yard into brilliant clarity. She discovered him with widening eyes and before he could open his mouth she darted away, doe-like, through the yard. Her speed shocked him. Even in the negligee she moved with a swiftness he couldn't believe, and by the time he'd found his voice, she was disappearing nimbly into the woods.

Chapter Eleven

April, 1951

He felt good tonight. He looked good too. The way Annabel watched him across the room, she wanted to get him alone, away from the party.

That was fine with Myles.

It was Maria that worried him. She was being more than usually flirtatious, going so far as to hang on David's shoulder as he stood next to Annabel. Myles watched his brother shift uncomfortably as the women eyed one another across his broad shoulders.

The band they'd hired was a good one. They even had a female drummer, a tasty little dish whose work on the brushes helped him forget about the drama being played out across the room.

Hoping Annabel would follow, Myles took his drink down the front hallway, past the smoking couples in the foyer, and outside into the cool spring air. On the front porch wrestled a group of kids whose moms and dads didn't dare leave them at home. Myles couldn't blame them. Four kids slaughtered in just under three years was an unsettling number for a parent. Especially in such a small town.

A red rubber ball skittered by Myles's shoes. A blond boy followed it, bumped him in the shin as he passed by. Prick, *Myles thought.*

"Watch where you're going Aaron," a little girl said to the boy as he came back with the ball.

"You watch it," Aaron said to the girl and stopped next to where Myles stood holding his drink. The blond boy dribbled the ball next to Myles's shoes to show the girl he wasn't scared of adults. Myles winked at the little girl. He held the glass of bourbon over the boy's head, let it trickle out over him, his blond hair going dark and sticky. "Hey," the boy said, tears welling up.

"Hah-hah, that's what you get," the girl said, pointing.

Myles descended the porch steps, threw a glance over his shoulder expecting to see Annabel coming down after him, but saw only the kids taunting one another.

He had a bad feeling about tonight, about the way Maria was goading her. He'd never seen Annabel angry, but he'd always known it was there, the potential, under that serene face.

Myles walked to the edge of the forest and listened. This time of year, it was quiet. A couple months, the hollow would be humming with life. For now, though, it was somber. He shook a cigarette out of his case, lit it.

A hand fell on his shoulder.

He pivoted expecting to find Annabel but discovered the lady drummer instead. She was a tiny little thing, mousy brown hair trimmed short like a little boy's. Smallish tits damn near poking out of her low cut dress.

"You want another drink?" She was holding out the glass.

He took it, sipped. Bourbon.

"How'd you know what I was drinking?" Eyeing her over the cigarette smoke.

"I know all about you, Myles."

"Is that so?" he asked, leading her toward the woods.

It was near midnight when he returned, the band long since having ceased playing, unable to do much without their drummer to keep time. He'd left the girl lying on a bed of bluegrass, dozing with his jacket covering her naked little body.

She'd been satisfying, and he wondered if he'd have anything left for Annabel if she was in the mood. But when he found her he knew sex was the last thing on her mind, that something had changed while he was outside with the drummer. He approached her cautiously.

"Party's winding down," he said.

"Where's David?" she asked. Coming right to it.

He noted the ferocious set of her eyes, the sharp edge the drinks had given her.

"I haven't seen him," Myles answered, careful to keep anything

insinuating out of his voice.

"That's not good enough."

He stepped back, really saw her then. She was livid. It was the first time he'd seen her that way, without her composure. Even during sex, her eyes wild and her body atremble, there was something in control that wouldn't let her surrender completely.

"I've checked outside," she said. "In their place by the brook."

Myles could only stare. If she knew about David and Maria, their spot in the woods...

But she beat him to it. "Yes I saw you and that girl, Myles. There's no need to be coy about it."

He could only grin and marvel at her.

Her expression darkened. "But my husband wasn't there. He's not in any of the guest rooms either."

"His car outside?"

"Yes," she answered, impatient. "And the whore doesn't drive."

A thought came to him and it was out before he knew what he was saying. "Have you checked your bedroom?"

Annabel froze. He felt his balls shrink. He knew he'd started something then, wished he'd never said it, but knew it was too late and there was no stopping her, no reigning her in, and whatever would happen now couldn't be prevented.

She moved past him toward the stairs. Behind him Myles could feel the partygoers watching. He could only follow, and as he did he sensed them following, too, drinks in hand, ambling up the stairs behind him, eyes glassy and wolfish. They'd been waiting for this for going on two years, waiting for Annabel to show her teeth. They rose up and up, creeping toward the third floor, hoping and dreading they'd find David and Maria rutting on the floor like animals.

When Myles came through the bedroom door after Annabel he knew it was true, that David and Maria had screwed in the bed where the married couple slept. He knew this even though the pair was fully dressed, David in his black trousers and white tux shirt unbuttoned to show the cleft of his hairless chest, Maria in her black dress with the different colored flowers on it, unzipped in back so that all who were crowding into the bedroom could see there were no panties under the dress.

When the partygoers came through the door they'd sigh at first because there were no naked people, their disappointment transforming into fascination when they noticed the way Maria sat on the bed smoking. David stood by the stained glass window rolling the ice around his empty glass. Both wore expressions at once intense and bland as if they dared Annabel to say something about their being there together.

Maria sat with her legs crossed on the bed facing David, only he mattering to her and Annabel insignificant, a nuisance she'd already dealt with, bested. Myles thought of saying something, of asking Maria if she were crazy, but if the death of her boy had unhinged her mind so utterly that she presumed to humiliate Annabel in her own house, in her own bedroom, *she truly was beyond help. Myles leaned forward on his toes and waited for the explosion.*

Annabel asked David, "Why?"

"That's some question coming from you," he said, still swirling his drink. "You're the one who can't keep your hands off my brother."

"Our bed," Annabel said in a voice barely audible.

From where she sat on the foot of the bed, Maria blew smoke toward her rival, a satisfied grin on her face.

"You deserve worse than that," Maria said.

The buxom girl moved to the window and stood next to David. "You don't deserve to sleep under the same roof with him. You should be outside with the animals." She wrapped a hand around David's waist right there in front of his wife. The crowd watched, stone silent, waiting for Annabel to retaliate. But it was Maria who went on.

"Why is it that all the kids who've been killed have been the sons and daughters of your enemies?" she asked, slurring her words. The crowd leaned forward, knowing the stakes had been raised. They murmured, wondering at this new accusation.

Sensing what might happen if things were allowed to continue, David stepped forward, silencing Maria. He stood up straight, his huge chest thrown out. Myles felt the men behind him in the doorway, all of them shorter and weaker than David, shrink.

"Okay, folks. Party's over. Get out of here," David said and turned his back to Annabel as if that decided it. Setting down his glass he gestured to Maria and made to leave. Maria took his hand and walked with him around Annabel, and as the Spanish girl moved around the tall

blonde her dusky shoulder nudged Annabel's out of the way, knocking her off balance. Myles observed it as he ushered the remaining partygoers out the door, the sounds of laughter echoing down the hallway, deriding Annabel, the cuckolded wife.

Maria and David were already beyond her when the change started, but from where Myles stood holding the door he noticed Annabel's body tense, the slim muscles in her back ripple. When she turned Myles saw and understood she still had control, she'd never not been in control. Her blue eyes smoldered beneath hooded lashes. Her face was down, her pointed chin lowered near her chest, her legs set wide like a man's.

Myles felt a chill whisper down his spine.

David and Maria were almost to the door, neither of them bothering to look at Myles.

"David," Annabel said in a low voice.

"What?" he asked without stopping.

"Look at me, David."

Turning, he obeyed.

"Fine, Annabel. I'm looking at you."

"Is she what you want?" Nodding toward Maria, who stood between the two brothers, glowering at Annabel in triumph.

But David said, "Is he what you want?" Cocking a thumb at Myles.

If Annabel was surprised, she didn't show it. David, though, was suddenly livid, his pent-up jealousy finally giving vent.

"My own brother? I knew you were cheap, but I didn't know you were that desperate. Jesus, you might as well have sex with the dog."

Myles couldn't stand it, the women fighting over David. He said to his brother in a low voice, "You're the one who strayed. She never did until you took this whore to the woods."

Maria whirled and hissed something at Myles but before she could finish David lunged past her and struck. His fist connected with his younger brother's temple and gashed him near the eye, but Myles surprised him by coming back with an uppercut. It stunned David, who staggered and stared angrily at the group of partygoers that had stuck around in the hallway hoping there would yet be fireworks.

"Get out!" David shouted at them and slammed the door in their *faces.*

Maria moaned, brought a hand to her mouth. It came away bloody. She stared at the blood uncomprehendingly, astonished she'd gotten hit in the scuffle.

Long fingers touched her shoulder.

"Are you alright, dear?"

She turned and discovered Annabel smiling sadly at her, looking for all the world the sympathetic host. As Annabel led her away from him and David, she seemed grateful for the help. Annabel wrapping her arm around her shoulders, saying, "There, there. It will be alright, dear."

Myles watched the taller blonde woman mothering the curvy Spanish one, their footsteps picking up speed as they crossed the room. Annabel's arm tightened behind Maria's back. Their pace accelerated until he could hear Maria beginning to shout questions, the questions melting into one long scream as Annabel propelled her toward the window, both hands now on Maria's back, and before David could break forward to stop it Maria was hurtling toward the stained glass windowpane. She crashed through face first, and before she disappeared into the night Myles watched a pink object hover in the air behind her, a severed ear, before it, too, disappeared through the jagged opening.

Annabel fell against the base of the window, the splintered glass bloodying her arms. David stepped forward just as a brittle thump sounded from the ground below. The sound of voices came, the sounds of people gathering around the dead woman, children screaming, thudding footsteps on the stairs behind them. Ignoring his bleeding wife, David dashed to the window and leaned out. Myles felt the door swing open behind him and men were rushing by, jostling him as he stared at Annabel sitting on the floor. He felt absolutely nothing, nothing for Maria as he heard the voices below confirm she was dead, nothing for his brother who leaned now on the broken stained glass, the shards piercing his palms, his broad shoulders wracked with sobs. Nothing for himself.

But looking at the slender woman sitting bloodied against the windowsill, whose terrible laughter now rose above the shrieking of the guests, he finally felt something, and what he felt was fear. Fear of her, and fear of what they'd let into their home.

Chapter Twelve

By six o'clock he'd killed a pint of whiskey, ridden the riding mower around the yard for an hour in no particular pattern before running out of gas and taking a nap under an elm tree. Then, he ate half a bag of pretzels by way of supper and read eighty more pages of *Ghost Story*. Once, a robin lighted on the grass a few feet from where he sat, but when he tossed a pretzel in its direction, it uttered a snobbish chirp and fluttered away.

The novel cheered him. That, at least, was a pursuit worthy of his time. While he killed brain cells with drink he could keep the ones that remained entertained. Switching over to beer, he carried the book and a small red cooler he'd filled with ice and a six-pack of Budweiser to the back porch for an evening of cheap entertainment. Studying the author's picture inside the back cover, the bald dome and intelligent eyes, Paul wondered how a guy learned to write that well. *Not by pickling his brain with alcohol and stewing in self-pity,* a voice inside his head answered.

"Piss off," he said aloud.

May was a good month to read outdoors, he thought. The lilac bushes near the veranda breathed their sweet breath, which mixed together amiably with the aroma of freshly cut grass. Inhaling deeply, he reached inside the screen door and flipped on the back porch light. The weather was just cool enough to keep the bugs from flitting and buzzing about his ears, and just warm enough to make a long-sleeved shirt unnecessary. Settling himself in the yellow lawn chair, he cracked open a beer, sipped it and read.

A bit later, he refilled the cooler.

The beer lasted until ten thirty. He was good and drunk, but he still had wits enough about him to move about the house. As he always did when he drank a lot, he entertained crazy notions. Calling Emily up and asking her to marry him. Driving back to Memphis to tell his father what he really thought of him. Jogging into town to raise hell at a local honkytonk. It was early yet—the idea wasn't all that bad. He could walk there, or better yet, hop on the riding mower and get there by eleven or eleven-thirty. There'd still be time to shoot a game of pool or sweet talk some local gal. The latter was probably out of the question though. He could smell his own breath—a rank mixture of cream cheese and beer—and in his stained tee shirt and tattered blue jeans he looked like he should be sleeping at the train yard.

What to do then? He wasn't particularly hungry, and he knew if he slept now he'd awaken too early. Mornings were best slept through.

He caught a glimpse of the woods through the parlor window.

Lovely, dark and deep, he thought, remembering a poem he'd read in high school. The forest was a mystery, a dark lady yearning to be explored.

Just one stop before he embarked.

The ballroom flared into brilliance, the twin chandeliers showering their lunar glow over the black and white tiles. Paul made a revolution around the large room, just avoiding the rich vermilion sofas, the brocade chairs, which sat around the dance floor like torpid spectators.

Stopping at the bar—marveling again that he owned it, as well as the sprawling ballroom reflected in its long strip of mirror—he fished out another pint of whiskey and crammed it into his pocket. Pushing away from the bar, he executed a spin and a leap and was proud when he stuck the landing. His shoes squeaked as he leaned and stumbled through the ballroom and the sounds of his crazy dance grew louder until their feverishness brought him to a listing stop, palms planted on knees, mouth dry and panting.

The sounds continued around him. Scraping, insistent.

It was the rats, of course. The place was acrawl with the verminous fiends though he'd yet to spot a single one. A deep, body-rocking shudder gripped him. The little bastards. If their aim was to chase him from the house, they were going to succeed. His skin throbbing and cold, he shivered as he heel-toed it down the hallway and out the front door.

The night air was a welcome warmth in contrast to the chill of the house. His jeans were a necessary evil, for how else could he carry the pint? His shirt, however, was dead skin to be shed. He left it lying in the gravel as he set off through the grass, carrying him to the forest's edge, to the inky mouth of the trail. Passing through, he thought again of Robert Frost, how Paul had it better than the guy in the poem. He had no promises to keep, no horse to water, no obligations to fulfill. He was free to haunt this hollow, to extend his naked arms and feel the cool new leaves kiss his fingertips, nuzzle his palms. He loved it all, the towering sycamores, the underbrush that hid what lived in the forest, though he could neither see nor hear any life save what was green and silent. An idea came to him then and branching off in a direction he and the sheriff had not taken, Paul clamped the neck of the bottle sticking out of his jeans and lifted it out, relishing the warm way the glass slithered up his thigh.

He was amused to find he was sexually aroused, both emotionally—as he always was when he drank—and physically, as he could almost never be when the alcohol had taken the verve from his loins.

He grasped the bottle like a baton and took off running down the trail. He was heading for a fall, he knew. Not only was he chronically inactive and apt to faint from exertion, but the forest was dark as hell. At any moment a root could upend him, snare his foot and give his ankle a savage twist. As he ran, chest burning, he pictured himself tripping and diving headlong into a tree trunk, or toppling end over end and snapping his backbone at the bottom of some rocky gorge.

Perhaps that's what happened to Ted Brand, he thought. The lawyer had gotten into Uncle Myles's stash and gone for a jog in the woods. Why, he could happen upon the corpse at any minute. Bloated and rotting, squirrels or rabbits nesting in his hollowed out gut. Rats feasting on his eyes.

That made him stop and rest against a tree. He hated the rats, hated the way they'd chased him from his home.

However, if it weren't for them, for their alien rustling, he'd never have discovered this new path in the woods. He leaned against a sycamore tree, its smooth curvy length filling the space between his shoulder blades, and sliding down, he unscrewed the cap and sipped.

Seated on the forest floor, he rested his forearms on his knees, closed his eyes and felt the back of his head thump against the tree. His breathing slowed, his chest rising and falling softly.

He awoke to the sound of something scurrying behind him. Sucking in breath, he shoved away from the tree and peered beyond it, straining his eyes in the darkness to find what had awakened him.

How long had he been out?

Backpedaling, he craned his head to look at the sky.

There were no stars, no moon to orient him. He wondered vaguely if he'd lost the pint before he realized he still grasped it.

The scuttling came again, sending him farther from the tree. He threw skittish glances over his shoulder at the unseen menace. When he'd gone what he hoped was a safe distance from the source of the noises, he pivoted and faced the place where he'd rested. Nothing but the lone tree stood out on the black tapestry.

A breeze rustled through the hollow, chilling his skin, making him glance over his shoulder. He turned back to the sycamore tree and stopped, breath catching in his throat.

He turned again and couldn't believe what he saw.

The graveyard filled the large oval clearing before him, its stone markers aged and standing at tired angles.

His feet carried him into the clearing, his eyes adjusting now to the blackness of the night. He peered about the graveyard, calculating his distance from home. The documents estimated Watermere's total acreage at well over a thousand. A territory that large surely encompassed this place, secluded as it was. No wonder he and the sheriff hadn't happened upon it. Barlow might not even know of its existence.

He wondered if anyone did. For the cemetery was overgrown, abandoned. Its markers were haphazardly arranged, some broken or cracked, others lying in the grass, swallowed up by weeds and time. A plump rabbit bounded toward him before veering off toward the engulfing forest. Some large black bird, a crow probably, sat perched on a faded ivory cross but didn't stir as he edged past.

Strange and varied were the gravestones. They ranged from puny rectangular slabs that lay flush with the weedy ground to elaborately carved sepulchers. Celtic crosses wrapped in marble ivy. A staring skull, its mouth full of teeth that themselves looked like tombstones. An open book with unreadable text adorned one cracked marker, the placement of the fissure injuring the carved book's spine. Paul gasped with delight upon spotting a tall, cubic stone cut to resemble a grandfather clock, replete with pendulum and a moon clock face. The hour and minute hands were permanently fixed at twelve o'clock.

He moved toward the back of the clearing. From the darkness a large marker emerged, the shadow of its burnished granite surface seeming to creep across the forest floor toward him. As he edged closer, he became aware of the silence. No bird twittered, no unseen menace shambled.

Face twisting with disappointment, he realized he wasn't the only living person who knew of the graveyard's existence.

Because for one thing, this stone was newer than the rest. No more than fifteen or twenty years old, he estimated. Yet there were more reasons than this to guess that others knew of the stone, this place. Where there should have been a name and an epitaph, there were instead deep, ugly gouges. A hammer and chisel and God knew what other tools had ravaged the marker so that its entire face was a nightmare of scars and trenches. The words WHORE and DEVIL were spray-painted in red. Near the bottom of the tombstone, the blood red letters, dripped and smeared, delivered the coup de gras: BURN IN HELL.

Stunned at the disrespect, he wondered what the occupant of the grave had done to incur such enmity. Scrunch his eyes though he might, he couldn't tell what the name was, nor what designs or sentiments had adorned the marker before the vandals had afflicted it. Sighing, Paul sat at the foot of the stone and nipped at the pint. Setting the bottle in his lap, he reclined on his palms and noted the strange feel of the ground. Unlike the surrounding area, the earth here was barren. No blade of grass grew, no weed sprouted. It was as though whoever had assaulted the tombstone had also sought to kill all the grass on the surface above the coffin. The charred-looking earth wasn't precisely rectangular, but it was clearly confined to the area above where the body would have been planted.

Musing on this peculiarity, he drank.

The alcohol warmed him, electrified his flesh, and again he felt the hot tingle of sexual desire. His whole body thrummed with the heat,

121

with visions of tongues and breasts and smooth open legs.

He frowned.

It was strange. He'd been sure the tombstone had been raped of all its carvings, but now that he observed it from this perspective, its imposing girth towering over him like some god or goddess, he saw there was indeed one design which had partially escaped the tip of the chisel and the insult of the spray paint. One florid wing, half of an angelic face, a tiny bare foot.

A cherub. A sweet, guileless creature of heaven.

Paul's eyes widened.

He rose, caressed the cherub's wing with the tip of his index finger, and inched away from the gravestone, eyes fixed on the childlike face. His breath quickening, he turned and moved with increasingly longer strides through the stones and weeds. As he reached the mouth of the trail his steps accelerated to a trot and then to a sprint. He moved as he hadn't in years, his arms pumping, legs a blur, his sneakers pounding down the forest trail. His body maneuvered through darkness, through myriad twists and angles, over crests, through dales, and soon he exploded out of the forest mouth, his pumping limbs compelling him across the silent yard and through the front door. He flew through the ballroom and took the curved stairway in four leaping strides. Past the library, beyond the bedrooms, into the lightless den. Without bothering with the desk lamp his fingers began to fly over the typewriter keys and within moments his hand shot out and slid in another blank sheet and with hardly a pause his fingers drummed again, sweat pouring from his matted air.

His typing continued long into the night. Sated, the sounds from the walls ceased.

Paul awoke.

And wished he hadn't.

The hangover was colossal. He felt like crawling across the room, opening the window and tumbling out. Problem was, he didn't even know what room he was in. He didn't dare open his eyes—if they hurt this badly when they were shut, how awful would the pain be if he exposed them to daylight? For a crazy moment, he wondered if he'd really gone through with his idea of the night before, driven the lawn mower into town and found some local dive. If so, he was probably in jail now. The air roiling in his mouth was close, dank, like the air of a jail cell. He ventured to open his eyes; what he saw did not reassure him.

Near his face was a wall. It seemed made of wood, like a coffin.

He realized he lay on a floor rather than a bed, and that the floor, too, was made of wood. His whole body screamed in protest as glacial chills passed through it, simultaneously chattering his teeth and broiling him with hot waves of nausea. *God, let me puke soon*, he thought. *If I don't throw up I might die of alcohol poisoning or bubonic plague or some other wretched affliction.*

On his back as he was, he found he could turn his head with some effort. Straining, he lifted his head and stared down at his toes. It was lighter down there. He began to sit up but had to stop when his forehead knocked a glancing blow against a hard surface. Whimpering, rubbing his aching head, he rolled over onto his stomach and pushed backward toward the light. He rose to his knees and realized why he'd thought of a coffin. He'd passed out and slept under the large mahogany desk.

Letting out a queasy breath, he braced himself on the edge of the desk and pushed to his feet. The fetid slime coating his mouth tasted like spoiled milk. He was about to make a dash for the bathroom and the cool porcelain toilet when something on the desk drew his attention.

His fingertips brushed the stack of pages. At a glance he estimated there were two hundred or more, neatly stacked, sitting in the center of the desk next to the typewriter. Beside that, a small snatch of lined notebook paper. Paul lifted the handwritten pages, thumbed through the small pile. Written in florid cursive, words filled the notebook, and even in the dim light filtering through the blinds, he could see the writing was not his own.

Setting aside the handwritten pages for a moment, Paul spied the chair a few feet away and rolled it to the desk. Forgetting the sick way his stomach growled and bubbled, forgetting the nausea tickling at his gorge, he sat and read.

THE MONKEY KILLER.

Under that, *A NOVEL BY PAUL CARVER.*

Pulse pounding, he lifted parts of the stack, amazed to see that the whole thing was full of typewritten words. He paused on a page about halfway through, expecting to find gibberish—"All work and no play makes Johnny a dull boy" perhaps—when he instead discovered that the writing was varied and formatted exactly as a story should be. He searched again and found passages of description, snatches of dialogue.

Paul chewed a thumbnail.

It couldn't be.

Dumbfounded, he looked again at the title page, set it aside, and began to read.

The sun was hot on Angela's shoulders, so she went to the pump for some water. Mrs. England was on the playground scolding a group of pupils who had crossed the lane to pick daisies. Angela heard her teacher now: "How dare you venture past the set boundaries? You should know better Carol Ledford, your father being the constable and all. You will all be in for a paddling if you do that again, and I mean it."

And on and on and on.

Angela let her lips touch the cool surface of the pump, the water flowing down her chin, dripping onto her white shoes.

She hated her white shoes. And her white dress and her stupid yellow hair ribbon. Her mother insisted on dressing her like a doll. Maybe her mother had not been allowed to play with dolls as a little girl so she had to make her daughter look like one.

She was tired of being a doll. A little princess. It was dreadfully boring. She wanted to be like Carol Ledford, who was a year older. Carol would never allow her mother to dress her in this silly garb. Carol got to wear pants and never wore yellow hair ribbons.

She heard the sounds of a kickball game starting up. Mrs. England getting everyone organized, the kids laughing at her but still minding.

Angela sighed. How she longed to get dirty, to stand in line with the other kids and boot the rubber ball high into the air, sailing red and lovely in the shiny spring sunlight. She was about to round the corner to sit on the bench and watch the game, as she always did, when something caught her attention near the woods.

It was the old kickball, the one that had got punctured by a rock last month.

Angela approached it and bent to pick it up.

She stopped, smiled mischievously.

Straightening, she reached out with her right foot instead and dragged the red ball back toward her, away from the woods. She was careful about it because just beyond the tree line, the woods dropped off into a steep ravine, and if the ball went down there she would not be able to retrieve it.

Once it was on level ground, Angela made to bump it through the grass with one white-soled shoe, but she could not feel the ball properly through her stupid shoe, so she stood trying to keep her balance as she took off one shoe and then the other. She was standing on her right foot, fumbling with her left shoe, when she heard the roar of the kids on the playground on the other side of the school. Carol Ledford had probably done something great, kicked the ball far or walloped someone running for home base.

Angela lost her balance and fell. She winced and giggled at her own klutziness. She looked about her and was glad to see no one was around. Come to think of it, she had not even asked to get a drink from the pump. It had not occurred to her then, but now she was happy she had not told Mrs. England where she was going. With all those kids to keep control of, the teacher would never miss her. Why, she could stay here until recess was over, and that was at least another twenty minutes.

She felt coldness against her leg and frowned. Springing up, she was horrified to see she had sat in a patch of grass down the hill from the pump and that the run-off had made a muddy puddle where she had fallen. Her fears were confirmed when she held out her white dress, felt the squishy fabric, saw the mud on the pretty lace. Her mother would be furious.

Squeezing back tears, feeling doomed, she made for the corner of the school building, hoping against hope that Mrs. England could get the mud out at the basin in the girls' bathroom.

Angela halted and glanced back at the red kickball.

She touched the soiled white fabric and knew there was no getting it clean. She was in for a good hiding, and that was that.

She might as well enjoy the rest of recess.

Fighting back tears but feeling a bit giddy, Angela ran barefoot through the empty strip of schoolyard. The grass felt tickly and soft against her bare feet. She giggled, toeing the half-deflated ball and nudging it out in front of her. She stopped, listening. The kickball game was growing from the sound of it. She guessed that all the kids had made their way over to the diamond. That was usually the way. The game began slow but grew in size and intensity and peaked just as Mrs. England blew her whistle for her pupils to go inside.

Angela reared back and kicked.

The lopsided ball smacked against the solid brick wall of the schoolhouse and bounced crookedly back to her.

She listened, hoping no one had heard.

The game continued, oblivious.

She was amazed at herself. She had never done anything like this. She had never gone to the pump without asking, never hid behind the schoolhouse all by herself. This was something Carol Ledford would do.

Booting the ball again, Angela reached up to untie her stupid yellow hair ribbon. It was caught, the knot hung on a tangle of her curls. Because she was absorbed with disentangling the ribbon, she did not see the kickball rolling toward the woods until it was too late. She gasped and made a dash for it but was too slow. The ball hopped over the lip of earth at the tree line and disappeared into the woods.

She stood between the trees, panting. She cast a fearful glance over her shoulder. There was time, she knew, to retrieve the ball, but if she did, would she be able to climb back up the hill? It was very steep, and some of it looked like mud. Her dress would certainly be ruined then, and how her mother would yell.

This did not even take into account it was against the rules to enter the forest. Especially after what had happened to the little boy in July.

Shivering, Angela backed away from the woods. She was halfway to the corner of the schoolhouse when she heard Carol Ledford's voice, loud and commanding, on the kickball diamond.

Carol would not be afraid of going into the woods, so why should she be?

Determined now, Angela walked past the tree line, reached out, braced an arm on a bent sapling and lowered herself down the ravine.

It was difficult with her bare feet, and more than once she stumbled and landed on her rear end, but within minutes, she had made it to the base of the hill. Picking the dead leaves and twigs off her dress, she stared out at the forest. She saw a small clearing, a series of rises and dips. And of course, she saw trees.

She did not see the ball.

She shook her head. It did not make sense that the ball was not here. She'd watched for it on the way down, and it was nowhere on the hill, stuck on a tree trunk or hidden under a bush. She glanced up the hill but was no longer sure where she had come down. The slope of the ravine was too messy to tell for sure, any footprints she had made only blended in with the muddy streaks on the ground.

Angela thought of working her way back up the hill, but she knew she would feel like a coward if she came up without the ball. Determined, she searched the forest for anything red.

She walked to her left, the soles of her feet blackening. The ground sloped a bit. She supposed the ball might have continued to roll this way. The ravine was very steep. The decline got steeper. She followed it down, hoping to spot the ball, when her bare feet slipped out from under her. Her head snapped back hard against the ground, the earth pounding the breath out of her. Dazed, she felt her dress push up as she slid down the steepening hill and was alarmed to see the ground drop away from her. Her face swung forward over her feet. The earth rushed up to meet her. Palms out to cushion her fall, she landed face-first in the mud at the foot of the slope. She was crying, she knew, and there was no stopping it. She thought she had broken some ribs. Her chest was a hornet's nest of sharp pains. Lying there on her stomach she tried to slow her breathing, and as she did so, she looked at the ground before her and saw the red lopsided ball sitting there in the dead leaves in front of her nose.

Her breath caught, her tears warming. She had succeeded. She was about to reach forward and touch the round surface when her hand stopped and her throat began to burn.

Beyond the red ball was a pair of boots.

Mud was caked on them, on their faded rubber soles. She pushed up onto her elbows and saw that a pair of legs connected to the boots.

She followed the legs up. They seemed to go on forever. Above them, around the waist of the navy blue work suit, was a belt. She pushed to her knees, eyes still traveling up the figure. She saw the wide chest, rising and falling, and when she saw the face, she felt urine scalding her thighs.

The figure wore a mask, the face red with black eyebrows and yellow cat eyes and short black horns coming out of the forehead.

As she gazed up into the devil's face, one enormous hand reached back, disappearing behind the blue work suit, and reappeared grasping a long, shiny knife with a wooden handle.

"Little monkey," a deep voice said.

As Angela sat paralyzed, the knife rose and the figure began to laugh.

Horrified, Paul read the next three lines, turned away from the pile of pages and vomited.

Book Two

Paul

Chapter Thirteen

He would read for a while, get up and pace, sit down again to continue, his curiosity mastering him. But before he got far another jolt would strike him and he'd step away from the desk, heart racing. The pile of papers came to remind him of an especially cunning snapping turtle, its ancient shell bleached white by the sun. Every damn time he ventured near it, the fucker would lunge at his fingers and wound him anew.

Maybe his drinking could account for the novel before him, but he couldn't see how. He'd said things while drunk before and not remembered them later. Once in college he'd slept with a girl and had little recollection of it the next day.

But writing an entire novel?

It didn't make sense. And if the words hadn't come from his liberated subconscious, just where had they come from?

Paul swallowed and stared at the pile of pages.

The Monkey Killer was a true story, or at the very least held particles of the truth. Its primaries were Myles Carver, his brother David and Annabel Carver, the woman who, though married to David, slept with them both.

The tale was spare and sickening.

Children were being murdered in Shadeland. The first child to die was the son of David Carver's mistress. The next victim the daughter of a woman who'd insulted Annabel during a party at Watermere.

After the second slaying, the police arrested a harmless old drunk who'd been seen in town the day before the girl was slain and didn't have an alibi for the time of either murder. The drunk was released when another murder occurred while he was in custody.

Two more kids were murdered.

Seeing the names of his relatives—people he knew something about, as well as ones like Annabel, who were mysteries to him—was jarring enough for Paul. When he read the word *Watermere*, he wondered if he were dreaming it all.

The final ten pages of the novel were the worst.

The killer's identity was found out when David Carver visited the tool shed for a sickle to clear a spot of underbrush. Frank McCabe, the Carvers' gardener and handyman, had acted suspiciously throughout the novel and the author—whoever that was, Paul thought sickly—had made it clear that McCabe was a suspect. In one scene the handyman spied on Annabel through a hole in the wall while she bathed, reminding Paul of Norman Bates. More than once David had wondered aloud where McCabe had been on the night of the murders.

So when David visited the tool shed where the handyman sometimes slept, and found a bloodstained pair of gardener's gloves under McCabe's personal effects, he told Myles they had to punish the man for his iniquitous deeds. Myles had no desire to apprehend McCabe, was weary of the whole business, so David pulled a gun on him, forced him into riding into town with him to gather up a posse to hunt McCabe down.

David was well-respected in Shadeland and had no trouble inciting his own private mob. The caravan of half-drunk vigilantes made its way to the woods near the limestone quarry, where McCabe was known to have erected a tiny ramshackle house.

Under a moon the color of oxblood, they moved through the woods, David in the lead.

They held McCabe aloft, marched through the forest with him on their hands like a jungle kill. Their flashlight beams swirled and bobbed like fearful birds. Myles looked askance at his brother. His jaw still hurt where David had slugged him. Just because he refused to help with the lynching. Myles didn't give two shits about McCabe, the idiot could hang for all he cared. He only wanted to get back to Watermere, to love on Annabel before David got to her first. Too many were the nights he had to play clean-up.

He followed the group through the woods, going God knew where. David stepped beside him on the trail. Myles looked at the .38, wondered if he could take it away from his brother, use it on him. The crowd might charge him, rend him to pieces, but he could take a few with him. The key was getting the gun away from David.

"Wait," he heard David shout. The men stopped, a single body, and listened for further instruction.

Jesus, *Myles thought.* They think he's some kind of messiah.

"Against the tree," David commanded. Myles wondered how they could know what tree he was talking about—they were in the woods, for chrissakes—when he saw and understood.

The great oak towered above the rest, its trunk a full ten feet around. There were no low-hanging branches, which confused Myles, for how could they lynch McCabe without a branch to string him from? He chalked it up to inexperience, waited for the men to discover their mistake.

David turned to one of the group. "Your boy send for him?"

The man grunted an affirmative. Myles wondered what they were talking about until he heard more voices, saw another traveling lightshow approach.

The arriving flashlights further illuminated the bizarre scene: McCabe on the ground, his scorched face clamped between the trail and David's large boot; David himself shirtless, his barrel chest sweaty from the closeness of the forest air, his square jaw set; men gathered around them in a loose semi-circle, drunken scarecrows in tee shirts and jeans, many of them holding bottles of cheap booze.

"Someone want to tell me what you all are doing to that man?" Sheriff Ledford asked.

"Isn't it obvious?" David returned. "We're taking care of this killer of children."

Ledford stepped forward, a stocky man with a sullen look. "I'm assuming you know it's against the law to drag a man out of his home, beat the hell out of him."

"He's gotten nothing he hasn't earned," David said. The men laughed, glanced sidewise at one another.

"You got any proof?"

"Ask him." David hooked a thumb toward his brother.

Sheriff Ledford glanced at Myles, his look going more sullen. Myles had bedded the man's sister the year before, never called her again. He

133

grinned at the sheriff.

"Well, asshole?" Ledford said.

Still grinning, Myles answered, "David here went snooping around McCabe's stuff. Found some bloody gloves."

"Bloody gloves," Ledford repeated.

"Uh-huh."

The sheriff turned to David. "That's it? That's why you drug this poor bastard out here in the middle of the night, made his face look like that? For Pete's sake, David," Ledford said, moving toward McCabe. "What'd you do to him?"

"He tripped and fell on the stove," David said and shifted his weight. Myles heard the gardener's cheekbones cracking as David leaned on his head.

"Tripped and fell," Ledford said.

"That's right."

"You better come with me," the sheriff said to David.

"He ain't goin' nowhere," called a voice from the crowd.

Ignoring it, Ledford said, "Come on, David. Let him go."

"Sure." David grinned, but showed no sign of letting McCabe up. "But do me a favor," he said and reached into the back pocket of his jeans. Ledford reached for his Colt revolver, but David was already holding out the crumpled sheet of paper.

"Go on," David said. "Take it."

Ledford did. He frowned.

"You find this with his things?" the sheriff asked. His voice was different now, huskier. Myles stepped around behind him to read what was printed on the note, the hand child-like, messy:

i like the sound the jafee girl makes. like a munkees wen she dies. eyes big lik that to. wen the nife go in her it feels so warm the blud. i got to stay out of town awile.

Myles finished the note, watched the sheriff's expressionless face. The man stood there reading it over, the only sound in the forest the whimpering from under David's foot. Myles looked down, tried to see McCabe's face, but the flashlights were all on Ledford now.

After a time, he looked up from the note, peered at David.

"You found this in his stuff?"

"Yes, sir."

"You think this is referring to the fourth victim, the Jaffrey girl?"

"I know it is."

"You'd testify to that in court?"

"We don't need a court."

The sheriff watched him, didn't seem to breathe. Ledford looked hard at David, who didn't look away. Then, the sheriff said, "Alright. But not here."

He gestured at the men behind him, deputies who often came to the parties at Watermere, drank and slept with women who were not their wives.

"Bring him," Ledford said.

He set off through the woods, the whole party behind him. Myles glanced at his brother, who seemed not to mind being usurped. He walked beside the man who was a great-uncle of one of the murdered children. Neither of them seemed to care one way or the other about McCabe's fate, were intent instead upon passing a bottle of gin back and forth.

The shack glowed dim. Without a word Ledford led his deputies inside. McCabe stumbled along with them, handcuffed and in a daze. Myles was amazed the man could still walk after all he had been through.

They went inside and the crowd grew silent.

A shot rang out.

The three lawmen left the shack, the sheriff holstering his handgun. Through the open doorway Myles could see the walls flicker and dance, watched McCabe's meager possessions shimmer as the flames spread. A fishing rod. A yellowing poster of Betty Grable.

The sheriff addressed the crowd in McCabe's front yard.

"We all know what happened here tonight," he said. "And we all know what might have happened had this thing gone to trial. We know from the note David Carver found that McCabe killed five kids, that he had to pay for it. Well, he's paid in this life and he'll pay in the next as well.

135

"Anyone asks you what went on out here, you tell them you were at the bars, drinking." Ledford laughed sourly. "That shouldn't be hard for anyone to believe."

He scowled at the men, who nodded at him, faces earnest. "You hear me? You had nothing to do with this and neither did we." Gesturing at his deputies. "We all wanted justice done. It's done. Let's not dwell on it. Main thing is, this stupid son of a bitch got what he deserved."

With no more fanfare the group broke up. Myles watched them go, lawmen back toward the house, no doubt to make sure it burned enough to destroy any evidence, most of the men toward the limestone quarry where their cars were parked. He did not see David among either group.

He knew he'd been caught dozing. David would take the car back to Watermere, celebrate his moment in the sun with Annabel, while he, Myles, would hold his pillow over his head and wish the walls were thicker. Annabel never moaned louder than she did with David.

His hands balled into fists.

An idea came. He took off through the forest, left the path the drunken men stumbled down. Leaping over deadfalls and rocks he headed for the quarry, knowing if he beat everyone there he would have a chance.

The distant sounds of their laughter told him he would make it. The woods thinned. He broke from the forest and made for Sheriff Ledford's patrol car.

The keys were in the ignition.

Knowing to dwell upon his good fortune was to risk it, he fired the engine, floored the cruiser. Not bothering with the lights, he relied on familiarity. He had lived in Shadeland all his life, knew every twist and turn by heart. Ahead, he spied a pair of taillights blinking like red eyes in the forest. David's Mercury was moving fast, but he had clearly not spotted Myles. Figured he was still back at the barbecue.

Myles swung the Panzer-sized cruiser onto the macadam lane behind the Mercury and accelerated.

The patrol car smashed into the Mercury's rear end, its left taillight shattering. David's car fishtailed, its roof shiny in the moonlight. Before it got traction Myles rammed it again, this time sending its right side careening onto the sloping shoulder. The gravel gave way under the Mercury's weight. Myles watched as David's car tumbled end over end, rested at the foot of the decline.

He pulled the cruiser over.

Knowing the lynch mob would be driving back this way to return to town, Myles hustled down the slope, moved around the side of the Mercury, which sat upside down against a tree. David lay unconscious inside the smoking hull, his blood staining the spiderwebbed glass.

Myles forced open the passenger's door, took care not to upset the balance of the car, which teetered as he climbed inside. His brother's forehead was a bloody mess, a deep scarlet gash running from his nose to his hairline. Myles put a finger to David's neck, felt a pulse, very faint.

Then, he put his hands over his brother's mouth and nose, waited until the breathing ceased.

Reaching into David's pocket, he retrieved a silver lighter. Climbing out, he flicked the lighter, held it over the exposed chassis, which glimmered in the starshine. Leaning closer, he saw a flicker and took off up the slope. The fire spread over the side of the car, engulfing it within seconds.

As he stepped toward the cruiser he perceived headlamps growing from the direction of the quarry. Multiple sets of them. Myles climbed into the police car, started it up. In the rearview he beheld a pair of brights less than a hundred yards away. He stomped on the gas, worked the wheel to give the patrol car some traction. Behind him, the oncoming lights reached out, sought his rear bumper. He got the car under control, sped off down the country road, putting distance between him and the car behind him. Then, he saw a flash of light, heard the Mercury explode. The cars behind him stopped to see what was happening.

Soon, Myles rolled to a stop outside Watermere. Its brick façade had never looked so good.

He expected to find Annabel in the master suite, but she wasn't there. He searched the library for her but it was empty. The den, the kitchen. Then he was outside again, the August heat baking his skin, and for the third time that night, he saw flames.

Near the wood's edge, in the back corner of the yard, stood Annabel, naked. Myles moved toward her, ready to tell her she belonged to him now, to rape her if necessary.

Tall, thin, she watched the flames. Her golden hair flowed over her shoulders, down her smooth pale back. He stared at her over the fire, her blond pubis shimmering in the heat, her nipples red and hard.

Myles said, "I killed him."

She smiled drowsily. "I know."

"I mean I killed David. I killed your husband."

"I know."

He stared at her, wondering at her tone of voice. But she was always a mystery to him. "You knew I would kill David tonight?"

"I knew you'd make it happen eventually."

In his throat was a thickness. He swallowed it.

"And how do you feel about that?" he asked her.

"Does it matter?"

He opened his mouth to answer, but her nakedness, her long curving body, silenced him. He had to avert his eyes, so he stared at the circle of flames between them, the little ring no wider than a washtub.

"You going tell me what you're burning?"

"Things," she said.

"Whose things?"

"David's."

"Because he's dead now?"

"Because they had blood on them that wouldn't come out."

He stopped, bit his lip. "McCabe's dead too."

Annabel stood silent.

"It's just as well," he went on. "There won't be a bunch of damn children playing on our porch now while we entertain."

"Oh no?" she asked.

"People will feel safe to leave their kids with sitters now that McCabe's dead."

"McCabe didn't hurt anyone."

Myles gazed at her, her shimmering smile.

"Say that again?"

Annabel watched him over the flames.

He asked, "Why did David's clothes have blood on them?"

"I think you know the answer to that." Her eyes lowering to the smoldering clothes, the scorched handle of the hunting knife.

"*David would never do that. He'd never murder a child.*"

"*He would for me.*"

Myles felt the tightening in his throat, fought it back. He strode around the circle of flame and belted her with the back of his hand. She dropped down laughing and lay in a bed of grass.

"*Shut up,*" he said, but she went on.

"*Shut up,*" he said, louder this time. Annabel only hugged herself, her mouth bloody.

"*God damn you.*"

He pounced on her, splayed her apart. He rammed her as she lay beneath him laughing and when he was spent he rolled over, stared with shiny eyes at the moon and hated her and still she laughed.

Later, as they lay in bed in the early dawn light, he went down on her, made her writhe and cry out. Shortly after that, there was a knock at the door and a shouting. Myles put on his boxer shorts to answer it.

Sheriff Ledford stood on the porch, fists clenched.

"*Help you, Sheriff?*" Myles asked and leaned in the doorway.

"*Wipe that sorry ass grin off your face and get in the car.*"

Myles nodded toward the cruiser, in which sat one of Ledford's deputies. The other one was pulling away in the car they'd ridden up in.

"*See you got your car back.*"

"*I told you to wipe that shit-eatin' grin off your face.*" Ledford fingered the butt of his holstered revolver. "*Listen, Carver. You're gonna burn for what you did to your brother. We all know what happened out there.*"

"*Funny you mention burning, Sheriff. Seems to me we've both killed tonight, haven't we?*" Myles scratched his belly, yawned. "*Only difference I can see, there're witnesses to yours. Mine, well, it might have just been an accident. Careless driving.*"

"*I'm not letting you off,*" Ledford said. His sullen face was unusually animated.

"*Oh you're not? You're going to tell a judge how I got to be in your car, how you got to be out at McCabe's? You really want them snooping around his shack, find his body, the bullet you put in his brain?*"

Ledford stepped toward him, jaw trembling. "*Why you son of a bitch.*"

"*I'm not the one killed a man tonight, Sheriff. I'm just a grieving loved one whose brother passed on.*"

"*You son of a bitch,*" Ledford repeated.

"*'Night, Sheriff,*" Myles said and nodded at Ledford. Then he shut the door and went up to Annabel's room, where they made love on David's side of the bed.

The End

Paul set the final page upside down on the stack. He'd not numbered the pages, but he was sure the tale was novel-length. And even as he fought off the nausea the narrative brought on, he wondered whether it were publishable.

For one thing there wasn't a single likeable character in the whole story. He felt sorry for McCabe, but that didn't make the gardener someone an audience could hang its hat on. Myles and David were scumbags, lechers and murderers.

Annabel was another story.

She was awful, inexorable. But she fascinated him too. He wished his uncle hadn't destroyed all evidence of her. Paul wanted to see her, see this woman who led others to murder and betrayal. A woman like that, she had to be a goddess, primal beauty and infinite evil in equal parts.

Paul left the den. It felt good to get out of there, to escape the curdled semen smell and breathe other air. Though he'd done his best to clean up the vomit, the room still reeked of it.

When he got to the library he stopped, listened. The scrabbling sounds were furious, louder than they'd ever been. His eyes darted nervously to the wall, expecting at any moment a pair of claws to scratch through, a floodgate opening and a tide of great black rats spilling out, a brood of rats tumbling onto the hardwood floor, the ragged hole in the wall broadening like a vagina giving birth.

Shivering, he continued on down the hall. The story pursued him. It was terrible, but did that make it unmarketable? And if the events chronicled in *The Monkey Killer* were true, did that change anything?

He thought of the gravestone then, the scarring and the blood-red spray paint. WHORE. DEVIL. BURN IN HELL. Those epithets could only be intended for one person. If that grave belonged to Annabel, if the things he'd written last night were true, she deserved to be called those things and worse. Though Maria was the only person she'd physically murdered, she was responsible for seven others: the five children, McCabe, her own husband. And since she was alive at novel's end, who else had she gone on to kill?

She was the true villain, and if *The Monkey Killer* revealed that to the world, who would protest? She was dead, her remaining relatives would not claim her, and who could blame them? For the first time Paul understood why his family never spoke of Myles, David, or the woman who'd married them both.

He'd make copies of the manuscript, send them out, and if they were rejected, what had he lost? But if some editor liked it, at least some good would come out of the tragedies. His bank account would get fatter, and everyone back home would know he was a published author. He thought of throwing the hardback version of *The Monkey Killer* at his father's feet and laughing in his condescending face.

In the ballroom he poured himself a vodka to take the edge off. As the liquid slid down, a question wormed its way through his headache.

But he didn't care to speculate about where his inspiration had come from or what had guided his hand, so he capped the vodka bottle, plucked his keys from the kitchen table and drove to town to research markets for his novel.

Chapter Fourteen

February, 1982

Cold as hell outside and stuck in here with his brother-in-law. Sam Barlow wondered why he bothered to visit Addie at all. His little sister spent all her time breastfeeding her twin boys, so he had to sit in the basement listening to his brother-in-law's stories. The guy was insufferable. Sam couldn't decide which of Raymond's two habits were worse, his answering his own questions or his insistence on talking about the hell he'd raised as a younger man. As a state trooper Sam had precious few vacation days. Why he wasted them sitting in a basement with a blowhard jackass, he'd never know.

"Were we drunker'n shit?" his brother-in-law was asking. "You bet your ass!" Guffawing like driving drunk down Shadeland's main drag was the funniest thing he'd ever heard. "Me and Fogerty, we were so shit-faced we couldn't see ten feet in front of us, but we still made it to the tavern."

Sam regarded Raymond sourly, wishing he'd give it a rest but knowing the asshole was just getting started. Raymond stared back at him, smiling with his mouth, his eyes daring Sam to say something, to judge him. What a creep, Sam thought. Not even noon yet, the guy already half soused. His poor wife upstairs with a baby on each teat, her sack of shit husband telling stories about the laws he'd broken, the women he'd screwed. Sam looked at the guy's weak chin, his receding hairline, wondered how he'd ever talked girls into sleeping with him.

"So I says to this redhead—and believe me, Sammy Boy, she was a true redhead—'You wanna have a little party? You, me, an' Fogerty here?'"

Sam rubbed his eyes, wished Addie would get done nursing so he could spend some time with her. Raymond prattling on about pulling a three-way with the redhead, all the time calling him Sammy Boy. The guy never stopped talking, only paused occasionally to break violent, reeking wind. Raymond had gotten to the part where he was riding the lady doggy style, slapping the redhead's ass while she gave Fogerty a blowjob, and Sam knew he had to get out of there.

He stood. "I'm heading into town."

"Great," Raymond said, standing. "I'd like to see what's shaking down at Redman's Bar. Shoot me some pool."

Sam thought of telling him no, he was going to the library instead, knowing that would put the guy off, but then he thought of Raymond here alone with Addie and the twins, drunker than drunk and telling his stories to her. How did she ever get mixed up with a guy like this?

"Alright," he said. "But leave the rest of that six-pack here."

Raymond slapped him on the back. "What's the matter, Sammy Boy? That badge makin' you feel uptight? I ain't gonna get us arrested."

Sam drove them to town in Raymond's rusted out Ford. The heater barely worked, and Sam could see the road below them through holes in the floorboard. His brother-in-law told him about a time he and Fogerty had set off cherry bombs outside the police station, daring Sam with his eyes to say something about it, tell him what a crazy guy he was. Instead, he held his tongue until they got to the bar, Raymond switching gears, telling dead baby jokes as they went inside.

Sam saw her the moment he walked in.

Long dark hair, cheekbones like an Indian princess. She stood there at the bar looking uncomfortable, not seeing him yet. Raymond was asking how many dead babies it took to feed an alligator, but Sam no longer heard. The bartender offered the girl a cigarette, hitting on her. She shook her head, stared at the slice of lemon on the napkin beside her glass of water. A million pick-up lines raced through Sam's head as he approached. Dismissing them all he wondered what she was doing here, in this dive, in the middle of a weekday. She looked like she should be in the movies, not sitting at a bar alone in this little burg. The jukebox played Merle Haggard, a song Sam didn't like. Raymond was droning on behind him. Back to his heyday again.

"Did we give a shit there were pigs sitting two tables over? Hell no we didn't! Fogerty says to the faggot waiter, you'll bring us another pitcher or I'll shove this empty one up your ass. One of the cops, he gives

143

me a look, but I just stare back at him like 'what the fuck you gonna do about it?' Waiter, he goes off an—"

"Shut your mouth for a second, Raymond," Sam said and stared his brother-in-law down. He was a full six inches taller, so that as he talked, his breath made the remaining hairs on Raymond's forehead wiggle.

"I've put up with your bullshit stories for two days. Your jokes about babies in blenders and how many colored guys does it take to screw in a lightbulb—"

"Now listen," Raymond said, hiking up his jeans.

"No, you listen, you stupid sack of shit. You're my sister's husband and I've got to be nice to you. Why she married your dumb ass I'll never know, but now you two have children, so I guess I'm stuck with you."

Raymond took a step forward, breathed beer fumes up at him. "What makes you think you can talk to me like that? That fuckin' badge in your wallet?"

Sam stayed put, stayed on top of his cresting anger. "You know what your problem is Raymond? No, you don't. You'll never know so there's no point in me breaking you in half." Sam poked him once in the chest, hard, lowered his voice so no one would hear. "But if you ever— and I mean ever—lay hands on Addie or the boys, I swear to God I'll rip out your liver and feed it to you. You hear me?"

Raymond's eyes shined, and he no longer smiled. He seemed about to say something, changed his mind and trudged over to the pool tables where two old men were playing eight ball.

When Sam turned, the girl was staring at him. He'd forgotten about her, so seeing her there at the bar was a surprise. She had the most striking green eyes, glittering jade ovals that reminded him of jungle creatures, jaguars or panthers maybe.

"You sitting with anyone?" he managed to say.

"Not at the moment."

"Someone's meeting you here."

"My ride's picking me up in a few minutes."

"You mind if I sit with you until your ride comes?"

Her eyes were very large. "As long as you don't rip out my liver and feed it to me."

He scratched his chin. "You heard that?"

She moved a thumb up and down her glass of water. "You talk to all your relatives that way?"

He smiled, sat on the stool beside her. "Uh-uh. Only Raymond. He's the only one brings it out of me."

They peered across the bar at him. Raymond had lit a cigarette, sat on a stool with a pool cue poised on his knees. A waitress swaggered up to him, took his order. Raymond stared at her ass as she moved away.

"He's quite a catch," the girl said.

"Oh, we really lucked out when Addie chose him," Sam agreed.

"So you're a policeman?"

"Yeah. I'm a state trooper." He motioned to the bartender, who looked at him blandly. "Budweiser, please. This isn't my territory, though," he went on. "I'm here on vacation."

"Great choice."

"It's the new Jamaica," he said and she smiled at him.

There was a pause.

"Sam Barlow," he said and offered his hand.

"Barbara Merrow."

He took the beer from the bartender, paid and told him to keep the change.

"Where is your territory?" she asked.

"North of here. What about you?" he asked. "What brings you to Shadeland?"

"I just graduated from nursing school. There was a job opportunity here, so I took it."

He sipped his beer, watched her dark skin in the neon glow coming from a royal blue Michelob sign. "What kind of opportunity?"

"An individual who requires a lot of care."

"You only have one patient?"

"Yes."

"Who is she?" he asked, then added, "Sorry. That's probably confidential, huh?"

"I probably shouldn't say."

Sam watched her. "Sounds like a good job, though. Only one patient."

"It's going to be harder than you think."

"Oh?"

"The patient isn't very stable. She has a condition that makes her dangerous."

"I don't like the sound of that. Why'd you apply for the job?"

"It's good money. I get my own house in the country. Free meals."

"The house is near where your patient lives?"

"Uh-huh."

He sipped his beer. "Free room and board. Good pay on top of that. Only one patient to look after. I guess you'll have it good out there."

She opened her mouth to speak and stopped. She was looking past him at the bar's entrance. He turned and saw a man standing there, a guy that looked like some old-time film actor. Black hair slicked over to the side, black sport coat over a starched white shirt open at the collar. The man was staring at Barbara.

"That your ride?" Sam asked, his stomach sinking.

She nodded.

Before he could stop himself, he said, "I don't trust him."

She looked at Sam, her green eyes unreadable, but said nothing.

"Can I see you again?" he asked. She stood and shouldered her handbag.

"Maybe," she said. "I don't know."

Sam glanced at the guy, who stood watching with arms folded, impatient for her to leave. "You're still allowed to date, aren't you?"

She smoothed her hair on her shoulder.

"Of course," she said.

She was almost past him when he said, louder than he'd intended, "I want to see you again."

She stopped, turned. Sam could feel the man's anger boiling out of him, trying to wither what had begun between him and Barbara. Refusing to let the guy influence them, Sam stood, looked down at Barbara.

"I need to see you again," he said.

Her eyes brightened and she tilted her head, appeared to consider.

"We'll see."

She gave him a little smile and walked away. Sam watched the man greet her, noticed the guy staring at Barbara as though she were a choice cut of meat. The guy took Barbara's hand, bent and actually kissed it. Then, without acknowledging Sam, he put an arm around her shoulders and led her out.

Raymond had moved up beside him, "Tough break, huh Sammy Boy? Tough to compete with a man looks like that. Fuckin' pretty boy's what he is."

Knowing his life had already changed, Sam asked, "Who was it?"

"Him?" Raymond laughed. "Myles Carver, the richest prick in town."

"He can't have her," Sam said.

"He will have her, Sammy Boy. His wife's got syphilis, crazier 'n hell. Your little dish there's probably his new piece."

Sam whirled, eyes flashing.

"Jesus, Sammy Boy. Relax already," Raymond said and backed away. "What's up your ass today?"

Sam shook his head, sipped his beer.

"Go shoot some pool, Raymond," he muttered.

Chapter Fifteen

By noon of the second day of his research, Paul came to the realization that he had no more ability to market the novel than he had to write one of his own. Sitting at one of the public library's computers he surfed writers' websites, browsed countless articles on how to write a good query letter, how to spot a publishing scam, how to get an agent. Every piece of advice was imparted with an air of haughty exasperation, as though the world of books had already reached terminal mass and needed no newcomers. Publishers pleaded with writers not to do this or that, all the while offering little tangible advice. Suggestions ranged from the obvious: "Be professional" or "Familiarize yourself with our guidelines" to the inexplicable: "Absolutely no sim-subbing," "Response times may vary from a few weeks to a year." Paul's favorite was "No unsolicited manuscripts."

Just how did one break in?

In the end, he purged his mind of what he'd read online, shoved aside the breadbox girth of the current market guide, tossed his voluminous notes in the trash and, as a final show of protest, stepped on the power strip button to shut off the still-running computer. He passed the unattended circulation desk and went out into the bright June day.

Flouting every speck of sage advice he'd absorbed, he walked his two Xeroxed manuscripts to the post office and sent them off to the publishing houses he'd seen most often on the spines of his favorite horror novels: Seizure Press and Twice Bitten Books. His query letter was short and direct, and if the folks at Seizure and Twice Bitten couldn't appreciate that, to hell with them. Paul didn't want to be published by a place that cared more about a manuscript's margin size than the quality of its content.

He was about to drive home when he remembered the market

guide checked out in his name, still sitting on the desk next to the computer at the library. They'd probably check it back in for him, but he couldn't be sure.

The library seemed deserted. When he got to his former workstation, he scanned the area but couldn't find the book. He walked along the aisles, searching for the grandmotherly woman who'd helped him the day before.

When he got to the circulation desk, he saw the girl.

Her back to him, she sat on her knees, sticking magazines into red plastic containers behind the desk. Her white, form-fitting shirt crept up her back each time she leaned forward, revealing smooth copper-colored skin. The artificial light glimmered there, made the flesh look warm and moist.

He thought of clearing his throat, of letting this exotic woman know he was there, yet the voyeur in him blanched at the notion. Why ruin a good thing? He watched in fascination, calculating which would be worse: startling her and risking her discovering him and his ogling, or being the good guy, making his presence known, and losing the free show he was enjoying.

The band of her tight black pants slid lower as she adjusted her position on the floor. A satiny line of pink panty peeked out over the seam of her pants. A trifle lower and he might see even more.

Then she was standing and speaking, not looking at him but talking to him nevertheless. How long had she been aware of his presence? He felt sick to his stomach and all at once he knew this girl was the same girl who'd come to his house in the night, the one who wore a white negligee in the pouring rain. She was repeating her question, but he couldn't calm down, couldn't hear over his jangling thoughts.

Eyebrows raised, she watched him, impatience clearly stamped in the set of her mouth and the flare of her nostrils.

God she was beautiful.

"Well?" she asked.

His hand rose, started scratching the back of his neck, but he forced it down. It wouldn't do to let her know how self-conscious he felt. As if she couldn't already tell.

Saying anything was better than nothing.

149

"I didn't know you knew I was here."

Hell. He sounded like a stalker.

"What I mean," he said, averting his eyes, "is that— You ever come up on someone, and you know that they don't know you're there? You don't want to scare them, but you know you're going to anyway. Like there's no good way to tell someone you're there?"

She waited, her green eyes burning him.

"I mean, you're waiting, and you're indecisive. And it becomes funny, sort of. Because you know, but they don't, that you didn't mean to—don't want to frighten them, yet it's inevitable once you're there. Unless you were to go out and come back in, which is just about impossible because then they'd hear you leave and be startled by the sound anyway."

The ghost of a smile played at her lips.

"So you start to laugh, inside at first, because if the laughing gets out, gets loud, then that'll become the sound that scares them. But the laughter came from the absurdity of the situation, from the irony of it. So at the moment you're the least threatening, you become the biggest threat to startle them. And then you do, and they jump."

She crossed her arms, her smile broadening.

"And the fact that you're laughing at them," Paul went on, smiling now himself, "makes them mad because they think you meant to do it, but the truth is the opposite, that you're only laughing because the last thing that you meant to do—scaring them—became the only thing you could do, and all because it was the last thing you wanted to do."

The look on her face might have been amusement or annoyance. His smile faltered.

"Can I help you?" she asked.

He chuckled. It came out harsh in the silence.

"I'm sorry about that. I should have made more noise on the way up to the desk."

"You didn't scare me."

"I didn't?"

"Uh-uh."

He liked her voice. Smooth like the curves of her lower back.

"Good," he answered, a trifle too brightly.

"Are you looking for a book?"

"Yes. Sort of."

She watched him.

"I got the book I needed yesterday. The older—the other lady helped me."

"Good."

"So," he shrugged, forgetting why he'd returned, "I guess I have no real reason for coming." He tried to eat his stupid, vacuous smile, but nerves kept his mouth from closing.

The girl nodded slowly. Why, he wondered, did he think of her as a girl? Maybe it was the lack of wear-and-tear on her unlined face. Or the intimidating tightness of her body. Minus his flab, Paul fancied himself a fairly attractive man. But this. This woman was out of his league.

"I guess I'll just look around," he said, and backed away from the desk.

"Are you a writer?" she asked.

Her interest, as she leaned on the counter, seemed genuine. Rather than feeling emboldened by her question, he felt both guilt and shame, as if she'd caught him in some immoral act.

"I checked in your book for you. Since it was about publishing, I thought you might be a writer. If you'd rather not tell me, that's okay."

"No." His eyes widened. "That's not it at all. Thanks for doing that, by the way. It's just that I've never talked about my writing before." He grunted and stared at his tennis shoes. "Of course, up until this week, there's been nothing to talk about."

"So you *are* a writer."

His eyes rose to meet hers. "I might be. We'll know sometime soon, I'm hoping. I really don't know."

She watched him with something that might have been exasperation.

"The fact is, I've always wanted to be a writer, but until very recently inspiration never struck." He ventured to take a step toward the desk.

"I didn't think it worked like that." Her triangular chin sat poised between her fists. The long lashes over her green eyes didn't seem to move.

"I don't know," he answered. "I guess I wouldn't know how it works. Except in my case that's how it did."

"What were you 'inspired' to write?"

"It's about a serial killer."

"Really."

"Yes," he said and forced himself to maintain eye contact.

"Whom does he kill?" Then, in a lower voice, "Or is it a she?"

Paul laughed, "Aren't all serial killers men?"

"Not necessarily."

"Well, mine is."

"Typical."

"You haven't even read the story."

"I don't have to."

He drew back a little.

"Your novel—I assume it's a novel?"

"That's right."

"—is about a jaded cop who lives alone with a dog—probably a bulldog named Rodney or Freddy or something—who gets a call about a gruesome double murder in the suburbs. The victims are a lawyer and his wife—maybe even their two little kids. We get a lot of internal monologue, a lot of his thinking that the human race is full of scum, that he wants some storm cloud to come and wash us all away so the world can start over."

Paul listened to her, enjoying it.

"The cop looks around, but neither he nor forensics—I hope you do good research, by the way. It's easy to spot a bad crime writer a mile away. They're always talking vaguely about fingerprints and dried semen, but anybody can throw out generic terms. That doesn't mean they know a thing about criminal science."

She pushed herself off the counter and he was a little alarmed to see that the girl was nearly as tall as he. He only had three inches on her, maybe four.

"How do you know about criminal science?" he asked her.

"I minored in it."

He nodded, tried not to be intimidated. "And your major?"

"Poetry. There's no trace of the killer, nothing to incriminate the murderous psychopath that chopped the family up and arranged their bodies in some cryptic pattern. Pictures of eyes clipped out of magazines and placed on top of the victims' empty eye sockets. One-word messages carved between their breasts.

"At the end of the first chapter, your cop is sitting in his office at the station after having an argument with his superior. The phone rings and one of his fellow cops tells him, 'You better get down here, Tom.'"

"That's the cop's name?"

"Yeah. Or Rick, maybe. So Tom or Rick goes down to the crime scene—it's raining—and there's a cop in a yellow parka shouting over the rain that he's never seen anything like it. He walks inside, past one or two younger cops who're very pale and shaking their heads like they can't believe what they've just witnessed and you just know by looking at them that the gruesomeness of the crime scene is too awful to be imagined, that it'll haunt them for the rest of their lives.

"But Rick is too jaded to show much emotion as he steps past the cop who's breathing hard into his hand after having just vomited. Rick ducks under the line of yellow tape and looks around the room at the blood smeared on the walls, smears that are either handprints or words. When he steps around the bed, which is also drenched in blood, he sees the woman lying there on the floor, her entrails removed and her shocked eyes open and staring blankly. Rick doesn't gasp or cry out like a scared old woman, but he's definitely shaken. You show us this by having him mutter a single word. 'Jesus', probably. Or 'Christ'."

"What about 'Hell'?"

"'Hell' would work, but 'Jesus' is better."

"You got all of this just from me saying the story was about a serial killer."

"Am I wrong?" She tilted her chin, challenging him.

"As a matter of fact, you are."

"Okay, what it's about?"

"Tell it right now?"

"You probably have better things to do."

"No, but this counter makes me feel like I'm in the way. Isn't this for checking out books and asking about the new Danielle Steel novel?"

"You read Danielle Steel?" she asked.

"I used to, but they just got to be too depressing after a while. Even though the women in the books end up happy, my ship never seems to come in."

She smiled and Paul felt some of his tension drain away.

"It's good that you gave them up then," she said.

"I've been much happier since."

Her broader smile showed her teeth. They were very white, very straight.

"Would you like to talk somewhere else?" he asked.

"Where?"

"Over lunch, maybe?" He held his breath.

"I ate already."

He took a deep breath. "Supper?"

"That's a little fast."

"I'll buy."

"That's even faster."

"Then you'll buy."

She cocked an eyebrow. "I'm not buying a stranger supper."

"But I'm not a stranger. You already know all about my book."

She smiled again. He knew she was sizing him up, putting her common sense up against her mild curiosity in him.

She bit her lip. "Can we make it lunch tomorrow?"

"Sure."

"But we're going Dutch."

"Whatever you say."

"That was the right answer."

He put his hands in his pockets and asked, "Do you want me to meet you here?"

"No. At Redman's. Eleven-thirty sound fine?"

"Perfect."

"Do you want to know my name?" she asked.

"Can I guess?"

"It's Julia."

"That's what I was gonna guess."

He made to go, was halfway to the door, when he stopped and turned. She'd gone back to her magazine filing. Before she could disappear below the desk, he said, "My name is—"

"Theodore Paul Carver," she answered without turning around.

"How do you—" he began to ask when it dawned on him. He answered his own question, "Library card."

She glanced at him over her shoulder.

"I go by Paul," he said.

She returned to her filing. "Have a good day, Paul."

He tore his eyes off her body. Walking down the steps outside, he suppressed an urge to raise his fists and bellow in triumph. She'd said yes, which was amazing. Even better, she'd looked at the registration he'd filled out yesterday to get his name.

Maybe, he thought as he drove home, that wasn't such a big deal after all. Really, how many new customers did the library get in a given day? In a town the size of Shadeland, probably no more than one or two.

Yet she had to be curious to have scanned the cards after hearing the older woman describe him. Unless she was there yesterday when he came, somewhere out of sight. The thought of her spying on him from the shadows was exhilarating.

And far-fetched. Why the hell would a knockout like her waste her time watching him?

No matter. He had a date. His first since Emily.

When Paul walked into Redman's Bar the next day, it didn't take him long to spot her. She sat in a corner booth in the back, her eyes down. Reading, he saw as he approached.

"Hello," he said and sat down.

"Have you been here before?" she asked him as she set her book aside.

Paul fought to pry his eyes off of her breasts, which pushed out impressively from her short-sleeved yellow top.

"I've gotten carry-out a couple of times, but I've never eaten here at the restaurant."

Julia looked around. "It's not bad."

He smiled. It felt strained. "Yeah, the food's pretty good."

She nodded politely. He felt like he was passing the time with a stranger in an elevator. Next they'd be commenting on the weather.

"What do you usually have?" he asked her.

"A salad."

"Caesar or regular?"

"Regular."

He pressed his lips together, nodded, drummed his fingers.

"Fascinating," she said, nodding with him.

"Yep."

"What type of salad do you prefer, Paul?"

He stared at her a moment. Then they both began to laugh.

By the time their salads came, he'd told her where he was from, how old he was, and how he'd come to inherit Watermere. Crunching a forkful of lettuce, she asked him how many things he'd had published.

Paul paused, wondering whether or not a lie would be prudent.

He decided against it. It was easier to be honest than to try his luck at keeping ahead of his lies. He didn't want to risk blowing this over something trivial.

"I haven't had anything published," he said.

"Had a lot of rejections?"

"No, I haven't had any of those either."

Her eyebrows arched as she took a drink of water.

Paul shrugged. "I've never submitted anything before."

"Why not?"

He flirted with another lie. It was on the tip of his tongue when he heard himself say, "Because *The Monkey Killer* is the first thing I've ever written."

"That's the title of your novel?"

"Pretty bad, huh?"

She sat back in her seat. "Not necessarily. Just different."

Paul went on with more confidence, "It's a little weird, I know, but it fits the story. It takes place here in Shadeland, not the Serengeti."

"Are there monkeys in the story?"

Paul's smile broadened. "No, no monkeys, dead or alive."

"Good. I don't like animal cruelty."

"Me either. Only human children die in my book."

"That's fine. Human murders don't bother me."

He bit into a tomato. The juice trickled over his bottom lip. "I'm the same way."

"So for how long are you here?" she asked.

"In Shadeland, you mean?"

"Sure."

"I hadn't thought about it. For good, I guess. I broke the lease on my apartment in the city. My family has all but disowned me, though they've been on the verge of doing that for years. I don't have a lot to go back to."

She sipped at her water. Paul liked the way the afternoon light shone red on her cheekbones. If she was wearing any make-up, he couldn't tell. No perfume either that he could detect, but when she'd leaned toward him once, he'd caught an intoxicating whiff of some citrus-scented lotion.

She stared out the window and asked, "Are you glad you came?"

"I am now."

She glanced at him. Paul blushed, realizing what he'd said.

"I meant, now that I have the novel done and sent off, I'm glad I came."

Immediately, he regretted saying it. What if she'd been flattered? If she was disappointed, she didn't show it.

He added, "The first couple months here were pretty rough. Creatively, I mean. I couldn't get anything to work. Not even a single page."

"I always imagined it would be tough to write a book."

"It is."

"All alone at a computer with nothing but the blank screen and your own self-doubt."

"Exactly," he said, feeling uneasy. They were back on how he'd written the novel. *Received it*, his conscience reminded. "Of course, I don't own a computer, so I use a pencil and paper. Or a typewriter."

157

"Really?"

"I had a computer when I was in college, but it broke and I couldn't afford to get it fixed. I wasn't going to ask my family for help, so I learned to get along without it."

"I don't have one either."

"We're probably the only two people in the world who don't have them."

"Why are things so bad between you and your family?"

He took a drink of his Coke. Much of the ice had already melted, so it tasted more like sweetened water. "I don't know." He chuckled without mirth. "It's not one thing, really. We just—haven't gotten along for a while, and things have kind of snowballed over the last few years."

"I didn't know anyone still wrote with a pencil and paper."

Paul blinked. Was she purposely trying to keep him off-guard, or was this just the way her mind worked?

"Well…" he trailed off, feeling vaguely guilty again. But why should he feel guilty? He'd written the damn thing, hadn't he?

"I imagine there are others who write that way," he went on. "It feels a little more intimate having to form the letters and dot your own i's."

They both looked up as their waitress unfolded a wooden stand beside their table. She set the platter down on top of it. Paul thanked her.

Julia had already begun to eat. He watched her for a moment and then asked, "How is it?"

"Good," she said around a mouthful of fettuccine. A noodle whipped up against her cheek before disappearing inside her mouth, leaving a slick, slug-like trail of white sauce on her skin. Paul grinned a little, watching her. He liked the way she ate, as though she couldn't care less what he thought of her. That was probably the truth, he realized. A girl this beautiful, why should she be worried about impressing him? He was a nobody in his mid-thirties. She could be on the cover of a magazine.

A few minutes later, she asked him what his novel was about.

He was determined not to lie to her, but it wouldn't be smart to talk about such things over dinner. Both to put her off and to go for broke, he asked, "What are you doing this Friday?"

She'd been spinning another mouthful of noodles onto her fork when he'd spoken. Now the fork was still moving but her eyes were fixed on his. He felt uncomfortable under her frank gaze, but he forced himself not to squirm, to meet her eyes and wait for an answer.

"I'm making you dinner," she said.

March, 1982

Sam knew it would take time with Barbara.

She was alone, but she wasn't easy. She was apprehensive about her new job, but she was too independent to rely on a man to make her feel more secure.

Sam couldn't tell how he knew all these things from one truncated conversation, but he was as sure of them as he was of the fact that he'd never get to know her if he remained on the state police force. His territory ended fifty miles north of Shadeland, so he wasn't going to run into her by luck. Neither would he increase the frequency of his trips to Addie's. He'd sooner drink bleach than spend more time with Raymond. He couldn't get a transfer to a more southern territory. The guys who worked those districts were all between forty and fifty, which meant they were going nowhere. Once a guy got settled in a place, he rarely moved.

That left him with only one option as far as he could see, and that was to leave the force. It made him sick to his stomach—being a state trooper was all he'd ever wanted in a career—but the thought of never seeing Barbara again made him even sicker. There'd been no wedding ring on her hand, but how long could he count on his luck to hold out? She was young, but girls that beautiful didn't stay single long. He considered himself lucky she hadn't been snared already.

So there was only one thing for it, and that was to turn in his badge and find work in Shadeland, which he did less than a month after they first met.

Soon he was working in the paper mill and asking around, as casually as possible, about the Carvers and their new nurse. It didn't take long for him to learn that his first impression of Myles Carver had been spot-on. The man and his wife—Barbara's patient—were bad news.

He couldn't get much out of his co-workers because he didn't want to sound overly interested. It wouldn't do to arouse suspicion. And he wasn't stalking Barbara, he reminded himself. He was admiring her from afar. He was looking out for her best interests. He was making sure everything in her life was safe and orderly.

Yet he knew something was wrong. Even after the first few days at the mill, he knew she was in a bad place, spent her time with bad people.

Sam went to Redman's every evening the first few weeks hoping he'd find her sitting at the same barstool. She never showed.

He spent every night in his new farmhouse thinking he'd run into her eventually, a town that small. Yet when two months had passed and he'd seen neither hide nor hair of her he decided to change his approach.

Addie suspected something. She found it curious he'd leave the force to take a dead-end job, and the thought occurred to him more than once that he'd thrown his career away to hear his brother-in-law answer his own questions and brag about dropping cowflops off the overpass.

Then, one frigid March night as he sat in a local diner, he saw her walk right by the window. She was wearing a thin jacket but no scarf, no gloves. He threw on his coat and plunged through the door after her.

She rounded the corner. He followed, terrified that Myles Carver would swoop out of an alley and take her away from him again.

But she continued on ahead, cold and shivering in the late-winter wind.

Sam wanted to spin her around, embrace her. Tell her all he'd done so they could be together. She took a left into a drugstore. He waited thirty seconds, followed her in.

He scanned the aisles. In the farthest corner of the store he spotted her, her back to him, browsing through the birthday cards. Moving toward her, he saw the tiny flecks of snow melting, becoming dew drops on her thin gray jacket.

Sam moved around the corner and stopped a few feet away. He stood before the magazines. Picking one up, he pretended to be engrossed in Cosmopolitan's *latest sex quiz. His eyes darted back and forth between Barbara and phrases like "inconsiderate lover" and "premature ejaculation." She was reading a birthday card with Snoopy and Woodstock on it.*

Stalker, *he thought.*

Brushing the thought away, he read: "Cunnilingus should occur no fewer than twice each week." *Sam glanced up from the sex quiz's answer key and found Barbara's eyes battened on his.*

"What are you doing here?" she asked. Her voice was soft, curious. No suspicion. At least not yet.

He hid the magazine against his chest.

"Visiting," he said, paused. "Actually, I'm…"

She watched him.

"…I'm working here now," he finished.

"For the police department?"

"No, I left the force. I'm working down at the paper mill."

"And reading Cosmo*?"*

Sam felt himself blush. Setting the magazine on the shelf, he asked, "Whose birthday is it?"

"My mother's."

"Oh. How's your new job?"

She frowned, checked her watch. "I really have to be going. My ride will be here soon." She turned away.

Sam took a step toward her. "Please don't go," he said.

Turning back, she regarded him. He knew she was waiting for him to say something, but what could he say? Of the endless combinations of words and phrases he could string together, how could he possibly know which one would keep her from leaving?

"I don't know what to say."

"No? I thought policemen were supposed to know how to think fast."

"I told you I'm not a cop anymore."

"So what exactly do you want?"

"To talk to you."

"Talk to me," she repeated.

"Yes."

She seemed to debate with herself. Shifted from foot to foot. She asked, "Why did you change jobs?"

"I wanted to be closer to my older sister."

"And your brother-in-law."

"He was the main reason."

She cocked an eyebrow. "Who could blame you?"

"Not a soul."

"Six o'clock."

"What?"

"Pick me up at six o'clock tomorrow evening. I'm the first left on County Road 500."

His mouth worked, but all he managed to get out was, "Great."

"Nice to see you again, Sam." She held out her hand.

He wondered if he should take it and kiss it the way Myles Carver had at the bar. But that wasn't him. He shook her hand, said he looked forward to seeing her again.

Then she was gone.

Julia watched him chew his food. He'd complimented her on the Jamaican chicken already. Too soon, she'd thought at the time, the first bite barely finished. Now he was halfway through his bowl, and he'd grown quiet. Was it her food or had it been her question? Thinking back, she remembered how strangely he'd acted when she'd asked about his writing at the bar.

"Everything okay?" she asked.

He looked up from his bowl. "Sure, everything's fine. The chicken is excellent."

She asked, "Do you not want to talk about your writing?"

Reaching out, he picked up his wine glass and took a drink. "To be honest with you, I don't know. On one hand, I'm very proud of it, but on the other, I'm afraid you'll think the subject manner is too awful."

"Try me."

He watched her doubtfully. Then he seemed to come to a decision. He set his fork down, folded his fingers and said, "Let's make a deal."

She waited.

"On Tuesday, I sent out two copies of the novel to publishers. As soon as I've heard back from them, I'll let you read the manuscript."

"But that could take months."

"True, but it could also be sooner. The books say there are publishers that respond within days, or even hours, if the novel's good enough. Or bad enough."

"That's fair. But only if you answer my other question."

"Other question?"

"About your family. Why you're estranged from them."

Paul sat back. The dining room light made his brown hair gleam. "Ahh...that."

"Well," he said, wiping his mouth with one of the red cloth napkins she'd pulled out and washed for the occasion. "That's a long story. I don't want to bore you."

"I won't be bored. I promise." She took a long, slow sip of the red wine. It was cheap but good. Paul had been embarrassed that none of the local liquor stores carried anything better.

"Alright, here goes. I've always been a bit of a disappointment. In high school, my grades were decent but not great; therefore, the college I went to was decent but not great."

"And that was?"

"It doesn't matter."

"Okay."

He paused. "It wasn't Harvard or Yale."

"Did your parents go to Harvard or Yale?"

"No, but that's not the point. My older brother did."

"Mm."

"So I bounced around between jobs before finally coming back to the bank."

"The family business?"

"Yes. My grandfather founded it, and my dad's the president. Oh, and my brother's the vice-president."

"What were you?"

"Nothing."

They both laughed, but when she heard the strain in his voice, she stopped.

She saw his eyes shift to the living room. He said, "That's a good-looking piano you have in there." He gestured over his shoulder. "Can you play?"

"A little."

"Will you play for me?"

The question was innocent enough, but she felt herself growing faint. The piano reminded her of Ted Brand. He was the last thing she wanted to think about tonight. Or any night. The cloying smell of oversweetened iced tea suddenly clogged her nostrils.

"How about we watch a movie instead?" she suggested quickly.

"At the theater or here?"

She thought of the vast, darkened room, the sea of staring anonymous faces.

"Let's stay here," she said.

She led him to the old trunk that sat beside her large console television. She watched him shuffle through the DVD boxes, discarding most of them without a second glance. He paused on *Rear Window*.

"You like Hitchcock?" she asked.

"Are you kidding? I love Hitchcock. *Psycho*'s one of my favorite films."

"And *Vertigo*?"

"Jimmy Stewart's best performance."

She sat forward. "He's better in *Rear Window*."

"I have a confession to make."

"Don't tell me you've never seen it."

He nodded. "It's true."

"That's it," Julia said, downing the rest of her wine. "Grab your glass. We're watching it tonight."

April, 1982

Things happened fast. Sam didn't dare think about how fast, choosing instead to forge ahead with the relationship as if scampering over a log that spanned a creek, afraid to stop for fear of falling. After a few dates, he was deeply, dangerously in love, and there was no going back, no returning to the safe side of the creek.

She didn't talk about her work, and he got so he didn't want to hear about it either. What she did share scared him, made him credit the stories the guys at the mill told on break. The ones about Carver killing his big brother, Carver's wife throwing some Mexican gal through the window. The worst of all was the one about the children, and for his own peace of mind he chose not to believe it. Barbara couldn't be working in a place with people like that.

It kept him up nights.

When Grace Kelly climbed over the balcony into Raymond Burr's apartment, Paul became aware of Julia's shoulder pressing against his. He'd sensed her burrowing into the couch as the movie's suspense grew, but this was the first time he'd felt her body. That citrus smell grew stronger, like freshly sliced oranges, but somehow purer even than that. Summery and vibrant and suffused with what must be the natural fragrance of her skin.

She stayed huddled into him until the movie ended, and when it did, she stretched, leaned against the arm of the couch with hugged knees and gave him an expectant look.

"Well?"

He chuckled. "It was wonderful."

But instead of seeming pleased, a pensive look darkened her face. He watched her brush a stray lock of black hair out of her eyes, a gesture he was sure was unconscious but that made him feel a little queasy inside. *What the hell are you doing with this girl?* an incredulous voice asked him. *Isn't it time to stop the charade?*

But I like this charade, he thought, and did his best to subdue his escalating insecurity.

Without looking up, she said, "Can I ask you a serious question?"

"That sounds ominous."

"It isn't about you personally." She glanced at him. "It's about men in general."

"Did I leave the toilet seat up?"

"I don't know, did you?"

He considered. "I don't remember."

She arched an eyebrow.

"I think so," he said.

"What I was wondering," she went on, "is whether men really only

165

care about one thing."

Paul took his time about it, mulled over the least offensive responses at his disposal. He said, "I assume we're not talking about football."

She gave him a wan smile.

He cleared his throat. "Before I answer, could I ask you a question?"

"I guess."

"Are you asking because of a bad experience?"

He'd never seen anyone visibly pale before, but Julia did. For a moment he really thought she might faint. "I've met a few jerks," she said quietly, "but mostly it's something I've read about. They say sex is the second-strongest need a man has."

"What's number one?"

"Being admired."

"And sex is second to that?"

She took a long sip of wine, but her eyes never left his.

He scratched the back of his neck. "I don't think I can speak for an entire gender."

"Speculate."

He glanced at the blackened television screen. "I guess it's important to most of us, sure. But not every guy treats women badly because of that desire."

He glanced at her hopefully.

"That's a pretty good answer," she said.

He tried not to show his relief. "Thanks," he said.

"You really liked the movie?" she asked.

"I told you I did."

She appraised him a moment longer, then nodded. "Okay. Then you'll get another date."

And though he laughed with her at that, he wondered if she'd been joking.

They had two more dates the next week. One to the local theater—

a crappy thriller about a psychic child and his overacting mother—and one to a restaurant Paul thought too expensive by half.

He knew he'd have to bring her to Watermere sooner or later, but his lack of housekeeping and his complete inability to cook anything fancier than spaghetti had put him off asking. On their last date, she'd mentioned Watermere twice, which meant she was either curious about the old place—a likely proposition given the proximity to her own house and the urban legends about Myles Carver she'd no doubt heard—or maybe she just wanted to see where he spent his days and nights. Put him in context, so to speak.

A week's cleaning and airing out did little to allay his fears. He was insecure about their age difference as it was, and something about the age of the place—the antiquated décor, the mustiness, the lingering stink of Myles Carver—brought acutely home to him what he was up against. He was thirty-seven and unemployed. True, he'd sent the novel to a couple of places, and neither had rejected him yet, but that didn't make him a writer.

At least he'd been drinking less since meeting Julia. Though his nerves demanded alcohol, he'd cut himself off after two drinks on each of their dates. More significantly, he'd begun to run up and down the lane to shrink some of the padding around his waist. After jogging up the lane and walking back, he'd measured it with the Civic's odometer and had been disappointed to find its total length less than a mile. The angry stitch in his side claimed a greater distance, but he knew the odometer was telling the truth.

Through pain, a suffocating dread of physical exertion and one particularly nasty fit of vomiting, he'd progressed to where he could trot to the road and back without walking or collapsing. And though he hadn't yet noticed a slimming of his waistline, he did feel a subtle increase in vigor. Even better, he'd taken to doing push-ups before bed and if he stared closely at his reflection in the bathroom mirror he thought he could see a new fullness in his chest and triceps. He knew he was no athlete, nor would he ever grace the cover of a fitness magazine. But he felt better, and that counted for a lot.

So it was that on the Fourth of July, Paul invited Julia to Watermere for the first time.

June, 1982

Myles Carver walked Barbara to the door, offered to give her a ride back to her house.

For the third day in a row she declined.

She claimed it was the nice weather, her need for exercise.

He knew better. It was her need for that cocksucker at the paper mill that had her treating Myles like a piece of fucking furniture. He got his hands on the big son of a bitch, the guy'd wish he'd never moved here.

And now the goddamn bell was ringing. He regretted giving it to her. Every time Annabel needed a drink of water, a snack, a softer goddamn pillow, she rang that bell. Slamming the front door he went to the ballroom to fix himself a stiff drink. In here, the ringing was louder than it had been in the foyer. He wondered how Annabel even managed to raise her hand in her condition, her arms and legs turning into sticks before his eyes. He wished she'd die already but knew she'd never go that easy. She had five more years in her, maybe more. The doctors said syphilis affected people in different ways. They said he should be grateful he'd not contracted it.

Grateful? Grateful for an invalid wife he couldn't fuck even if he wanted to?

Christ. He drained his bourbon. Fucking doctors.

"I'm coming," he shouted at the ringing bell.

He took his time making his way to the third floor. When he got to the master suite, he frowned, for the sound wasn't coming from in here. The odor of a heavy bedpan hung in the air. Of course. That noisome shit-and-piss smell never disappeared. Myles made a face and sighed. As he was about to leave the bedroom he paused. The ringing had ceased.

He scanned the gloom of the master suite for her. He was walking toward the bathroom door when he noticed the bell sitting on the nightstand beside her bed.

What the hell?

Movement behind him made him whirl and cry out.

The sound, a secret slithering, continued. Yet Annabel was nowhere in sight.

He called her name but was answered only by another sound, an *alien rustle inside the walls.*

"Myles."

Her voice came from outside the bedroom, somewhere down the hall. Sweating, he listened and moved down the corridor. He heard his name again and knew she was in the library, probably reading some of her weird magic shit.

He opened the library door, felt the blood drain from his face.

Annabel was standing naked before the hearth, the room around her freezing cold despite the fire she'd built and the heat of the summer day. She no longer looked wasted and frail. Her back was to him, and looking at the cleft of her buttocks, the smoothness of her legs, he felt the old desire kindle and grow. The shadows of the flames flickered and danced over her creamy skin, and Myles was moving toward her, time folding in on itself until he was back with her by the bonfire on the night he'd killed his brother.

She stood there with arms out and palms up, her feet wide and knees slightly bent. The fire, like a molten lover, seemed to lick her body, and though Myles felt chilled to the marrow he could see the sweat trickling down her contoured back.

He stood behind her and for a moment glimpsed her portrait above the hearth, the painting of her in those old-fashioned clothes, the white dress and the jewels. He'd asked her where she'd had it done and who had painted her, but she'd only laughed and changed the subject, and for the first time he wondered whether she'd really been playing dress up, whether the truth of the portrait were stranger, less comprehensible. He'd met her when David had, at one of their parties, but even then he'd thought she'd looked familiar, as though they'd seen each other as children or sometime else in the distant past.

He smelled the lust breathing out of her, and all around them came the sounds of the unseen creatures, the stealthy rustle and click he'd heard in the bedroom. Aching with the need to be inside her and trembling in fear of what hid behind the walls, Myles reached out.

And screamed.

For she'd swiveled her head to leer at him with blood red eyes, her fish-white teeth too long and too sharp. Her breasts swam and moved under her flesh, her pubic hair a nest of tiny vipers slithering in a shifting black clump, their diamond heads slithering into her vagina and out again.

He fell then and flopped onto his stomach. He buried his face in the crook of his arm to block out the sight of her, to escape her terrible scarlet eyes and her slithering flesh, but when he opened his eyes to find the door, the cold had gone and the rustling sounds had given way to the ringing bell. Myles glanced over his shoulder at the empty hearth, which gave no sign of having been used in months.

Whimpering, he pushed to his feet and back toward the master suite. When he entered, the ringing of the bell did not stop, and Annabel, in her white nightgown, lay watching him. Above the bedclothes he could see her thinning arms, pallid and frail from the sickness.

The bell dropped from her hand, landed on the rug beside the bed.

"What is it?" he asked, struggling to regain his composure.

Her eyes crawled over his body. "Why are you sweating?"

"None of your goddamn business. What do you need?"

"I'm cold, Myles."

"Then why didn't you have Barbara give you an extra blanket before she left?"

"Because I don't like Barbara."

Myles felt the chill return, icy fingers caressing his spine. He took a blanket from the dresser and spread it over her, careful to avoid eye contact.

"I said I don't like her, Myles."

"That's ridiculous," he said. His throat felt dry and dusty, cornhusks in a drought. "She does a good job of looking after you."

"And you do a good job of looking after her."

"Don't let's start on that again," he said.

As he drew the blanket over her arms and tucked it under her pointed chin, her eyes snared him. Try as he might, he couldn't look away.

Annabel said, "Don't touch her."

He laughed but it came out wrong. "You're deluded. Every girl you see you think I want to screw."

She watched him, eyes large.

"I mean it, Myles."

"Go to sleep, Annabel." He turned from the bed and left the room. As *he passed the library, he could almost pretend the sounds he heard were in his head and not the walls.*

Chapter Sixteen

Sam was on edge. Though he hadn't learned a single thing about what happened to Ted Brand, the more he learned about the man himself, the more he felt his disappearance wasn't such a bad thing. Brand was no criminal, but he was no saint either. By Sam's count, he had at least five girlfriends, a couple his age, the rest of them younger. He favored strippers and waitresses, brunettes mostly. None of them knew a thing about Brand's whereabouts.

To make matters worse, it was only ten in the morning and Daryl Applegate was already driving him nuts

The deputy was breathing loud. The guy made sounds like an iron lung, strained and wheezy. Out of the corner of his eye he watched Applegate, mouth open, filling up the squad car with his eggplant breath.

"Daryl."

Applegate turned.

"Yeah, Sam?"

"Close your mouth when you breathe."

Daryl's face pinched. "You know I got sinuses."

"We've all got sinuses, Daryl."

"Yeah, but mine are stopped up on account of my allergies. I can't even breathe out of my left nostril."

Sam sat quiet.

"Had surgery on it," Applegate went on. "Doctor said it was a real roto-rooter job. Didn't do any good though. Still can't breathe with the left and can barely breathe with the right." Daryl made an exaggerated sniff to illustrate his point. "See? It's like breathing through one of those coffee straws."

"Okay, Daryl."

The car turned onto County Road 500, asphalt becoming gravel. Sam rolled down his window and spat. The summer air felt good on his face, so he thumbed the window down all the way and cocked an elbow in the opening. The sounds of the tires crunching on gravel drowned out some of Daryl's wheezing.

He came to Julia Merrow's lane, turned.

"Now make sure you keep quiet and let me do the talking."

"Sure, Sam."

"Julia's a good girl, so don't treat her like a suspect."

"Right." Daryl undid his seatbelt, reached down, shifted his gun in his holster.

"What the hell you doing with that?" Barlow asked. The stupid oaf carried his Ruger everywhere, was always messing with it, tempting fate.

"Nothing, Sam. Just making sure it's holstered right."

"Why do you need a gun anyway?"

"We're interrogating a witness."

Sam hit the brakes. Applegate slid forward and caught himself on the dash.

"What's the matter?" Daryl asked.

"One, she's not a witness. She said she didn't see anything, and I believe her. I'm just double-checking because we've got nothing."

"It could be she's lying," Daryl said and nodded down the lane toward the house, which was barely visible through the dense pines and firs.

"She's not," Barlow shot back, loud in the squad car. "And secondly, this isn't an interrogation. An interrogation happens at the station. This," he said, nodding toward the house, "is a private residence. And the girl who lives here hasn't done anything wrong."

"Fine," Daryl said, wounded. "All I meant was it's better to have a gun and not need it than need a gun and not have one."

Sam let off the brake. "You've seen too many police shows."

"It's still true. Why would you talk to her again if you didn't suspect her?"

"It's just a precaution," Sam replied.

Sam chewed the inside of his mouth. He knew he should have left Applegate back at the station, but the dumb shit was driving Patti nuts, and as a favor to her Sam took custody of him for the day. Now, he wished he'd dropped him off on the roadside somewhere.

The cruiser pulled up next to the little white farmhouse, and Sam felt his heart ache for a moment. Applegate made to get out of the car, but Sam grabbed his arm.

"What?" Daryl asked.

"What are you gonna do in there?"

"Keep my mouth shut."

"What are we doing here?"

"Just talking. She's not a witness and we're not questioning her. Alright?"

They both looked up. Julia stood on the porch.

They climbed out of the car. Sam could smell the forest around them, the dandelions dotting the yard. Julia watched him, no expression he could read. She wore a red tee shirt, tight, and beige shorts.

"Morning, Julia."

"Hello, Mr. Barlow."

"Now darn it," he said, approaching the porch, "I told you to call me Sam. Makes me feel old when you start saying mister and sir."

"Okay," she said and smiled, though he could see her heart wasn't in it.

"Remember me?" Daryl put in.

Barlow shot him a look. Julia watched him without speaking.

"We used to have the same piano teacher when we were little. Until I gave it up to focus on sports."

Julia didn't respond.

"Mrs. Weybright?" Daryl said. "Remember her? Used to make you start all over if you hit a wrong note."

"I only went to her for a little while during kindergarten. My grandma taught me after that," Julia said.

"Yeah, she wasn't much of a teacher. Dead now." Daryl cleared his throat. "Julia, we'd like to ask you a few questions about the night of April the Fourth. Do you remember where you were that evening?"

Julia looked at Sam. "I thought we already talked about this."

Sam was watching Daryl, seething. Glaring at the deputy, he replied, "We did, Julia. Deputy Applegate is speaking out of turn."

Daryl opened his mouth to reply but Barlow cut him off, looking at Julia now. "The problem is, we've had no luck finding him. I know you had nothing to do with whatever happened to Ted Brand, but I'm hoping you've maybe seen or heard something that could help us."

She shook her head slowly. "Not that I can think of."

"I know it's an inconvenience, but would you mind if we came in?"

Julia glanced at Applegate, seemed about to demur, then her expression relaxed and she said to Sam, "Of course."

She moved toward the door, Applegate following. Sam gripped the deputy by the arm. "You talk again and I'm gonna shove that revolver up your ass."

Sam held Daryl's eyes a moment longer.

With a sour grunt, Sam mounted the steps and opened the screen door. It banged Daryl on the shoulder as he passed through.

Out on his run Paul remembered he'd forgotten to check the mail the day before. When he spied the envelope from Twice Bitten Books, he felt his stomach flutter.

He exhaled, reading the rejection. A form letter.

Disappointed and relieved, he jogged home.

The girl was sitting at the kitchen table, the hanging light making a shiny oval on her forehead. Barlow scooted a chair up to the head of the table, beside the girl. Daryl sat across from Julia, watching her. Her red tee shirt stretched taut on her breasts, and as he stared at them, at the supple skin of her throat, he saw goosebumps materialize, and when he looked up he realized that she was watching him watch her. She folded her arms to cover her breasts. He felt his throat go dry.

"Julia," the sheriff said to break the silence, "you'll have to forgive Deputy Applegate. He's not around people much."

Daryl grinned, then realized what the sheriff had said.

But Barlow had gone on, "To be honest with you, we don't know what we're dealing with here. It could be serious or it could be Brand decided to take a vacation. What would help us—what would help us a great deal—is if you could expand on what you told me at the library."

Daryl leaned forward. "We know you told us all you know, but—"

"Could you wait outside, Deputy Applegate?" the sheriff said without looking at him.

Daryl sat up straight and opened his mouth to speak.

"Deputy?" Barlow repeated.

Daryl shrugged. "Sure." He stood and nodded at the girl, who stared at the tabletop in front of her.

The morning air felt good against his face as he wandered across the lawn. It was getting warmer, the dew on the grass evaporating. The mist hung in smoky sheets over the long yard. Applegate followed it, liking the way the moisture coated his skin. Away from the house, nearer the woods, the air was redolent with wet buds, dripping branches.

He watched his rubber-soled shoes slick through the unmown lawn, and when he first noticed the garden, he was almost upon it. Nestled as it was back by the forest, it was no wonder he'd missed it. A pair of tomato cages had toppled over and lay threaded with weeds. Wild rhubarb struggled here and there to gain traction in the tufted ground.

Daryl frowned.

Then, an ugly grin curdled his lips.

Before he could move forward, pick up the shovel lying discarded in the grass, he heard the screen door knock shut. He spun and jogged toward the house. Seven years ago, he thought as his footfalls slowed, during his days as a three-sport athlete he could've made the distance in five or six seconds. But by the time he rounded the corner of the house and saw Barlow leaning on the porch rail saying his goodbye, Daryl's lungs were burning with a feverish heat.

As they climbed into the car Daryl asked, "Did she give you anything?"

Without speaking Barlow started the cruiser.

Daryl watched the sheriff turn around in Julia's drive. "Think we got ourselves a lethal hottie?"

The sheriff scowled at him. "Remind me to leave you at the station next time."

Though the house still smelled to Paul like an unwashed armpit, he decided there was no sense in Windexing the windowpanes again, sweeping the foyer or dusting the wooden surfaces one more time. The place was as clean as it was going to get.

He'd gone halfway to the Civic before pausing and staring off through the large green lawn. He rolled the keys around in his fingers, considering. Checking his watch, he realized that he was very early; he wasn't to pick up Julia for another forty minutes.

In the middle of the lawn, he saw the firepit he'd dug. At the brook he'd found enough stones to border the hole. He imagined roasting marshmallows tonight with Julia. It was corny, but he didn't care. He couldn't wait to see her again.

Paul breathed deeply of the late-afternoon air. It was humid, but the air whispering out of the forest still carried the scent of green, vibrant life. Even better, the grass he'd cut yesterday with the ancient lawn tractor looked like a golf course. He'd bagged the grass and dumped it in the woods so that their legs and feet would not be itchy tonight as they sat watching the fireworks.

He hoped he'd estimated rightly. The Fourth of July display was to take place in the city park, only four miles from Watermere. Unless the town skimped and used low-flying rockets, the fireworks should be easy to see from his back yard. He'd driven twenty miles to buy good wine for them to sip after they grilled out. He'd even considered buying his own bag of fireworks, though in the end he guessed she'd rather laze on a blanket than run around playing sparkler tag.

The winding screech of the cicadas began to sound hesitantly from the woods around him. He loved July. Pocketing the keys he wandered out into the yard, thinking about the night to come. If the smell didn't bother her, he was sure she'd love the house. From the outside it was a stunner. He couldn't imagine a woman with her literary imagination being unimpressed by such an exquisite Victorian structure. The inside, too, was looking better and better—less like a dilapidated museum and more like the center of town social life it must have been back in his uncle's prime. Paul tried to see the house through her eyes. The carved mahogany banisters serpentining downward toward the black and white checkered tile of the ballroom. The vast great room with the cathedral ceiling and marble fireplace. The carvings and paintings, many of them done by Myles Carver himself.

Yes. She'd be impressed.

Even the mosquito-fogger he'd puffed through the yard last night seemed to have worked. Though the sounds of insects echoed through the forest, there were no buzzing flies, no persistent throng of gnats seeking his ears.

He checked his watch again: 5:25.

He peered at the Civic, but it was looked incongruous with the beautiful things surrounding it. That decided him.

He set off toward the path to Julia's. Though he'd only taken it once—and that with the sheriff—he thought he could trace his way through the rises and shallows to her little farmhouse.

The wooded air filled his lungs, its languid heat drawing a mist of sweat on his chest and temples. Rather than oppressing him, the sweat felt good on his skin.

His tromps up and down the lane were helping. He'd been walking for—he checked his watch—ten minutes, over knolls and through overgrown places where he had to crouch or sidle to pass through, and he felt as strong as he had before he'd begun.

Thinking about Julia, he took an alternate route toward her house.

One that wouldn't take him past the graveyard.

"Fashionably late?"

She sat on the porch, reading. He sat down below her on the bottom step and leaned against the base of the steel rail.

"I'm sorry. I thought I'd left myself plenty of time to get here, but those trails..." He gestured vaguely toward the woods. "They're a little confusing. Not for you, I'm sure, but I've only been on them a few times, and most of those were in the dark." He looked up at her, squinting through sweat. "You're mad, aren't you."

She cocked an eyebrow at him. "To tell you the truth, I'm kind of impressed."

"Impressed that I'm fifteen minutes late?"

"Impressed that you're walking now instead of driving everywhere. It's good for you, even if it does make you late."

"What can I do to make it up to you?"

"That's up to you. I'm not making it easier on you."

"I'd kiss you, but I'm too sweaty."

"What would that accomplish?"

"Ouch."

She marked her page and ran a hand through her long black hair. "I told you I wasn't going to make it easy on you." She set her book on the porch. *The Collected Poems of Lord Byron*, Paul saw. Pulling herself up by the porch rail, she dusted off her backside and offered him a hand. He took it and was shocked at how easily she pulled him up. Standing as he was, three steps below her, his face was bare inches from her exposed midriff. He liked the way her flat stomach tapered down before disappearing under the khaki rim of her shorts. The skin there was dark and smooth, and for one crazy instant, he considered embracing her waist, drawing her to him and running his tongue along her stomach. He could even smell her as he stood there before her, feeling like a worshipper before some pagan goddess. Whether it was the scent of the flowers blooming in her window planters or some light perfume she wore, the smell streaming into his lungs was maddening.

She said, "You're pitted out."

He smiled uneasily and took a step back. He was in the process of peeling his sweaty shirt away from the skin of his chest when she descended two steps, reached out, and placing one long-fingered hand on the sweaty nape of his neck, drew him forward and kissed him. They'd kissed only once before, on their last date, also here on the porch steps. The kiss had been brisk and dry and dizzying.

Yet this kiss was searching, needful. Her full lips moved against his, her tongue sought and licked, and for a moment, he felt her thighs press into him. The erotic, summery smell of her made him harden.

She pulled slowly away and led him toward the trail that would lead them to Watermere.

They sat on the fuzzy blue blanket with their sweating bottles of beer leaning against the cooler. Paul had worried about the height of the trees but they were able to see the fireworks just fine. Each time a rocket went off he would turn a little to watch the moonburst reflection in Julia's eyes, a billion little stars falling to earth on a light green canvas. She was so beautiful she made him self-conscious. Most of the time he was able to bullshit himself into playing things cool, to let things come rather than forcing them. But tonight her silences were too long, his need to keep her entertained too great. She was content to watch the light show and listen to the booms and crackles as the rockets broke up over the woods. He remarked how nice it was to be able to drink and not worry about driving home, meaning she could drink more than one or two glasses of wine if she wanted. What it came out sounding like was either he expected her to leave at some point, was dropping hints about it, or he was trying to liquor her up. Neither was true and he was pretty sure she'd taken his intended meaning, but he felt the need to explain himself. He started to when a thunderclap spawned glittering purple rivers and she kissed him, letting it linger as the rivers dried on their way to earth.

She touched his chin. "You're quiet tonight."

"I was thinking the same thing about you.

She arched her eyebrows. "So you're not bored by my company?"

He leaned forward, kissed her and lowered her to the blanket. They lay on their sides facing one another, the aromas of cut grass and cold beer swirling around their bodies. A few feet away the embers burned a dusky orange in the firepit.

He said, "I can't believe no one's snagged you yet."

"No one's ever interested me enough." Her pretty face resting on her arm. "Or I've never interested them."

"Then you've only met idiots."

She grinned crookedly. "That include you?"

He rolled her onto her back, kissed her deeper.

When he pulled away, she sighed. "That was nice."

"Just 'nice'?"

"I don't know," she said. "Try me again."

Paul leaned toward her, a flurry of flashes exploding above the trees.

She said, "That was even better."

"Good," he said. "I was worried I might be losing my touch."

"Oh yeah?" she asked. "How long has it been?"

He paused.

"Did you have a girlfriend?"

He nodded. "Emily."

"Pretty name," Julia said and sat up.

"I guess."

"How long ago did you two date?"

He looked at her then, the fireworks ringing her head in a dazzling corona. "Pretty recently, actually."

"Yeah?"

"We broke up just before I came here."

Julia watched him. Thinking it over, he could tell. Over her shoulder a firefly glowed, darkened.

She said, "Do you miss her?"

Paul thought about it. After a time he shrugged. "Not really. I was afraid of being tied down, I guess."

She lay on her back beside him, a hand behind her head, the other on her stomach. "Are you still afraid of commitment?" she asked him.

Paul watched the long fingernails move slowly on her belly, the strip of bare skin. The way her stomach rose and fell as she breathed, he could look down her shorts, see her panties, low-cut with little frilly things near the top. He felt his face grow hot.

"I'm growing out of it," he answered.

She watched him for a moment, touched his face. She drew him to her and kissed him long and deeply. He leaned forward and let his chest rest on hers.

They kissed.

She wanted to see the library.

Paul said great, that was fine with him, held her hand as they walked up the stairs together. He felt quivery, wondering if they'd retire from the library into the bedroom. It had been so long since he'd slept with a woman, he wondered if he'd remember what to do. He caught Julia smiling at him so he smiled back, hoping she couldn't read his thoughts.

Once in the library she became engrossed scanning titles, making comments about books she'd read or needed to read. Most of the time Paul only grunted, not wanting to sound stupid. He'd only read a handful of the titles she called out. Her tastes were more refined than his.

She was making her way along the south wall when she spotted the manuscript, the one he couldn't remember writing, sitting beside the crushed velvet chair.

"Um," he started to say.

She picked it up and gave him a questioning look.

"I meant to get rid of it," he said, furious with himself for leaving it out.

"Why would you get rid of it?" she asked, all eyes now, one finger tracing a pattern over the front page.

"Because it's terrible," Paul said, approaching. "It's a first try, and to be totally honest, it's embarrassing."

"But you sent it out," she said.

"Yes, I sent it out and got a very negative response."

"From how many places?"

"One."

"How many places did you send it to?"

"Two."

"That's all?"

"It's best if we put this away," he said and reached for the stack of papers. But she turned away, her mischievous grin telling him he was in trouble, that he'd either have to get serious about it, ruin the wonderful mood they had going, or let her read it and hope for the best.

Both possibilities posed a risk.

But she decided it for him by wheeling and dashing out the door. He stepped out of the library in time to see the office door close. He took a step in that direction, heard the click of the lock and stopped.

Morosely, he moved back into the library and sat down. She'd either think him talented or depraved, possibly both. It was out of his hands now, though that didn't make the waiting any easier.

He thought of telling her the truth about the novel, then discounted the idea. But if he did nothing, what had begun between them might end tonight.

He felt her slipping away.

Sucking in a breath and covering his face, he was shocked to find he was close to tears. *Son of a bitch*, he thought. *I'm a loser* and *a crybaby.*

Paul dropped his hands and stared morosely at the wall. What was the use of waiting? Go to her now and come clean. *Look, Julia, here's the story. I know you won't believe me but it's important to me to tell you the truth about that awful book. I didn't really write it, though my hands did record it. It was something or someone that got to me in the graveyard and made me do it. I'll take you there and show you the marker where it happened. Tell you the truth, I don't remember much about it at all, except the feeling that I had to get the movie playing in my mind down on paper. It was possession of a kind, not Linda Blair pea soup possession, but possession nonetheless.*

He was thinking this when he noticed something about the wall he'd not noticed before. Below the empty discolored rectangle where there'd obviously been a piece of artwork before, to the right of the fireplace, there was a tiny gap, about three feet tall and no more than a centimeter wide. Standing, he walked over to it and tried to wedge his fingers in the gap. It was too small. He looked around for something to slide into the aperture and then stood staring at it. He reached out, pushed the wall, and watched in amazement as it gave slightly and swung out a couple of inches. A tinge of old cedar tickled his nostrils.

He gaped at the trick door and the darkness beyond, not believing he'd found a secret passageway, telling himself those things only happened in Sherlock Holmes stories.

But the door did open wider when he tugged at it, giving easily, making an opening about a foot wide. Afraid suddenly the rats would appear, he took a step back. Lightning flashed outside, startling him. Seconds passed, and the answering thunder rumbled through the woods. He guessed the lightning was a few miles away.

Paul turned to the opening.

He knew he should get a flashlight, knew there was a small one in the kitchen and one of those big square ones in the garage. He squinted into the shadows, already seeing a tall thin shape leaning against one inner wall. Outside, raindrops began to pelt the window, thunking like thick fingers.

He held his breath, scooted forward on his knees, and reached out. The thing was well inside the dark space. By the spare light Paul could see a gilded edge, like a picture frame. He slid it toward him, expending some effort because of its weight. As the thing came out of the compartment, he realized it was, after all, a painting. Its back was to him, so he slid it the rest of the way out and propped it against the fireplace.

The woman in the portrait was ravishing. Her blue eyes blazed with an unnerving intensity. He felt himself growing lightheaded staring back at them. He forced himself to look away.

His eyes moved back to the portrait.

The woman's blond hair, done up in a complex network of braids and ringlets, had little hints of strawberry in it. The set of the mouth was hard to read but the eyes were laughing and that made him think she was smiling too. The nose was small. Her earrings were tiny pendants with pearls on the ends. Her chin was slightly lowered, as if she were daring him to approach. The alabaster throat, too, was inviting. Paul was a little embarrassed to find himself aroused at the sight of the cleavage pushing up out of her light blue dress. The low neckline—Paul hunted for the word—the décolletage, displayed her perfectly shaped breasts to dizzying effect. He stared at the gloved hands, the thin waist made thinner by a corset, the bare forearms resting on her lap.

Was this woman, then, the woman in the graveyard, the woman who was so loathed that her tombstone was a scarred ruin?

Was this Annabel?

Thunder rumbled through the woods, vibrated the foundations of Watermere as Paul stared at the portrait, the heat of arousal returning, shame attending it because this woman was dead, might have been his relative. And that didn't even take into account that the woman he was falling in love with was in the next room.

The rain came hard then, battering the house until the sound became a continuous roar. He fancied he could smell the rain through the window. It comforted him. He was staring at the window when lightning strobed, three quick flashes followed by a fourth, this one sustained, and in the pane's reflection he saw he was not alone in the library. He cried out, whirling, and saw the dead woman glaring in the silver light. He stumbled backward, and as thunder shook the house he saw it was Julia, only Julia, holding the manuscript and watching him strangely.

He blew out ragged breath and braced himself on a chair. He giggled and wiped a hand over his forehead, which was clammy, iced with sweat.

"You scared me," he said.

As Julia approached, Paul moved the painting behind a chair so she wouldn't see it.

His gaze went from the manuscript in her hands to her watchful green eyes, back to the manuscript again.

"Well?" he asked.

She threw the pile of pages in his face.

The storm grew severe.

More than once the lights dimmed, threatened to go out. Paul wished they would. That way he wouldn't be able to see the way Julia was staring at him, as if she were seeing him for the first time and not liking what she saw.

They sat across from one another in the library. Her eyes were hard as she watched him. He wanted to go to a different room to speak, get away from the painting, but Julia insisted on having it out here, now.

At first he'd been grateful she'd sat with her back to the painting. He could keep an eye on it that way, keep both women in sight so he could keep the two separate.

What scared him most was how Julia still looked to him like his deceased aunt. Physically they were different; Julia with the fuller figure, the green eyes instead of blue, the dark hair and skin that made her look exotic, like a maiden from some remote Pacific island. She

185

looked nothing like the woman in the painting, not really. It was the way they both watched him, relishing secret knowledge about him, knowing how weak and insecure he felt around their beauty, that bound them in his mind.

"Paul?"

He jumped, realized he'd been staring beyond Julia, into the face of the dead woman, her pale throat, her round breasts.

"Sorry. I've been a little off today."

She waited.

He cleared his throat, sat forward. "I guess you didn't like *The Monkey Killer.*"

"It's not right," she said.

"Could you expand on that?" he said and regretted his smartass tone.

"Is this why you came here?"

The look on her face, which he now recognized as suspicion, stunned him into silence.

"There are things in there," she said, pointing to the spray of papers on the floor, "that you can't possibly know."

When he only stared dumbly back at her, she went on, "Things about your uncle—*uncles*—that might not even be true."

Paul felt his heartbeat in his throat.

"So what happened? You went through your grandfather's stuff in Memphis, came here to dig up more dirt, get the rest of the story, and made up the rest? Then you sent out your lies to get rich?"

"Julia—"

"Did you expect to impress me with this trash?"

"Wait a second."

"Because that's what it is, Paul. Garbage."

"It's only a story," he said thinly. He saw their relationship near the edge of some black abyss, ready to tumble over.

Her voice grew louder. "It's slander."

Paul sat forward, mind frozen like the gears of some unoiled machine. "Julia, please don't overreact. For one thing, I don't even know those people," he said and glanced at the pages for help, as though they'd verify his story. "I mean, let's say for a moment it's true.

186

Even if it is, everyone in that book is dead now."

"I was afraid you'd say that," she said, her voice flat. She stood, walked toward the door.

"Wait," he called. He moved toward her. "Why do you care so much about the people in the story?" He allowed himself to say it. "They're my relatives, not yours."

She turned then, and as she did he was afraid she'd see the portrait leaning against the chair. She shook her head, eyes down, chin trembling. When Paul reached out to touch her shoulder her hand shot out, slapped him hard across the cheekbone. Pain exploded and he staggered, just managing to keep his balance.

"Go to hell, Paul."

Holding his cheek with one hand, he was reaching out for her again when he saw her eyes flare, her face contort.

Withdrawing his hand, he asked, "Can't we talk about this?"

Julia's jaw flexed. "No, we cannot talk about this, Paul. You sent this out to publishers, right?"

"One of whom already rejected it," he said.

"He was right to," she said, going.

"Please don't leave."

She faced him from the doorway, the skin around her mouth drawn tight.

"I never want to see you again."

"What's wrong with you? I'd understand if you hated my book, but you act as though I killed someone."

She was watching him with an expression he couldn't read.

He went on, "Hitting me in the face? You'd think Myles was your father or something."

Her eyes widened.

"Oh my God," he said.

He took a step toward her, but she was already turning away.

"I'm so sorry, Julia."

He started after her, but by the time he'd gotten to the back staircase the front door was slamming shut.

She was gone.

Halfway home, the rain ceased. When she emerged from the woods and trudged through the yard to the farmhouse, her clothes damp and clingy on her skin, the stars shone so brightly that she could not only make out the lightning bugs as they flashed but could see their wings keeping them afloat, their pill-shaped bodies hovering above the grass. They were mating, she thought, celebrating the end of the thunderstorm. In another frame of mind she might have appreciated the lightshow, but all she could think of as she watched them signal to one another was how sorely she'd misjudged Paul.

He was airing people's dirty laundry for a profit, which was one thing. It was another thing entirely that he was doing it to his own uncle, whether he knew the man or not.

The one saving grace was the likelihood the trashy novel would never be published. It flowed easily enough; she'd give him that much. But the subject matter was lurid, and the offhanded way he dealt with it was nothing short of ghoulish.

Maybe that was the real Paul, she thought as she got rid of her soaked shoes and walked through the dark house. A human buzzard feasting on the carrion of his family's skeletons.

The moon was so bright there was no need to mess with the living room lamp. Knowing nothing would take away the sick betrayal she felt, she sat at the Steinway and played a somber Bach sonata she knew by heart. The song choice was a bad one, she realized, and she once again dissolved into tears. She hated herself for wallowing in self-pity, but reasoning with it was no use. She'd really thought she and Paul had something meaningful.

A voice said, "Are those tears of remorse?"

She whirled, falling against the piano, her elbows crashing discordant notes.

"Who's there?" she asked.

"Just relax," the man in the rocking chair said. A wide-brimmed hat made his head huge in the shadows.

She rose from the bench. In the lurid moonlight bleeding in through the window she watched an arm reach slowly out and twist on the lamp.

Daryl Applegate sat staring at her.

"You can sit down," he said.

Julia opened her mouth uncertainly.

"I said sit down."

Reluctantly, she did.

He sat rocking in her mother's chair. She felt her anger return.

"You have no right to be here, badge or not. Where's Sheriff Barlow?"

"Home. Or he might have gone over to Redman's after the fireworks."

"Who do you think you are, breaking in here?"

"Cut the crap, Julia."

She laughed once, harshly. Then she stood and walked over to the phone.

"You wiped your prints off Brand's car."

She stopped, depressed the receiver.

"What are you talking about?"

"What I'm talking about is that bullshit story you told Barlow at the library. I know you were in Brand's car the night of his death."

"Sheriff Barlow said Brand might still be alive."

Applegate snickered softly and shook his head. "Barlow might think that but we know better, don't we?"

She tried to brush it off. "I don't know wh—"

"Like I said," he interrupted, "let's cut the crap, alright?"

She watched him. In the dim glow of the lamp his eyes looked black.

Applegate stared at her breasts. The deputy's belly sagged over his belt, a hint of hairy white skin peeking out at her from between buttons. He rocked slowly in the wooden chair, serene, his hat brim bobbing up and down.

"What do you want?" she asked.

"How about you tell me what you got planted in your garden."

"Nothing yet."

"Tomatoes?"

"Not this year."

"Cukes?"

"No."

"My grandma always plants cukes. Makes them into this creamy salad stuff. Tastes great with corn on the cob. What else you got in there?"

"I told you nothing."

"What about dead lawyers?"

Julia met his stare. "I don't have any idea what you're talking about, and I don't care for the accusation, either."

"You shouldn't have killed him, you don't care for the accusation."

The way the chair groaned when he rocked in it, she was afraid his fat ass would bust through the wood.

"Come on, Julia. Help me out here." It was the first time he'd spoken her name. She didn't care for it.

"Other than the fact that I'm innocent, don't you need a search warrant to break in here?"

"Door was unlocked."

"You know what I mean, damn it. I have rights."

He stopped rocking. "You really want me to get a search warrant? Tell Sheriff Barlow about this?"

Her lips thinned but her eyes held his.

"Maybe I won't tell Barlow what I find out there," Applegate said, nodding toward the backyard. "Maybe I don't give a shit about some hot shot from the city. Maybe that lawyer got what was coming to him."

She allowed herself a smile. A small one.

Applegate smiled too. "So. Are we gonna be friendly about this?"

Julia crossed her legs. "I still don't know what you're talking about, Deputy, but you're welcome to stay for some coffee if you'd like. I was just about to brew some."

"Sure you were," he said. "That's fine then. I'd love a cup of coffee. Haven't had one since breakfast."

He followed her into the kitchen. She could feel his eyes on her ass. Underneath, her panties were soaked through with rain, uncomfortable in the muggy kitchen.

She rounded the table, her fingernails skating over the Byron collection she'd been reading, and glanced back at him. He'd taken off

190

his hat, revealing a dented pelt of thick black hair, the kind that rejected water completely, made it bead and run off like canvas. Julia set the coffee to brew.

She made to excuse herself as Applegate sat down, but before she made it past him, he barred her way with a long arm. "I don't think so," he said.

"I'm going to change clothes. Where do you think I'm going to go?"

"To get your gun maybe."

"I don't have one."

He eyed her, thinking. Then, he grinned magnanimously. "Okay, then. You want to slip into something more comfortable, I'll let you."

She moved past him and disappeared up the stairs.

When she returned in her white sports bra and her low rise gray running shorts, Applegate was sitting at the table, scowling over one of her books, *Mansfield Park*. When he looked up, his face reddened. His eyes flitted from her bare stomach to her breasts.

"Enjoying the book?" she asked. As she poured the coffee, she could feel him staring.

"It's real nice."

"I'm glad you like it."

Setting down the cups, she sat across from him. He put the book down and sipped at his coffee. Other than the sound of his stertorous breathing, the house was silent.

"Cream?" she asked.

He set the mug down and examined it. "How'd you do it?"

"Do what?"

"How'd you do it?" he repeated, still watching the mug.

"I have no idea what you mean."

He looked at her then, but before long his eyes sank to her cleavage. She had an urge to cover herself but instead allowed her shoulders to glide back and touch the chair, felt her breasts push against the stretchy material.

"Let's try this another way," he said to her tits. "*Why* did you do it?"

Her thumb went up and down the handle of her cup, her eyes willing his to meet hers.

191

"He try something on you? Make you act in self-defense? If he did, you're not gonna get in trouble for it."

She spoke slowly. "I don't know what you're talking about, why you're here, or what you want from me. If you don't have any more questions, I'm going for a run."

He met her eyes. "You do, you'll regret it."

She stared at him, waited for him to look away first.

He did. "Damn it," he said. He leaned back in his chair, licked his lips. "Come here."

Her shoulders leaned against the seatback, her breasts teasing him.

"Now, Goddammit," he said.

She set her cup on the table and stood. The kitchen was too warm. Sweat glistened on her bare stomach. She moved around the table and stood next to him. The front legs of his chair hung a foot off the ground, the back of his seat resting on the edge of the counter.

Applegate motioned her closer.

She took another step, her hip brushing his shoulder.

Applegate scratched his matted hair, licked his lips. He reached out with a tremulous hand. His large fingers touched her stomach just above the navel. She watched his fingers pressing her dark skin, the fine blond hair on her stomach tickling at his touch. His mouth was open, his breathing very loud in the kitchen. The withering odor boiling out of his mouth made her gorge clench, but she did her best not to show it. He traced an index finger along the muscle over her hip, toward her abdomen. When his finger reached her waistband, it glided there, back and forth, pushing down the elastic band of her shorts, probing lower.

His eyes came up as the sizzling coffee pot swung toward his face. An arm flew up and blocked her wrist, the burning pot spinning loose and shattering against the cabinet behind him. Steaming jets of coffee scalded the back of his neck. Hissing, he caught her wrist, twisted it savagely, while his other hand gripped his blistered neck. With her free hand Julia raked his cheekbone, four deep trenches blooming in his flesh. He screamed and twisted her arm. She felt a wrist bone crack. Desperately, she kicked at the back legs of his chair and felt him release her as the chair started to fall.

Before he could prevent it, the chair toppled backward, the base of his skull smashing the hard counter edge. His body followed, landing in a heap.

She kicked at his face. He surprised her by dodging and snagging her other foot. He pulled it toward him. Both her legs went airborne, the hard wooden floor rising up to meet her back. Her head followed, whacking the floor with a sick thud.

Dazed, she saw him gaining his feet and reaching toward her. Feebly, she batted at his hand. He slapped her hand aside, stepped on her injured wrist. She cried out. He dropped a knee into her ribs and let his weight follow, laughing at her agonized cry.

"Innocent, huh?" He seized a handful of her hair. "Then why'd you attack me? Trying to kill me too? *Fucking cunt!*" he roared, jerking her head up and slamming it on the floor. She lay semi-conscious, a thin rill of blood trickling out of one nostril.

Daryl wrestled her onto his shoulder and carried her into the backyard. By the time they reached the garden he was ready to faint. He dropped her on the moist garden bed.

She landed with a thump. She rocked over on her side, trying to regain her feet. She reminded him of a turtle rolled over on its shell. He measured, reared and planted a kick in her kidneys. She moaned and bent backward, holding her lower back.

"Think you can get away, huh?" Daryl reached down and grabbed the shovel lying in the grass. She was on her back, face squeezed tight in agony, her arm pinned beneath her holding her side. He'd gotten her good.

"What's wrong, honey? You got a pain?" He straddled her, brought the edge of the shovel up, cupped her chin with the blade. She cried out as he pressed the dirty shovel tip into her throat. She tried to lift her chin to get away from the pressing tip, but he followed her, kept the steel point pressed in her flesh.

He felt her kick at him, aiming for his balls, but she was too weak and had a bad angle. She kicked the underside of his buttocks instead. He pulled the shovel away, raised one of his size fourteens and stomped her in the belly.

Daryl grinned. The bitch deserved it. Raking him with those

193

goddamn Freddy Krueger fingernails, dousing the back of his neck with scalding coffee. He touched his neck and grimaced. The raised blisters back there hurt like a motherfucker.

She was curled up like a pillbug and retching. He dropped down next to her, cradled the back of her head. She writhed away, so he snatched a handful of her hair and drew her face to his. "It's just you and me now," he said. "No one's gonna stop me from doing what I want, least of all you."

Crying now, she batted weakly at his face. He headbutted her, saw her dazed expression and felt his cock growing hard. With both hands he grabbed ahold of her long hair and kissed her. She struggled beneath him, but he only mashed his face harder, his tongue out and squirming to get between her closed lips. She bucked beneath him, battered his shoulders and neck, but he wouldn't let go. He let one hand drop to her breasts, squeezing them, kneading, his other hand slide lower, down over her slick tummy and work its way under her waistband. She thrashed beneath him, and just when his fingertips found her pubic hair, he felt a screaming pain in his right ear, knew she'd sunk a fingernail in there, through his fucking eardrum.

He yelped and rolled onto his back, his legs bicycling in the air, running through the agony. Daryl howled, felt tears stinging his cheeks.

He remembered himself after a time and sat up, one hand holding in the ganglia oozing through his fingers.

The bitch was crawling away.

He scrambled over and grabbed the shovel. As he got to his feet he saw what bad shape she was in. She'd made it only a few feet from the garden. He followed her, but his balance threatened to betray him. The bitch and her goddamn fingernails had screwed up his equilibrium, but he still had the upper hand. He had to do it quick, before his spinning brain pitched him over onto the wet grass. He stood above her, feet straddling her back.

Daryl lifted the shovel over his shoulder, brought it down hard, flat end clanging dully on her skull. Her body flopped on the grass, went still.

He stared at her long shiny body, face down, curvy and limp and silhouetted by the moon.

He wondered how he'd explain this to Sam.

Knowing she was out for a while, maybe for good, but still wanting to keep an eye on her while he dug, he reached down and grabbed the waistband of her shorty shorts. He felt the silk of her panties on his fingertips, lifted, meaning for her body to come with it, but instead of lifting her off the ground, her shorts and underwear slid off her hips, revealing her beautiful round ass.

He dropped her, panting. He stared at her glistening buttocks, pallid and full in the moonlight.

He wiped his mouth. There would be time for that later, after he dug up Brand's body. Not bothering to pull her shorts up, he lifted her feet and dragged her like that until she was lying next to the garden. He eyeballed her exposed rump, imagined how it would be, her out cold, him violating her however he chose, for hours. He could incorporate it into his story later on. How she'd called him, asked him to come out to her place. *I knew it was wrong, Sam, but she was so pretty and so aggressive. It was after we'd already had sex that she confessed to me about Brand, thinking I wouldn't tell on her. When I came out here to see if her story was true she attacked me with those scimitar nails of hers. She slashed my face and probably cost me my hearing in one ear. It was self-defense then, and even though I didn't want to hurt her, I had to, to save myself and to get justice for Brand's wife and kids.*

Laughing, Daryl thrust the shovel into the dirt.

He dug, working leisurely at first, then feverishly when he realized she'd buried the lawyer down deep. By accident he tossed a shovelful of dirt on her back and shoulders. He watched how still she was, wondered for a moment if she'd died on him. Then he saw her ribs rising and falling and knew she was still alive even if her skull was busted. It didn't matter, as long as she was alive when he took her. He threw another clump of dirt on her, this one thumping on her lower back, dirty crumbs of earth collecting in the crack of her ass. He leaned on the shovel, enjoying the sight. Bitch thought she was too good for him, what'd she think about herself now? Face down in the mud, dirt in her buttcrack, she wasn't such a princess now, was she?

He dug lower, four feet deep now, wondering why he hadn't come to it yet. The ground was getting stony, sparks flicking up when he struck. Was it possible she'd fooled him, buried the body somewhere else? The blade struck something solid. Too solid, he thought. It felt like a big rock, but Brand's body had been underground for a while now. Maybe it was petrified.

Daryl chuckled, set the shovel aside and worked the rocky soil with his hands, scraping the earth away from the hard object beneath. Its surface was at least a foot wide. The lawyer's torso, maybe? It was awfully flat for that.

Steeling himself for the putrefied stench of rotting flesh, he felt around down there on all fours. He realized what he felt was only a stone. With the realization came the knowledge she had not buried the lawyer here after all, couldn't have. The rock was too large for her to manage on her own. She couldn't have pulled it up, put him under it, shoved it back again. Disappointed, he stood in the hole and put his hands on the lip of the opening to haul himself out.

The shovel tip whistled down and crunched through his wrist. Too shocked to scream, he looked up at her, holding the shovel and standing at the edge of the hole. She jumped and landed with her bare heels on the edge of the shovel blade. Daryl bellowed as he watched the dirty steel sink into the ground, his wrist bone snapping in half, his hand severed, the blood already muddying the soil between wrist stump and shovel. He gripped his jetting wrist, held it before his eyes with his remaining hand. He grew faint at the sight of the gushing red fountain.

He staggered back to the edge of the opening, saw the girl land in a crouch before him. In the hole with him she stood erect, brought the shovel up. Before he could lift his arms to ward off the blow, the blade was whizzing through the air, sideways, so that the sharp tip caught the side of his open mouth, sliced through the stretched skin, cleaved his lip on the other side as well. Blood gurgling, choking him, he sank to his knees and tumbled forward onto his belly. Waves of dizziness dulled the pain, but it was still there, awful, gigantic in his mouth and where his hand used to be.

Losing consciousness, he flopped onto his back and gasped for breath. He glimpsed Julia above him, upside down and snarling. The shovel came down on his chest, puncturing his skin. She stood on it again, balancing as he batted at the blade. It disappeared into his chest, sank through his lungs, parted his vertebrae.

Chapter Seventeen

The thing about the eyes of the lady in the painting wasn't the way they followed you about the room—which they did—but rather the way they absorbed you and dismissed you, turned you into an irrelevancy.

Men are playthings to me, those eyes told him. *What makes you any different?*

Paul couldn't say why he spent so much of that week, the week after it fell apart with Julia, in the equatorial heat of the third-floor library where the central air's reach never seemed to extend. It wasn't to admire the painting; the woman above the fireplace was too striking to be lingered on.

Maybe it had something to do with the way that gaze of hers, the one that prickled the nape of his neck even when his back was turned, spoke to him. *You're no more to me than these other men,* the eyes said, *but you're no less either. There's more in you than you know, Paul. I'll bet you could show me a good time.*

It was both sick and strange, he knew, to think such thoughts about his great aunt, but because he'd never met her, he was able to rationalize away his instinctive revulsion, to forget the incestuous elements of his feelings for the woman and revel in the way she made him feel. Thinking of her, he was able to ignore the way the rustlings in the wall had ended.

In the days since Julia left him—for good, it seemed—he'd grown stronger. His jogs had become daily affairs, and soon he was running twice a day and for greater distances. He'd converted a second story bedroom into a workout area, complete with equipment he'd had delivered from the local sporting goods store.

Ten nights after Julia rejected him he dreamed of Annabel for the first time, and since that night he'd dreamed of nothing else. In his dreams he pursued her the way he'd pursued Julia through the yard the first night he'd seen her. But when the lightning flashed this time he could see it was the woman in the painting, her knowing eyes and confident grin. He gave chase, but with barely an effort she remained ahead of him.

He grew closer to the woman each succeeding night, and her delays, when she'd turn and stare at him, were more frequent and sustained.

Because he wanted his dreams undiluted by alcohol, he'd sworn off drinking, going cold turkey. He shocked himself by sticking to his resolution. He found he was able to run even farther each morning without the encumbrance of a hangover and that without the liquor in his system his body recovered more briskly from each run.

One day in late July he diverged from his normal routine and took the route his nervousness had forbidden him from taking. After all, he told himself, he couldn't stay away from the cemetery forever.

He did not immediately go to the grave on the extreme edge of the clearing, instead moving up and down uneven rows, searching for names he could use for his characters. He'd gotten the idea shortly after Julia deserted him that he might, without the aid of whatever power had gripped him before, be able to write a novel of his own, one that would not cause editors to send him polite, slightly pitying responses.

When he reached the large black tombstone, all he could do was stare.

He was not surprised to find the grass above whatever body was entombed there sprouting in delicate tufts. He'd first come out here in May, and there might have been morning frosts at that time of year that could account for the blighted grass he'd seen. Now, the ground that had before been scorched and black was improving, though still a good deal less lush than the earth around it.

What astonished him was how drunk he must have been that fateful May evening, for he now realized that the name on the marker was quite clear.

The tall narrow letters read, ANNABEL CARVER

And below, 1930-1988

So this was, after all, his great aunt. The name fit the woman in the painting, so much so that he found himself whispering her name. He realized how quiet the forest had become, how the diesel symphony of the cicadas had subsided, the cawing of the blackbirds all but ceased.

He looked down at the grave.

There were no truculent messages, no red spray paint. He supposed they could have been washed away, though that didn't make sense. The scars were still there, gouged into the granite surface of the marker.

Yet staring at the gravestone now, he couldn't believe he'd not seen it before.

In a way he supposed it made sense. If he'd been so drunk that he couldn't even read a mildly vandalized tombstone, it was no wonder he'd blacked out upon touching it. The possibility that it was really he who had written *The Monkey Killer* and not some emissary from beyond seemed perfectly reasonable to him now. Sure he'd been drunk, but weren't there people who'd committed crimes when asleep? Was it really that improbable that his imagination had taken control once liberated by drink, had surmounted his self-doubt when it was too muddled to hinder him?

He stood, feeling his muscles ripple in the hot, close air. He wished now he'd taken pictures of his former body, the one with two chins and puffy cheeks.

He lay down in the patchy grass and watched the overhanging leaves stir in the weak summer breeze. He tried to imagine Julia's face but could only see Annabel's, the blue eyes replacing the green, the tawny skin draining of color.

He closed his eyes and pictured Annabel turning toward him, beckoning him, allowing him to slide his hands over her sides, his tongue into her mouth. She laughed as he tore the thin shoulder straps of her white dress and he took a moment to look at the white pool of fabric around her feet. As she stood there naked his eyes traveled up her slim, powdery body, his hands caressing her legs, massaging her.

Paul opened his eyes and sucked in air.

What the hell was wrong with him?

It was one thing to find a woman in a piece of art attractive. It was another matter altogether to be so attracted to her that he could find no other outlet for his imagination than fantasizing at her gravesite. Feeling decidedly less suave than he'd felt moments earlier, he trotted out of the graveyard and through the forest, intent on outrunning his shame.

The exertion and the heat did little to faze him, his breathing quick but measured as his long, loping strides brought him closer and closer to home. He was sure he was seeing things as he approached the mouth of the trail, for across the yard, near the garage, he was certain he perceived flashes of glass, glints of gold. Paul focused on his arms, pumping his elbows front-to-back as his feet whirred over the grass of the back lawn. He passed the place where he and Julia had spent that last enchanted evening.

Then Paul saw the car. It was familiar to him, yet it wasn't until he turned and beheld the woman sitting on the front porch that he realized the car was Emily's.

November, 1982

"I want you to leave there."

Sam promised her on the phone he'd give it a rest, let ten minutes go by without telling her what an unwholesome place Watermere was, what a ruthless bastard she was working for and what a soulless bitch she was looking after. But his thoughts hovered over it like a stalled storm system, raining on their first date in a week.

Barbara looked at him with a pained expression. Seeing her lovely face pinched that way made him ache. She could be anything in the world, but she had to be a nurse. Annabel's nurse. Sam wished the insane woman would die and save them all the trouble.

Last time Sam and Barbara had seen one another, he'd made a remark, something about the poetic justice of Annabel's condition, her getting a venereal disease after using her body to screw up so many people's lives. Barbara said it wasn't her job to judge her patients, what they did to get sick was none of her business.

That set him off because it was the same damn argument lawyers made, like they couldn't help defending and getting guilty people off, using technicalities and lawyer-speak to prevent child molesters and rapists from getting what they deserved.

"So you're telling me," he'd said, knowing they were headed for another blow-up, "that you'd condone saving the life of a serial killer even if you knew he was guilty?"

"I'd do everything in my power to help him," she said, defiant.

"What if you knew the D.A. couldn't get a conviction, that the only hope the public had—the families of the victims had—was for the slimeball to die on the operating table?"

"I can't believe you'd ask me a question like that."

"And I can't believe you'd put some bullshit nurses' code over doing the right thing."

That had sent her toward the door.

Now here they were again, on the edge of the cliff, ready to tumble over, kicking and clawing each other all the way. He didn't know how many more falls their relationship could take, and though he was bothered by her ethics, he loved her a hell of a lot more than he disagreed with her.

Barbara was watching him, her expression saying he was a selfish jerk. It made him mad. What the hell, he thought. If wanting the woman he'd fallen in love with to stay away from that nest of vipers, to for chrissakes move in with him instead of living in this farmhouse in the middle of the forest, then yeah, he was selfish. He looked up at the plain white house, thought of the episode with Reverend Hargrove and his family, what Myles had done to Mrs. Hargrove.

He bit the inside of his mouth. "Look, I know you're pretty pissed at me these days, and I know you've been putting in a lot of hours at your job. You're doing your best to help that...woman, and I want you to know I respect your motives."

She laughed, bitterness changing her voice into something he didn't recognize.

He fought through it. "And if we disagree on some things, well, a man and a woman were never intended to agree on everything. And we agree about enough things to make up for the other."

The way she looked at him, she was listening. Which was a start. He struggled to find the words, to choose them with care, so he could maybe lead her back to him.

"I love you. You know that. I changed my life around for you, and—"

"I never asked you to do that."

"I know," he said, trying not to show how hurt he was, "and I'm a grown man who's responsible for the things I do. It's just," he paused, thinking. "It's just the stuff I know about those people—though they don't deserve to be called people—are so—"

"That's what I'm talking about." Her face, her voice, were suddenly fierce. "You talk about Myles and Annabel as though they were less than human, like you've never sinned or done anything you're ashamed of. What makes you so vicious toward them?"

Sam gaped at her. "What makes me so vicious? What do you think, I've made everything up? That everyone in town doesn't hate them, isn't scared to go out there because of the terrible things they've gotten away with? Barbara, those stories predate my arrival here, it's not like I'm the one who made them up. They're true. Those people are the worst kind of scum. They were responsible for the death of five children. Of too many men and women to count."

"You're impossible," she said and reached for the passenger door handle.

"Wait," he said and reached for her.

She swatted at his arm. "Don't touch me."

He sat back in his seat, unbelieving. "Jesus, Barbara, I'm not trying to hurt you."

She opened the car door, put one foot on the ground. "No, you just want to own me."

"Own you?" he asked, getting out of the car. He faced her over the roof. "Where's all this coming from?"

Her green eyes flared. "From you, Sam. That's where it's coming from."

"Will you just get back in the car so we can talk?"

She was heading toward the porch. "I'm done taking orders."

"I've never told you what to do." Seeing her climb the steps, he felt something in his chest constricting.

"Whatever you say," she said. She reached for the door.

"Wait," he called. He moved around the old black car, the one that had replaced his state cruiser. His stomach was a frozen knot. "I'm sorry if I've been a pain. I'm not very good with words sometimes."

She turned, looked down at him, and the woman he loved was gone. In her place was someone distant, a woman who was moving on.

"You know what, Sam? Sometimes I think you were a trooper too long. You've let it go to your head. You take people and put them in one category or the other—good or evil—but people aren't like that. We're all of us good and bad at the same time. I know Myles has his faults, but there's also nobility in him."

"Nobility?" he said. For a moment he forgot his fear of losing her. "You've got to be joking."

"Sure, Sam. You believe that." She opened the door, saying, "You go on believing you and Myles are from different species, that you're the saint and he's the sinner."

He opened his mouth to protest, but the slam of the screen door and the bang of the heavy wooden door behind it stole his words.

Seeing Emily again was strange, particularly because of the way she was looking at him.

Her brown hair, usually shoulder length, was shorter now, and as usual, she wore no make-up. She didn't need to. He'd always secretly considered her his opposite. Naturally healthy, untinged by chemicals and substances, she looked like an actress in a commercial for facial wash. She wasn't a bombshell like Julia, but she was pretty in her own way. The white skirt she wore showed her figure to good advantage. As she came down the steps, her eyes wide with incomprehension, he noticed she was barefoot as she usually was and hoped she hadn't hurt her feet walking across the sharp gravel.

He was surprised at how short she looked. He couldn't tell how much of their height disparity could be attributed to his improved posture, but standing there in the fading afternoon light she seemed tiny, like a child.

He liked the way her eyes kept traveling from his face to his torso and back again, and he could almost hear her wondering how it had happened. He tried putting himself in her place, remembered times when he'd seen people after long periods of separation, been amazed at the weight they'd gained or the hair they'd lost.

But this was the reverse, and he could tell she'd expected the opposite, for him to fall apart here all alone. He couldn't blame her. He had expected that too.

She reached up, ran a hand over his cheek.

"You're so thin," she said. "What's happened to you out here?"

"Too much to tell." He looked down at her, at her happy face, her brown eyes and her straight white teeth, and remembered how it'd been when they first met.

She moved in and gave him a hug. He returned it, though something deep within him held back.

When she released him he asked, "How did you find this place?"

"You left your landlord the address in case any mail needed forwarding."

"You're quite a detective."

"You've been lifting," she said, her eyes scanning his chest, his shoulders.

"Running, too. Can you believe it?"

She grinned, shaking her head.

"It's okay," he told her. "You can say it."

"No, it's just," she paused, met his eyes. "It's just a pleasant surprise." Her face clouded. "Maybe getting away from Memphis really was what you needed."

He shrugged. "This is a better life for me."

She took in the woods around them, glanced back at the house.

"That's not to say I haven't thought of you, though," he said.

She stayed quiet, watched him.

He turned his head, stared at the garage a little sadly. "I've thought a lot about how things ended. The way I acted. Choices I made."

"Yeah?"

"Yeah." He nodded toward the house. "Let's talk about it inside."

February, 1983

"Can I come in?" Barbara asked him.

Sam had been asleep. Had actually dozed off after too many beers and too much solitude. He saw on the clock over the couch it was only five-thirty in the afternoon. Christ, he thought. Not even six yet and already in the bag.

He followed her through the kitchen out to the screened-in porch. It was where they always sat, enjoying the quiet of the cornfield that bordered his back yard. In the summer it was nice, but now it was freezing. Sam watched her, worried about her thin jacket, the way her breath turned to smoke when it hit the air. She looked bad. Her nose was red, her eyes wet, and if he didn't know her better he'd guess she had a bad cold. As it was, he suspected what was on her mind had more to do with her appearance than any flu.

"We could sit indoors," he said. "I had a fire going the other day." It was a lie, but he didn't like her thinking of him sleeping and drinking away his time in a cold house.

She shook her head, distracted. "It's good for me. I've been inside all winter."

"Does Myles drive you back-and-forth from the farmhouse?" he asked, trying to keep the bitterness out of his voice.

She nodded, wiped her nose.

He waited. She was looking out at the patches of snow, the dead stalks of corn laid out like starved refugees.

He thought of asking her why she hadn't returned his calls, had ignored him when he saw her at the grocery store. He'd even tried writing a letter, and if that didn't show he cared about her, he didn't know what did. He hadn't written a personal letter since the sixth grade, and that was to impress a girl who'd gotten her titties before everyone else.

He watched Barbara and thought of telling her how she'd hurt him.

Instead, he said, "It's nice having you here again."

It made her cry. Alarmed, he sat forward on the cold chair and wondered what he'd said wrong. He put out a hand to touch her shoulder, pulled it back. The last thing he wanted was to scare her away.

"Can I help?" he asked.

She shook her head, face frozen in a sob. She had bags under her eyes. He wanted to wipe her nose for her, do something to help the crying.

"Is it Myles?" he couldn't help asking.

That doubled her over, her sobs coming in convulsive waves. After a time, she got it under control, took the tissue box he'd brought from the living room.

She blew her nose, looked at Sam gratefully.

"You're so good to me," she said, her voice breaking.

"You're my girl."

It set her off again, and seeing the way her tears were frosting her cheeks he took her arm and forced her to move back inside. He left her on the couch to get a few wedges of firewood. She didn't look up when he returned.

"Now tell me," he said as he knelt to open the grate, "what's got you so shaken up."

She looked up, saw him feeding wood into the hearth, and said, "Really, Sam. I can't stay."

She stood.

He couldn't keep the impatience out of his voice. "Will you tell me what's going on? I'm not going to yell at you, for chrissakes."

"Something's happened," she said.

"I figured that." He stood, watched her from across the room. She was facing the door, but hadn't yet moved to leave.

Barbara said, "I should have known this would be the hardest part."

"Did he hurt you?" Sam asked. He imagined getting Myles down, bashing his face until there were no features left.

"I did it to myself."

Sam felt ill, though he couldn't say why. "Barbara, what are we talking about here?"

"I did it to you, too, Sam."

He waited, dread gripping him by the throat.

"The first time was New Year's Eve. He brought me home and invited himself in. He'd been so good to me, and I'd been drinking…"

Sam turned to steady himself on the mantle. He felt the beer in him sitting like lead in his belly. He wished she were making it up, but he knew it was true.

"It happened more often then," she continued, sniffling. "The other *morning, I felt sick."*

"Is it..." he stopped, having no idea what to say. He hadn't the strength to catch his breath.

"I'm going to have it, Sam."

He turned then, looked at her. She didn't look up.

"I'm going to have his baby."

The tears surprised him because he felt nothing at all now. He buried his eyes in his shirt sleeve, leaned on the mantle and willed her to leave, which she did. He let himself down on his knees, sat back on his heels and went over on his back. After he lay there awhile he went into the bedroom, took the lockbox from under the bed. His fingers closed on the little gray box inside. As he walked through the house and out the back door the velvet on the box felt stiff, frozen. He crunched over snow and brittle grass. With a final effort, he planted and hurled the box and the engagement ring into the field, dropped to his knees in the snow, cursed God and Barbara and Myles Carver.

Myles Carver most of all.

The real Emily surfaced.

"The bar looks nice," she said, and from the look on her face it was obvious she was asking if he'd been drinking. He opened his mouth to tell her she need not worry about that, he'd gotten it under control, but stopped, wondering why he felt the need to explain himself.

"It's one of my favorite parts of the house," he said.

She was watching him, he realized, with a look that was part curiosity and part anger. She was waiting for him to tell her how much he'd missed her.

"Do you want a drink?" he asked.

She gave him a thin look. "What do you think?"

"Should we go outside?" he asked.

She strolled up to him then, a languorous expression altering her face. "Maybe later."

She drew him down and kissed him. Julia filled his mind and he pulled away, but then he remembered her angry voice, her eyes full of loathing.

"Come on," Emily said, crowding him. She kissed his chest, snaked her arms under his. "Let's be friends again."

Though he kissed Emily back this time, his thoughts tended first toward Julia, then Annabel. He closed his eyes and imagined making love to Julia on the blanket under the fireworks, grew furious with himself that he hadn't. The vision of Julia's glorious body brought him alive, intensified his kissing of Emily. She responded, kneading his rigid back muscles and moaning against his lips.

He thought of Annabel gazing up at him from the forest floor, the earth soft and cool beneath them, golden glints of sunlight slanting through the canopy of branches.

Emily pulled away and spoke his name. Staring into her unbelieving face, thoughts of Annabel vanished.

"What is it?"

"Over there," Emily said and pointed with a trembling finger. "There was someone in the window."

He followed her gaze. "What are—"

"A woman," Emily said, a hand massaging her throat. "She was staring at me like she wanted to kill me."

August, 1983

Barbara's screams went on into the night.

She hated Myles for taking her to the basement. The midwife argued for the hospital, but he'd shouted her down. The midwife told him Barbara would be more comfortable in her bed and Myles told her he'd be damned if he'd have her bleeding all over his sheets. He'd fathered the child, so she'd damn well do what he said. He reminded the midwife he'd also paid for her, and poked the old woman in the chest to drive home his point.

Barbara asked for painkillers; Myles refused. Barbara asked for Sam, and Myles smacked her in the mouth. Half the night she wept. By dawn the head was visible, Barbara fully dilated. Forty-five minutes of pushing and the old woman wrapped the bloody baby girl in a wool blanket, scooped a finger through the baby's mouth to get rid of the slime.

Myles's attitude changed then, and what Barbara had feared—his being disappointed if the child were a girl—never materialized. Instead, he stared at the baby, fascinated. He and Annabel had never conceived, though he never doubted his ability to father a child. Barbara wondered how he could be so sure, but wrote it off to his supreme arrogance. She'd been shattered when the doctor told her she was pregnant, but now, as she accepted the baby from the harried old woman, she forgot all about Myles and Sam and illegitimacy and lost herself in the little girl's stunning green eyes.

"Julia Grace," Barbara said, and holding the baby to her chest, wept.

They walked through the forest, Emily making sarcastic comments about Indiana.

They'd eaten lunch at one of Shadeland's two Chinese restaurants. She'd said the soup tasted like dishwater, that it was nothing like the place in Memphis she frequented. He said the selection wasn't as varied in a small town as it was in a city of two million, and she said you're not kidding.

Then they sat in silence.

It was the way all their conversations seemed to go. It dawned on him that she'd come to Watermere not to check on him, not to assure herself of his well-being, but to retrieve him, to rescue him from the sticks and deliver him to the city, to his old job and his old life, and she was disappointed he didn't need rescuing. She did not like the way his face had emerged from its cocoon of fat. His hair, short and styled rather than longer and askew, bothered her. She said it made him look like he thought he was still in his twenties.

That pissed him off.

She loved reminding him of the passage of time, as though he weren't aware of it without her pointing it out. In times past she'd used his age as a means of scaring him into a marriage proposal. She'd joked about the two of them standing at the altar on walkers, having a nursing home ceremony. Now, she was using the same tactic for an end more cruel. His youth was gone, she was reminding him, his workout regime and new image were a desperate attempt at recapturing it.

It was terribly ironic.

For years she had harped on his lack of cardiovascular fitness, his lack of ambition, and now that he was doing something about it, making the most of the time and resources he had, she was criticizing him.

He was thinking of how unfair she was being when she gasped with delight and left him on the forest path. She was already through the break in the trees before he realized where she was going.

Feeling a trifle light-headed, he followed her into the graveyard.

And damned if she didn't head right to Annabel's tombstone. He lingered near the mouth of the trail and hoped she'd lose interest. But the marker had grabbed her the way it had him, and soon she was calling him over, insisting he take a look at it with her.

He made his way past the smaller markers—several of them guarded by surly crows—and suppressed an irrational fear of her finding out about the novel. She was saying something about how disrespectful it was for people to desecrate so elegant a gravestone, but what got his attention was the way the designs on the marker had gotten clearer since earlier that day. Now not only were the name and dates unscathed, the rest of the carvings had largely recovered as well.

Near the bottom, inches above the sharp rectangular base were two designs. On the right side of the marker was a full moon peeking out of a bank of clouds. On the left was a woman's face, and when he bent to touch it Emily said something that he missed. His breathing slowed and as his feet edged backward through thickening grass, Emily put out a hand, and though he knew she was speaking he no longer heard her voice.

He walked out of the cemetery and down the forest trail. Though she spoke sharply, her words were a muddled haze. He saw a woman in a white gown, her blue eyes bloodshot above her gaunt cheeks. He saw a younger, dark-haired woman who reminded him of Julia. He heard them shouting at one another, and when he returned to the den and the typewriter, he recorded what they said.

Chapter Eighteen

Emily stood outside the house, irresolute. After finally finding Paul locked away inside the office, she rapped on the door and asked him why he'd left her in the forest. He refused to answer her questions or even acknowledge her presence. She'd stood outside the office door listening to the typewriter keys clack away far too rapidly—Paul had always been a hunt-and-peck typist who'd be lucky to crank out thirty words a minute. Finally, she gave up and came outside.

Now, without anything else to do, she decided to take a shower. Her pores were a horror of oil and travel grime, and if she didn't wash up soon, she'd go crazy in her own skin. In fact, she was already feeling a little unstable, the sedatives she'd taken reacting with her regular heart medicine. She knew she shouldn't mix the two, but darn it she needed to calm down.

Emily turned and regarded the old house, the solid red brick that had lasted over a hundred years and would likely last several hundred more. The water, when she'd gotten a drink from the tap, had tasted surprisingly pure. The shower water would be no different.

She thought of the face in the window, the woman's hateful eyes.

Though a shiver plaited down her spine at the memory, her reason nevertheless won out. Even if, she thought as she climbed the porch steps, there was some backwoods voyeur wandering around, the woman was unlikely to bother Emily while she showered.

She went in and stopped at the first bathroom she found. Just off the kitchen, adjacent to what looked like a servant or guest bedroom, she found a tiny but perfectly good toilet, sink and shower stall. *Well,* she thought, *the tinier the better. Fewer places for vermin to hide.* She'd heard them earlier, skulking in the shadows of the ballroom, and had no desire for a further encounter.

Quickly, she retrieved her black travel tote from the kitchen table and returned to the little room. The décor left much to be desired: pink wallpaper with a paisley design, chocolate brown pedestal sink and toilet, a hazy glass shower stall with more than a little rust creeping up its metal frame. An odd falling sensation tumbled through her, and she grasped the sink edge to steady herself. God, she better not mix her meds anymore. Though she'd never experimented with drugs, she supposed this weird, unsettled sensation was how they made a person feel.

When the room stopped tilting, she opened the shower door and looked with repugnance at the swirling rust stain, the ancient drain grate gone black with age. Emily twisted on the hot and cold knobs and was pleasantly surprised at the clearness of the water that spewed forth. Within moments the water was hot enough to steam up the mirror. All the better. She had no desire to see any more than she already had of the room. Renovating it would be, she decided, one of the first jobs she tackled at Watermere.

The clean white towel she'd brought curled in a ball on the edge of the sink, Emily peeled off her shirt and stepped out of her jeans. The steamy air was exhilarating on her bare skin. God, how she'd been craving a shower. The smell of the hot water, lazy and faintly metallic, routed the dank scent of must that had until now predominated. Her bra unclasped and hung over a towel rod, she drew down her underwear and tossed them aside. Immediately the drowsy mist moistened her pubic hair. The sultry air caressed the skin of her bare buttocks. Emily reached out and rubbed clear a circle on the mirror. The condensation wetted her hand, but rather than drying it on the towel, she slowly drew her palm along her belly, just under the navel. Her nipples hardened.

Making sure the lock on the doorknob was fixed in place, she crossed to the shower and gradually made her way under the scalding water. Ordinarily she hated too-hot showers, but this one felt sublime. The painful needling on her skin, the steam filling her lungs and nearly stealing her breath... God, it was so good it was all she could do not to faint. One hand braced on the white wall beside the showerhead, she leaned forward and took her time with it, her right hand kneading her breasts. Her fingers crawled down her tummy, massaging. The delicious burning water sprayed over her forehead, her eyelids, pure sweet runnels of it lapping over her lips, her teeth. She drank in the tropical spray, the wall upon which she leaned changing, growing pliant, rubbery, the warm surface writhing beneath her fingertips—

Emily froze.

She opened her eyes and saw the outline of a face and a large pair of hands reaching toward her. She opened her mouth to scream but couldn't.

She watched the large finger shapes in the wall swelling and closing over her hand, the face pressing forward, leering, the pupilless eyes mere inches from her own, the showerhead itself bowing up from the strain of the undulating wall.

Emily screamed.

She pulled away, and in the moment before her elbow crashed against the stall door, she saw—she *felt*—the large fingers pulling her hand into the wall, the staring face grinning in triumph.

Emily landed on the pink tile and dove for the door. Her wet fingers fumbled about the lock for an eternity before she ripped open the door and dashed to the foyer. She'd never in her life been out of doors without clothes on, but she scarcely noticed her nakedness as she sprinted over the biting gravel driveway to the Camry. Her hands were shaking so wildly she was barely able to work the ignition, and she cut the wheel too severely as she swerved out of the garage. The edge of the driver's side bumper scraped against the wooden garage as she arrowed the Camry toward the lane, the car sluing as rocks spattered the surrounding grass.

She had to calm down, had to corral her galloping heart. She'd escaped, that was what mattered. If she spiraled out of control now, she would only have herself to blame.

There, she thought as she pulled onto the empty country road. *That was better. Safe and away from the house, from the staring, ravenous face and those horrible writhing hands.*

Then, a thought jolted through her, and Emily's foot recoiled from the accelerator. The Camry decelerated quickly, the gravel road grabbing her tires as if refusing to let Emily leave. She stopped the car, moved the gearshift to park.

What on earth was she doing?

She thought of the sedative her doctor had prescribed...Zolpidem, that had been its name. He gave it to her for insomnia, but when she looked it up on the Internet she learned it also had hallucinogenic qualities. And that didn't even take into account how it might interact with her heart medication, her birth control.

So what was more likely? That she'd experienced an upsetting—and incredibly vivid—hallucination brought on by prescription drugs or that a monstrous male figure living in the walls of Watermere caught her masturbating?

She slumped forward on the wheel, a weary laughter taking hold. To think she'd nearly thrown away this new life with Paul because of a fluky drug reaction. Was she really so skittish? She continued to laugh as she pointed the car toward the shoulder and began the process of turning around. By the time she was heading back to Watermere, she'd all but managed to discount the idea that there were spirits inside the old house, that there'd been rubbery hands growing out of the tile walls. As the Camry moved down the lane, she was able to dismiss nearly every detail of the hallucination.

But try as she would, the leering white face would not completely fade.

Timmons and McLaughlin sat across from Sam, and Sam could tell by their faces that they'd rather be discussing anything but the disappearance of Daryl Applegate. Though no one could stand the guy, his vanishing had clearly shaken both deputies.

He couldn't blame them.

Sam knew they'd come up with the same thing—nothing—that it was a waste of time, but he knew he wouldn't get much done today anyway, so what was the use of pretending it wasn't on all their minds? He wished he'd met them somewhere other than the police station. Lately, he hated coming here, as though the dual disappearances of Brand and Applegate were proof he didn't belong here, didn't deserve the job.

Doug Timmons started them off. "Deputy Applegate's car was found at the quarry, near the back part that's never used. No fingerprints were found inside Deputy Applegate's—"

"I think we can call him Daryl," Sam said.

He noticed his two deputies studying him, imagined what they saw. Eyes bloodshot from too much drinking and too little sleep, three days' growth of beard, the shirt of his uniform even more wrinkled than normal, a coffee stain on the belly. He didn't worry so much about Doug Timmons, who was thirty-five and had a wife and three daughters. But Tommy McLaughlin was younger, more impressionable. He was looking at Sam like a boy whose dad just struck out to lose a father-son baseball game.

Barlow sat up in his chair, tried to get it together. "Go on, Doug. You were talking about where Daryl's car was found. As luck would have it—bad luck, I should say—the cruiser wasn't discovered until three days after he was last seen. We'd assumed—wrongly, it seems—that being the screw-up he was, he just knocked off early on the night of the Fourth and went home. He wasn't due back to work until the sixth, and none of us really worried about him until the seventh."

"When the foreman at the quarry called," McLaughlin said.

"Right," Sam said. "So we know the last anyone saw of him was the evening of Independence Day, and that was me."

McLaughlin said, "No one saw Daryl leave here, so we can't say for sure when our window starts and ends."

"Say eight o'clock," Sam said. "I left the station at seven that evening to take in the fireworks, and Daryl wouldn't have left right away. So we've got from eight o'clock on the night of the Fourth to three p.m. on the seventh, when the quarry called."

"That's a pretty big window," Timmons said.

"Let's talk specifics," Sam said, feeling better to be discussing facts, even if they'd been covered a dozen times before. "Daryl's car was found on the north side of town, inside the limestone quarry behind a mountainous pile of rocks."

"Whoever drove the car there was probably not Daryl," Timmons said, "so the car was put there to hide it."

"Or to make us think Daryl had disappeared there," McLaughlin added.

Sam nodded, said, "Whoever ditched the car—if it wasn't Daryl, and I agree with Doug it probably wasn't—either had an accomplice who picked him up from that point and drove away, or else left on foot."

"The quarry's in the middle of nowhere. If someone walked away from there, he had a long way to get back to wherever he was going," Timmons said.

"And the county boys found nothing?" McLaughlin asked.

"Not a thing," Sam said.

"Just like Ted Brand," Timmons said, voicing what they'd all been thinking.

Sam crossed his arms. "Let's go down that road, Doug. We've discussed it already, but there might be something we missed." He put his feet up on the desk. "Both missing persons are men between the ages of twenty-five and forty-five. One was a good-looking guy with an affluent job and a nice car. The other one was..."

"Daryl," McLaughlin said.

"That's right," Sam said. "Not exactly twins, but not completely different either. Brand had a history of skirt-chasing, and we know Daryl liked women an awful lot too."

"It's all he talked about," Timmons said. He opened his mouth to expand on that, but stopped. Sam commiserated. It was the way all their brainstorming sessions went. They danced around it, but the truth was that Daryl was bad news. Sam knew the guy had been a heel, but the more he heard from his two remaining deputies, the more he realized Applegate had held back when he was around. Timmons had gotten on Daryl's computer and found a good many nude pictures of teenage girls. McLaughlin talked about Daryl's extensive porn collection, how the tapes were just lying around the house. Sam knew a lot of guys who got into the stuff, but to leave it lying around in plain sight, to make no effort to conceal it from people who might stop by...

Which brought him to another revelation about Daryl Applegate. The guy was a total loner. He'd suspected as much, but he'd never realized to what extent Daryl craved yet almost never received human contact. The bartenders down at Easter's Tavern—a shithole if ever there was one, a place Sam wouldn't be caught dead in and only visited when there was trouble there—said Daryl was a regular. He'd come in four or five times a week to drink and shoot pool.

But after he'd been there awhile he'd just stare. A waitress said it creeped her out. Like when he was drinking he forgot how impolite it was to ogle a woman for minutes on end. What bothered Sam, one of

216

the many things he found out about Applegate while investigating his disappearance, was the way Daryl had spouted off about being a cop if anyone ever called him on his behavior. He'd play that card every chance he got, it seemed. A boyfriend or a husband got tired of him eyeing his girl or wife, Daryl would pull out his badge, remind him he was still a cop even if he was off-duty. But Applegate hardly ever got lucky. He was too drunk and too grating for even the easiest of the local barflies.

Realizing both deputies were watching him, wondering what was on his mind, Sam said, "We know that Daryl had no shortage of enemies. There were enough people he'd written tickets for, mouthed off to, that the perpetrator could be any number of people. How'd your latest check go, Doug?"

Timmons counted off the leads on his fingers. "There were four guys who had run-ins with Applegate who also had criminal records. One of them has since moved to Arizona. Of the other three, one has an airtight alibi—he was at the fireworks with his family, home with his family, or working at the trailer factory during the period we're talking about—one is in jail, and the other, well, the other we're still looking into."

Sam knew the suspect Timmons was talking about. Everyone but Kenny Sayler was alibied out.

And Kenny Sayler hated Daryl Applegate.

Sayler was a drunk whose only alibi was that he'd spent most of that time working on the slipshod deck he was trying to slap onto his rundown house. What bothered Sam was the interval between the guy's last dispute with Daryl and Daryl's disappearance. They'd had a run-in over a year ago about a traffic violation that had carried over into Easter's Tavern. Sayler had threatened Daryl, and the witnesses said Applegate had tried to arrest him but was too drunk to actually do it. None of them thought Kenny Sayler was capable of murder, but Sam wasn't ruling him out. He lived on Gordon Road, which Ted Brand would have traveled the night of his disappearance. Could Sayler have been the motorist who gave the lawyer a ride? Might Ted Brand's body be buried under Sayler's new deck?

He'd interviewed the man already, and he seemed clean. Stupid, a bit truculent, but probably not a killer. Still, it was all they had.

Sam said, "Doug, I want you to go to Easter's tonight, see what you can find out."

"We've all three been there already."

"Not during happy hour. Maybe they'll say more when they're drunk. Watch Sayler, see how he acts."

"Okay," Timmons sighed, resigned.

"Tommy," Sam said, "you talk to Sayler's co-workers at the gas station. See what they have to say about his altercation with Daryl. Maybe he let something slip."

McLaughlin followed Timmons to the door.

"I'm going to meet with Daryl's father to tell him we don't have jack," Sam said.

McLaughlin grinned. "Tell the selectman we send our regards."

On the drive over Sam thought of how Daryl had looked at Julia, how the guy had gone quiet whenever she was mentioned. It made him think of Ted Brand, of how a guy like him would have gone crazy over a beauty like her. How Brand might have stopped to offer her a ride, hoping to get more.

Thinking of that got him remembering what happened fifteen years before, and that got him dialing through the radio, hoping to find a song that would bring his mind back to the present. He found one by George Strait, "The Fireman." One of his favorites. He tried singing along but his heart wasn't in it. Not for the first time that day he wondered if he'd done the right thing back then.

Or whether he'd created a monster.

Emily decided to wait outside for Paul.

She wondered if she could find her way back to the graveyard, see that stone he'd freaked out about. It certainly was unique—elaborate designs scarred by ugly hands, the sheer size of the stone and its obsidian hue—but did that warrant Paul's reaction? He acted like touching the thing put him into some kind of trance. Then that childish show of his newfound athleticism, the mad dash through the woods. Proving to her he still had a lot of growing up to do. But wasn't that why he needed her?

To her left, the undergrowth rustled. Emily pivoted that way, scanned the brush but could see nothing. Of course it was nothing. Funny, though, how much it had sounded like a person.

Her stomach growled. She thought of turning back, either forcing him into talking to her or getting something to eat. But the way Paul talked, he was going to be at it awhile. What was more, seeing his new streamlined frame had rendered her self-conscious. In the past she'd thought her body better-shaped than his, but now his muscles made her more aware of her little pot belly, her thick ankles. It wouldn't kill her to skip a meal.

She thought of how he'd acted, so intent on locking her out of the den. Emily pursed her lips. It was just another boyish display meant to show her how changed he was. His attempt to prove once and for all his moving here had been the right thing. Well, if that's what it took for him to feel vindicated, she'd let him have his little delusion. As for her, she'd believe he was a writer when she saw his name on the bestseller list.

She turned and though she was far too deep in the forest to see the house, she pictured him up there, in the den window, typing in that pathetic way he had. She wondered what tripe he was trying to pawn off as fiction.

It was getting dark. She started back toward the house, amazed at how much time had passed. The last place she wanted to be was within those walls without Paul by her side, but it would soon be night, and she couldn't stay out here.

Unbidden, the leering white face loomed in her memory.

"*No*," she said aloud, shaking her head. Her heart stuttered painfully in her chest, her throat suddenly desiccated by fear. If it wasn't a drug reaction, there was no explaining what had happened to her, but not everything could be explained, could it? Look at Paul, who was almost an entirely new person, so different from the uncertain man she'd known.

You mean the man you could dominate, a voice whispered.

Emily's nostrils flared as she sucked in frustrated breath. Yes, the old Paul had been more tractable, but hadn't he been a little boring, as well? A bit too predictable?

She remembered their kiss earlier, the only real contact they'd had before he went loony tunes and left her in the graveyard. His mouth

219

had been hot, his tongue strong and sensual. The feel of his muscles bunching under her fingertips, the broad outcropping of his chest pressing into her.

The woman watching from the window.

Gasping, Emily whirled, half-expecting a tall female figure to be bearing down on her. But the driveway and the surrounding woods were untenanted, quiet save for the swelling chorus of insects.

Soon it would be dark. And she was certain she hadn't imagined the woman in the window.

Shivering, Emily jogged up the porch steps and reentered Watermere.

September, 1988

The girl was excited to finally explore Watermere. Though she knew she shouldn't have snuck away from her mom, the thrill of seeing the whole place for the first time more than made up for her guilt. She'd thought she'd be scared once alone in the vast house, but a velvety sense of calm fell over her as she stepped inside the library. The scents of old books and worn leather comforted her. The view of the forest made her feel like a princess in some enchanted castle. Even the large painting over the fireplace brought with it a peculiar reassurance. The woman in the light blue dress had to be Annabel, her mom's patient. Her mom had said some bad things about the woman, but with a face like that how bad could she be?

"What a nice surprise," a voice croaked from behind her.

Julia whirled, backpedaled away from the haggard woman limping through the doorway. The woman's appearance was unpleasant enough, but after seeing how Annabel had once looked, the sight of the woman's red eyes and cracked lips made Julia's throat constrict.

Annabel was saying something, but the only word Julia caught was "whore."

Julia watched Annabel with wide eyes. "What?" she asked.

"I said, you should know your mother is a whore."

"What's a whore?" the girl asked.

"A creature who sleeps with other women's husbands."

"Oh."

"Your mother is one, dear."

"Oh."

"You should also know I don't treat whores kindly." Annabel winked with one watery eye. *"The last time one made a play for my husband—this was my second husband, dear, and many years ago—I made sure she never did it again, to anyone."*

The girl's face clouded. She cocked her head.

"But my mom takes care of you."

"How old are you, dear?"

"I'm six."

"As young as that?"

Julia nodded, wished there were a way to escape the library without passing by this hideous creature.

"Then I'll give you some advice, darling. Appreciate your mommy now." Annabel grinned. *"While you still have her."*

It felt good to get back inside the house. But the good feeling faded when, halfway up the third story stairs, she heard the clatter of the typewriter. She could volunteer to type for him, she knew, but that would be an endorsement of his new diversion, and what he needed was a swift kick in the rear end. He needed to reclaim his old job at the bank.

She knew James, his older brother, would welcome him back. His father would be a tougher sell, but in the end she knew she could soften the man's heart enough to smooth the way for Paul. She sighed, moving down the stairs. Paul still had to apologize to his father for leaving, and Paul was fantastic at screwing things up.

Emily was thinking this when she heard the scratching sounds.

They filled the ballroom, sent chills through her body. She realized she had to urinate, that the sounds weren't helping her hold it in.

What on earth?

They increased, changing. It sounded like dying birds writhing in a field of skeletons, and my God, what else did she hear?

Laughter, faint but undeniably real.

Hands at her throat, Emily backed toward the bar, sure that at any moment a black throng of demons would swarm over her and pick her bones clean.

"*Stop it,*" she shouted. "*Stop laughing at me!*"

But the noise grew, doubling in intensity until she found herself scuttling around the edge of the bar, taking refuge in the shadows between the bottles and the wall. She sank to her knees, hands clamped over her ears, screaming now, entreating the voices to stop and wondering why the hell Paul wasn't coming. Couldn't he *hear?*

On all fours now, Emily stiffened. *My God,* she thought, *maybe that was it...maybe he didn't hear.*

Maybe the sounds were all in her mind.

Just like the face you imagined in the shower, the groping hands.

No.

You felt guilty for masturbating, so you created a leering white face to punish yourself.

Absurd.

How else to explain it, Emily? the voice cajoled. *How else if not your overactive imagination and your weak heart?*

"Got to relax," she told herself. Her forehead beaded with sweat, Emily lay on her belly and rested her right cheek on the cool wooden floor. There, that was what she needed. Something to moor her, to make her feel solid and in control again.

She had lain that way for some time when she realized the noises had ceased. She raised her head, the skin of her cheek making a peeling sound that reminded her of removing a sticker from plastic. She listened hard but could hear nothing but the muted tick of a clock.

Exhaling a long breath, she slumped to the floor and stared at the wall opposite the bar. She felt protected here, the liquor bottles behind her and the white wall under the mirror forming a pleasant enclosure, a talisman against the machinations of her fancy. Nothing could harm her, and what was there to fear anyway? Dust? The occasional rodent? This house was no more haunted than—

Under her the floor moved.

Emily's eyes stretched wide, her body tensing into one hypersensitive knot. She was sure she'd felt something ripple just above her navel. Impossible, yes, but she knew what she'd felt, and regardless of what her mind told her—

The wood beneath her palms squirmed.

Emily stared in stunned dismay as wooden fingers laced with hers, the floor somehow malleable and very much alive. All around her the cool surface flowed and rippled, and though she tried to disengage her hands, the brown fingers clutched her, squeezed, pulled her toward a face materializing in the wood, deep eye sockets gaping, the hideous grin worse than before. It had lured her here, she realized, sent her scurrying back here for safety so it could have its way, and as she strained to lift her chin away from the open mouth, she felt something brush her thighs, something curved and hard.

When Emily glimpsed the gigantic wooden phallus she screamed and thrashed, one hand slipping loose but the other one still gripped tight by the laughing, leering monster whose body was now farther out of the floor than it was a part of it, the muscular arms freed to the elbows, the hips actually thrusting upward in an effort to rupture her underwear, to impale her with its filth.

In desperation she seized the first object her free hand touched. She lifted a large brown bottle and shattered it in the leering face, and the ballroom exploded in a fusillade of screams. The hand that bound her let go, and Emily lunged against the wall. The arms groped toward her, the face now contorted with horrible longing. Within the shadowy wooden maw she could see the tongue darting in idiot lust. She pressed her shoulder blades against the wall, sidled away from the male figure, which was now only connected to the floor by a few umbilical strands of writhing wood.

Powerful white tentacles enveloped her. She slapped at them, shrieked with what strength remained, glimpsed pale knuckles, ghostly white fingernails.

Something bit the middle of her back.

Emily leaped forward, but the steely fingers caught her and jerked her back to the wall. She strained against them, whirled, and now she was staring at her own reflection, at the long strip of mirror above the bar.

For a moment, she couldn't even scream.

In the mirror's reflection she saw the walls of the great hall alive with male figures, their faces stamped with agony and lust and lunatic wrath. In the floors, the walls, the wainscoting, everywhere she looked, the surfaces of the ballroom were attenuated with flexing fingers, the striations of leg muscles, the obscene sickles of engorged penises.

Emily closed her eyes against the hellish scene, and only then did she realize the hands grasping her arms, her skirt, were dragging her ever closer to the wall.

Three inches from it she opened her eyes and beheld the silvery face forming in the mirror. She opened her mouth to cry out to Paul and then the mirrored lips closed over hers, Emily's image swallowing herself in a smothering kiss. A hard, slick tongue filled her mouth. A pulsing phallus thrust under the edge of her skirt, bumped feverishly against her, bruised the skin around her labia. Scrabbling fingers tore at her underwear, a sea of arms pinioning her legs against the wall, offering her up for the demons who dwelt there. The mirrored face was half out of the wall now, one of Emily's legs already swallowed up, as if she were being absorbed by the creatures.

Please God no.

Weeping, Emily summoned what strength she still possessed and shoved against the mirror. A bright burst of pain stitched her fingers. She glanced at them and realized she still grasped the jagged neck of the bottle. Without thinking she thrust the gleaming brown shards into the side of the mirror creature's face. She felt the creature scream, gagged as its hard wormy tongue slithered out of her mouth.

A rush of heat swam away from her and she felt herself released, her body slumping in an enervated pile. Groaning, she crawled away from the wall and saw they were still coming out of the walls, their unholy births nearly complete. Their faces were enraged now, grimly resolute. As she rose unsteadily to her feet she saw, dear God, an ichorous black substance trickle slowly down her leg.

Under her bare toes, the floor undulated.

Hissing, Emily broke for the hallway, made it, plunged through the reaching arms that slapped and clawed at her shoulders, her face. She made it to the foyer and discovered a figure rising from the tile, the black and white squares stretching, adhering to the brawny shoulders, the enormous arms banded with ropes of muscle. She sidestepped the articulating figure, careful to avoid the walls, and stumbled out into the night.

April, 1990

Annabel threw the bedpan at her, cackled as hot black excrement spattered Barbara's face. Gagging and spitting, Barbara ran for the door. The wraith rose from the bed, her gown a sheer curtain draping bony shoulders, and razored one walkingstick finger at her.

"You're a goddamned whore!" she shrieked.

Weeping, Barbara stumbled into the hallway. The stink from Annabel's shit wriggled into her sinuses, sullied her thoughts.

The smell overwhelmed her. She dropped to her knees at the top of the stairs. Her gorge clenched. Her chest contracted and her breathing ceased. Then the burning chunks dragged agonizing claws up her throat and exploded through her mouth and nose. She retched and moaned and another wave seized her and now there was blood in the bile and digesting food.

"No," she pleaded. "No."

In moments the dry heaving stopped. Barbara looked at the vomit-stained carpet between her hands. This was it. Her attraction to Myles was as nothing next to her deathless loathing of the chortling invalid who now haunted her very dreams. The time to leave this place was years ago. She knew her life was misspent, her reputation ruined. That did not mean her daughter must also fall prey to the wickedness dwelling between these walls. And inside them.

Barbara shut her eyes against the terrible memories of what she'd seen. To escape them, she thought of her daughter.

She still had Julia.

Julia, who had grown into such a beautiful little girl. Julia, who was only in the first grade, yet smart enough to read the classics. Julia, who could not understand why they almost never visited her father even though he lived so close.

Thinking of her daughter, of how much fun they would have as she grew up, Barbara pushed herself onto her feet and felt a pair of bony hands shove her forward over the top stairstep. Crying out, she tried to brace herself with an outstretched foot. Her heel skipped off the edge of the step. She felt her leg folding under and a red pain ripping through her groin. The cackling laugh accompanied her tumble down the stairs.

Each step found a new body part to punish. Her temple banged the edge of a stairstep, her sprained left ankle ricocheted off the banister. Her head twisted as her body toppled over her and just as she was certain her neck must snap, she felt the wooden floor beneath her.

"You think you can have him once I'm gone but you're wrong," *Annabel growled.*

Opening her eyes, Barbara stared up at the ballroom ceiling. Her neck screaming in protest, she leaned forward and glimpsed the figure in the dirty white garment limping her way down the stairs. How could an invalid, backside chancred with bedsores, move so swiftly?

Unless she'd been feigning weakness, biding her time.

Barbara pushed herself toward the front door. Annabel's feet, made ghostly by the pale morning light, slapped the foyer tile. Something flashed at the crazy woman's side, and Barbara spotted the scissors clutched in her left hand.

Barbara chided herself. How could she have been so careless? One did not leave a lethal object on the bedstand of an insane person.

Annabel was coming fast now, her yellow teeth bared. Chin glazed with spittle, she towered over Barbara and raised the scissors. Wincing at the grinding in her ankle, Barbara rolled away as the steel points thunked on the floor where her throat had been.

Where was Myles?

On her bad ankle she was not swift, but she was still able to drag herself across the foyer, gain her feet, and escape through the door. Feeling sure she led Annabel by twenty or thirty feet, she allowed herself a look over her shoulder and it was then that the demon burst through the door and threw her wasted body on top of her. Barbara screamed and felt her feet leave the porch. A moment later, the wind was knocked from her as they hit the ground in a tangled heap. They struggled there on the concrete, Annabel's hand grasping the scissors, Barbara clutching Annabel's wrist to keep the scissors from descending. Barbara forced a palm under Annabel's chin and arched her back to rid herself of the woman's weight. Annabel swatted her hand and lunged at her throat. Barbara howled as rotting incisors pierced the soft flesh under her chin. Desperate, she dug her nails into the skin of the woman's shoulders. Annabel gasped and came away, mouth bloodied and covered with bits of Barbara's flesh. In terror, Barbara swiped at

Annabel's exposed throat and laughed in satisfaction as the skin parted in crimson grooves. Gurgling, Annabel rolled off and clutched her throat. The two women regarded each other.

Even now, blood seeping through her shriveled fingers, Annabel mocked her with her laughing blue eyes.

Barbara whimpered and scrambled to her feet. The first step on her bad ankle sent pain lancing up her leg. She hopped on her good foot, using her bad ankle only as a crutch. As she neared the forest path she cast a glance back at the porch and was amazed to see Annabel rising to her feet. It was impossible. The woman was losing too much blood.

Her white gown drenched red, Annabel bent low as she ran, her varicose legs carrying her through the yard toward her prey.

Barbara wiped the tears from her eyes and disappeared into the woods.

Behind her, she heard the woman follow.

Barbara clenched her jaw. She knew these woods as well as Annabel. She concentrated on the path ahead and blocked out the sound of the crazy woman calling out to her.

"Steal my husband will you? Get rid of me so your little whelp can have a daddy?"

Barbara felt her ankle giving way. She tried to hop without landing on it but that only made it worse when she did. This was no sprain. She knew by the way it jiggled and swung loose that it was broken, busted and dangling, a useless appendage. If she survived this she would be in a wheelchair for a long time, and that was an ugly irony. Annabel had allowed her to believe she could not walk and now it was clear that all that time she'd been planning this, waiting to attack when Myles was away.

It was no use. Barbara could not escape on one leg. She had to fight. Barbara knew it would be to the death. Stopping, she steeled herself for the final confrontation. She lifted her hand for a swipe at her enemy's eyes.

Her hand falling, Barbara stared in disbelief.

Annabel was gone.

Barbara's eyes strained into the trees. To get off the trail, Annabel would have to have climbed up an embankment. To do that, she had to have considerable strength left.

227

Barbara should not have been surprised, she knew. Annabel's strength, even as the disease ate away at her body, was uncanny. It was the only reason Barbara had not slain the woman in her sleep. Poison was out because Annabel made her taste everything before handing it to her. She could have used conventional means to murder her, but a superstitious dread always choked her courage. Knives could miss their mark. Guns could jam. The only sure way was to allow the disease to take her by degrees. If she had known it would take seven years to wring the life from her, she wouldn't have waited.

Keep moving, she reminded herself.

She had just started running again when the shadow swept over her and the unspeakable pain ripped through her back.

As she drove down the deserted country lane, she concentrated on keeping to the center of the road, to for god's sake *not* end up in a ditch.

Though she fought to keep her mind off it, Emily remembered the chalky feel of the white fingers scraping her flesh. *God.* She shivered, the little hairs on her hands bristling.

Would those things...get Paul?

Who cares? the voice of self-preservation answered. *You're out of there, and that's all that matters.*

Are you really that callous? her conscience rejoined.

Moaning, Emily punched the wheel.

She still loved him, she realized now. He had his faults—and they were serious ones—but he also had many endearing traits.

And now he was alone in that house of horrors.

She had to do something.

That's right, the practical part of her shouted. *You need to get the hell out of here and back to Memphis, where the walls aren't full of monsters trying to rape you.*

Ahead and to her right she spotted the dim glow of Shadeland. Another country road was approaching. She could either keep going and eventually hit the state road that would lead her to the interstate, or she could turn right onto the gravel road, head into town and tell the police that Paul was in danger.

Emily blew hair out of her eyes and thought of the police's reaction. They'd think her crazy.

You're going to let your fear of ridicule keep you from saving Paul?

"Dammit," she said. She flicked on her brights and turned toward Shadeland.

The gravel road was pitted and dark, the woods on either side dense and overflowing. Her heart stuttering ominously, Emily bit her lip. Had she made a mistake? If Paul had lived there safely all these months, why would he be in any danger now? It was her they wanted, not Paul.

Time to go home, Emily. Paul can take care of himself.

She slowed, ready now to turn around and head back toward the state road, but there was little room to maneuver, and the last thing she needed was to get stuck in a rut and have to hike back to town. She thought again of Paul, of his obsession with horror movies and books, and remembered one of the novels he'd all but forced her to read. She forgot the name now, but it had scared the living crap out of her. The setting, she remembered, was very much like this. Deep in the woods, far from any living soul. The branches smacking the side of her car, her wheels jouncing on the primitive road all sounded like a tribe of demented cannibals. She resolved to never read another scary book again.

Emily gripped the wheel tighter, thinking of the creatures that had nearly raped her, nearly killed her. She thought of the tongue poking around in her mouth, the penis befouling her skin. *Damn you, Paul,* she thought. *Damn you for leading me to such a horrible place.*

The woods closed in on her bouncing car and she thought of the horror novel, the scene in which the main character had glanced at the rearview mirror and seen the killer staring at her from the backseat.

"Oh God," Emily said. The hair on the nape of her neck tingled. She willed her eyes to stay on the road, but knew she had to look. She thought of the leering faces in the walls, the vile laughter surrounding her.

Emily glanced up at the mirror. In the gloom she could barely see the backseat.

It appeared to be empty.

Relaxing a little, Emily turned her attention back to driving and saw the woman in the white dress standing in the road, grinning at her.

Emily screamed and wrenched the wheel. All she could see was the woman's leer, the hateful blue eyes, as the Camry left the road and soared over the lip of the ravine, the front end dipping and heading for a huge stone.

She opened her mouth to scream again, but the weight of the car crushed her on the rock. The car continued over, flipping and settling on its blown tires.

Emily lay limp in her seatbelt, her eyes seeping blood.

April 1990

Julia looked up from her reading. Someone had knocked on the screen door. Setting her book of poems on the floor beside the rocking chair, she moved through the silent house. She hoped her mother had come home. She opened the screen door.

And saw the bad woman in the hospital gown disappear into the woods.

Julia looked down.

Her mother lay in the grass below the porch, the skin around her face gone. She walked down the steps and stared at where her mother's face had been.

She saw her mom's white skirt had been raised, her underwear taken off. Sticking out of her, only the circular handles visible, was a pair of scissors.

Book Three

Annabel

Chapter Nineteen

Paul ran to get it out of his system, the polluted way he felt after the automatic writing, if that's what it was. He caught a glimpse of himself afterward, a shadowy reflection in a picture frame in the den. He'd glanced at his reflection first, not liking what he saw. Then, he pulled focus and saw what was in the photograph.

In it were his uncle and a woman not his uncle's wife. The lady looked an awful lot like Julia. Myles had an arm slung around the woman's waist in a casual way, like he was used to doing it.

What really caught his attention, though, was his own face, transposed on top of his uncle's. Myles was shorter, a bit more compact, but absent of that, the resemblance was unsettling. Rather than lingering on it, he went on a run.

Around him the shadows were marshaling over the forest. The droning whir of the cicadas swallowed the sound of his padding sneakers.

Emily was gone, had probably been gone for hours. The only guilt he felt was at not feeling guilty. He knew he should, they'd been together for a long time before breaking up. Yet stripped of his needfulness, the relationship crumbled. Since he was no longer her project, there was really no need for them to pretend. He'd not been surprised to see the red car gone from the driveway, was actually relieved she'd come to the same conclusion on her own.

What scratched at his thoughts was the new novel. It was a sequel of sorts to *The Monkey Killer*. He'd gotten a bit of the first notebook, the red one, down in type, read through it absently as he hunted and pecked. Annabel and Myles were again the main characters, though their relationship had begun to change in much the same way as

Annabel's relationship with David had.

Paul had a hard time believing it was all true. Though he didn't like to linger on the identity of the author behind the work, he couldn't help but wonder if it was Myles, Annabel, or his own subconscious. Reason dictated the first two choices were outlandish. The notion of a literal ghost writer was the stuff of horror novels. Much more likely was the possibility of his cobbling together the elements he knew—Barlow's story, the snatches of innuendo he'd overheard from his parents growing up, his own exploration of Watermere—and fashioning them into a coherent narrative with his own imagination.

Then why did he feel so helpless? And why did he remember so little of the writing?

He'd heard authors say they created the characters and let them do their thing. Was this how it felt? His characters were already created for him, their internal logic innate. Was it really that much of a stretch to suppose he was capable of recreating the past?

And who was to say the novels were really true? Julia recognized enough of her father in *The Monkey Killer* to be enraged. That meant there had to be a dark pearl of truth in the narrative. Yet she didn't believe the tale completely. Just the opposite, she refuted it, insisted he was telling lies about the dead.

He thought of Julia as a child, how it must have been for her. No wonder she had trouble trusting people. The sight of her mother, brutally murdered, must have caused irreparable damage.

Maybe he could help. It had taken the unfortunate episode with Emily to show him how much Julia meant to him, but the point was, he realized it now. She was the best thing that had ever happened to him. Wasn't it possible she could forgive him?

Feeling better, Paul chugged through the forest and wondered where the story would go.

Julia was sitting on her porch when he emerged from the forest. She watched him approach and did her best to keep her expression neutral.

He was looking at her now with an expression she couldn't place. His face was thinner than when she'd seen him last, his body sturdier.

His arms were fuller, roped with muscles that reminded her of the pictures she'd seen of her Uncle David.

"Julia," he began. "I—"

But she cut him off. "I miss you," she said.

It stopped him.

"I miss you too," he replied. "I'm sorry about the things I wrote."

She nodded, moved closer. He seemed taller than before, and that, too, reminded her of David Carver.

She said, "I've heard writers say that they have to write, they don't really have a choice."

The way he gaped at her, she'd caught him off guard.

"Is that true?" she asked.

"Well, yeah," he said. "As a matter of fact, it *was* like that."

"And I can't fault you for wanting to make money."

"I didn't write it for money."

She watched him for a moment. Then, she stepped onto the sidewalk. He stood up straighter now, and that too made him seem larger than before.

"I'm glad you came," she said. She laced her fingers behind his neck, liking the sweaty feel of his skin on her wrists.

"Yeah?"

"Very much."

She almost kissed him then, but waited, wanting him to do it. She felt him growing hard against her, felt herself go a little dizzy from wanting him. Their argument seemed very distant, her anger disproportionate to the situation. Standing here with him, the late summer air close and humid, all she wanted was to go inside, to give herself up to him, her windows open and the heat drowsing over them as they lay in bed.

His frown stopped her.

"What is it?" she asked.

He wouldn't meet her eyes as he said, "I think I've messed things up again."

She waited.

"Remember me talking about an ex-girlfriend? The one I wasn't very good to?"

235

"Yes," she said, pretending to think. "It was Emily, wasn't it?"

"That's right." He grew shamefaced. "The thing is, I don't know how to say this to you without ruining the moment."

"Then just say it."

"After you and I stopped seeing one another, a lot of time went by—at least, it felt like a lot of time."

"A month," she said.

"It felt like longer."

She waited.

He said, "Emily showed up again."

"Did she?"

"Yes."

"Is she still with you?"

He met her gaze then. "No. She went back."

"To Memphis?"

"I guess so. She never told me."

"She just left?"

He shrugged. "Things didn't exactly go well. I realized how different things are now."

"How do you mean?"

"I don't know. Lots of things. Like the way she always talks to me. I never noticed it before, but it's more like a parent scolding a child than a man and woman talking to each other."

"So you broke it off?"

His expression was pained. "Yeah, I did, but that's not what I need to tell you."

"Go ahead."

"While she was here," he said, "last night..."

Though she knew what was coming, had seen it all through the windowpane, she had to fight to keep her voice even. "Yes?"

"We kissed," he said.

She sank her nails into her fingers.

"You're angry," he said.

She said nothing, waiting for the rest.

"I'm sorry, Julia. I thought you and I were done."

236

Her nails dug, the blood wet on her fingers.

He went on, "I know it's hard for you to believe, but that's all that happened."

She stopped. "You didn't sleep with her?"

He shook his head. "I don't know if I'm in love with you or not, but what I feel for you is more than I ever felt for Emily. I don't say that to be cruel to her. I only mean you're the one I think about all the time, the one I wish would come over and enjoy the house with me."

"The house," Julia said.

"Not the house itself, but the experience of it. The spending time there. Making it beautiful the way it used to be."

She felt her anger abating. "Close your eyes," she said.

He did. It gave her a chance to wipe her bloody hands on the seat of her black shorts.

"Can I open them yet?"

"Sure."

"Don't I get a surprise or something?"

"That depends on what else you have to say."

He said, "I screwed up and I'm sorry."

She didn't know whether to laugh or be furious with him, but she must have smiled because he was grinning and moving in to kiss her. She put a hand on his chest to stop him, and then regretted it when he stopped, stared at her hand.

"I cut it gardening," she said.

He took her hands, examined them.

"There are cuts all over your palms."

She pulled her hands away, angry at being scrutinized.

"You did that to yourself," he said.

She turned. "No, you did it to me by kissing someone else."

His eyes fell. "I know. I'm sorry. I'd take it back if I could, and if I'd thought there was still a chance to make things right between us I'd never have let her in my house."

She thought of the long nights, the mid-summer days she'd spent wondering about him. "You didn't do much to get me back."

"When you left that night it seemed so final. I've never had anyone that mad at me."

"Wouldn't you have been?"

"I guess so, but it wasn't like it was intentional. I didn't realize you were related to Myles."

"Which brings up the question of incest," she said.

He smiled a little. "We haven't had sex yet."

"Yet?" She cocked an eyebrow.

"It can't be incest if we haven't consummated anything."

"But what if we do?"

He shrugged. "Didn't Poe marry his second cousin or something?"

"I hardly think we should use him as our model."

"Hell of a writer though."

She grinned despite herself.

"Look, I'm probably going to regret this," he said, taking her hands, "but I'm tired of leaving things unsaid. You and I didn't see each other that long, but the time we spent together was wonderful. I shouldn't need someone else to help me find myself, but that's exactly what happened. It was like there was this other version of me I'd always wanted to coax into existence but never could. When we were together, I began to figure out how to bring that person out, to become more like him."

"You do look great."

"That's not what I'm talking about. It's more a state of mind than anything, a way of looking at things. Before, I was so damned lazy, so weak. I hated myself because there was nothing about me I liked. I look back at the way I was and cringe. A self-pitying, do-nothing alcoholic."

That raised her eyebrows. It was the first time he'd talked about it.

"It's the truth. I had to lose you to realize how much you meant to me."

"And how much is that?"

"A lot," he said. "I know how lame that sounds, but it's true."

He averted his eyes. Then, he seemed to decide something.

"I was starting to fall in love with you," he said.

She couldn't stop her mouth from falling open.

"I don't deserve another chance," he said, "but I'd like one anyway."

As she stared at him there on the sidewalk, she remembered the way he'd looked in April, standing on the veranda at Watermere, staring out at the forest in her direction but not seeing her where she crouched. She'd watched him that way every evening, to take her mind off Ted Brand, speculating about him and whether or not, like Brand, he was concerned only with himself. The manuscript she'd read seemed to confirm her worst fears, and yesterday, when she saw him kiss his ex-girlfriend, she hated him. It was all mixed up inside her now, the rage and the lust, and beneath it, the tender feelings she had, the thought of a future together.

"One more chance?" she asked.

"Just one."

She pretended to deliberate. "And when were you thinking of seeing me?"

He leapt on it. "What are you doing tonight?"

"I'm reading a book."

"Eat dinner with me instead."

"Only if you get carry-out."

"Chinese?"

"Extra fried rice."

"Done," he said. He gave her hands a squeeze, backed toward the forest. "Give me an hour," he called out and was gone.

She stared after him, smiling. When she thought again of his Poe comment, her smile grew troubled. Poe had written a poem, "Annabel Lee," that she didn't like to think about. She'd read it first with her mother the summer of her death. Her mom had tried to skip over it, going from "The Raven" to "Ulalume," but Julia persisted, and Barbara Merrow turned pale as her daughter spoke the name. After much arguing, they read it together, read about the jealous angels conspiring to murder the beautiful girl named Annabel.

But it was Barbara who died two months later, and it was no wind that took her.

April, 1990

A moment after they told him the news, Myles heard her laughing.

Doc Trask, the spineless weasel, had shown up at his door with Sheriff Hartman. They were asking him where he'd been that day, who could vouch for his whereabouts. In truth, he'd been boning the hooker he'd taken to a hotel in the city, but he wasn't about to tell them that.

Then they told him about Barbara, and he'd come unglued.

Though it wasn't for show, his breakdown helped convince Hartman and Trask of his innocence. Now that he knew the story of his little Asian prostitute would keep him out of jail, he told them everything, right down to the club where he met her. The sheriff vowed to check his story, said it in such a way as to get a rise out of him, but Myles was too sick with the loss to muster much heat.

He hadn't really loved Barbara, but that didn't mean he wouldn't miss her. She was an incredible lay, and she was the mother of his only child. Without her around, his plans for Julia would fall apart. Since he wasn't her legal guardian, he might not be able to raise her, to groom her to take her mother's place.

He had no idea how, but he was sure she'd murdered Barbara Merrow. And when Annabel began to laugh, he thought the crazy bitch had slipped up, had finally incriminated herself by gloating within earshot of the sheriff and the coroner.

The men asked if they could speak to his wife.

Myles welcomed them in.

On the way up to her stinking lair he wondered how she'd done it, how Annabel had finally rid herself of the one woman who had bested her. But when he opened the door to her room and saw her, he knew she would never be convicted of the crime.

She looked embalmed.

Seeing her lying there in the middle of the king-sized bed was like seeing an old wasp dying on a windowsill. Her emaciated limbs were waxen and bruised; her eyes were hollowed out cavities, the eyes of a skeleton. Her head lay on its side, facing them, and behind him Myles felt the sheriff and the coroner recoil, apologizing already for intruding on such a sickly creature.

Myles bade them enter. They did, hesitantly.

When Sheriff Hartman asked Annabel about the last time she saw

Barbara Merrow, she only watched him with those filmy eyes, appeared not to understand. Hartman asked again, and Myles was surprised at his gentleness. Hartman had taken over for Sheriff Ledford decades ago and had inherited all of the man's hatred toward the Carvers. He'd no doubt heard many things about Annabel, had even investigated Watermere a few times over the years, but he'd never found enough probable cause to arrest either of them. Twice, prostitutes had gone missing, and though Myles and Annabel had indeed used them and slaughtered them, they had always concealed the bodies well enough to remain free.

But all of that was history now. At least, judging from Hartman's quiet questions. It was impossible that this dying husk of a woman could make it to the bathroom, much less traverse the distance from Watermere to Barbara Merrow's house, where Barbara's body had been found by her daughter.

Making matters more difficult, Myles later found out, was Julia Merrow's shock. According to Trask the girl hadn't spoken since she'd found her mom, scissors sticking out of her vagina like a lethal sex toy.

"What's to happen to the girl?" Myles asked as they stood next to Annabel's bed, both men studiously avoiding eye contact with the woman. And, he noticed, fighting off the gag reflexes the smell in the room had triggered.

"She'll live with her grandmother until she's eighteen," Hartman answered, clearing his throat into his fist.

Myles swallowed. "And the house?"

"The house?"

Myles tilted his head. "Who's to get it?"

"I don't see where that's relevant," Trask said.

But Hartman overrode him. "Barbara Merrow left all her worldly possessions to her daughter. They'll be held for her until she's of legal age."

Myles felt like strangling them both, Hartman and Trask, for coming here, for telling him such awful things, for ruining the delights Julia Merrow surely had in store for him. She already favored her mother, but the uncanny thing was she sometimes looked like Annabel too.

"Mrs. Carver is obviously not well today, and I think Doctor Trask would agree that she had nothing to do with this business," said the

sheriff. "*We will need her statement eventually, Mr. Carver, to establish time of death and possible clues, but for now I think we should focus our efforts elsewhere.*"

It was said innocently enough, but Myles could tell the guy thought he was guilty. Trask was staring at Annabel thoughtfully, as if he weren't convinced of her condition. For once, Myles found himself hoping Trask would succeed. The guy had been trying to bring them down one way or the other since the late forties. Annabel was his white whale.

Still, he couldn't reconcile the brutal slaying of Barbara Merrow with the motionless sack of bones before him. "*Let's go,*" *he said to Hartman.*

They did.

And as Myles turned to leave he saw something that made his blood freeze.

Annabel's mouth had fallen open, and between two shallow breaths, a black, forked tongue whispered out of her mouth, inviting him once again into her bed.

Her sly grin followed him down the stairs.

They were eating chicken lo mein in the middle of the ballroom floor when Julia stood and unbuttoned her blue jeans. The noodles dangling out of his mouth, Paul watched as she pushed the jeans down her smooth tanned legs and stepped out of them. She turned, leaving him sitting on the black and white tiles, the opened cartons of Chinese food surrounding him like solemn parishioners. As she walked away, he saw she wore a thong, white like her tight tank top, her perfect buttocks round and flexing as she moved up the curving staircase.

Numb, he finished chewing and set his chopsticks down—she'd made him fumble around with them for her entertainment, she said—and followed her. The way she disappeared around the corner, the shadows swallowing her whole, reminded him of that first night in the rain. Just out of reach yet tantalizingly close. Now that she was giving herself to him, he couldn't believe it was true. Something had to intrude, had to ruin it for them. Paul took the stairs two at a time. He caught a glimpse of her gliding up the staircase to the third floor. When he reached it he saw her disappear into the master suite.

He passed through the doorway and found Julia standing in front of the open window, facing him. Her stomach was dark above her white panties, and in the evening sun he saw soft golden fuzz on her skin. He approached her and knelt, his tongue tasting the flesh around her navel. He caressed her buttocks, slid his fingers beneath the thong. Her hands touched his hair, massaged his scalp, and he let his tongue pass over the outside of her underwear, going lower, his saliva melting into the wetness between her legs. Increasing the pressure, he felt her push into him, quivering now, the hands grasping his hair needful, frantic. He took his time, let her lean over him and knead his shoulder muscles. He moved her underwear aside and heard her moan. A few minutes later she hooked him under the arms, led him toward the bed. He took off her white tank top and bra and began kissing her breasts, his tongue loving the large firm taste of them. When they were fully nude, he paused and looked at her for a moment. She smiled languidly. In moments they began. He knew then it was her first time, but rather than alarming him, the knowledge made everything better. At the end she clung to him, shuddering. Awhile later they made love again and with greater passion. Then she was crying out and covering his mouth with kisses.

They lay naked most of the evening, comfortable with each other's bodies. It was well past midnight when she fell asleep. Careful not to rouse her, Paul stood and moved to the large window beside their bed. Was this the window, he wondered, that Annabel hurled Maria through? If it was, some of Annabel's blood would have splattered here and there on the floor, for that was how his first novel told it.

The second novel was lying in the office, half-typed. In it, Barbara Merrow had just been murdered, leaving her daughter motherless. He fought the urge to go in there, finish reading what he'd written. Julia was in the book. What else would he learn of her? It brought him fully awake. Reading terrible things about her was the last thing he wanted to do now. He was in love with her, he knew. He thought she felt the same. His writing had only caused them problems. The first novel had already been rejected by one publishing house and was sure to be shot down by the other. If *The Monkey Killer* almost ruined their relationship, what would *Song of Annabel* do to them?

That decided it. He slipped out the door and moved to the office.

Gathering the notebooks he'd filled, the pile of typed pages—even the paper with one sentence on it still in the typewriter—he hustled down the stairs to the kitchen. He grabbed the lighter and moved toward the door.

The laughter stopped him.

It was a woman's voice. Lilting, playful.

Paul glanced about the gloomy foyer but found nothing to account for it. It continued, louder now, less pleasant. It came, he realized, from the ballroom. The voice had grown deeper, menacing now. Paul backed toward the door as the laughter swelled. It drove him out of the house, walking backward down the porch steps, following him through the door he hadn't shut.

He refused to let it faze him. In a way it made perfect sense. The house had secrets, had seen terrible things. How could it not but retain some of the evil that had taken place within its walls?

Paul looked at the pages in his hands.

These were remnants of blacker days. Maybe by giving voice to the thoughts contained in them he'd propagated the darkness.

Paul's jaw clenched.

But these were not bad times, he reminded himself. This was the beginning of a glorious era. He was stronger now, healthier than when he first came. He and Julia loved one another, and that would prove more powerful than whatever flickering shadows still resided within Watermere's walls.

He took a deep breath, marched to the lawn to the fire pit he'd dug for the Fourth of July. There was no breeze, so it was easy to light the pages, watch as the flames licked them, curled them in on themselves, the terrible words blackening to smoke. Paul savored the sharp tang of it, but even more so the truth it represented. The past could not harm them. Whatever Annabel was, she was gone. Myles and David too. They'd had their time.

The notebook was taking longer to burn. In the scant light cast by the fire Paul could see the florid hand, the writing that was not his own, combusting slowly, reluctantly. Eventually, though, it became a blackened twist of illegible pages.

Paul felt the skin on the nape of his neck tingle. He whirled, certain he'd see Annabel in the library window, escaped from her portrait and come to haunt him.

But it was Julia he saw, nude, standing in the picture window of the master suite. She spread her arms for him, and though for a crazy moment he was sure she'd jump, he soon realized she was beckoning him back to bed.

Paul returned.

"You look happy today."

Julia glanced up at Bea, who was staring at her over her bifocals with a look that begged details.

"I am," Julia said.

"And may I ask why?" Bea set her copy of *Good Housekeeping* on the desk.

"I'm in love."

Bea's mouth worked, her hands kneading one another excitedly. "That's *wonderful*, dear. How did this happen? Who is it, the Carver boy?"

Julia laughed. "He's not exactly a boy."

"He is to me." Bea frowned. "I thought you two were through. You sulked your way through most of July because of it."

"I forgave him."

"Did he deserve to be forgiven?"

"I think so. We all deserve to be, don't we?"

"Most of us, at least. So when did this start up again?"

"Recently."

Bea waited.

"Last night," Julia said, and they both laughed.

The older woman stood, fidgety in her giddiness. "Oh, dear, I hope this is the one. Why you've never married is something I've never understood. I've lost sleep over it."

"You needn't have."

"You don't know how it is. Bill and I never had children, so I suppose my maternal instincts get dumped on you."

"I wouldn't use that word," Julia said and took Bea's hand.

"*Used* on you. How's that?" Bea said.

"Better."

Bea turned, clouding. "Now I feel guilty about tomorrow night."

"Don't be."

"But spending your Friday night here helping me with the book sale is probably the last thing you want to do. When I asked you I thought you were single."

"I am single," Julia said, smiling.

"Perhaps," Bea answered. "But maybe not for long."

Had he seen Snowburger upon entering the bar, Paul would've left right away and things would have turned out differently. As it was, he didn't notice the exterminator until Julia's expression changed and she said, "Do you know those guys?"

Paul turned and knew there'd be trouble. Snowburger and a larger man that could only be his brother were staring at him from the back of the bar where they stood leaning on pool sticks, the smoke skirling about them obscuring their faces. Snowburger, his red hair slicked back ridiculously, would gesture toward Paul and the larger guy would nod and grin an ugly barracuda grin.

Under the table Paul's hands bunched into tight knots.

"You want to go?" Julia asked.

Not taking his eyes off them, Paul said, "Why would we go?"

Julia cast a worried glance over her shoulder. "They look like they're planning something."

"So let them."

"You know you don't have to impress me, right?"

Paul didn't answer, watched a third man join Snowburger, a scrappy-looking guy with a permanent scowl and a chin so deeply cleft it looked like a pair of butt cheeks. The guy stared boldly at Paul, said something to Snowburger and made to approach. The exterminator, his sleeveless denim shirt stretched tight by his immense belly, stopped him with a hand on his shoulder. The scrappy guy acted mad at being touched. Snowburger patted his shoulder placatingly and moved ahead.

Julia said, "I wouldn't think less of you if we left and went to a movie. The food's not that great here anyway."

"This is where we had our first date."

As the men neared, Julia said, "Let's go to the movie."

"We're still going to do that," he said. "After we're done here."

"And when will that be?"

"Soon."

"Soon," she repeated. "And I'm supposed to act casual, as though these guys aren't—"

"Here they are."

The biggest guy was in the lead, his bushy red beard making him look like a mutant goat.

"Heard you picked on Bobby," the Goat Man said. He was enormous, six-and-a-half feet tall at least. He threw a thumb at the exterminator standing a few feet away. The Goat Man was definitely Snowburger's brother. This close, the resemblance was uncanny. They even exuded the same repellant body odor. Paul imagined a pack of bologna split open by the noonday sun and squirming with plump maggots. The only difference between the two brothers was their size. Snowburger was fat but only as tall as Paul. The Goat Man was a giant.

"Heard you refused to pay him what you owed," the scrappy little guy said. Paul had not seen him move up next to their booth, but now he appraised the crooked nose, the flesh of the forehead mottled by scars.

"You threaten my brother?" the Goat Man asked, placing a huge freckled hand on their table.

Paul glanced at the middle-aged couple sitting in the booth behind Julia. The look on the guy's face, he wanted to help but was afraid he'd get beaten to a pulp. Between the two Snowburgers Paul glimpsed the bartender, on the phone with someone. Sheriff Barlow, he hoped.

"He's gonna shit himself," a familiar voice said.

It was the first time Bobby Snowburger had spoken. He was confident standing behind his mountain of a brother. Paul couldn't blame him.

"He get it up for you?" the scrappy little guy asked Julia. "Or he like you to strap it on and give it to him?"

Paul stood up in the booth. It was hard, the way the table pressed against his legs.

"Don't," Paul said.

The little guy seized the neck of Paul's tee shirt, twisted. "You gonna do something, Carver? With a name like that you probably like to hang around playgrounds, kill little kids like your uncle."

Paul raised his fist to smash the guy's sneering face but Snowburger's brother was too fast. The gigantic knuckles pounded the side of Paul's face, knocking him into the corner of the booth. The little guy was on him then, assailing him with short painful jabs to the face and chest. Paul heard Julia shout something. There was a crash. Through the hands he'd thrown up to protect his face from the little scrapper he saw the Goat Man sitting on Julia, holding her immobile with his leviathan girth. He had ahold of her arms so that her nails hung useless in his grasp.

The exterminator was moving up behind the little guy. Paul realized what the crash had been: a broken bottle, shattered jagged and held by the neck. Bobby Snowburger tapped the little guy on the shoulder. "Hey, Kenny. Back off a second."

Kenny did.

Before Snowburger could slash him with the broken bottle, Paul slammed a foot in his gut. Ignoring the pain and the blood trickling down his cheeks Paul yanked himself forward, out of the corner of the booth where Kenny had cornered him, and straight at Snowburger.

Paul tackled him low, under the belt, so that when they went over, the back of the exterminator's head cracked the table behind him. He yelped as Paul followed through, driving with his legs, until the fat man smacked the floor, his head cracking a second time.

The little guy made to jump on him but before he could, Paul shot an elbow back and grinned savagely when he felt it connect with the little guy's mouth. Paul spun and saw the guy spitting bloody teeth into his palm, and beyond him a trio of men with shocked faces.

Paul stepped toward the little guy, crouched and threw his whole body into an upper-cut. The impact sent the scrapper erect, turning and then tumbling face first onto the grimy floor. Paul looked in surprise at the prone bodies of Snowburger and the little man and thought, *Only one more.*

"You cocksucker," the Goat Man was saying, but he was struggling to get out of the booth where he'd been sitting on Julia. As the huge man stood, Paul heard him cry out and for a moment all he could do was stare at Julia, who glared at the back of the man's neck with such triumphant hate that it made his skin go cold. The Goat Man whirled and Paul beheld what Julia had done to the back of his neck. Flesh hung in bloody strips where her nails had torn him. The Goat Man advanced on Julia, who swung at his face again. The huge man staggered backward to avoid her nails, and as he did he backed right into Paul. Reaching up, Paul thrust a forearm under the guy's chin in a chokehold and reared back.

It caught the Goat Man off guard.

Going to his knees, the big man flailed his hands at Paul's arms, trying to free himself of the chokehold, but Paul only squeezed harder. As the big man went limp in his arms he felt someone shaking him from behind. He looked up at Julia, who was staring at him, frightened. Paul relaxed his grip, felt the Goat Man slide to the ground. He whirled, ready to strike again, but it was only one of the three men who'd been watching. When the guy saw Paul's raised fist he raised his own hands to show he wanted none of it. Above the din he heard someone saying, "Over here. Quick."

Paul turned and watched the bartender leading Sheriff Barlow over to them. For the first time he noticed the overturned tables, the shattered glass and spilled beer. Barlow was staring at him as though seeing him for the first time. So was Julia. A patron was kneeling over the Goat Man, checking for a pulse.

"He dead?" Barlow asked.

The guy who was kneeling over the Goat Man shook his head, said, "He's alright."

Barlow looked at the little guy lying face down in a puddle of blood and beer. "Sayler start this?" he asked the bartender.

"All three of them did," the bartender answered, though he was looking at Paul with something like fear. "Jimmy here threw the first punch." Nodding at the Goat Man.

Paul heard someone crying and from the sound of it he thought it was some old woman who'd been struck by a piece of glass. Looking down he saw it was Snowburger, doubled-up, too ashamed to make eye contact with anyone.

"What'd you see, John?" the sheriff was asking one of the men who'd been at the next booth over, a guy in a red seed store cap.

"Same thing he saw," John said, nodding at the bartender. "These two were just sitting here when Kenny Sayler and the Snowburgers attacked them."

Barlow looked at the middle-aged couple standing behind Julia. The man and the woman both nodded, though they kept a safe distance.

The sheriff sighed, removed his hat and passed a weary hand through his hair. A deputy had moved up next to Barlow. Looking at Paul, the deputy said, "Everyone's saying the same thing. That these two," nodding at Paul and Julia, "didn't do anything until these dumbasses started it."

"Alright, Doug," Barlow said. The sheriff surveyed the scene disgustedly, put his hat back on. "Cuff these idiots and get them into the cruiser."

Barlow glared at Paul.

"Go home," he said.

As soon as they pulled out of Redman's parking lot, she was on him. With one hand she grasped his penis, with the other, the back of his neck. She licked his throat, his ear. Feverishly, Julia pushed up his shirt and bit the skin below. Straining to focus on the road he slid his free hand under the top of her shorts. His fingers moved along the crack of her ass, then delved lower. He rubbed her as she undid his shorts, then her own. He gasped as she took him into her mouth.

Paul stomped on the gas, sped down Gordon Road.

She pushed off her shorts, her underwear, but his angle was all wrong, and he couldn't touch her the way he wanted. Frustrated at the Civic, he veered onto the lane to Watermere and skidded sideways. Throwing it into park even before the skid was done, he grabbed her and tried to kiss her. But she pushed away, threw open her door and climbed out. Paul watched her beautiful, perfect ass flex in the moonlight. Then he followed.

Backpedaling, she pulled her top over her head, let fall her brassiere. Paul tossed his own shirt into the underbrush and pushed his boxer briefs and shorts the rest of the way off. She grinned at him, eyes glimmering, as she backed into the forest.

She turned to run, but he was already on her heels. He allowed her a small lead, relishing the way her tawny skin reflected the pale light filtering down through the overhanging boughs. Sweat poured from her as her strong legs pumped. She curled around a stand of evergreens and went off the path. Paul raced after her, his erection growing. Ahead, near the brook, he spotted the glowing bower of bluegrass beside the little path. That was where he'd take her, he decided.

She threw an exhilarated glance over her shoulder, tried to elude him. But with a cry he bounded forward, fell on her. They landed in the grass. She pushed up to one knee, but he toppled forward onto her, pinned her on her stomach in the bluegrass. Shoving into her immediately, he squeezed her breasts, kneading them savagely, and pumped his hips into her. She spread her legs wider and moaned into her forearm. Soon Paul was moaning too.

When it ended he sat back on the grass, the brook trickling a few feet behind him. Closing his eyes, he let the sound of it soothe his painfully throbbing penis.

He gasped as daggers jabbed his inner legs. He looked up just as she landed on him. She slipped him inside her, cried out as she pumped her hips. Fiery pain bloomed as she dug sharp nails across his chest. He raised his head to see her face, but the darkness shadowed it. He imagined it was Annabel riding him, and as the shadows shifted she seemed to sense his thought. She pumped her hips in a frenzy, leaned back. He stared at her full, beautiful breasts in the moonglow as they moved to the rhythm of her hips, and she screamed, teeth bared.

She slumped on him, breathed into his shoulder. He told her he loved her, but she only laughed.

Chapter Twenty

The sheriff was waiting at the house.

They strode through the lawn, Julia making no effort to cover herself as they emerged from the darkness. Barlow studied the ground in front of him, said he'd wait for them to get some clothes on.

When they got to the master suite, Barlow waiting for them in the ballroom below, Julia said she had nothing to wear. Paul glanced about the room, as if women's clothes would be draped over the furniture.

"I'm sure Annabel had something you can wear," Paul said.

They both stopped. Paul felt his chest constrict. It was the first time he'd said her name aloud.

"I think Myles got rid of all her stuff," she said.

"All except that painting," he said.

"I can't wear that, can I?"

Paul rummaged through the bureau, came out with a tee shirt and a pair of jeans. "These do?"

She put them on.

When they came back down Barlow was sitting at the bar nursing a drink.

Paul sat down on one of the red velvet couches. Julia sat beside him.

Without turning Barlow said, "You two need to stop this."

Paul laughed once, harshly.

"I mean it."

"What's wrong, Sheriff Barlow?" Julia said. Her eyes were coy as she stared at him, played with Paul's hair.

Barlow faced them. "What's gotten into you?"

She rested a hand on Paul's crotch.

"Jesus," Barlow said and turned away.

"Are we in some kind of trouble?" Paul asked.

The sheriff sipped his dark amber glass. "More than you know."

"You heard the witnesses," Paul said. "Those three morons started the trouble, not us."

"This isn't about that," Barlow said.

"Then what is it about?" Julia asked.

"When's the last time you saw Daryl Applegate?" Barlow asked her.

"Your deputy? The time you two were at my house."

Barlow watched Julia a long moment, then said to Paul. "You and I need to talk. Alone."

Julia stood. "That's fine. I have something I need to take care of anyway."

Paul followed her, but she stopped him with a hand on his chest.

"I'll be back in a few minutes."

"You don't have to go," Paul said.

She kissed him, long and deep. Winking at the sheriff she said, "Have fun, Sam."

Barlow watched after her, said to Paul, "What's gotten into her?"

"I don't know, but she's taking my car." They listened to the Civic pull away.

Barlow went back to the bar, sat on his stool.

Paul moved around the edge and stood before the long mirror. Pouring himself a whiskey and ice, he asked, "What was that business with your deputy?"

"You ever meet him?" Barlow asked.

"Applejack?"

"Applegate. And you might not want to joke about him. He's been missing for a month." Barlow sipped his drink. "Haven't you heard?"

Paul stirred his own drink. "I don't really hear much out here. I like it that way."

"What about Emily Henderson?" Barlow asked.

"What about her?"

"Have you heard from her?"

Paul paused, staring at the ice cubes bobbing in the amber liquid.

"No," he said, "I haven't."

"You're lying."

Paul returned the sheriff's gaze. "How's that?"

"You heard me."

"Why do you think I'm lying?"

"Because it's the first time you have. Up until now you've told me the truth. I can tell when I've been lied to."

Paul set his glass on the bar, eyes narrowing. "Why are you asking me about Emily?"

"Because," the sheriff said, "she's disappeared too."

It stopped him.

"Disappeared," he repeated.

"Her parents think she might've come to see you. She'd been talking about you a lot lately. They think she might have tried to reconnect."

Paul frowned, pretended to think. "Well I haven't seen her. I'm worried about her, though. It's not like her to run off and not tell where she's going."

Barlow nodded. "That's what her father said. He said she only acted like that where you were concerned. That's why he contacted me."

"I told you I haven't seen her."

"Yeah, you told me that."

"You don't believe me."

"No. I don't."

"Then I'd like you to leave."

Barlow grinned. "I'm not going to."

"What the hell does that mean?" Paul edged around the bar. "You need a warrant to come in here."

"You invited me in."

"And now I'm inviting you out."

"It doesn't work like that."

"You son of a bitch." Paul crowded Barlow where he sat.

Barlow downed the rest of his drink, said, "Because I don't think you're all bad, I'm going to forgive that." The sheriff stood, his girth dwarfing Paul's. "But that's the only one you'll get."

Barlow moved close, inches from Paul's face. "I'm going to tell you something, and then I'm going home to get some sleep. We've had three disappearances in four months."

"I told you Emily was never here."

"I know you told me that, and you know I don't believe a word of it. People have a way of coming here and not being seen again."

Paul opened his mouth but Barlow overrode him. "I don't know if you're the cause or not, but I'm going to put a stop to it one way or another." The sheriff turned, made for the hallway, but stopped before he got there. "And one more thing. I don't like you and Julia together. It's bad for both of you. The girl I know wouldn't act the way she's acting without someone else's influence. I've seen what a bad man can do to a good woman and you're not going to do it again."

"What the hell," Paul said. "You think I'm gonna kill her or something?"

"What I'm talkin' about is worse than death."

Paul laughed. "Jesus you've got a vivid imagination."

Barlow's teeth showed. "That's not what I'm talkin' about."

"I have no idea wh—"

"Damnation," Barlow said, "is where you two are headed, and that's a whole lot worse than dying."

The sheriff turned to leave.

"You know, she's not her mother," Paul said to Barlow's back.

The sheriff stopped. "How's that?"

"She's Julia, not Barbara Merrow. Just because a girl broke your heart and a relative of mine happened to be involved doesn't mean I have to take the blame."

Barlow's voice was hollow. "How did you know about that? Who told you those things?"

Paul laughed, loving the ashen hue of Barlow's face. "What's it matter, Sam? That's all this is really about, right? Your inability to let go of the past."

Quicker than Paul would have thought possible Barlow crossed the room and seized him by the collar.

He glanced at Barlow's hands. "I don't think you're supposed to do that."

Barlow's voice went thin. "Tell me how you know all this."

Paul was about to tell him about the graveyard, about the two manuscripts, everything, when they heard Julia come through the front door carrying a black athletic bag.

"Did I interrupt something?" she asked. Without waiting for an answer, she disappeared up the stairs.

Barlow watched her go, then returned his stony gaze to Paul.

"Your time's almost up. I find anything to tie you to Brand, Applegate, your ex-girlfriend, you're done."

"Thank you, Sheriff," he said.

The door slammed shut. A moment later, the cruiser rumbled and drove away.

Paul went to the bar and got his drink. Then, he went upstairs to search for Julia. She wasn't in the library. Nor was she in the master suite. Then he saw the shut door of the master bath, the tiny sliver of light shining beneath the door.

Sipping his drink, he waited for her. To pass the time he counted the seconds as they ticked off the grandfather clock in the hallway. He was glad he'd wound it. It enhanced the ambience of the old house.

When the clock struck three in the morning he realized he'd been asleep. He heard the latch click on the bathroom door.

Julia stepped into the room.

Paul sat straight up in bed, his drink spilling.

"How do you like it?" Julia said.

Paul tried to answer but could not. The light blue dress—the same dress Annabel wore in the painting—was too tight for Julia, but he knew the sight of her cleavage bulging over the top of it should have turned him on. It would have, too, if not for the smell that still attended the dress. And though he knew the fragrance couldn't be familiar, it was just the same: Annabel's perfume.

The dress slithering over her skin, Julia stepped toward him with a voracious look in her green eyes. "Now rip it off me," she said.

256

Chapter Twenty-One

July, 1996

Myles slid out the drawer and bent to see inside. Newspaper clippings and faded photographs. The moonlight was too dim to see them by, but he dare not risk turning on the light. Annabel was beyond hurting him in her weakened state, but he'd still rather her not know of his snooping.

He watched her motionless form on the bed. Her body was bent and sunken with the disease, her limbs little more than flesh-covered sticks. How she'd lived so long he'd never know. She hadn't been out of bed without a wheelchair in over a year.

Yet she still frightened him.

Myles gathered what he'd found and stole out of the room.

Inside the office he shut the door and listened. Satisfied he'd not been discovered, he flipped on the desk lamp and studied what he'd taken.

The pictures were all of Annabel. Seldom was anyone else featured. He or David popped up here and there, as did other men she'd bedded, but most of them were Annabel by herself. She stared at the camera, through time, straight at him.

Something rustled.

He whirled, standing, and stared at the closed door. Was Annabel on the other side watching him through the keyhole?

His heart pounding, Myles reached out, twisted the knob.

Darkness.

Peering left and right down the shadow-filled corridor he could see nothing save empty space. He shut the door and cursed himself for being so skittish. Seventy years old and acting like a frightened child.

A stack of papers, clipped together and brown with age, drew his attention. He riffled through them and saw they were the obituaries of the dead children, the children his brother had murdered. *Murdered for Annabel.*

Under the child obits were others—Maria Ustane, Jane Trask, Barbara Merrow, others he'd forgotten. He set the clippings aside and studied the pictures. They went back to Annabel's teenage years, apparently. In them she gazed at the camera, that strange knowing look in her eyes.

The rustling came again.

As he turned it got louder, and instead of reminding him of autumn leaves scraping together in a pile, this time he thought of thick little claws clicking on plaster, black rodents teeming inside the walls, pink tails trailing heavily behind them.

What the hell?

One didn't go from a pest-free house to complete infestation over the course of a few minutes. But that was exactly how it sounded, the walls around him alive with black wiry hair and sharp fangs.

Repulsed, Myles started to leave. He was out the door before he remembered he'd forgotten the desk light. As he reached out to extinguish the lamp, the chorus of rats grew louder, their noxious symphony swelling.

Then, something caught his eye.

Another, thinner stack of clippings sat untouched on the desk. More obituaries. These names, though, were unfamiliar to him. What was more, the dates on them were over a century old. Why on earth had she collected these, and why throw them in with things relating to her?

Then he saw it.

A picture of Annabel in the newspaper. Atop a large yacht, she stood next to a man, her slender body leaning out over the water, his large hands supporting her. The caption read Robert and Annabel Wilson at the Wintergem Yacht Club. *In the upper corner of the clipping, the date:*

May Fifteenth, 1889.

Myles turned.

Annabel stood in the doorway.

He cried out, attempted to hide the clipping.

She smiled.

Myles struggled to control his breathing, to play off being caught, but her smile burned into him.

He forced himself to return her gaze. "What are you doing out of bed?"

She watched him.

He fought the urge to bolt past her into the hall, down the stairs and out the door.

He said, "You should be in bed."

"I'm in bed all day. I want to spend the night with my husband."

Myles stared at the scarlet moons under her eyes where the flesh was paper thin, felt his skin prickle.

He cleared his throat. "I'll take you back to your bed."

He led her into the hall, forcing himself to touch her back. The ribs there stuck out like kite frames, her vertebrae so pronounced they raised her yellowed nightdress like children's blocks beneath a blanket.

He got her into bed and was about to leave when she said, "Stay with me, Myles."

He opened his mouth to protest.

"Stay with me, Myles," she repeated.

He got into bed beside her, held his breath against the fetid odors of mildew and dirty diapers. The nurse did a terrible job keeping Annabel clean, but she was cheap and he was finished spending money on his dying wife. He wondered how long it had been since the last sheet change.

"You took my portrait down."

He sat up on an elbow and stared down at her. Her eyes were shiny and black in the scarce light.

"Yes," he answered.

"Where is it?"

He studied the taut skin covering her cheekbones, an olive tent held in place by bony stakes.

"Tell me something, Annabel."

"Mm."

He tried to keep his voice from shaking. "One thing about that portrait always bothered me."

When no reply came, he went on, "You put that painting in the library when you and David married."

An almost imperceptible nod. He realized she was nearly asleep.

"Where did you say it came from?" he asked.

She said something, but he couldn't make it out.

"I always wondered that," he went on. "You said your parents commissioned the painting, that you owned the dress. But if your family was as poor as you said they were, how could they afford it? A dress like that, old-fashioned and silky, all those ruffles. It must have cost them an arm and a leg."

Annabel lay still.

Myles said, "And the artist, the guy who drew you. How much did he charge your parents?"

"My parents didn't pay for it."

"But you said they did. You told David that. You told me too."

"Did I." It wasn't a question. In a voice so faint he scarcely heard her, she said, "It's been so long I don't remember anymore."

"I remember," Myles said, lying back. "I remember you showing up at our house in those old-fashioned clothes. The other women made fun of you. At first."

He waited.

"Where did you get those clothes, Annabel? Why didn't we ever meet your parents? Not even at the weddings. It was almost as though they didn't exist."

He waited for an answer, but her breathing was deep and restful.

He lay there watching her a long time.

Chapter Twenty-Two

Their lovemaking was awkward, frustrated. As they lay there afterward, he said, "I don't want us to act like anyone else. I want us to be us."

"Who says we aren't?"

"I don't know." He scratched the underside of his jaw. "But don't you feel strange now, like we're doing things for the wrong reasons?"

"I don't know what you mean," she said, but she didn't meet his eyes.

He took a breath. "Julia, why did you wear that dress?"

"Because I felt like it."

"Okay, but why did you feel like it."

She looked at him, eyes narrowed. "What are you asking me?"

He opened his mouth and shut it. A few moments passed before he said, "I don't think we're in control anymore."

She looked away. "That's ridiculous."

"Is it?"

"Yes."

"Tell me you're acting normally."

"What is normal?"

"I don't know what normal is, but I can sure as hell tell you what normal isn't. It isn't losing control in a bar..."

"Paul—" she said, but he was going on.

"...or beating the shit out of people and enjoying it. It isn't telling off the sheriff—"

"So who is in control?" she demanded. "If we aren't, who is?"

He shook his head, unable to meet her eyes.

He said, "Tell me you haven't had dreams about her lately."

She opened her mouth. Then, she looked away.

"Tell me you haven't been thinking of her."

She would not meet his gaze.

"Tell me she's not getting ahold of us."

"You want to know why I wore her dress?"

"If you wanna tell me."

"Are you sure?"

"Hell yes, I'm sure."

"Do you really think I don't know where you go in the middle of the night?"

Paul opened his mouth.

But Julia went on, "Do you really think I don't know about your fascination with her?"

His stomach was a knot, and though he wished to say something, he knew that nothing would make the situation better.

Julia said, "So I thought I'd save you your late night trips down the hallway by acting more like her myself."

Paul didn't respond, instead stared down at his hands. The silence drew out. Dawn was beginning to show through the windowpanes, and the milky light slanting onto her pretty face helped undo some of the effect her dress had had on him. Her body fuller, more voluptuous than Annabel's, she was definitely her own, not a copy of the dead woman. Julia sat in the window seat.

"What did you and Sam talk about?" she asked.

"The disappearances."

"The lawyer and the deputy," she said.

"And my ex-girlfriend."

He saw her face cloud. Something in his mind clicked.

"Julia," he said.

Without looking at him, she answered, "Yes?"

"What do you know about Emily's disappearance?"

"Nothing."

"Then why are you frowning?" he asked.

She took a deep breath, then shuddered as she let it out. "Because I saw you two together."

Paul shook his head. "But there's something else."

"Paul—"

"Something else you're not telling me."

She regarded him, and for a while, neither spoke.

Then, she said, "What do you want to know?"

He swallowed. "Everything."

Her gaze intense, she said, "Have you told me everything?"

"I'm sure I haven't," he admitted.

"Tell me then."

"I didn't write the novels."

"You didn't tell me there was a second one."

"You're in it."

She stared.

"You were only a child when I stopped…transcribing it, I guess."

"What did I do in the novel?"

"Nothing. You were only a child."

"You're serious about this."

"I read," he swallowed the lump in his throat. "I read about what Annabel did to your mother."

He could see tears welling in her eyes.

"I'm sorry, Julia. I didn't really write them. I got the ideas when I was next to the grave—"

"The grave," Julia's voice was thin.

"Out there," Paul gestured, "in the forest. I got the ideas and they just flowed out of me." He went on, though. She got up and started pacing about the room. "I don't even remember writing them."

"Where's the second novel?" she asked. "The one I'm in?"

"It's gone."

She stopped pacing. "Where—"

"I burned it. I didn't want it near us."

She looked at him in disbelief, seemed about to say something. Then, she put her face in her hands.

Paul rose and led her back to bed. Lying beside her he said, "I'm sorry for not telling you about it, but frankly I was ashamed. I wanted to be a writer, but I'm really... I've never written a thing. I can't. I tried when I got here, but I was terrible."

He lay beside her in silence and wondered whether he'd lost her again. When her body stopped shaking, he cupped her chin. "Julia, I'm sorry. I'm truly sorry for not being honest about—"

"It's not that," she said, "it's something I've done, something I've got to tell you."

"Whatever it is, it can't be as bad as—"

"Paul."

"—because I've been awful to you. I really have, and—"

"*Paul*," she said, and the flatness of her voice silenced him.

She wiped a tear off her cheek, glanced up at the ceiling. "I've done things I shouldn't have," she said.

"Did you see someone else while we were apart?" he asked.

Her eyes flared. "Damn it, Paul, it's got nothing to do with that."

Chastened, he waited for her to continue.

She said, "I know where Brand is."

He frowned. "Yeah?"

"I know where Daryl Applegate is too."

His temple began to throb. "Where are they?"

"Which one?"

"Either of them." When she didn't respond, he said, "Applegate."

"He's dead."

"Julia."

"I'm sorry, Paul."

He edged away from her.

"What are you telling me?"

"He's buried in my yard."

He stared at her, his heartbeat devolving into leaden thuds.

"In the garden," she added.

He sprang off the bed and grabbed a pair of boxer shorts.

"Paul, wait."

"For what? For you to tell me you chopped him up into little pieces? What the hell is wrong with you?"

"I didn't mean to. He tried to blackmail me. The rest was out of my control."

"You killed him."

"I didn't want to kill him."

"Jesus," he shouted at the wall. "I can't believe I'm hearing this."

"Paul, listen."

"I don't want to listen." He put on his jeans.

"There's more."

"You tell me you killed a cop and buried him in your garden and there's *more*?"

"The lawyer," she said.

"Don't tell me."

"Ted Brand. He came on to me and when I wouldn't sleep with him he called me names. Later on, he tried to kill me, but that was because I tied him up to keep him from hurting me."

"What the hell are you talking about?" Paul clutched his temples.

"He's buried in the woods."

"These woods?"

"Yes."

He stared at her. "You killed him and buried him on my land."

Her voice was choked. "Paul."

He gritted his teeth. "And you parked his car on my lane to make it look like I did it."

She looked pleadingly at him. "I didn't know you then."

"No you didn't, but you sure as hell made life fun for me when I got here, didn't you?" He pulled on his shirt. "Interrogated by the police..."

"I'm sorry, Paul," she stood, started to touch his arm.

He jerked away. "You're sorry? For what, that I'm a suspect in a murder case because of you?"

"Nobody knows it was a murder."

"Nobody but me," he said, tapping his chest.

She lowered her eyes. "Are you going to tell Barlow?"

"Tell him what? That you're a serial killer?"

"Serial killers are different."

"Yeah? How?"

"Serial killers kill people for no reason. I didn't mean to kill anyone."

"You murdered two men by accident?"

"Brand wasn't an accident," she said. "It was self-defense."

"And the deputy? What about Appleton?"

"Applegate. Definitely self-defense."

"So he came to arrest you and you defended yourself by what, poisoning him?"

"I told you. He wanted to barter sex for silence, and I wouldn't do it."

"You killed him instead."

"*I didn't want to kill either of them,*" she shouted. "All I wanted was you."

He chuckled mirthlessly and turned to go.

She took him by the shoulders, brought her face up to his. "You're all I have."

The naked sorrow in her voice stopped him. He said, "How can you expect me to forget this? Hell, how can you expect not to be caught?"

"I haven't been caught, have I?"

"It's only a matter of time."

"Why? They don't even suspect me."

"That's because they suspect *me*."

"Not anymore."

"How can you know that? What about the deputy's family? What about Brand's?"

"Did Barlow ask you about them?"

"He asked me about Emily."

"What did you say?"

"I told him I hadn't seen her."

"But you did. You kissed her."

"I know that," he said, voice rising. "I lied and I have no idea why."

"I'm sure she'll turn up."

"And if she doesn't?" he said. "For all I know you killed her too."

"That isn't fair, Paul."

His shoulders slumped. He regarded her in the darkness. "I'm sorry. You didn't deserve that."

She took his hand. "You didn't deserve the trouble I caused you. It was a mistake." Her wet cheek touched his. He felt her breasts press against him. "Please don't leave me, Paul." She kissed his neck. "You're all I have," she said.

"I can't do this," he said.

"You love me."

"That's not the point."

"What else matters?" she asked. She kissed him and he could feel her fear of losing him, her desire for him beneath it.

"Julia," he said, trying to recall his anger.

"Paul," she said with such longing that he let his hands touch her, linger over her hot bare skin.

"You love me," she said.

He kissed her, his tongue finding hers. They lay back.

"Say it," she said.

He kissed her again, and she climbed on top of him.

"Say it, Paul," she whispered, her breath hot in his ear.

"Damn it, Julia."

"Say it."

"I love you," he said.

"We belong together," Julia said.

He made love to her, but he couldn't shake the image of her in Annabel's dress. In his mind's eye, Julia looked much as she had earlier—the body, the skin, the smile—but the eyes were Annabel's. They were red-rimmed and enraged.

The thought of those infernal blue eyes kept him up long after Julia had fallen asleep.

Sam Barlow sat on his screened-in porch and stared into the field behind his house. In a just world Barbara would be sitting beside him, drinking a wine to go along with his beer. It would be dusk, and their children would be visiting from out of town, maybe bringing the grandchildren with them.

But he sat there alone instead, sucking on a bitter tasting can of warm Budweiser, the gloaming still hours away.

He thought of his sister, Addie, killed in a drunk driving accident when her boys were in high school, of his brother-in-law Raymond, moving to West Virginia and remarrying. At that moment, Sam mused, Raymond was likely torturing his second wife with dead baby jokes and stale beer farts.

He wondered why life turned out the way it did. Why things never worked out for some people, why the bad guys too often won.

He looked at the lock of Julia's hair he found when he jimmied open Brand's car and wondered why he'd never sent it to the lab.

He scowled at the unnaturally tall cornstalks and shook his head. Of course he knew why. She was a murderer, and he didn't want to admit it, and though she'd probably also killed Daryl Applegate—who undoubtedly deserved what he got—Sam didn't want to admit that either.

And now there was this other girl, Emily Henderson. Her parents and friends were worried sick. Her bosses said she'd taken the week off, so that at least was normal.

Yet she'd never made it to Watermere, if Carver was to be believed.

Sam took a swig of warm beer. Carver wasn't to be believed.

He'd tried to like the guy, he really had. If he listened to Paul Carver speak, joked around with him, he could forget for a while that he was related to Myles. But the more he looked at him—at the uncanny resemblance—the more he hated him.

And then last night, that show the two put on for him.

Julia walking right up to him naked as the day she was born, the girl he'd known since birth, the girl who should have been his own, the girl who would have been his own if only Barbara had been willing to leave, to get the hell away from that godforsaken family.

But she hadn't. He told Barbara he didn't care her daughter was sired by another man. He begged her to live with him in town, but something about Myles Carver held her.

And now look at her daughter.

Sam glared at the cornfield, his stomach souring.

Julia, in the space of a couple months, going from a sweet, smart girl to the kind that paraded around wearing nothing but a smile, fondling Carver right in front of Sam, daring him to say something disapproving. Christ, it really was like she was his own kid, taunting him like that.

But she wasn't.

She was a killer.

Carver was innocent of the murders, or he seemed to be. And as much as Sam cared for Julia, he knew the time had come to end it.

He would go out there tonight, confront the two of them. If it turned out Carver had something to do with the killings, with Emily Henderson's disappearance, Sam would enjoy locking the bastard up. That at least would heal some of the wounds festering inside him.

He wouldn't enjoy dragging a confession out of Julia. He wouldn't enjoy locking her up. Fact was, it would tear him apart, which was probably why he'd been avoiding it this long.

But it had to be done. Her boss said she'd never missed work until recently. Then, the weeks after Brand and Applegate go missing she's absent nearly every day. He asks Julia about Brand and she says all the right things, but he knows in the deepest part of him she's lying, the same way Paul Carver was lying when asked about the Henderson girl.

He thought of the way Applegate had looked at Julia. Not just undressing her with his eyes but ripping off her clothes and raping her with them as well.

Applegate goes out to accuse her. Applegate, the moron who refused to listen to anyone. Applegate, the porn addict who couldn't get laid in a whorehouse. Applegate, with blackmail material on the most beautiful woman in town.

Applegate, the murder victim.

It all fit. The circumstantial evidence, the timeline, and most of all the personalities involved.

Brand the lecher.

Applegate the potential sex offender.

Julia Merrow, the object they both desired, the woman with too much of her mother's pride to be taken advantage of.

And Emily Henderson, the rival.

Whether Julia acted alone on that one or had help from Carver, he could see her taking drastic measures to eliminate her competition. Girl like that, her mom taken from her at such a young age, raised in a dreary house by her grandma, never finding a man worthy of her.

Until she fell for Carver.

That was what cinched it. Julia's similarity to her mother. A wonderful, tenderhearted girl with one besetting sin: a dark stream of lust pulsing through her that attracted the worst kind of man.

Even if Sam had nothing else to go on, he had this.

With both hands, Barlow held the strand of long black hair up to the western sun.

The hair he found in Ted Brand's BMW was Barbara Merrow's as much as the green eyes in Julia's face. He'd recognize that hair anywhere. Thick. Black and shiny like a serpent.

He'd arrest her tonight if it killed him.

Barlow wrapped the strand around his thumbs, drew them apart until it snapped.

Damn it all to hell, he thought.

He'd do it tonight.

To clear his head Paul decided to run longer than usual. When he'd doubled his usual distance, he decided to continue on, explore paths he'd never traversed. He checked his watch as he emerged onto the gravel road that formed the western perimeter of his land. He'd been running for over an hour. Over rugged terrain in the febrile August heat, he'd been running the entire time and hadn't even begun to tire. As he crossed to the mailbox he wished he had a mirror nearby to see himself. He imagined his body a machine, lathered in sweat, his muscles surcharged with boundless energy. He'd never felt so good, couldn't believe he'd lived so much of his life so lazily. Now that he'd found himself, now that he'd found Julia, he'd never fall prey to indolence and self-doubt again. He'd ask her to marry him tonight, to move into Watermere with him. She could leave the old Hargrove place behind. It was surrounded by his land—soon their land—and he saw no reason to sell it off. Their children could use it in some future time. It would be their playhouse, somewhere they could go with their friends at night to tell ghost stories.

Paul opened the mailbox, found a single letter inside. The sender, Seizure Press.

Paul held his breath and ripped open the letter.

He read it, folded it and placed it in the envelope. Clutching it, he recrossed the gravel road and sprinted toward home. Paul laughed as he ran.

Now they had another reason to celebrate.

August, 1996

Sam Barlow saw the smoke rising from the forest.

Hands tightening on the wheel, he made a left off the gravel road and guided the cruiser down the lane. He came out here regularly, but for one reason or another it had been a couple of weeks since his last visit. Sam cut the headlights.

The first thing he saw, other than the smoke, was a car he didn't recognize. Then he saw an upstairs light was on and grew angry. Take it easy, he reminded himself. If a few teenagers came out here to get their kicks, they didn't mean any harm. They don't know what the place means to you. Probably a few of them smoking pot upstairs, the rest down in the yard having a bonfire. But how did they get the electricity turned on? Stopping behind the car, he climbed out and moved around the edge of the house. He'd been right about the bonfire, but not the teenagers.

It was like seeing Barbara again. The girl was tall and gangly, all bones and wild energy, but he knew right away it was Julia Merrow. An older woman he recognized as her grandmother was standing across the bonfire from her, both of them holding sticks with hot dogs impaled on their blackened tips. He felt suddenly embarrassed for intruding, wished he could drive away before they spotted him.

But Julia was staring at him over the fire, the flames dancing on her young face, and instead of apprehension he saw recognition, happiness. She dropped the stick, the hot dog landing on the burning logs, and raced around to give him a bear hug. He was amazed she remembered him. Of course, he had been the only man around in those early years, the guy that showed up with groceries now and then and ventured to make her mother laugh. He remembered walking on hands and knees

271

while a four-year-old Julia sat on his back and called him Horsey.

It made him tear up, thinking about it. If only Barbara had felt the things for him he felt for her...if only she'd let him take them to town with him so they could get away from Myles...Barbara would still be alive, and this precious young woman he was holding would still have a mother.

"Hello, Mr. Barlow," Julia's grandmother said.

He nodded at her. "Evening."

Then, patting Julia on the shoulder he wiped his eyes, looked down at her and saw she'd been crying too.

"What I can't figure out," he said, grinning, "is who this pretty lady is."

Julia laughed, and he could have adopted her right there. But not wanting to make anyone uncomfortable, he led her back to the bonfire to stand next to her grandma.

"You coming back here to stay?" he asked.

Julia started to say something, but her grandmother overrode her: "Just a visit."

He tried not to let his disappointment show.

"That's great. How long will you be staying?"

"Not long, I hope. We'll be gone by month's end," the grandmother said.

"You got the electricity on, I see." Sam nodded toward the house.

"Not that we need it. All this girl does is play the piano and read books."

"That true?" he asked Julia.

"What's wrong with that?" she asked. God, she was like her mother. Feisty, good-humored.

"Not a thing."

The grandmother pointed at his badge. "When did you become a trooper?"

Sam grinned. "Sheriff, actually. About six years ago. Less than a year after..." he trailed off, wishing he weren't such a clumsy lout. Why not tell them the rest? a voice in his head asked. Tell them how Sheriff Hartman nearly went nuts trying to solve Barbara Merrow's murder and how he finally resigned because of the stress of it. How you took the job hoping you could bring down the Carvers, Myles most of all. Tell them all that. It'll make nice conversation.

"Less than a year after Julia moved away," he finished.

The silence spread around them.

To break it, he said, "Could I have you two over for dinner while you're here?" Looking at the older woman but really asking Julia, hoping she still wanted a father figure. The grandma was divorced, he knew. Probably married some unworthy son of a bitch, same as her daughter did.

It was Julia who answered. "We'd love that."

"Wonderful." Sam grinned, gave her a one-armed hug, and said, "Saturday evening work for you two?"

The old woman was staring at him with an expression he couldn't read. "Saturday would be fine," she said.

He said goodbye and walked to the car, wondering what he'd cook.

As it turned out, he didn't cook anything Saturday night.

Because on Friday there was a murder.

Barlow showed up around nine, just as the sunlight was dying in the yard. Paul didn't look up, kept chopping wood on a stump beside the weathered gray shed. Determined to let the sheriff speak first, Paul lifted the axe, slammed it down on the squat section of log he'd chainsawed earlier. He loved the way it split neatly in half, the fresh white wood inside smelling green and reminding him of how little he'd known when he first came, how naïve and pathetic he'd been. Barlow had bullied him then, he now saw. Paul had been flabby and self-conscious, and even though he'd done nothing wrong, the bigger, stronger man had treated him like his whipping boy, judging him for things Paul's ancestors had done.

He swung the axe, teeth bared, the green scent of fresh wood filling his lungs. He felt the sheriff's eyes on his back, standing ten or fifteen feet behind him.

Let him look, Paul thought. *Let him see my new muscles, bigger than Myles's, harder than David's.* Paul took a deep breath, stifled the grin that threatened to spread over his face. He'd taken the best parts of both of them and done them one better. Paul was the next stage in the evolution. He and Julia. Their children would be beautiful. Her stunning green eyes and his literary mind. He positioned another log on the chopping stump and as he did he felt the acceptance letter in his hip pocket, thought of how Julia would react to it. They'd make love to his success, to their future.

Paul swung the axe.

Barlow said, "I'm not going to let you do it."

Paul wiped sweat from his brow. "Do what, Sheriff?"

"Corrupt her."

Paul swung. The wood split and fell. He muttered, "You're being absurd," and raised the axe again.

"Put that down," Barlow said.

Paul smirked and glanced over his shoulder at Barlow, whose right hand rested on the holstered gun. "Or else what? You gonna shoot me?"

"If you don't put the axe down."

"Aren't threats like that against the rules?" he said. He placed another fat block of wood on the stump.

"What do you know about rules?" Barlow asked. "What do any of you care about them?"

Paul hammered the log, left the axe in the stump. "What are you talking about, Sam?" he asked, turning. "I'm the only one here."

"You and Julia," Barlow said.

"Let me tell you something." Paul approached. "You've got some serious issues that need worked out. All this stuff you're hung up on. My uncle—my great uncle, actually—the business with the Hargroves, my *corrupting* Julia. It's all in your mind."

"Think about the way she's acting now and tell me that's all in my mind."

Paul moved closer and Barlow tensed. "Don't take another step," the sheriff said.

"Like now," Paul said. "You're about to draw your gun for no reason at all. As though I've killed someone." He grinned slyly. "Or stolen your girl."

Barlow swung and Paul felt fire erupt in his jaw. Staggering back, he stared up at the larger man.

The sheriff said, "I told you not to come any closer and you did. Now I'm telling you to walk over to my car and put your hands on the roof with your feet apart."

"Hit a nerve, did I? Is it because you haven't gotten over Julia's mother screwing another guy, or is it you want Julia for yourself?"

"You son of a bitch," Barlow said, advancing.

Eyes on the gun—still holstered—Paul backpedaled. "That's what it is, isn't it? Lost another girl to a Carver. First Barbara, now Julia." He laughed, seeing the tears in the big man's eyes. "You should really be ashamed, Sam. A girl that young, she could be your daughter."

That did it. Barlow leapt forward with a roar and swung at Paul's head.

Dodging, Paul avoided the punch but caught a powerful shoulder in the chest. Barlow drove him down, knocking out his wind and crushing him with his weight. Somehow the sheriff had gotten handcuffs out. A gleaming steel loop was open, yearning to imprison him. Paul clutched Barlow's wrist and squeezed, and the sheriff sucked in surprised breath. The cuffs dropped from his hand and landed in the grass beside them. With his free hand Barlow smashed Paul in the chin. Paul bucked, lifted the sheriff off him long enough to plant a knee in the big man's groin. Grunting, Barlow rolled off and pawed for his holster. Paul lunged for it then realized he was too late. As the gun came up Paul scrambled toward the woods.

Barlow shouted at him but he was off and running. For a horrible moment Paul was certain he'd be killed, but for whatever reason, Barlow didn't pull the trigger.

Why didn't he?

No matter. With Paul's new speed the sheriff no longer had a chance to gun him down. He pumped his arms in a sprint, reveled in the way the trees flashed past him.

The work boots and jeans weren't suited to running, but at least he wore no shirt. He knew the man following him was in shape, but the sheriff hadn't a chance in this race.

Barlow called his name, but the voice sounded a mile away, as if the sheriff had already given up or taken a wrong turn. Paul would make for the northern edge of the forest, head into town.

To do what? a cynical voice asked.

His forehead creased. What could he do? The authorities would never take his side instead of the sheriff's. Barlow *was* the authority. No matter what Paul did, he would catch the blame.

Then, he got an idea.

Veering back toward the house, he called to Barlow, led him where he wanted him to go.

Sam heard Carver calling his name.

The bastard.

He'd show the guy. He might not have the speed of the younger man, but he was in better shape than Carver knew. He could run all night. Eventually, the guy would get tired, take a rest somewhere.

He followed the sound of Carver's voice. The bastard taunting him, calling him all sorts of names. Saying things about Barbara, goddammit. He'd throttle the son of a bitch until there was nothing left of him.

Hearing Carver's voice, closer now, he slowed. Was the guy doubling back on him, trying a sneak attack?

Sam halted and knelt. He gripped the .45 Smith & Wesson and scanned the woods.

No sign of him.

He had to be careful now. If the guy was anything he was cagey. Sam had made the mistake of underestimating him earlier, letting him get away. Carver wouldn't get away twice.

The voice again. Closer this time. Less than fifty feet away.

Sam noticed the other sound then. The bubbling trickle of water. Carver was straight ahead of him, near the brook. As he moved on hands and knees toward the sound of Carver's voice, he thought of Julia, Julia as a child as she wept at her mother's funeral. Julia as an adolescent needing a dad.

She was his reason for doing this. With a little work he could make Carver for all three murders, if murders they were. He had to get the bastard to confess. He'd get a confession the honest way or he'd beat it out of him. Regardless, once he found out where the bodies were stashed he could make up anything he wanted to and he'd be a hero for it.

Julia would have to choose, then. Either go along with it, pick up the pieces and start a new life, or refuse to accept it, in which case he'd have to make public her role in the crimes too.

It would be up to her, though. He'd wait for her tonight at Watermere. She'd no doubt be coming there after getting done at the library. Her boss said she'd be working late, until midnight maybe, to get ready for the book sale. Nice old woman, Julia's boss. Able to keep a secret, holding off telling Julia about their conversations until everything was sorted out.

He came to the clearing.

The bluegrass beside the brook was soft and matted, as though someone had been there recently. Sam searched the elms around the clearing, looking for movement.

Pain exploded at the base of his skull and starbursts popped in his eyes. Sam fell forward, scrambled for his gun, but before he could grab it, a boot shot out, sent it skittering toward the water's edge. He made a dive for it, but the gun went over, the clear water swallowing it up with a plop. Sam rolled onto his back, stared up at the man holding a rock the size of a grapefruit in his hand.

"Let's end this," Carver said.

Paul stared down at Barlow, who lay on the ground blinking at him. The sun was almost dead and they were only silhouettes in the twilight. Paul became aware that Barlow was grinning.

"Something about this amuse you?" Paul asked.

The sheriff said that it did.

Paul shot out a workboot, tattooed the older man between the eyes. Watching the pain in the sheriff's face was heartening. He tossed the smooth rock into the water.

Rolling over, Barlow coughed and rubbed at his face, but beneath the coughing Paul heard the sheriff chuckle.

"What's so funny?" Paul asked.

"You're not very smart, are you?"

That brought the boot out again, catching Barlow in the gut this time. Bunched up, the sheriff spat and moaned. It was Paul's turn to laugh. The big man looked pitiful doubled up that way. Through the coughing he heard the sheriff say something, but he couldn't make it

277

out. He knelt over him, smacked him in the face to let him know he was still there. Barlow eyed him.

"You're not much, are you?" Paul asked.

The sheriff spoke, his voice hoarse: "Have you gone to your uncle's grave yet?"

It stopped him. "What?"

"You even know where it is?" Barlow was smiling again.

"Of course I do," Paul said, nodding toward the graveyard. "It's over there with his wife's."

"No it isn't," Barlow said. "It's in Greenview Cemetery, next to the city park."

"I don't understand," Paul said.

"That's right. You don't. So ask yourself why a husband would want to be buried separate from his wife."

"I don't have the first clue."

"Because he was afraid of her. Because in the end he understood what she was."

"You're a fool," Paul said.

The sheriff laughed. It infuriated him. He made to slap Barlow again, but the sheriff surprised him by feinting the blow and smashing a meaty fist into his ear. Head ringing, Paul stumbled and tried to remain standing, but the larger man was on him too swiftly, dragging him down like a lion. The sheriff on his back, weighing him down, Paul shot out a desperate elbow. It caught Barlow in the kidney. Bellowing, the sheriff went down again, his big body mere feet from the edge of the brook.

He jumped on Barlow's chest, pounded him with his fists. The sheriff tried to fend him off but Paul was too quick, his advantage too great. Again and again he snapped jabs at the sheriff's face, aiming for and connecting with his eyes, his bloody mouth. Not wanting Barlow to lose consciousness, wishing the older man to feel every possible scrap of pain, he grasped him by the chin and shouted into his face: "It doesn't matter where Myles is buried, don't you understand that? He's gone, you lousy old piece of shit!"

"He's gone," Barlow wheezed, "and you've taken his place."

"That's right. I've taken his place." He scowled at the sheriff, who was laughing again, harder now, and spitting up blood.

He yanked Barlow up, yelled into his face: *"Don't laugh at me."*

But the sheriff did. He went on laughing until Paul, sick with anger, let his head drop to the forest floor. He stalked back and forth, waiting for Barlow to stop. When the laughter had finally abated, Paul said, "You're the reason it's come to this, you know."

"*She's* the reason."

"Julia?" Paul stood over him. "I don't blame her for anything."

"You're a fool if you believe that." Barlow said. "But Julia's not the one I'm talking about."

"Then you're the fool."

"You don't know her."

"I know all about her."

"You don't know anything," Barlow said, his voice rising.

"I know I'm a published novelist. I know I'm enough of a man to keep a woman."

Barlow said, "She'll keep you."

Paul pounced on him, raised his fist and slammed the sheriff in the nose.

His hands over his face Barlow said, "Haven't you noticed her changing?"

Paul shook him. "Tell me what you're saying."

"I'm saying she's not Julia anymore."

Paul froze, hands clutching the sheriff's collar.

"You haven't even thought about it, have you?" Barlow said. "The stuff she's done, the people she's killed. That's not her. Julia would never have done those things."

Paul's face twisted into a snarl. "Crazy old bastard."

"She even looks like her now," Barlow said, ignoring him.

"I've heard enough," Paul said and stood.

Still holding onto Barlow's collar, he dragged the larger man toward the water's edge.

"The same mannerisms, the same expressions." Barlow's voice rose, pleading now. "Last night she even talked like her."

Paul let go, Barlow's head dangling over the water.

"You know I'm right," the sheriff said, a thick stream of blood drooling out of his mouth. "She's either Annabel already or becoming her."

Paul watched him, eyes veiled. "That's enough."

But Barlow went on, "Or maybe you've planted her seed in Julia's womb."

"Shut up." Paul straddled the sheriff, pushed down on the man's forehead.

"Listen to me," Barlow said, voice panicked. Paul gazed into the sheriff's white, wild eyes. *"I'm trying to help you."*

Paul watched his face disappear into the turbid water, which gurgled, the big white bubbles rising and bursting. Barlow seized Paul's shirt, lifted himself out of the water.

"Please," the sheriff said, sputtering, *"please listen to me...it's Annabel..."* He coughed blood and murky water. *"Don't you see that this is what she wants? If you'll only—"*

Barlow's voice was swallowed up by the water rushing over his face.

"Fool," Paul growled. He leaned back, avoiding Barlow's flailing arms.

The sheriff's face breached the surface. Paul saw the man's mouth forming words, but no sound escaped save the retching and gagging. Doubling his efforts Paul drove with his forearms, dunked the sheriff's head again, and now the large man was beginning to weaken. His frenzied hands batted at Paul's shoulders, fought in vain to loosen his grip.

Paul grinned. He saw Barlow's eyes under the surface, huge and frightened. Teeth bared, Paul held him there. He discerned his own image on the water, rendered brilliant by the charnel light of the moon. He laughed, for the reflection made it seem as if he were drowning himself, his own face. Then, Barlow's hand splashed again and the illusion vanished.

Paul held Barlow under.

He pushed to his feet and stared at Barlow's motionless body. He lifted the sheriff's ankles and shoved them toward the water. His huge limp body somersaulting, the sheriff toppled into the brook. It was just deep enough to move him along with the current. He watched the sheriff's feet disappear as the body floated around a bend. For a moment, Paul's breathing slowed.

Then, as if awakening, his whole body tensed.

What the hell was he doing?

"*No*," he said. He took a step into the brook. Its depth surprised him. He tumbled forward, the cool water rushing over his mouth and eyes. He began to tremble. He splashed to his feet, the water chest high, and began running downstream, his muscles rendered useless by the water's resistance. He flailed his way forward, thinking the sheriff might still be alive, he had to be, but Paul's progress was negligible. As if in a nightmare, he felt the water pushing against his limbs, impeding him. He fell forward, the waters closing over his head. Under the surface he heard laughter, and he knew it was Annabel. He thrust forward and up, his hands breaking the surface. He opened his mouth to curse her for making him do this. He reached the water's edge and heaved himself up, and through the coughing and gagging he cursed her, cursed Annabel for making him kill the sheriff.

Lying on his stomach, he let his cheek rest on the wet grass. The coughing was under control now, and he could think more clearly. It hadn't been like the automatic writing because he remembered everything, remembered the sheriff's panicked eyes as Paul shoved him under. Yet it was like that in a way because he didn't hate the sheriff, didn't truly believe the thoughts that led to the confrontation.

But Barlow was dead and Paul couldn't take it back.

He and Julia would have to go away. Barlow's body would be found soon.

Paul mashed his face in the grass and the mud. It smelled like a freshly dug grave.

Soundlessly, he began to weep.

Chapter Twenty-Three

The late hours were hard on her.

In years past Bea Merten had looked forward to the book sale. Staying up until midnight or beyond. Using her muscles more than she was accustomed to, loving the fact that she and Julia could do the work all by themselves.

Bea's expression grew troubled.

She had no idea what it was Sheriff Barlow thought he knew about Julia, but she didn't like keeping secrets from her, speaking furtively with the sheriff at her house rather than here at the library where they might be discovered.

The questions he asked were about that lawyer, Ted Brand, who'd come to Shadeland but had never left. And then about the night of Independence Day, when she knew Sheriff Barlow's deputy, that cretin Daryl Applegate, had disappeared.

She'd tried not to think about it, but that was like not thinking about a pink elephant. The more you tried not to think about it, the more you did. She'd lost sleep lately, and trying to act normal around Julia was exhausting what meager energy she still had.

Bea ripped off a rectangle of Scotch tape and stuck it on the sign. Careful to keep the sign level, she taped it to the front window. That done, she stood in the foyer, thinking of what else she could do to prepare for the sale.

What she could do to avoid Julia.

Bea thought of the younger woman down there in the bowels of the library, standing on the step ladder, pulling boxes of books down from the tall shelves where they kept the ones that hadn't sold last year. Terrible work. It was always hot and muggy down there, and Julia had been at it for hours already. The girl was so helpful, so loyal. It wasn't possible that Julia was involved with all that nasty business the sheriff kept calling about. Bea knew that Julia was no killer.

So why was she afraid of being alone in the basement with her?

Bea pressed a hand to her chest to calm her racing heart. She'd known the girl for going on six years. Julia was like a daughter to her. It wasn't a stretch to say she loved the girl, but why on earth had she been absent so much lately, and why had she taken to wearing heavy makeup? In April Bea had asked her about the darkness around her eye. Julia said she tripped in the woods.

She was lying, Bea was certain. And why would she lie, if not to protect herself? Bea gazed down the wide staircase leading to the upper basement, where the children's books were. Julia was under there somewhere in the lower basement, in the catacombs, sweating away.

While Bea stood up here quaking in her shoes as though her assistant were Jack the Ripper.

It was ridiculous. Julia had nothing to do with the disappearances, and Barlow had gone off his gourd. Smiling, Bea took a step toward the stairs.

And screamed when someone knocked on the door behind her.

She whirled, thinking it could only be the sheriff at this time of night.

No one was there.

The area outside the glass door was unoccupied. It was a bright, clear evening so there could be no mistaking it. Bea squatted to see under her homemade BOOK SALE sign.

Nothing.

Kids, then. Playing tricks on her.

You're two months early, she thought wryly. *The practical jokes aren't supposed to begin until October.*

Irritated at the way her chest was tightening, she flipped the lock on the door and pushed out into the warm night. Kids would be kids, but they should be smart enough not to play their tricks on an old woman with a heart murmur. She'd have to take an extra water pill before she went down to help Julia carry the boxes up.

Bea stood on the porch steps and scanned the quiet street before her, the houses around the library. Nights like this always made her think back to her younger years. The courting and the secret kisses.

It calmed her heart.

Maybe tonight she'd wake up Bill when she got home. They hadn't made love in months, seldom did anymore, but they still slept in the same bed. She thought of his warmth, the comforting way he looked at her.

A susurrant breeze had begun; it caressed her skin. Bea sighed. She loved the night air, but there was work to be done.

She grasped the door to go inside but stopped when she discovered what the kids had done to her sign.

Angry now, she turned and scanned the bushes flanking the porch. She descended the steps and moved down the sidewalk, hoping to catch a glimpse of them, the white of an eye, the glint of malicious little teeth. *I'll teach them to write wicked things on my sign,* she thought. *BURN IN HELL, of all things.*

The words unsettled her, though she couldn't say why.

The memory came then, and though she tried to hold back the sick fear crashing down on her she could not. Bill and his dalliances. Her years of secret hurt, her pleasure at the whore's affliction. The spray can her only means of retribution once the hideous woman had died.

But they couldn't possibly know about that, kids who'd not yet been born.

Fists balled, she stepped off the sidewalk and onto the path that led between the library and the Catholic church. They'd be here, she was sure, hiding in the darkness, hoping she'd go back inside so they could wreak more mischief at her expense. Make her heart stutter the way it was now.

From the corner of the building, where the bushes and dogwood trees nestled right up next to the brick, she noticed something gauzy and white. It fluttered in the breeze, sheer and delicate.

Curious, she approached.

As she neared she saw the patch of white disappear around the corner. She'd not let them get away. Their parents would see what they'd done to her sign, hear about how terribly they'd frightened her.

Bea turned the corner and felt her heart seize.

Her eyes widened in horror.

Then a pale hand lashed out and removed her face.

August, 1996

   The girl sat in the grass, reclining on her elbows.

   After a time, her grandmother's window went dark.

   Instead of rising right away the girl tilted her head so the moonlight shone full on her face. Her hair swept the moist grass, the little dewdrops there absorbed by her raven tresses. She inhaled the night air, cool and crisp and tinged with the acrid smell of wood smoke. She passed a hand over her abdomen. She could feel herself changing, the pains that meant she was becoming something different. Rolling, she felt the ground massage her growing breasts, the muscles of her stomach. She pushed herself to standing and disappeared into the woods.

   Twenty minutes later she emerged from the gloom of the forest and stepped into the lawn. His car was gone, as she knew it would be. She clucked her tongue. A man his age and still visiting the city for its brothels and strip joints. She did not understand such things, but then, she'd never understood Myles Carver.

   Julia stared up at the third floor, at the black window near the left corner of the huge house.

   Not bothering to conceal herself, she took her time walking through the yard. In five years, she'd return. The house she and her grandmother were staying in would be hers and hers alone. She would escape the old woman and her strictures. Five more years and she could come here whenever she wished.

   Getting to Watermere had been difficult. Thirteen years old and no means of transportation meant convincing her grandmother to spend a few weeks in Shadeland. Visiting the place where her only daughter had been murdered had not sounded pleasant to Julia's grandmother. But Julia was persistent, mentioning the trip more and more often as summer approached. Ultimately, the old woman acquiesced.

   She had planned on waiting until Saturday night to complete her mission, but Sheriff Barlow's dinner invitation changed that. With him around she could not do what she needed to do.

   Julia moved up the porch steps.

   The front door was unlocked, as she knew it would be. Instead of using the front staircase the girl passed down the hallway into the ballroom. Her bare feet caressed the tiled floor. In the mirror over the bar she saw herself in shafts of moonglow, a tall, thin ghost of a girl.

Without touching the banister she ascended the curved staircase. She focused on the steps ahead of her and listened for sounds in the old house. But she heard nothing save her strained breathing.

She reached the third floor.

Fighting the urge to enter the library, she fixed her gaze on a closed door at the end of the corridor. She moved toward it. When she reached the door she thought of the Poe story they'd read that year in school. The old man in the story had been innocent, the narrator insane. How different from these circumstances, *she thought.* How very different.

Turning the knob she let the door swing open.

The smell hit her. Cloying, fecund, it threatened to muddle her thoughts, shake her resolve. Steeling herself with the thought of her mother, of all that had been stolen from her, she strode into the room, careful to avoid the blankets on the floor.

The figure lay on the bed, her wasted body covered by a thin nightgown, her face covered by a washcloth.

Julia inched closer and stood over her.

The sick woman's body was like some dying insect's. Segmented and discolored, the creature on the bed was a knobby relic.

Julia took the hatchet from her waistband.

She was about to strike when she thought of her mother. It would not do to slay this monster in her sleep. Julia would not deprive her of the pain she deserved. Reaching out, Julia lifted the washcloth.

The woman's eyes shuttered open.

Annabel rose, her goblin's grin even worse than her cadaverous insect body.

Julia retreated, disbelief chilling her blood as the woman climbed out of bed, her insect arms and legs moving effortlessly.

"I'm glad we're alone, dear," Annabel said and reached for her.

Julia swung the hatchet.

It tore through Annabel's cheek. Julia stared in horror at the exposed teeth, the frothing gums.

Annabel's white jawbone leered at her.

Her teeth clicking like a skeleton's, the sick woman unbuttoned her nightgown until her shriveled breasts showed, the bones of her sternum and ribs tenting her white skin.

"Here, darling," Annabel said, offering her naked chest. The skeletal face nodded at the hatchet. "Put that here."

"Goddamn you!" Julia shouted and brought the hatchet down. It crunched through Annabel's collarbone and stuck there, the blood spewing out around it a black flood in the moonlight.

The dying woman chortled at her, followed her into the hallway as though the hatchet weren't embedded in her chest. Annabel's hands whispered out of the shadows, fell on Julia's shoulders.

"Oh God no," Julia cried.

She thrashed her head from side to side to rid herself of the grinning face hovering toward her, but the mad eyes loomed closer until the stench wafted over Julia, enveloping her.

"First mommy, now daughter," Annabel croaked.

Julia felt the skeleton fingers dig into the meat of her shoulders. Her knees buckled. She tried to scream but no sound escaped as her back met the floor. The grinning woman landed on her. The blue eyes were avid as Julia reached up, grasped the handle of the hatchet.

The dying woman did not react when the hatchet chunked out of her collarbone but Julia gasped when a long black forked tongue slid out of the bloody mouth and licked at her. Gasping with revulsion, Julia threw Annabel off.

Julia stood and stared at the creature lying on her back.

"Here," Annabel croaked, touching the waxy skin above her heart. "Put it right here."

But instead, Julia brought the hatchet down between the woman's eyes.

The black blood spraying from her forehead, Annabel still laughed.

To silence the woman's laughter, to end the lunacy once and for all, Julia leaped on her, seized her by the throat. Again the tongue snaked out, licked at her face.

Shoving away, Julia stared aghast at the laughing creature on the floor. She wanted to back away, to flee the house forever, but her determination was gone. In its place descended a suffocating dread. She'd been a fool to believe she could march in here and kill Annabel so

287

Jonathan Janz

easily.

The woman was rising, the hatchet handle pointing insanely out of her forehead. Annabel groped toward her.

The feel of the woman's fingertips on her throat galvanized Julia.

She fled.

Down the hall to the stairs, which she took three at a time. Once in the ballroom she risked a glance over her shoulder, but the maniacal woman was nowhere in sight.

Crying with relief, she crossed the foyer to the front door.

It was locked.

Muscles locking in atavistic terror, she pulled feebly at the door. It would not give.

"Julia," said a voice behind her.

She whirled and saw the woman coming toward her. Annabel's feet did not seem to move. Behind the dying woman Julia could see the slick trail of blood dripping off of her like rancid menstruation.

Instinct propelled her toward the first door she could find. Opening it, she fell into darkness. A shoulder slamming wood, feet somersaulting wildly, Julia tumbled down the basement stairs until she crashed into the concrete wall where the stairs turned. Her head woozy from the knocks it had taken, she glanced up at the open door.

Annabel stepped through it.

Hysterical with fear, Julia tried to stand but found that her ankle would not cooperate. It threw her headlong down the second, shorter flight of stairs. As she struck the floor she felt her hip jostle something heavy. It listed over her and fell, landing beside her on the ground.

Julia stared into her own face.

Forgetting for a moment the woman trying to kill her, Julia reached out, touched the statue.

It was smooth, made of wood.

It was Julia.

"He wants you," Annabel said.

Julia gasped, pushed away from the woman, who was now standing and watching her at the base of the stairs. She could not read Annabel's expression in the scant light of the basement, but she could hear from the woman's voice that all the humor had gone.

288

With an effort she pushed to her feet, stared at Annabel.

"Look around you, dear," the bleeding woman said.

She did. Wooden statues of Julia filled the basement. In some she was just a child. In others she was older, more mature.

In all of them she was nude.

"I took his nurse away," Annabel said, "so now he wants fresh meat."

As Julia glanced at the wooden images, her vision started to gray. She opened her mouth to speak but Annabel had disappeared. Julia whirled and scanned the basement for the woman, but everywhere she turned she saw herself. It was like being in a hall of mirrors. The pallid light showing through the cobwebbed basement windows made it difficult to tell whether the figures were wood or flesh, lifeless or animate.

"He can't have you," a voice at her ear whispered.

Julia gasped and swiped at the voice but her hand slapped cold wood, her middle fingernail snapping off.

"Go to hell!" Julia shouted.

Laughter, a rustling from the shadows.

"Just let me leave," Julia tried to shout, but her voice dissolved into tears.

A hand fell on her shoulder.

Julia recoiled and crumpled to the floor. She knew she was beaten. She'd been wrong to come here so soon. Had she waited until she was older she might have been strong enough, but a girl her age was no match for the malevolence here. Through her tears she heard Annabel's voice, wheedling.

"Do you imagine him between your legs, dear? Your own father?"

Julia ground her palms into her ears to rid herself of the voice.

"Do you imagine him bouncing you on his lap, dear?"

"I hate you," Julia whimpered. "I hate you."

"I think you hate yourself, dearest, for wanting what you can't have." Annabel's face drew closer. "Just like your mother."

Julia's sob caught in her throat. Raising her head she saw Annabel's stick legs, the varicose veins like black licorice in the near darkness. Gazing higher she saw the hatchet handle pointing out of the woman's head.

Julia grasped it, pulled.

If Annabel was surprised she made no sign. Instead, she stood there motionless as Julia rose, brought the hatchet above her head.

"Someday," Annabel said as the blade cleaved her skull.

Chapter Twenty-Four

The sweat dripped into Julia's eyes. It stung horribly. It had to be over a hundred degrees down here. It made no sense, she thought. Heat rose, didn't it?

Yet down here, more than two dozen feet below the ground floor of the library, the atmosphere was stifling, suffocating. The books smelled of congealing mushrooms, the dank walls bled moisture and moss. Julia felt like a medieval prisoner, left here to die on some wicked king's whim. The grungy metal bookcases watched her like stolid sentinels.

Feeling dizzy, she dismounted the ladder and mopped her brow with the front of her blue tank top. The movement only smeared the sweat around, made more of it drip through her eyelashes. She glanced about for something dry to absorb some of the sweat but saw only unwanted books, and she'd have to be more desperate than she was to use them.

Anxious to get to Paul and ready to have this miserable work behind her, she surveyed the boxes she'd already filled and the shelves she'd yet to scavenge for sellable books.

Only half done.

Julia sighed.

If Bea weren't so good to her, she'd tell the old woman to shove her books. If tomorrow were anything like usual, they'd end up toting most of the boxes back down here anyway, for who really needed forty-year-old science textbooks and moldy collections of children's poetry?

And speaking of Bea, where had the woman gone? It wasn't like her boss to shirk hard jobs. Now that she thought about it, the woman had acted strange all week, as though harboring some secret grudge.

Twice Julia asked her what was wrong, and neither time did the woman really answer her, changing the subject instead to something banal.

"*Julia,*" a voice whispered.

She whirled, scouring the long room for her boss.

"Yes?" Julia asked, smiling. Her friend was always considerate, warning her before her presence could startle. When no answer came, she said, "Bea?"

She strode around the corner of the tall metal bookrack nearest her and peered down the aisle. Nothing but more racks, more books, and a disquieting collection of bunched shadows.

Julie blew out trembling breath. Was she being put on? Bea was no practical joker, but wasn't it possible the woman was feeling unusually playful?

She decided to go with it. Hunkering low so she'd be harder to see, Julia made her way down the single aisle, past the shelves she'd already picked through.

Movement ahead and to her right. Julia grinned, imagining the gray-haired woman standing just outside the sub-basement door, waiting to jump out at her.

She'd give her friend a scare she wouldn't forget.

Careful to avoid the books she'd boxed, Julia kept her gaze trained on the place where she was sure Bea was hiding. There was a blind spot on the landing, an outcropping wall where someone could conceal herself until her unsuspecting prey was upon her. Bea was there, waiting.

Julia took care to tread lightly, her sneakers making no sound on the damp concrete. She crouched, then sprang around the corner.

No one was there.

Disappointed, she peered up the stairs. The door to the main basement was barely discernible in the gloom. Now that she'd come this far, Julia wondered if now would be a good time to go upstairs for a water break. Bea would be down soon, but what about the meantime? Her throat was dry and papery, her skin sticky with sweat and grime.

Julia bit her lip. She cast a glance over her shoulder and saw the boxes lined up along the aisle. She realized she'd made it farther than she'd initially thought. She scrunched her brow, counting. Of the eighteen metal bookracks she only had seven left to go. It seemed silly to quit now. With Bea down here the work would go much faster. Rather than toting armfuls of books down the ladder she could lower them to Bea, who could arrange them in the cardboard banana boxes they used. With luck they could be done by half past midnight. That would put her at Watermere by one—or earlier if she allowed Bea to take her home.

That's just what she'd do, she decided. Giving her a ride was the least her boss could do after leaving her down here to do the dirty work for—she checked her watch—nearly three hours now.

She walked back to where she'd left off. She climbed the ladder.

This shelf might take awhile, she decided. Unlike the four shelves below, this one was promising. No outdated almanacs or science textbooks here. Reading the authors she felt the familiar love surging within. Thomas Hardy. James Joyce. Hemingway. How could she have missed these last year?

Steadying herself by holding the rim of the shelf, she stepped onto the top of the step ladder so she could read the titles at eye level. Julia gasped with delight. Her very favorite writers, the romantic poets. Shelley, Byron, Keats, Wordsworth. Upon seeing a collection of Robert Browning's poems that appeared to be in great condition, she stifled a cry of joy. It was unfathomable that writing this good should rot away down here in the darkness. Smiling, she pulled the Browning collection from the shelf.

And saw the blue eyes staring at her from the other side.

Chapter Twenty-Five

All that mattered now was Julia. She was coming later, though how much later he didn't know.

Paul took a path that would lead him to the brook, upstream from where he'd drowned the sheriff. Slowing, he angled toward the water. Little glints of quicksilver glimmering on its surface, the brook looked cool and pure in the moonlight. He knelt at the water's edge. For a moment he perceived his reflection staring up at him. He leaned over and kissed it, his lips forming ripples in the still water. He let it swallow his face, his hair. He leaned out as far as he could without falling in. Then, he lay on his stomach and dunked his arms in the cool water. It calmed him a little. Standing, he started for home.

As he moved through the hollow, he was captivated by the spectral glow enveloping him. He'd never seen so many stars. Glancing askance, Paul was not surprised to find he'd chosen the trail that passed the graveyard. He took a step toward the clearing and stopped.

Staring through the trees he could see the high grass, the black stone shining.

"God damn you, Annabel," he said and turned away.

Jogging, he made the trek home.

Emerging from the forest, he strode into the yard, arms spread, the moon and stars baptizing him. He felt the light on his strong, chiseled chest, his rippling stomach. He felt it on his round shoulders. Paul stopped and looked around sadly. This would be his last night at Watermere. He'd always remember it, remember how he arrived one way and left as something quite different. He was no longer a wanderer, a man without a purpose. He had Julia now.

Yes, he thought. Thinking of Julia took his mind off of what he'd done.

He imagined her naked body beneath him, breasts shifted slightly outward, their sweat mingling together as she moaned.

Paul unlaced his boots, peeled his sweaty socks off. He unzipped his jeans. Pushing them down, he rid himself of his boxer shorts as well. He closed his eyes and let the breeze sough over his bare skin. He already felt Julia against him, her smooth body, her long blond hair.

He opened his eyes.

It was Annabel he was imagining, he realized. When he made love to Julia, it was Annabel's face he saw.

Paul shivered. Yes, it would be good to get away. He and Julia could make love one more time, and then they'd leave without packing. They could ditch the Civic in a few hours and board a plane after that. There was plenty of money from the inheritance. Hopefully, he could wire for some of it in the morning, before anyone got wind of what happened to the sheriff.

Paul entered the house thinking of Julia, of flying away with her. It didn't matter where they ended up. He would drink to her, his true love.

He reached the bar and selected a bottle of Johnnie Walker Red. He relished the sound of the whiskey splashing over the ice cubes in his glass. Alcohol tasted so much better now that he didn't need it. He finished his drink in three gulps.

Paul poured again.

Not wanting to deaden the sensations the night would bring, he decided his second drink would be his last and set the whiskey bottle under the bar. He moved across the ballroom and up the stairs. Knowing he'd stay in the library if he entered it, he passed by the doorway with an effort. He relaxed a little. Annabel's hold on him was broken now. As long as he stayed away from the painting, he'd be safe.

Paul went into the master suite. He pushed the covers aside and let them pool on the floor. He sat on the edge of the bed, sipping his whiskey, staring out the window at the starlit night.

He felt the room begin to change. The sheer curtains stirred, the breeze cooling the bedroom. The air became charged with her energy. He felt his skin tingle with longing.

Julia had come.

He set his drink on the nightstand and lay in the middle of the bed, aching with his need for her.

She stood in the doorway wearing a white gown that looked very much like the one she'd worn that first night, the night he'd lost her in the rain. He remembered those first glimpses of her. Her large breasts pushing up against the rain-soaked nightie. The black triangle of her pubic hair wet and visible through the sheer white material. Her long black hair flowed over her shoulders. She'd been beautiful that night, but tonight she was even more radiant.

He watched her lithe form in the far corner of the bedroom. He willed her forward, dying to enter her, to hear her whimper for more.

She drifted across the room.

He could see her sleek body in the moonglow. When her thigh brushed the edge of the bed, he leaned forward to lift her gown, but she pushed his hand lightly away and he could feel her smiling down at him. She wanted to control their lovemaking tonight, he could tell.

He would let her.

Lying back, he rested his head on a pillow and watched her move on hands and knees over his body. She kissed his toes, his ankles. Her hot tongue passed along his calves, over his knees. Every nerve alive, he fought to lie still, to let her have her way with him, but the way her mouth teased was maddening.

She climbed up his body and straddled him.

She guided him in, and it was like nothing he'd felt before. She was alive inside, her sexual muscles massaging him as she rode, her hips sweaty and rhythmic, and he began to moan. Her sweat dripped on him and he tasted her. She'd put in a lot of hours at the library and her scent was muskier than usual, almost sour, but her kneading hands and the hot slick sensation of her sex were driving him crazy.

The moon shone full on them and he opened his eyes to watch her pelvis slapping against his, to see their bodies joining, when he sucked in breath, his body frozen beneath her.

The maggots squirmed in his pubic hair, writhing against his scrotum, the little white worms tumbling out of her vagina each time her hips lifted.

Gagging, Paul shoved her away. He scrambled out of bed, and as he did he saw the woman rise, the starlight full on her face.

"*Mine,*" Annabel said.

Mouth frozen in a wordless scream Paul backed away from the woman on the bed. She stepped down, her blazing blue eyes never leaving his.

He backed out of the bedroom and Annabel followed, and though he turned to run, each time he looked over his shoulder she was only a few feet behind. He passed the library and his fleeting glimpse revealed the portrait, illuminated, laughing at him in the silent house. As he ran he realized it wasn't Annabel's voice he heard, but a deafening return of the rats. God, their fulsome bodies scraped and writhed behind the walls, and it was all he could do not to—

Fingers brushed his neck.

Paul cried out, lurched toward the stairs. He jumped forward in a blind panic, tripping, the damage to his knees not registering. Paul tumbled down the last few stairs. He pushed to his feet. Something moved ahead and to his left, and while he veered away from it without difficulty, he caught a glimpse of a face, a pair of arms stretching out from the walls, and, Jesus, it looked like Myles Carver.

Forget it! his jangling nerves demanded. *For Christ's sake, she's coming!*

Without looking back he sprinted through the ballroom toward the French doors. He was sure they were locked but he couldn't stop, could almost *feel* Annabel's hot breath on the back of his neck. Lowering his shoulder, he slammed against the doors and staggered onto the veranda.

He started toward the car before remembering he'd left the keys in his jeans, which were still on the lawn. Desperately, he raced through the yard to find them, certain they had somehow disappeared.

He spotted them, lying where he'd left them.

Sobbing with relief he snatched the jeans from the grass and without bothering to put them on, he hurried toward the Civic as his hands probed the pockets. It was impossible, he told himself, that she had returned, that he'd made love to a corpse, but he knew what he'd seen was no illusion, none of this a bad dream.

His fingers closed on the keys. With a cry Paul yanked them out and bolted toward the car.

A white shape glided down the front porch steps, barring his way.

"Oh my God," he whimpered. As he fled the white figure something flashed in his periphery, and he knew she was about to overtake him. He lengthened his strides, and focused on the opening in the woods ahead.

Paul left Watermere and felt the smooth forest floor meet his bare feet. He ran as he never had before, the sanity that remained in him guiding him toward Julia's house.

Ahead, the figure appeared on the trail.

Paul screamed and wheeled off the path. He jumped over a fallen branch and dashed madly into the forest. Blindly, he barreled through the trees and undergrowth, stones twisting his ankles, thorns opening his flesh. Knowing at any moment Annabel's hand might close on his shoulder, he bulldozed his way through a twisted snarl of brambles. With one hand he covered his privates, with the other he flailed to clear the way. A sharp branch pierced his torso under the armpit and ruptured the skin through the nipple. Weeping with pain and terror, Paul surged forward through the last of the branches and fell forward onto the grass.

He gasped when he saw where she'd led him.

The graveyard was resplendent, its markers glittering like hideous gems.

Paul staggered to his feet, but the blood drizzling from his multitudinous wounds sullied his vision. He tripped, fell to his knees and felt his face crash against something sharp.

The air around him cooled, a breeze whispering over his supine form.

Paul raised his head, read what was printed on the small white rectangular marker:

ANNABEL SADLIER 1901-1928

Paul crawled away from the gravestone and read the taller one beside it:

ANNABEL LILITH WILSON 1850-1893

"Jesus Christ," he said.

Paul rose and turned.

And sank to his knees as Annabel extended her hand.

"Please don't hurt me," he said. His wounds pulsed agonizingly, the blood pumping out of him onto the tall grass. "Please don't kill me, Annabel."

Fingers touched his shoulder. Gently, he felt her helping him to his feet. He was aware of her smell, no longer sour. Now her scent was sweet and cool, lilacs and spring. Not wanting to see her face again, her awful, half-restored face, Paul read a cluster of markers: WILLIAM SADLIER 1896-1939, MARTHA SADLIER 1898-1922, JEREMIAH SADLIER 1909-1922, DESSA SADLIER 1920-1922.

He felt himself growing faint, the arm locked with his supporting him.

The grandfather clock gravestone loomed to his left, and in the brilliant light Paul read ANNABEL GENTRY 1786-1839. Through the waves of lightheadedness he read other names and dates, Gentreys and Wilsons, Singletons and Shadelands.

A larger granite marker to his right read DAVID CARVER 1917-1950.

Beside it, an open grave.

"That's meant for me," he said.

Tears rolling down his cheeks he forced himself to look at Annabel, to ask the question again. He opened his mouth to do so but was transfixed by her almost beautiful face. The words *gradual resuscitation* flashed through his mind, though this creature didn't look resuscitated. She looked like what she was—a supernatural creature who wasn't quite immortal. She had to die in order to live, and because of this necessity, her body had decomposed as any body would. Even now, despite the substantial restoration, the hair wasn't quite rid of the graveyard dirt. One eye socket still gaped black, the long ago worms and centipedes that feasted there now surely dead too; ragged holes on her forearms and her jaw still in the process of regenerating.

Yet despite these flaws Annabel was already obscenely breathtaking. Her cheeks, her breasts, her sex...the sleek, muscled legs that seemed to never end... God, even her bare toes made him ache.

Then she swiveled her head slightly to see something beyond him, and the spell of her beauty was broken. He watched in aghast fascination at the membranous flap growing out of her head, a new ear where none had been. The nascent skin bulged a moment, then a maggot as wide as his middle finger wriggled out of the hole and tumbled into the grass.

Bile rising in his throat, Paul turned to see what she was staring at, and when he saw it he clapped a hand over his mouth and dropped to his knees.

Julia hung suspended, her naked body pinned with ropes against the enormous black gravestone. Paul followed the ropes to the giant oaks standing sentinel beside the gravestone, which now clearly read ANNABEL LILITH CARVER. No date was listed, but beneath the name the epitaph read LOVE ENDURES.

On hands and knees Paul stared at Julia.

She watched him wild-eyed, the rope around her throat stealing her voice. Her arms and legs were crushed against the marker by the thick rope. Dried blood traced black lines on her flesh. She mouthed something to him but he could not understand it. He felt himself blacking out.

Steely fingers coiled around his neck.

"*Time*," the voice above him croaked.

Paul whimpered, cowering in her grip.

"*Choose*," Annabel said.

He opened his mouth to ask her what she meant. A hatchet landed on the grass before him.

Paul looked at it, then at the empty grave beside David Carver's.

The hand on his neck squeezed. Paul felt the vertebrae there crunch, the cartilage giving way.

"*Choose!*" she thundered.

He lunged sideways, trying to rid himself of her, but the grip on his neck tightened, her muddy fingernails puncturing his skin.

"Please don't," he said.

Wordlessly, she dragged him toward the hole.

He felt his feet sliding over the grass, his flaccid member dripping blood. His face moved over the lip of the grave, his shoulders.

Paul felt himself going forward, falling into darkness.

"*Wait*," he cried.

She held him there, suspended.

"I'll do what you ask."

She pulled him away from the lightless pit. Weeping, he crawled back to the huge gravestone and grasped the hatchet.

Standing, he regarded Julia.

She watched the hatchet, horror washing over her features. Squirming against the smooth black stone she fought against the ropes but they refused to budge, holding her as surely as an insect under glass.

Paul shut his eyes. He felt acid sizzling in his throat. He gazed at the hatchet in his hand.

"What will happen to me?" he asked.

He felt Annabel's grin. *"You will take his place,"* she said.

He turned away from Julia and saw Annabel standing there, the starlight dyeing her blond hair silver, her limbs glowing ethereally. Within hours and perhaps even minutes, he knew, her new body would complete. Beneath the roiling nausea and paralyzing terror, he was appalled to feel another stirring of lust.

Forcing himself to look away, he turned and studied Julia's splayed arms, her pinned legs. He could see how the rope at her throat had made wounds there, the fresh blood shiny.

She was dying. He peeled his eyes off Julia's glistening body and met her eyes, which regarded his mournfully. Her gaze flickered back and forth from Paul to Annabel, the vengeful wraith at his shoulder.

Paul saw Julia's eyes widen.

"I'm sorry," he said.

He raised the hatchet.

Turned and brought it down on Annabel's head.

It felled her, yet even as she crumpled he knew something had gone wrong. He stepped back from her shuddering body, sensed Julia squirming behind him.

He watched Annabel rip the blade out of her temple. She cast it aside. When she faced him he could see the wound closing, the angry ripped flesh knitting itself.

She stepped toward him and fingernails like scythes swept his forehead. As he fell the flap of torn scalp folded over his eyes. He batted frantically at the loose flap of skin. Through the blood spewing out of his forehead he caught glimpses of Annabel leaping forward, teeth bared, her nails rending and tearing at Julia's exposed flesh. He heard

Julia's strangled cries and watched in sick horror as Annabel set to work on her neck and her face. Annabel's head twitched as she fed, the arterial spray soaking her white gown. Julia convulsed as Annabel's snarling teeth ripped through tendons and cartilage.

Paul held the loose flap of skin to his head and tried to look away as the spasms ceased, Julia's body hanging limp against the gravestone.

Her features painted red, Annabel turned and grinned at him.

He tried to crawl away but she was already on him, digging at his exposed crotch. His hands moved to block her.

She tore them apart too.

He felt his consciousness dissolving in a blackening tide of agony. She stood and seized him by the hair. He felt himself dragged through the grass. Then his body was plummeting into the darkness of the open grave. He landed on his back, his eyes glazing.

The last thing he saw as the dirt poured over him was Annabel's grinning red mouth. She said something about the walls of the house, but he couldn't quite make it out. Then, as he began to suffocate, he realized what she meant and why he'd seen Myles Carver's face in the wall. It brought on one last scream, but the falling soil swallowed it up.

After

Watermere was alive.

Even out here on the veranda, Tommy McLaughlin felt the carnal energy, the throbbing desire charging the air. The band playing inside had the couples worked into a frenzy, the guitarist going off on a chaotic riff, the drummer and bass player following wherever he went. The salacious odors of hard liquor and cigarette smoke wafted out of the open French doors.

Tommy had seen Sheriff Timmons stealing up the stairs with a woman much younger than his wife. Mrs. Timmons, liplocking with a cute little redhead, didn't seem to mind. McLaughlin had never pegged her as the bisexual type, but there she was, her long fingers massaging one of the redhead's pert breasts through her dress. He never would have guessed the Timmonses were swingers, yet lately it was all the rage, the whole goddamn town intent on sleeping around until marital vows were punchlines.

Maybe it was in the air, the hot thrum of lust driving them all crazy. Maybe it was the warmth of the summer night after the months of snow and rain and investigations and mourning. Maybe the booze had something to do with it, though Tommy suspected it was something far less obvious, some fundamental alteration in the collective psyche.

Whatever it was, he had to steal out here into the moonlight to get his thoughts in order.

He'd recovered from Sam's disappearance, though he still wondered about him sometimes. It was assumed that the sheriff had gone the way of Ted Brand, the Memphis girl who used to date Carver, that poor old woman from the library, Julia Merrow and that dumb shit Daryl. Yet unlike the others, Sam's body had never been recovered, and it wasn't as if that maniac Paul Carver had bothered concealing all his victims. Despite the midnight shroud of sultry air baking him, Tommy shuddered at thought of the Henderson girl, dead in her car. The craziest part about it—even crazier than the fact that she'd made it all the way to Shadeland only to crash on a stretch of road about as safe as a city sidewalk—was the look on her face. Or what was left of her face. As if she'd gotten the world's worst scare. Tommy took a big swig of whiskey and fought to put the image out of his mind.

And speaking of scares... Jesus, he still couldn't believe the number Paul Carver did on the Merrow girl. Her once terrific body—which, if he was absolutely honest, he'd lusted violently over and had often fantasized about until he was too sore to piss—looked like it'd been gotten at by a pack of machete-wielding werewolves. Add to the five dead bodies Sam Barlow and you had a bona fide serial killer, the first ever in this part of the state.

Tommy shook out a cigarette—Annabel had gotten him started on the things—and lit up. He thought of Julia's mutilated throat, the rope marks on her arms and legs...

Yet Paul Carver was still on the loose. Thinking of Carver, Tommy sipped his whiskey, glared at the forest surrounding the yard. God, what he'd give for five minutes alone with the vicious son of a bitch. He'd make him scream for every rip in Julia's flesh, every bite mark on her once-beautiful throat. And the librarian... What the hell had been her name? Merten, he thought, Bea Merten. Who the hell did something like that to a defenseless old lady? Her whole damn face torn clean off her head, the only thing left a pink tongue lolling from a red-stained skull.

Thinking about Paul Carver, Tommy brought the cigarette to his lips, drew hard on it. He grunted, blew out a plume of smoke. Yep...Carver—*Great name for a serial killer*, Timmons had joked—was as dangerous and twisted as a person could get.

Of course, there were other theories, but none of them made much sense. Some said Sam had been in on it from the beginning, that he and Carver were a killing team, that they'd escaped to Mexico and were trolling the beaches for fresh senoritas to screw and slay. Another scenario had Sam as a cannibal. Never mind that Julia Merrow was the only victim found with bite marks, the idea here was that the reason

Carver had never been found was that Sam Barlow was the real killer and that Sam had eaten him. Tommy took another drink and almost smiled at the thought of Sam going all Jeffrey Dahmer on that bastard Carver.

Tommy furrowed his brow, moved over to the veranda railing.

If Sam wasn't one of Carver's victims, Tommy often wondered, how else could his disappearance be explained? If Sam had decided to jump ship in the middle of it all, how could Tommy reconcile that with what he knew of the man? The Sam he knew stuck things out until the bitter end. Had the events of the summer driven him mad?

Regardless, he was gone. It was a blow to the town, a loss to him personally. The man had been like a father to him. He compressed his lips, stared sourly down at the lawn. When Tommy's parents died a month after Sam disappeared, killed senselessly in their sleep by a house fire, he thought life couldn't get any worse.

He met her at the funeral.

The tall blonde woman said she knew his mom from his mother's time as an elementary school teacher. Annabel had been her pupil.

They hit it off right away, Annabel holding him as he wept, her shedding some tears too. She was the first girl who really looked at him, really gave two shits about how he felt. She was the one who'd suggested he use his parents' insurance money to bid on the old Carver house.

The idea seemed absurd to him when she'd first suggested it. Why would he want to live in the house where the killer had lived? If any place was cursed, he reasoned, it was Watermere. And what if Carver decided on a homecoming? If Tommy saw him again, the guy'd wish he'd never stepped foot in Shadeland. If Tommy didn't see him coming, however, and if Carver was canny enough to get the drop on Sam...

He won't bother us, Annabel had insisted.

Tommy said no way, he wouldn't bid on Watermere. The place was cursed.

Annabel had laughed at that, the idea of a cursed house.

The look in her eyes, as they sat there in her cramped little studio apartment near the library, told him that possessing Watermere meant possessing her too. He couldn't say why he felt that way. It just was.

He won the auction and had money to spare for renovations. They spent the spring working on the place, getting it ready for summer.

They married.

When they arrived back from their honeymoon two weeks later Annabel said, "It's time."

She was right. It was time.

Although he knew the town needed a diversion, something to get its mind off the tragedies of the previous year, he had no idea its need was this great. Nor did he know how brazen some men could be. Not even bothering to do it discreetly, to humor him at least, they watched Annabel like jackals salivating over a new kill. Tommy felt a weird kinship with the men's wives, feeling as indignant as they did at the way their husbands eyed Annabel.

One, though, was taking it too far. As a matter of fact, here she came...

"Have you seen Doug?" Karen Timmons asked. She'd left her redhead inside.

"I haven't seen him," Tommy answered without looking up.

"Oh no?" Karen asked. She smiled a slow, lazy smile. "And what about your wife? Have you seen her?"

Tommy tensed. "Are you implying something, Karen?" He dared her with his eyes to say more. Sheriff's wife or not, he'd wipe that fucking smirk off her face.

She returned his stare. "I don't have to imply anything about that whore."

His arm was out before he knew it, his fist smashing her front teeth. She went down, holding her mouth. McLaughlin glanced about to see if anyone had witnessed it, but the veranda was deserted.

"How dare you?" she mumbled, but he could tell by the cowed look on her face she'd backed down. For now.

"Go find your redhead," he said.

Karen Timmons stood and straightened her dress.

"Doug will hear about this."

"Doug's too busy to care right now. And he's not with my wife."

It hit her hard. Karen dabbed at her bloody lip, watched him to see if he was joking.

"Go on," Tommy said. "He's upstairs with that waitress from

Redman's if you want him."

Karen crossed the veranda and passed through the French doors.

Across the yard, Annabel emerged from the forest. Her light blue dress hung low on her chest, her creamy skin luminous. She fixed him with her hypnotic eyes and held him there as she ascended the steps and stood next to him. He handed her his drink.

Working to keep the suspicion out of his voice, he asked, "Out for a late stroll?"

She looked toward the woods. "It's lovely tonight."

"The trees or the house?" he asked. "Or the party?"

"All of it," she said, and he had to wrap her up, kiss her as deeply as he could. Even there with her he felt she might disappear at any moment, that her interest in him would soon flag. She wiggled against him, her perfect body naked beneath her dress. In her heels she was taller than he was. He was dizzy with his need for her, the cleft between her legs achingly close to him.

"I love you," he said.

She stiffened and pulled away.

"What's wrong?" he asked.

She cast a glance toward the house. "I saw you talking to Karen Timmons."

McLaughlin grunted. "She thinks you've got eyes for her husband."

He waited for her to refute it, but she stared into the forest.

"I punched her," he said.

She nodded.

"Are you mad at me, hitting a woman? It's not something I usually do." His voice went lower. "In fact it's the first time."

"It was necessary," she said.

"Necessary."

"But it won't last." Annabel's voice had gone flat, lifeless.

"It won't?" he asked. He felt himself getting lost in her voice, as he did more and more often lately.

"Something will have to be done about her."

Tommy McLaughlin watched his wife, waited for her to laugh.

She didn't.

After a long time, he began breathing again. His cigarette had burned to a line of ash. He tapped it on the concrete ledge and stared out at the forest.

"Tell me what you want me to do," he said.

And taking his hand, she did.

About the Author

Jonathan Janz grew up between a dark forest and a graveyard. In a way, that explains everything. His debut novel, *The Sorrows*, which FEARnet called "a wickedly fun read," is available in both ebook and trade paperback editions. His follow-up novel, *House of Skin*, is his second Samhain Horror release. He has also written two novellas (*Old Order* and *Witching Hour Theatre*) and several short stories. His primary interests are his wonderful wife and his three amazing children, and though he realizes that every author's wife and children are wonderful and amazing, in this case the cliché happens to be true. You can learn more about Jonathan at jonathanjanz.com, or you can find him on Facebook and as @jonathanjanz on Twitter.

Something is trapped in the castle, and it wants to feed!

The Sorrows
© 2011 Jonathan Janz

The Sorrows, an island off the coast of northern California, and its castle have been uninhabited since a series of gruesome, unexplained murders in 1925. But its owner needs money, so he allows film composers Ben and Eddie and a couple of their female friends to stay a month in Castle Blackwood. Eddie is certain an eerie and reportedly haunted castle is just the setting Ben needs to find musical inspiration for a horror film.

But what they find is more horrific than any movie. For something is waiting for them in the castle. A being, once worshipped, now imprisoned, has been trapped for nearly a century. And he's ready to feed.

Available now in ebook and print from Samhain Publishing.

SAMHAIN
P U B L I S H I N G

THE BEST IN HORROR

Every month Samhain brings you the finest in horror fiction from the most respected names in the genre, as well as the most talented newcomers. From subtle chills to shocking terror, experience the ultimate in fear from such brilliant authors as:

Ramsey Campbell

W. D. Gagliani

Ronald Malfi

Greg F. Gifune

Brian Moreland

John Everson

And many more!

THE HOUSE OF HORROR

SAMHAIN

PUBLISHING

It's all about the story...

Romance

HORROR

Retro
ROMANCE

www.samhainpublishing.com

CPSIA information can be obtained at www.ICGtesting.com
Printed in the USA
BVOW031104131212

308137BV00002B/141/P

9 781609 289218